Forge of Freedom

THE AMERICAN
PATRIOT SERIES
~BOOK 7~

J. M. HOCHSTETLER

ELKHART, INDIANA
46514 USA

Published by Sheaf House. Requests for information should be addressed to:
Editorial Director
Sheaf House Publishers
1703 Atlantic Avenue
Elkhart, IN 46514

jmshoup@gmail.com
www.sheafhouse.com

Library of Congress Control Number: 2022935265
ISBN: 978-1-936438-48-8 (softcover)

All scripture quotations are from the King James Version of the Bible. Scripture verses quoted on p. 122 are Psalm 127:3-5*a* and 128:3*b*-4; on p. 276, Matthew 7:5; on p. 420, Ruth 1:16*b* and Philippians 3:13-14*a;* on p. 423, John 14:1-3; on p. 426, Isaiah 6:9-12.

Cover image: American General George Washington resigning his commission as commander-in-chief of the Continental Army to the Congress of the Confederation at Annapolis, Maryland, on December 23, 1783, by John Trumbull. This work is in the public domain. It depicts George Washington's resignation as commander-in-chief of the Army to the Congress, which was then meeting at the Maryland State House in Annapolis. This action was of great significance in establishing civilian, rather than military rule, leading to a republic, rather than a dictatorship. Washington is shown standing with two aides-de-camp addressing the president of the Congress, Thomas Mifflin, and others, such as Elbridge Gerry, Thomas Jefferson, James Monroe, and James Madison. Mrs. Washington and her three grandchildren are shown watching from the gallery, although they were not in fact present at the event. The painting was commissioned in 1817 and placed in the United States Capitol rotunda in Washington D.C. in 1824, where it is still located today.

Back cover image is of Muchalls Castle in Scotland.

Cover design by Marisa Jackson.
Map by Jim Brown of Jim Brown Illustration.

Manufactured in the United States of America

Praise for Forge of Freedom

"Richly researched and brimming with emotional depth and spiritual truth, *Forge of Freedom* places you right alongside the beloved, unforgettable characters of the American Patriot Series who bring America's hardwon history to vivid life. Both literary feat and reading feast, *Forge of Freedom* is a triumphant finish to a stellar series!"

—Laura Frantz, Christy Award-winning author
of *The Rose and the Thistle*

"*Forge of Freedom* is a beautiful and satisfying final installment of an amazing series! I was sorry to say goodbye to characters I've followed for so long, characters so vivid they could indeed have lived among the historical figures scattered throughout the tale. I can't speak highly enough of the author's attention to detail and passion for preserving the wonder of our nation's history, even with all its missteps and blemishes."

—Shannon McNear, RITA® finalist, SELAH winner, and author
of the Daughters of the Lost Colony Series

"*Forge of Freedom* is an exciting, satisfying, and often heart-wrenching finale to J. M. Hochstetler's The American Patriot Series. Weaving together a compelling fictional romance with actual historical events, Hochstetler gives readers an opportunity to see the American Revolution up close and on a very personal level. Through Carleton and Elizabeth, we experience the hopes, fears, faith, courage, and sacrifice every Patriot must have faced as the Revolution achieved victories and suffered defeats. Through real life historical figures, we see their very human sides as they struggle to establish a new nation unlike any other in the history of the world. This series should be required reading for every high school student."

—Louise M. Gouge, award-winning author

"In *Forge of Freedom,* the author has again brought us another view into Elizabeth Howard and Jonathan Carleton's compelling lives. Ms. Hochstetler's research into the events and attitudes of the era is impeccable. While the Revolutionary war drags on we experience the emotion and witness the love, joy, separation, adventure, and faith that encompasses Elizabeth and Jonathan's lives. My concern is that there won't be a continuation of their fascinating story."

—JANET GRUNST, author of *Setting Two Hearts Free*

"*Forge of Freedom* is the satisfying conclusion of Joan M. Hochstetler's American Patriot Series. Written in an engaging fashion, the reader is pulled into the story and transported back to the end of the Revolutionary War. I highly recommend reading these books in order. Together, they complete an epic series of beautifully researched American history surrounding the fictional story of ordinary people pushed to do the extraordinary. Populated with actual historical figures and events, this series illustrates the personal struggles and sacrifices required to birth a nation."

—PEGG THOMAS, award-winning author of *Sarah's Choice*

Forge of Freedom and The American Patriot Series as a whole are dedicated to the one true and only God, the Creator of heaven and earth. The series' spiritual theme is that throughout the ages, by his great mercy and grace, God has used flawed human beings to advance his kingdom and ensure true liberty for all his people. I pray that this series inspires and encourages readers to walk as faithful disciples of Jesus Christ, always looking forward to his appearing.

Ye are come unto mount Sion, and unto the city of the living God, the heavenly Jerusalem, and to an innumerable company of angels, to the general assembly and church of the firstborn which are written in heaven, and to God the Judge of all . . . and to Jesus the Mediator of the new covenant . . . Wherefore we, receiving a kingdom which cannot be moved, let us have grace, whereby we may serve God acceptably with reverence and godly fear: For our God is a consuming fire.
—HEBREWS 12:22-23a, 24a, 28-29

Now the Lord is that Spirit; and where the Spirit of the Lord is, there is liberty. But we all, with open face beholding as in a glass the glory of the Lord, are changed into the same image, from glory to glory, even as by the Spirit of the Lord.
—2 CORINTHIANS 3:17-18

If the Son therefore shall make you free, ye shall be free indeed.
—JOHN 8:36

This is the Lord's doing; it is marvelous in our eyes.
—PSALM 118:23

J. M. Hochstetler is the daughter of Mennonite farmers, a graduate of Indiana University, a professional editor, and a lifelong student of history. An award-winning author, she is a proud member of Daughters of the American Revolution.

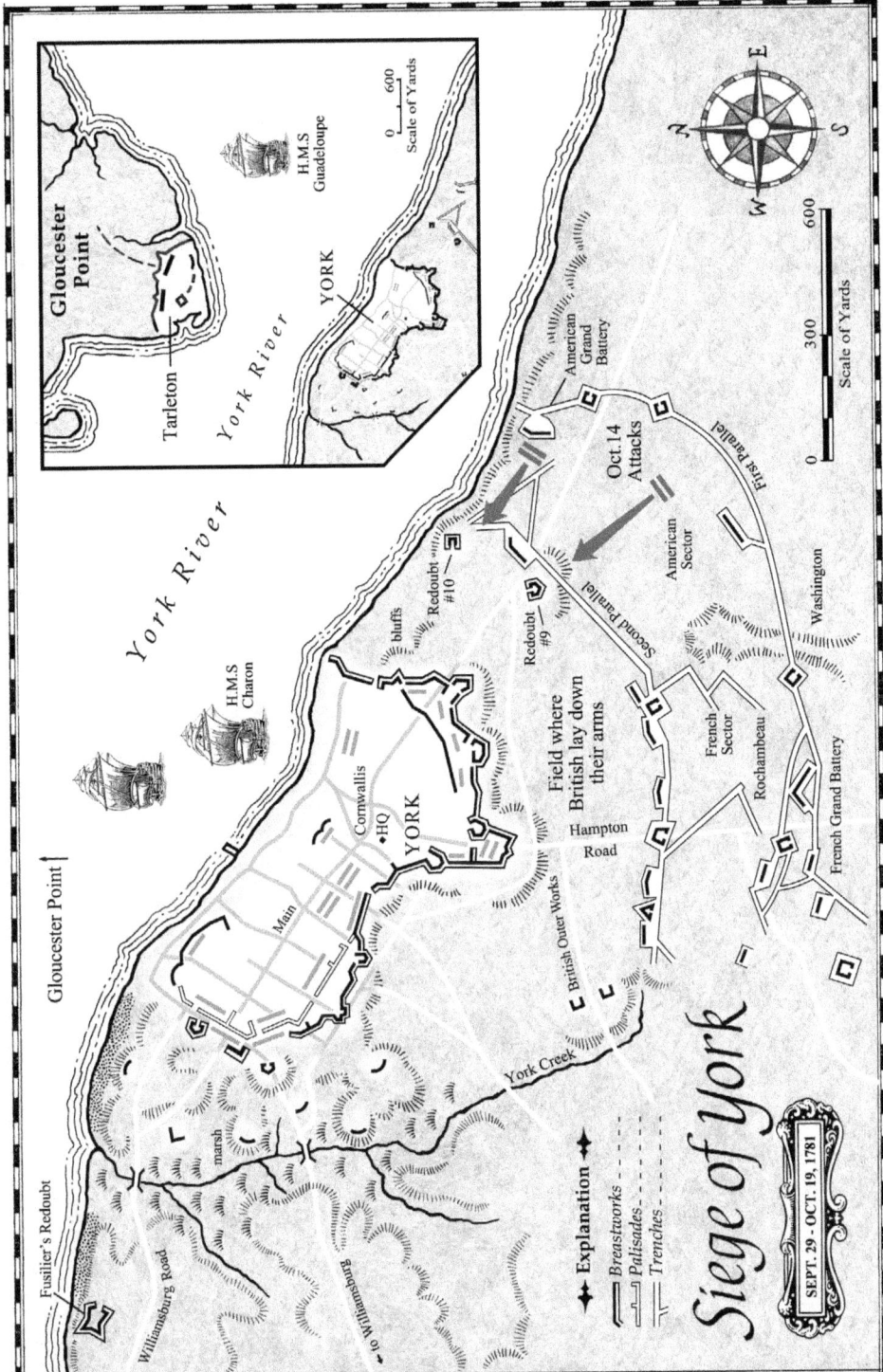

Siege of York

SEPT. 29 - OCT. 19, 1781

Explanation
- Breastworks
- Palisades
- Trenches

York River

Gloucester Point

H.M.S Charon

YORK

Cornwallis
HQ
Main

bluffs

Redoubt #10

Redoubt #9

American Grand Battery

Oct. 14 Attacks

First Parallel

American Sector

Second Parallel

Washington

French Sector

Rochambeau

French Grand Battery

Field where British lay down their arms

British Outer Works

Hampton Road

York Creek

marsh

Fusilier's Redoubt

Williamsburg Road

To Williamsburg

Inset: Gloucester Point

Gloucester Point

Tarleton

H.M.S Guadeloupe

York River

YORK

0   600
Scale of Yards

0   300   600
Scale of Yards

Chapter One

WHEN ALL APPEARS LOST, *what's needed is a madman.*

His own words mocked Major General Jonathan Carleton as he poised atop the railing of 40-gun American frigate *USS Bonhomme Richard*'s forecastle. He clung to the foremast backstay with one hand, grapnel line in the other, while cannon and small arms shot screamed through the choking clouds of gunsmoke that enveloped his surroundings.

What utter lunacy had induced him to give in to the urging of the rogue American John Paul Jones, newly elevated to commodore, to join his latest adventure? And what an entertaining expedition it had been, especially since every other ship in this tiny, vanity-riven squadron were commanded by an overbearing, pompous French captain—regardless that they officially sailed under the American ensign!

Having taken on this nonsensical assignment, however, why the devil had he listened to even one word Jones spoke thereafter, much less made no objection to this confrontation with one of the Royal Navy's newest, fastest, and most heavily armed warships? He had a wife he adored, a baby on the way, and every reason to live!

A musket ball blasted past so close the hot lead burned his arm. *Oh, aye,* he reflected, grimacing at the ball's sting. He had meant to wreak vengeance on the British for decimating his privateers and capturing his most formidable ship, *Destiny.* His first priority, however, had been to free the captured crewmembers who still lived, among them, he hoped, *Destiny's* captain, William Eaden; surgeon Jean Lemaire and nurse Marie Glasière; and Pete Moghrab, son of the colonel commanding his Rangers' black regiment.

He had accomplished none of it. As far as he was concerned, their efforts had been for naught despite the capture of several enemy vessels with their cargoes and crews. It had become painfully apparent that in terrorizing the populace along Britain's coast, Jones's raids had only served to alert the British to their presence and intent. The thought that as a result he might never see his new wife, Elizabeth, again or hold their first child, soon to be born, filled him with rage and despair.

He sucked in a sharp breath as a fiery cannonball tore through the air, far too close. It took with it two of his men and left a deep gouge along one side of the tottering foremast, casting razor-sharp splinters through the air.

Resolutely he shoved self-doubt and recrimination back into the dark recesses of sub-consciousness. If he was to have any hope of surviving this debacle, he had to focus on the urgent present.

He cast a quick glance to either side at the motley pack of sailors and Marines clustered around him at the ready. Pikes, axes, cutlasses, picks, and pistols flashed back the intermittent gleam of moon rays, battle lanterns, and the blaze of cannon fire.

A shoulder belt carrying a keenly honed cutlass and another bearing bags of powder and shot crisscrossed his lean, hard-muscled torso. From his belt swung a brace of loaded pistols and a tomahawk, and a sheathed knife dangled from a leather thong around his neck. His face, bare chest, and arms were streaked with gunpowder, sweat, and blood from multiple cuts and raw scrapes caused by flying debris. But, God be praised, so far he had suffered no injuries likely to be fatal—a condition that threatened to change at any moment.

Like the rest of *Richard*'s crew, he had stripped off his shirt to prevent battle-filthy cloth from becoming embedded in bullet wounds and causing infection. His long blond hair was covered with a black silk kerchief

Chapter One

WHEN ALL APPEARS LOST, *what's needed is a madman.*
His own words mocked Major General Jonathan Carleton as he
poised atop the railing of 40-gun American frigate *USS Bonhomme
Richard*'s forecastle. He clung to the foremast backstay with one hand, grapnel line in the other, while cannon and small arms shot screamed through the choking clouds of gunsmoke that enveloped his surroundings.

What utter lunacy had induced him to give in to the urging of the rogue American John Paul Jones, newly elevated to commodore, to join his latest adventure? And what an entertaining expedition it had been, especially since every other ship in this tiny, vanity-riven squadron were commanded by an overbearing, pompous French captain—regardless that they officially sailed under the American ensign!

Having taken on this nonsensical assignment, however, why the devil had he listened to even one word Jones spoke thereafter, much less made no objection to this confrontation with one of the Royal Navy's newest, fastest, and most heavily armed warships? He had a wife he adored, a baby on the way, and every reason to live!

A musket ball blasted past so close the hot lead burned his arm. *Oh, aye,* he reflected, grimacing at the ball's sting. He had meant to wreak vengeance on the British for decimating his privateers and capturing his most formidable ship, *Destiny.* His first priority, however, had been to free the captured crewmembers who still lived, among them, he hoped, *Destiny*'s captain, William Eaden; surgeon Jean Lemaire and nurse Marie Glasière; and Pete Moghrab, son of the colonel commanding his Rangers' black regiment.

He had accomplished none of it. As far as he was concerned, their efforts had been for naught despite the capture of several enemy vessels with their cargoes and crews. It had become painfully apparent that in terrorizing the populace along Britain's coast, Jones's raids had only served to alert the British to their presence and intent. The thought that as a result he might never see his new wife, Elizabeth, again or hold their first child, soon to be born, filled him with rage and despair.

He sucked in a sharp breath as a fiery cannonball tore through the air, far too close. It took with it two of his men and left a deep gouge along one side of the tottering foremast, casting razor-sharp splinters through the air.

Resolutely he shoved self-doubt and recrimination back into the dark recesses of sub-consciousness. If he was to have any hope of surviving this debacle, he had to focus on the urgent present.

He cast a quick glance to either side at the motley pack of sailors and Marines clustered around him at the ready. Pikes, axes, cutlasses, picks, and pistols flashed back the intermittent gleam of moon rays, battle lanterns, and the blaze of cannon fire.

A shoulder belt carrying a keenly honed cutlass and another bearing bags of powder and shot crisscrossed his lean, hard-muscled torso. From his belt swung a brace of loaded pistols and a tomahawk, and a sheathed knife dangled from a leather thong around his neck. His face, bare chest, and arms were streaked with gunpowder, sweat, and blood from multiple cuts and raw scrapes caused by flying debris. But, God be praised, so far he had suffered no injuries likely to be fatal—a condition that threatened to change at any moment.

Like the rest of *Richard*'s crew, he had stripped off his shirt to prevent battle-filthy cloth from becoming embedded in bullet wounds and causing infection. His long blond hair was covered with a black silk kerchief knotted at the base of his skull, which, added to his weapons and loose sailor's slops, lent him a properly villainous air. He took perverse satisfaction in the thought that as long as the British considered him a pirate, he might as well look the part.

Beneath the battle clamor he suddenly caught the rattle of *HMS Serapis's* anchor chains and at once guessed what was coming. "Hold on!" he shouted to his men.

As though on cue the 44-gun British warship with which they grappled in mortal combat jerked to a halt like a galloping stallion sharply reined.

It was Thursday night, 23 September, 1779. Moments before, outgunned and outmaneuvered, with his ship hulled below the water line and the carnage rapidly mounting, Jones had ordered his sailing master to bring *Richard* around in an effort to extricate her from the enemy's bloody barrage, lay her athwart *Serapis's* bow, and direct a shattering broadside down her length. But as *Richard* had begun sluggishly to fall off, the light breeze suddenly died away, stalling her directly in front of the enemy's bow. And then, while *Serapis* attempted to steer around her, the frigate's bowsprit had ripped through *Richard's* mizzen rigging, entangling both ships.

Taking advantage of this unforeseen gift, Jones and the sailing master had wasted no time in roping the enemy's jib boom to *Richard's* mizzenmast. That done, the commodore had ordered the boarding attempt for which Carleton and his party had been poised.

Now it occurred to Carleton that *Serapis's* captain must have dropped anchor in the hope that, carried forward by the strong tide, *Richard* would break free and drift helplessly toward the British coast. *Serapis* could then come about and blast her into oblivion. Instead the sluggish old mechantman arrested with a bone-jarring jolt that caused Carleton to teeter dangerously on his perch and the men crowding *Richard's* blood-slicked decks to stagger.

Clawing back to balance, Carleton cast a swift, assessing glance upward, past the ship's courses, hauled up for battle, with yards chained to prevent their falling if struck. The topmen in the platforms high on the masts of both ships clung to any available handhold as the tall spars swayed violently against the serene, cloudless silvery heavens.

A sixteen-year-old midshipman commanded *Richard*'s foretop directly overhead, crammed with every Marine and sailor who could be squeezed into it, including Carleton's servant, Private James Stowe, at the moment blocked from sight by his mates. Carleton transferred his anxious gaze to the maintop captained by twenty-four-year-old Connecticut midshiman Nathaniel Fanning and bursting with an even larger number of men including—astoundingly—Red Fox.

Still disbelieving his eyes despite the weeks they had spent together since leaving Thornlea, his Virginia estate, Carleton stared in amazement as the elder of his Shawnee cousins leaned fearlessly over the platform's low railing to grin down at him. Indeed, the warrior had never feared heights. Only . . . large bodies of water.

There was certainly enough of that element below him to instill terror. Yet he appeared no more daunted than he had on their first voyage to France a year earlier on a futile mission to negotiate with Louis XVI of France—and incidentally for Carleton to finally make Elizabeth Howard his wife. Red Fox had subsequently returned across the ocean to rejoin Carleton's Rangers with no apparent qualms. Even more astounding, in July after Carleton had delivered Elizabeth to Thornlea, Red Fox insisted on accompanying him back to France to join in the present adventure.

The ways of the Almighty were not to be reckoned.

The two ships righted, and Red Fox turned hastily back to aim his musket. Every man in the fore-, main-, and mizzentops resumed a blazing fire directed at their British counterparts ensnared short yards across from them. By now they had dropped or driven most of the enemy from their perches, and return fire had noticeably slackened.

Abruptly Carleton became aware that *Richard* was still moving, revolving ponderously from her entangled stern. Just as he concluded that the two ships were going to collide, Jones's shrill shout reached him from across the ship.

"Ready grapnels!"

Clutching the forestay for balance, Carleton swung down onto the deck. "Steady!" he sharply admonished the men clustered around him.

In a deliberate half arc, *Richard* swung full around until she faced opposite to *Serapis*. The two ships' hulls came violently together, bow to stern, with a grinding crash that sent a shock through every object and person aboard. *Serapis*'s jib boom snapped, and sailors on both ships staggered and toppled. Carleton and his mates grasped the nearest rope, rail, or mast to keep to their feet.

The instant the ship settled, he vaulted back onto the forecastle rail, commanding his party to follow. As one they obeyed and heaved their lines. A flight of grapnels soared across the narrow space between the two ships and clawed into *Serapis*'s rigging, bulkheads, and railings. British sailors and Marines swarmed across her decks, furiously tossing off loose grapnels or using axes to chop at the lines of any that found purchase. Pouring a blistering fire across the enemy's decks, *Richard*'s topmen drove them back.

"Don't let her loose!"

Carleton directed a baleful glance toward the quarterdeck, where Jones screamed orders. He looked a veritable fiend with his craggy face blackened by gunpowder and dirt, an array of pistols ornamenting his belt, the short jacket and trousers that clad his slight figure befouled and torn.

Chafe though he might at Jones's hardheaded obstinacy, it was far too late to reverse course now. And as a mere volunteer Carleton had no option but to do whatever he could to stay alive.

Movement in *Serapis*'s foretop, now hovering directly above *Richard*'s poop deck, caught his eye. The British foretopmen were furiously hacking with knives, axes, and swords at the ropes supporting their boom, hopelessly entangled in *Richard*'s mizzen shrouds.

Carleton shouted a warning just as the heavy beam let loose. It plummeted onto *Richard*'s poop deck with a thundering thud, scattering the French Marines clustered there. Jones, standing on the quarterdeck below with his back to them, hardly flinched.

Carleton immediately directed his party to throw more grapnels across the narrow gap between the two ships. Men all down *Richard*'s length joined the effort with alacrity, some throwing additional lines while others fired on the British defenders. This time the grapnels held.

"Secure the lines!" Carleton ordered.

With a mighty heave at their ends, they tethered *Serapis* snuggly alongside, inextricably binding the two ships together.

"Well done, my brave lads," Jones cried out, brandishing his cutlass in triumph. "We've got her now!"

Right, Carleton thought. With a sardonic laugh he pulled free one of his loaded pistols.

A FULL HARVEST MOON had just begun to climb out of the North Sea, emerging from of a veil of wispy clouds off *Richard*'s bow as she glided across the eerily still, glass-smooth water toward the approaching British warship and her escort, a small, lightly armed sloop-of-war. Perfectly framed within the rising golden orb, the enemy frigate, trimmed in the British Navy's distinctive black and yellow colors, gleamed with sinister magnificence in its rays.

Pale wisps of smoke from the slow matches ready at the Americans' cannon had wafted delicately upward along her upper gun deck in the light, cool breeze. Off their stern the beetling chalk cliffs of England's shore glimmered white in the serene moonlight—roughly three nautical miles to the southwest, Carleton calculated. All sound seemed damped as though the night waited in suspense.

Early that afternoon, with Yorkshire's Flamborough Head rising out of the sea off their starboard bow, the lookouts had sighted the sails of more than three dozen merchantmen of Britain's Baltic fleet to the southeast, no doubt returning from Norway laden with a rich cargo of shipbuilding supplies. But this enormous prize had not tempted Jones.

It was the convoy's escorts that held his attention. Glory lay in being the first American to capture a British warship, and Jones had signaled to his squadron to lay on sail.

He was making a foolhardy challenge, one they were not likely to win, Carleton had reflected grimly. But Jones had already ignored Pierre Landais, the French captain commanding the frigate *Alliance,* who urged a swift retreat. And knowing Jones's lust for fame, Carleton reckoned it a waste of breath to voice his own objections.

Over the following hours, while the merchantmen scuttled off to safety like a clutch of fat hens, the ships had drawn inevitably together as though pulled by a magnet. With the sun declining, drummers had stamped briskly down *Richard*'s decks to the shrill call of the bosun's pipe, beating a tattoo that sent men to battle stations. The ship had been rapidly cleared for action, courses furled and yards braced, parquet decks sanded to aid traction once their planks were slicked with blood. The French Marines in their bright red jackets and white breeches took their posts at the companionways to prevent anyone from fleeing, while below decks bulkheads were cleared away, moveable items stowed in the hold, the surgery readied in the cockpit.

Equally speedy action had been visible aboard the approaching warships. The larger drew up her own courses in response and dropped the port covers on both upper and lower gun decks to expose the menacing black mouths of her 18-pounders, their gun crews starkly outlined in the lantern light spilling from behind them.

As though in synchrony, the ship's white and red St. George ensign fluttered down from her stern flagstaff. Carleton had watched through his spyglass alongside Jones as *Serapis*'s captain personally nailed onto the pole the Royal Navy's enormous red ensign.

Extra rations of rum had quickly been distributed to *Richard*'s crew to fuel courage. A double ration and casks of water were issued to the topmen before they scrambled aloft to the platforms high on the masts, armed with an array of weapons. Meanwhile, ignoring their commodore's signaled orders, *Alliance* and the other two ships in the squadron scattered God knew where.

When the length of a pistol shot lay between *Richard* and the enemy, the silence was broken by a hoarse challenge: "This is Captain Pearson aboard His Majesty's ship *Serapis*. What ship is that?"

At Jones's command the sailing master returned, *"Princess Royal,"* the name of a British merchantman of similar size.

Pearson had shouted suspiciously back, "Where from?" Receiving no reply, he followed with, "Tell me instantly from whence you came and who you be, else I'll fire a broadside into you!"

The game clearly up, Jones had immediately signaled for *Richard*'s British colors to be hauled down and replaced by the bold red, white, and blue Continental Navy ensign. As the latter ran up the flagstaff, musket fire crackled from *Richard*'s tops, touching off simultaneous broadsides from the two ships at point-blank range in a deafening, reverberating roar that shattered the still air and rained a cataclysm of death and destruction across both decks.

Richard had gotten the worst of the confrontation from the first. While maneuvering for advantage each ship had rammed the other. But *Serapis* had easily outsailed the converted former French Indiaman with her high, old-fashioned poop deck, giltwork, and elaborate carvings that made her look like nothing more than a floating confection. The enemy had repeatedly raked her fore and aft, sending 18-pound shot straight down the length of her.

In short order *Richard*'s few 18-pounders had all been silenced, with a couple exploding when fired. Her yards and sails had been decimated, her masts riddled. The French colonel commanding the poop had been driven down to the quarterdeck with his surviving Marines.

Now, while the world revolved toward midnight, the battle was entering its third hour beneath the moon's radiant light. With the wind becalmed, the current vainly tugged the two ships toward England's hostile coast against the drag of *Serapis*'s sea anchor, each held fast to its opponent, hulls grinding together. And the slaughter continued unabated.

The warning the Shawnee women's peace chief, Nonhelema, had issued against seeking vengeance rang in Carleton's mind. Ironic to what lengths the lust for revenge would drive a man when he'd denied to others and specifically to himself that that was his motive. Yet in this matter it was, and by heaven he was going to have it.

At least as long as his survival and God's will aligned, he corrected himself with black humor. The trouble was that only the Almighty knew what he had in mind. For Jones appeared to be as mad as Benedict Arnold leading repeated charges against the British at Saratoga until shot from the saddle.

Chapter Two

I MIGHT AS WELL BE IN SCOTLAND.

Beguiled, Elizabeth Howard Carleton studied the rear of the brooding building that loomed before her atop a low rise where a loop of the Thorn River enclosed three sides of a wide clearing. The imposing grey limestone manor of her husband's Virginia estate could not possibly have looked more like a Highland laird's domain with its steep slate roof, crow-stepped gable ends topped by massive chimneys, and bartizans at each outer corner.

Adding to the effect were the lilting strains of fiddle and pipe that reached her from the almost denuded kitchen gardens at the back of the nearby laundry house. She smiled to see several of the Scottish and Irish servants taking a brief break from their duties by dancing an exuberant jig.

She had stepped out through the rear door of the large stone carriage house, converted for use as the Rangers' hospital, only to stop, as she often did, arrested by the picturesque view. Yet even in these peaceful surroundings war made its uneasy presence known.

Indeed the vista would have given the impression of a blissful, dreamlike idyll were it not for the armed, uniformed troops and Indian warriors in native dress riding or striding purposefully along the pathways and lanes between the property's outbuildings. The muted hum of voices, distant rattle of wagons and harness, nearby plop of hoofs, and scuff of footfalls sounded on all sides.

Although remote in its mountain fastness, the estate was normally as bustling as any town, even more so since Carleton's Rangers had occuied it the previous spring. Nominally Continental troops under the command of General George Washington, in reality Carleton's division was an independent force that he personally funded and that answered to him alone.

A cool breeze tugged at her plain blue linen petticoat and white apron, causing her to draw her creamy white wool shawl more closely around her shoulders. Absently she tucked loosened, wind-teased strands of her unruly dark auburn curls back under her linen cap.

What she could see from where she stood behind the manor's south wing was but a small portion of the sprawling estate her husband owned —or had, for he had transferred ownership of the entire property to her on their marriage. Vast forests blanketed the high mountains of the Blue Ridge that walled the secluded valley on either side and sprawled onto the valley floor.

North of the manor toward the valley's mouth spread verdant, tree-dotted meadows, where fenced fields produced wheat, oats, barley, rye, and flax in their seasons. Amid them lay the dairy barns, poultry yards, and gristmill. Other open areas north and south of the manor provided pasturage for large herds of cattle and horses and the flocks of sheep that provided meat, wool, lanolin, and butter-soft skins. Several miles south at the valley's far end, wooded uplands provided forage for hogs left free to roam.

"Quite the idyll, isn't it?"

The well-loved voice drew her around, smiling with warm affection at her father, Dr. Samuel Howard, who paused in the doorway behind her, drying his hands on a linen towel. She noted with a pang that his stance was not quite so erect as she remembered from earlier years. During her extended absence in France deeper lines had furrowed his face, and his black, curly hair was more thickly threaded with grey. For the first time it struck her that, although he was not yet an old man, the years were passing more quickly than she wished.

"Exactly what I was thinking, Papa," she returned, forcing a cheerful tone.

"We're too much alike, Daughter."

She regarded him, one eyebrow raised. "Obstinate, you mean?"

"*Romantic* was the word I was thinking of!" he answered, eyes narrowing.

Her laugh drew a grimace. He dropped the cloth on the table just inside the doorway and turned to speak briefly to his young chief of surgery, Captain Elias Lawton. Then grabbing his dun-colored uniform jacket with green facings from a peg on the door's other side, he slipped it on and came to join her.

She leaned on the arm he offered, her attention returning to her surroundings. It was shortly past noon on Thursday, 23 September. High above in the sky's limitless clear blue, the sun's golden orb cast fingers of light and shadow across the valley, setting the high ridges on either hand in vivid relief. The chime of birdsong drew her gaze to the tall trees interspersing the buildings.

The wind fanned the leaves' hues of crimson, citron, and amber to flame like wildfire racing among the dusky greens of pine and cedar and holly. It stirred as well the smoke rising from campfires over which hung bubbling kettles filled with stew for the Rangers' afternoon mess, while the manor's kitchen chimneys sent up their own smoky columns.

She drew in a deep breath of the crisp, smoke- and pine-tinged air. The place appeared to date to a distant century, yet during his too brief stay after delivering her to the estate in July, Carleton had told her that his uncle and adoptive father, Sir Harrison Carleton, had built it in 1732, only forty-seven years earlier. His intent had been to recreate his clan's ancient ancestral castle in Scotland, which had fallen into wrack and ruin after suffering extensive damage during earlier Jacobite wars. Carleton's grandfather had eventually abandoned it for Stoughton Hall, a larger, more modern manor.

She knew that Sir Harry, the Scottish laird's elder son, had fled his homeland for Virginia in 1715 after the British defeated the Highland clans at Sheriffmuir. The death of his father on the battlefield and Harry's flight to the colonies to escape the coming reprisals had left his younger brother, Oliver, Carleton's father—a child at the time—to assume the clan's lairdship. And their mother to pretend a fervent loyalty to George I to stave off forfeiture of their landholdings and secure the hereditary title of marquess for her younger son.

The persistent ache in her back intruded on Elizabeth's reverie. Releasing her father's arm, she pressed her hands against the sore muscles and stretched to ease their stiffness. A protesting ripple caused her to grimace, and she ran one hand tenderly along the curve of her rounded belly, smiling at the vigorous kick her touch elicited.

"Are you all right, Beth? You aren't having any pains?"

She looked up to meet her father's worried gaze. "It's nothing, Papa. My wee one is just restless, as usual."

"You've been working too hard," he chided. "Caring for the troops is more than you should take on, but adding Thornlea's employees too—"

"I'm working no harder than you, Papa. And I'm in perfect health. There's no reason why I shouldn't continue my usual activities."

He fixed her in a keen gaze. "You're absolutely certain you've yet two months before the birth?"

"I don't think it could be any earlier." She considered the evidence of her seven-months' pregnancy dubiously. "Though I am increasing more quickly than I expected."

"I can't imagine that crossing an ocean in the midst of a naval war benefited your condition!" he huffed.

She released an exasperated sigh. "Papa, you know very well that I gave Jonathan no choice. Either I'd sail with Uncle Alexandre's heavily armed squadron, or I'd travel to Amsterdam alone and cross in a Dutch merchantman. But return home I would!"

When her father opened his mouth to object, she cut him off. She had heard every possible objection from Carleton; Caledonne; Carleton's business agent, Louis Teissèdre; her Aunt Tess and little sister Abby; and Caledonne's daughter, son-in-law, and granddaughter, she reminded him.

"I missed my own country after being so long in France. And I wanted you and Mama with me when my babe is born."

"Well, I won't argue with that," he conceded. "I'm just glad your aunt and sister had the sense not to accompany you. I can't think of how your mother and I would have suffered if you'd been lost at sea, but all three of you would be a blow too great to endure." His voice choked.

"That was a very large consideration for us as well," she said earnestly. "Besides, you know Uncle Alexandre refuses to be parted from his bride any longer than his duties demand, nor would Cécile and her family relinquish either Aunt Tess or Abby."

"I do miss my little girl very much," he replied wistfully. "But Alexandre was right. Your mama and I could not have asked for a better situation for her." His gaze sharpened as he frowned down at her. "And for you, too. I'm not excusing your pigheadedness—"

"It was no such thing! I did a fair bit of sailing while I—" She broke off when he raised his hands, giving her a reproachful look.

"I'm sure there were many things you did as a spy that your mother and I are better off not knowing." He raked his fingers through his hair. "That aside, equally irresponsible, you rode—astride!—well over a hundred miles here to Thornlea instead of hiring a carriage."

She rolled her eyes. "I've been riding since I was a child, and the Shawnee women ride without harm when they're pregnant. Considering the state of the country roads so far out west, taking a carriage would have been much slower and rougher, if not impossible in places. Riding was far more comfortable and safer, too, as I could wear masculine garb. And you know Jonathan treats me as if I'm made of glass. Between him, the midwife and nurse he hired, Jemma, and the other women aboard ship, I was so hemmed about by caretakers that I could hardly move without tripping over someone."

She laughed at his droll expression, then continued with a shrug, "As you see, none of the dire predictions everyone made came to pass."

"Complications might still arise when your time comes to give birth."

She waved his comment away and quickly changed the subject. "You were not the only ones surprised by our arrival, you know. When Jonathan and I discovered you here serving with the Rangers, we both concluded that the Apocalypse was at hand."

He chuckled, then his expression turned grave. "What you suffered at the hands of the British, even being forced to flee to France for safety, was quite convicting. When Charles wrote offering me command of the division's medical department at the rank of major, well, I simply couldn't justify sitting idle any longer while others waged the fight on our behalf."

"At my age I'm not much of a soldier," he continued with a sigh. "But I can at least shoot straight and serve the sick and wounded. And as your mama missed her girls even more after our visit to Passy last winter, she wouldn't let me leave her behind. So having you and Jon turn up without notice was certainly a happy surprise."

"We almost didn't," she admitted, smirking. "We never received your letter, for one thing. And even after receiving Charles's report that the Rangers had been attached to the army's Southern Department and he intended to establish his headquarters here, it took every wile I could conceive to overcome Jonathan's objections. He was beyond exasperated with me."

"He's getting a foretaste of the rebellious nature your mother and I have had to deal with ever since your birth!"

"Of course, *you're* the most amiable and biddable of men, Papa," she teased. "No rebel, you—nor your sister."

He conceded a grin. "My mother, an exceptionally strong-willed woman herself, called it the mother's curse. Beware, daughter. You, too, might have a strong-willed child."

"Forewarned, forearmed," she replied with a laugh. Sobering, she bit her lip. "Jonathan promised to send a letter assuring us of his safe arrival as soon as he reached L'Orient. Surely he must have gotten there by now."

"Considering how much time it takes for correspondence to cross the ocean—if it arrives at all—a little more than two months isn't unusually long to wait."

Looking down, she nodded mutely, fighting to hold back the tears that stung her eyes. He gently encircled her shoulders with his arm.

"There's no reason to worry, my dear. His letter will arrive in due time."

She met his concerned gaze with a smile. But she couldn't help wondering, heart aching, where Carleton was. Or, in light of the ongoing naval war, if he even still lived . . . She added another anxious, silent plea for his safety to those constantly hovering in her thoughts.

They were interrupted by Blue Sky, General Charles Andrews' tall, willowy Shawnee wife and Elizabeth's adoptive sister. Stepping out of the doorway behind them, she said. "Corporal O'Hara just awoke from the surgery. He is in some pain, as to be expected, but otherwise seems to do well."

Laughing Otter, Red Fox's wife, followed, closing the door behind her. "Captain Lawton will send for you if the corporal's condition worsens."

Dr. Howard nodded to both women. "Thank you. I'll check on him again after dinner. Thankfully we have a good supply of rum on hand for the pain."

"You're going back to your camp?"

"Little Elk will be hungry, and he has little patience," Blue Sky said with a chuckle, referring to her and Andrews' nine-month-old son.

"We will see you at dinner, Healer Woman," Laughing Otter added, using Elizabeth's Shawnee name.

"Oh, that's right—it's Thursday!" Elizabeth exclaimed as the two women took their leave. "I'd forgotten it's our day for the officers' dinner."

"We only do this every week," Dr. Howard teased.

Elizabeth grimaced. "It's too easy to lose track of time in this place."

Her gaze followed the native women down the path until they moved out of sight. Then her father led the way around the side of the hospital to the carriageway at its front, where they turned toward the manor's outer courtyard.

The building's immediate environs sat athwart the road that bisected the broad Thorn Valley—named for its graceful stands of black locust trees and dense growths of hawthorn shrubs, according to Carleton. He had described the river's headwaters, which poured from a narrow gap in the mountain's high summit in a spectacular, thundering cascade to form a large pond below. From there the river snaked back and forth northward through the valley's forests and across its tree-dotted meadows on its way to join the larger Staunton River a little over a mile outside the valley's mouth.

She sighed. Because of her pregnancy, viewing the falls and exploring the valley's southern end, with its secluded glens carved into the folds of the ridges' flanks, would have to wait. For now she could only imagine its beauty, for Carleton had warned that farther down the valley the road dwindled to a narrow, rutted, stony path before disappearing altogether. He would take her there in the spring after she had recovered from their child's birth, he had promised.

Suddenly her gaze blurred. *Long before then, in God's mercy, Jonathan will have returned, and our babe will be safely born,* she assured herself resolutely.

As though he sensed her turmoil, her father's hand tightened over hers. "He's in God's hands," he said quietly. "We all are."

Blinking back tears, she nodded, her throat too tight for speech.

❋ ❋ ❋

Hearing the measured patter of hoofbeats approaching from the direction of the valley's mouth, Elizabeth stopped on the threshold of the open gate in the high, crenellated wall that enclosed the manor's courtyard. Her father turned back with her as a small company of Rangers came into view from behind the trees at the road's far bend. In moments the detail passed the charming stone chapel over which Major James McLeod, the Rangers' chaplain, currently presided, set a short distance off the courtyard's north end.

At their head rode Andrews. A couple of inches shorter and more slenderly built than Carleton, with clear blue eyes and light brown hair, he wore the Rangers' striking uniform, as did the men riding behind him: snugly fitted dun-colored French-dragoon-style jackets faced in forest green, his distinguished by a general's epaulette on each shoulder; buckskin breeches; black knee-length boots; and forest green leather helmets adorned with gold chains and a flowing, blond horsehair crest. A dark grey shoulder belt carrying a sheathed sabre crossed each man's chest, and two pistols and a carbine were secured in holsters on each side of their saddles.

As the party drew to a halt before the arched courtyard gates a small boy burst through them and ran gleefully toward Andrews. "No'tha! No'tha!"

Close behind came Elizabeth's mother, Anne Howard, her fair beauty, delicately modeled features, and slender, graceful form hardly marred by her forty-two years. She captured the hand of another little boy who trailed her to keep him from straying too close to the horses.

"Leads the Way!" she admonished the first boy anxiously. "Be careful! Please don't run and shout or you'll scare the horses. And call your father Papa!"

"Papa, Papa!" he responded, bouncing on tiptoe, as he reached urgently for his father.

"Mama, please!" Elizabeth remonstrated.

"Charles's sons need to learn to speak English!"

Andrews exchanged a meaningful glance with Elizabeth as he dismounted. "Indeed they do, and Blue Sky and I are doing our best with both of them," he said before catching up his elder son. Laughing, he tossed the squealing child high into the air, catching him safely in his arms as he fell.

He Leads the Way was a strikingly beautiful child, tall for his not quite two years, with expressive dark eyes inherited from his mother and a tawny complexion that held some of the duskiness of hers, though softer in tone. To Elizabeth the contours of his sweet, rounded face reflected what his father must have looked like as a child, although his eyes were hazel rather than blue and his hair was darker, the rich color of ripened wheat.

The second boy, Jimmy Douglas, was shorter and stockier, with dark hair and eyes. Mary McLeod's son by her late husband, a Continental soldier killed in action, was barely two days older than his inseparable friend and shared his energy and sweet nature.

"Where's my wife?" Andrews demanded, turning to Elizabeth.

"She and Laughing Otter headed back to the warriors' camp just a few minutes ago."

Andrews dismissed his escort. The men touched their fingers to their plumed helmets in salute, then, nodding respectfully to Elizabeth and her parents, rode off in the direction of the Rangers' camp.

Setting Leads the Way on his feet, Andrews reached to ruffle Jimmy's hair before straightening. "I hope the boys aren't being a bother."

"Not at all, Charles. I'm enjoying having little ones around again— and am looking forward to more." She directed a pointed glance at Elizabeth.

"Which I'm beginning to think might be sooner rather than later," Dr. Howard muttered with a worried look in Elizabeth's direction, to which she returned a frown.

"These boys are inseparable," Anne continued, undeterred, "and Leads the Way already has Jimmy using Shawnee words. You must remember that your children will have to live in both worlds, Charles. You can't start early enough teaching them how to speak and behave in proper society."

Andrews muttered something under his breath that Elizabeth couldn't hear. She gave him a sympathetic glance.

"They're half White, after all," Anne continued, oblivious to their by-play.

"And their mother is all Shawnee," Andrews returned, tightlipped. "Our boys will never be fully accepted in the white world. But I am accepted in their world."

Dr. Howard had been following their conversation with an unreadable expression and now offered quietly, "As a practical matter, perhaps it would make things a bit easier for the boys if they had Christian names, Charles."

"Tell me your English name," Andrews immediately prompted his son.

"Joshua!" Leads the Way exclaimed, bouncing on his toes.

"And Little Elk's English name?"

"Daniel!"

"You didn't tell us," Anne chided before adding firmly, "We'll call them Joshua and Daniel from now on then."

Elizabeth bit her lip, but Andrews only conceded a faint smile and shrugged. "They'll answer to either."

Looking down at Leads the Way, Anne took his hand. "Come along, Joshua. And you too, Jimmy."

"Treat!" Leads the Way insisted, skipping as she led them through the gate and into the mansion's front courtyard.

"I want cake!" Jimmy echoed happily.

"We'll see." Anne glanced over her shoulder with a smile as the others followed. "It seems they've developed a particular attachment to me."

"What do you expect, Mama, if you persist in feeding them sweets all day long?"

"It's not my fault! Salome supplies the most irresistible delicacies, and if I didn't share, I wouldn't own a gown I could fit into."

All of them laughed, and Dr. Howard scanned her with an admiring smile that drew her blush. "I see no ill effects to your figure, my dear. In my opinion, you're as blooming as when we first met."

Thornlea's head cook was a small, sprightly, black woman in her late forties. Her husband, Rufus, a burly, muscular man, oversaw the estate's livestock and the herdsmen, shepherds, and dairy and poultry workers. When Carleton had freed the slaves he inherited at Sir Harry's death, they had chosen to stay on as paid employees. A small number of others had done so as well, including the wives and children of the men who enlisted in the Rangers.

Elizabeth sighed. "Perhaps her skills are the reason I'm increasing so quickly. What delights is she preparing for dinner?"

"A great herbed beef tenderloin done to perfection, I'm sure, as only she can, along with all the trimmings," Anne answered as she led the boys up the mansion's wide stone steps to the massive double oaken doors, Dr. Howard on their heels. "You've still time to change before dinner if you don't dawdle, dear."

"I'll retrieve the boys in a few minutes," Andrews called after them. "Please only one small biscuit apiece!"

Anne laughed in response. The butler opened the door, and she, Dr. Howard, and the boys disappeared inside.

Elizabeth lingered with Andrews. "Charles, I'm so sorry that Mama persists in—"

"I understand her point of view," he broke in, waving Elizabeth's apology away. "Not so long ago I'd have shared it. But both your parents need to understand that I'll not deprive my wife and children of their kin, whom they love and who love them. Nor will I ever allow them to feel ashamed of their heritage."

She gave him an approving nod. "Quite right. I feel the same way. Jonathan's Shawnee kindred are mine and will be our children's as well."

Her gaze took in the flagstoned courtyard. Its wall enclosed the area on two sides, forming a rectangle with the L-shaped manor's main building and its south wing. In the event an enemy attempted to storm the entrance, she noted, defenders could direct a deadly enfilading crossfire not only from the upper floors' windows, but also from those in the lower floor, built halfway into the ground.

A short wing with a matching gabled front projected from the main building's northern end, the shallow protrusion of its upper floors supported by a row of decorative corbels. A semicircular tower housing an interior spiral stairway occupied the angle where each wing joined the main building. And at the second floor, matching corbelled bartizans with narrow, diamond-paned windows and conical roofs extended from the structure's outer corners.

"I'm still amazed that Jonathan grew up in this place," she mused.

Andrews chuckled. "It isn't what one would expect to find in the Virginia wilderness, that's certain."

She studied the Carleton coat of arms carved into a large limestone block above the main entrance. The ornate Norman shield was divided into quarters emblazoned with mountain, cross, blazing torch, and sword, the banner above inscribed with the motto *numquam cedere.*

"Never yield," she murmured. "The clan motto does seem rather appropriate, don't you think?"

"So it does. Did you know that the crest dates to Norman times when Duke William came over to conquer England, bringing Jon's ancestor among his knights?"

She nodded. "Jonathan told me. He said the symbols represent one's land, Christian faith, light, and strength. If he's an example of his forebears, they were certainly intractable men." She stopped abruptly.

He fixed her in a sympathetic gaze. "I know how hard it is to be separated—"

"Yet again." Sighing, she took his arm. "I don't mean to whine, Charles. You and Blue Sky have suffered separations too."

His expression softened. "She couldn't be happier to have her sister with her again, you know."

"Both of you are a comfort to me. And to Mama and Papa, of course." Forcing a smile, she looked up to meet his gaze. "I hope their comments about the children don't offend you too much."

"To be truthful, it is aggravating at times," he admitted. "But Blue Sky and I are grateful that they take such a kindly interest in her and our boys and wish the best for them."

"Even if they're often wrongheaded?"

He laughed. "Even so. I do like your parents very much and try my best to hold my tongue when we disagree."

"It's such a joy to be with you and Blue Sky and your little boys again. But I can't help wondering what separations and sorrows the future still holds for all of us in this war . . . " She let the words trail off, unable to go on.

He took both her hands in his. "He'll be back, Beth. As long as he lives he'll move heaven and earth to come to you. But should the worst happen, God forbid, you'll always be surrounded by those of us who love you and will protect you and your child."

"I know." She dashed away her tears with the back of her hand.

Taking his arm, she said brightly, "Well now, you'd better come along and collect the boys before Mama overstuffs them with treats. I'm sure Blue Sky is wondering where you are, and I'm looking forward to hearing the news you've brought from General Lewis at Richfield," she added cheerfully as they ascended the stairs and went inside.

Chapter Three

IN A TOWERING FURY Carleton wove through the carnage on *Richard*'s crowded waist, dodging the multitude of jagged craters cannon shot had punched through the deck. Deafened by the din of shouts, cries of the wounded, and reverberating blasts of gunfire, he choked with every labored breath on the overpowering stench of gunsmoke, sweat, and blood.

The point at which any sane mortal would have struck colors on one side or the other had passed an infinity ago. But both Jones and Pearson had clearly thrown all reason to Hades, bent on victory at any cost no matter if that meant annihilating both ships, their entire crews, and themselves into the bargain.

There was no tactical finesse involved in this battle. It was sheer butcher's work.

Serapis continued to blast gaping holes into *Richard* at close range with her 18-pounders, senselessly sending more men to perdition. *Richard*'s few remaining 12-pound cannon had been silenced as well, and only two 9-pounders were still in action. By now both her upper and lower gun decks had taken so much damage that she had been reduced to a virtual skeleton amidships with the majority of the enemy's shots passing unhindered straight through the hull and out the far side.

Amazed that the ship still topped the waves, he took what comfort he could in the fact that enemy frigate had suffered telling hits as well.

Gunners servicing one of the 9-pounders at the rear of *Richard*'s quarter-deck targeted *Serapis*'s defenders with vicious blasts of grapeshot. The other pounded her masts with solid bar shot in the effort to take them down. The enemy's mizzenmast shuddered, supported only by a tangle of rigging.

Several fierce blazes had ravaged the enemy's decks and climbed tarred shrouds and masts to engulf the lower sails, with flames springing across to *Richard*. Countless times all guns on both vessels had stilled while their crews desperately battled raging conflagrations. Blistered patches reddened Carleton's hands and arms from helping to beat down flames.

The incessant small arms fire from the naval and Marine marksmen stationed on the platforms atop *Richard*'s masts was doing the deadliest work. Their furious volleys had finally succeeded in silencing the British tops, and several men had swung across on the enemy's yards, wedged tightly against *Richard*'s, to take possession of *Serapis*'s platforms. Adding grenades and combustible flasks called stinkpots to their arsenal, they were very close to owning their foe's upper decks as well. Only *Serapis*'s starboard guns beneath the forecastle on her lower gun deck still kept up the punishing bombardment.

Half an hour earlier Carleton had helped Jones and one of the gunners wrestle one of the 9-pounders across the quarterdeck to the starboard side for a better angle from which to fire at the broad yellow-painted trunk of the enemy's enormous mainmast. The sensation that the ship was noticeably settling had sent him hurrying below as soon as they finished, leaving Jones slumped on the chicken coop as wearily as the beleaguered creatures inside huddled in a limp, feathery clump, no longer capable of a single protesting squawk.

He had found the lower gun deck strewn with bodies and wrecked guns. The cockpit on the orlop deck was crammed with wounded and dying men, the surgeon and his mates overwhelmed. Farthest down, five feet of water sloshed in the hold. Oblivious to the British prisoners screaming that they were going to drown, exhausted crews desperately worked the three pumps that still functioned, steadily losing ground to the seawater pouring in through the hull's multiple gashes.

Hysterical rumors swirling among the men that Jones and his officers were dead, leaving no one in command of the ship, had sent him racing back topside. Jones was not where he had left him, and his gut clenched.

Without warning, as if to mock the last fraying thread of hope, a deadly barrage of round, bar, and grapeshot shrieked through the murky air from beyond *Serapis*'s bow. It exploded across *Richard*'s ruined poop and down the length of her waist to her forecastle.

The planks beneath Carleton's feet swayed and bucked like a careening bull, the whirring, high-pitched keening of the blast sounding like banshees riding the wind hell-bent for doom. He had to brace against the mainmast to keep from pitching to the deck. Swearing with profound violence, he turned one shoulder to the whips of rigging, sails, and dagger-sharp splinters that flung across his back and the deck on all sides.

At length the ship steadied and the debris settled. He straightened to stare aft through the gloom, squinting to make out the source of the attack.

By the battle lanterns' wavering light he could just distinguish the dark shadow of what appeared to be a frigate passing off *Serapis*'s bow. From the sailors' screams and Jones's raging curses, he gathered that the attacker had been *Alliance*.

Carleton had been put off by her captain from their first meeting. Landais's supercilious manner had warned him that the French officer was unlikely to obey any command Jones issued. And so it had turned out.

The return to France had been fortuitous enough to ease his initial concerns—a swift voyage with only one sighting of unidentified sails on the horizon, from which they had easily slipped away. They had made port at L'Orient on Saturday, 14 August, to find Jones's squadron preparing to weigh anchor. Certain of God's leading, Carleton had thrown his baggage aboard *Richard*, Red Fox and Stowe following, as eager for adventure as beagles on the hunt.

Too late he had learned that the squadron had inexplicably been reduced from seven ships to four. And the scent of spices still wafting from the hold of the former *Duc de Duras* of the Companie des Indies had reminded him forcefully that Jones's flagship was a converted old-fashioned merchantman, sturdily built but not designed for combat.

The ships had hardly cleared the harbor for the open sea before Carleton's heart had truly begun to sink. *Richard* was top-heavy, wallowing in ocean swells like a fat sow in a mud puddle. Far from being the fast ship Jones had insisted he must have in order to sail into danger, she quickly turned out to be the slowest and least maneuverable vessel in his squadron.

Equally disconcerting was that, although they sailed under the American flag, every one of Jones's ships was either on loan or purchased from France except the 36-gun *Alliance.* The best warship built in America and the squadron's fastest and most maneuverable vessel, she, however, was under French command, as was the 32-gun frigate *Pallas,* and the 12-gun brigantine *Vengeance.* And that the vessels were manned by motley crews of American, French, Scottish, Irish, Portuguese, and Maltese sailors seeking glory and prize money and soon carried a number of British prisoners acquired in their raids was as troubling a situation as one could ask for when bearding a formidable enemy in its den.

From that point things had swiftly unraveled. Following an argument with Jones early on, Landais had announced that he would no longer follow Jones's orders. Thereafter *Alliance* had abandoned and rejoined the squadron at her captain's whim.

After an absence of two weeks Landais had reappeared at dawn on 23 September, returning the squadron's strength to four ships as they neared Flamborough Head. Then with battle in the offing, he had sailed off again. And now he reemerged at the worst possible moment to fling a broadside at the enemy's bow—against which *Richard's* stern was tightly grappled—raining death and destruction across *Richard* as well.

At the sight of yet more dead and wounded gunners sprawled among their shattered gun carriages, Carleton gave his ire vent in furious obscenities. But *Alliance* was already sailing serenely off, with Landais either oblivious or indifferent to the screams and curses, shaken fists and desperate signals of his commodore and the flagship's crew.

It was just possible that Landais's only intent was to lend aid, Carleton reckoned, blood boiling. But with bright moonlight pouring down on *Richard*'s black hull and *Serapis*'s striking yellow trim, there could be no mistake in identifying the combatants. And considering the acrimony between him and Jones, Carleton would not have put it past the churlish Frenchman to intentionally target his commander's ship.

As Carleton balefully watched the frigate disappear into the night, his attention was drawn to the rapid flashes and flicker of cannon fire in the distance, visible through brief rents in the battle smoke, though their thunder was indistinguishable beneath the clamor close at hand. Hope welled up that at least the rest of Jones's squadron might be profitably engaged with *Serapis*'s escort.

There was no time to consider that welcome possibility. Shouts from behind him brought him hastily around. Flames again licked up *Serapis*'s rigging and erupted across *Richard*'s entangled cables. Men on both sides were casting weapons aside to beat down the fires.

Carleton wasted no time locating Jones, brass gunner's level in hand as he bent with the gunner over the repositioned 9-pounder on the quarterdeck to adjust its elevation. Determined to slap some sense into the man, Carleton shoved through the swarming mass of sailors, marines, and the terrified powder monkeys who lugged heavy cartridges toward the guns.

He was halfway up the quarterdeck companionway when more frantic screams caught his attention. As he sprang up the last step, he saw the gunner's mate, the ship's carpenter, and the master-at-arms clustered on the port side waving a white flag.

"Quarter, quarter! For God's sake, quarter!" they screamed. "Our ship is sinking!"

Before he could storm across to throttle them, they ran up onto the ruins of *Richard*'s poop, evidently intending to tear down the ship's ensign, which, Carleton noted, had already been shot away along with its staff. Realizing this at the same instant, the three men swung around and stumbled back down to the quarterdeck, still pleading for quarter.

"Quarter? What blasted rascals are them? Shoot them—kill them!" Illuminated like a veritable devil in the intermittent flicker of lanterns and gunfire, Jones glared at the men, pistol aimed, body shaking as he lunged in their direction.

Apparently reflecting that he had already shot at seven of their comrades for deserting their stations, had even peppered the shins of his own nephew, one of the lieutenants, all three ran for the port ladder at the same moment Jones pulled the trigger. No reverberation followed.

Having gained the waist, the carpenter and master-at-arms promptly vanished through the hatch. The gunner's mate lingered a moment too long, however. Face contorted with rage, Jones hurled his pistol at the man. It found its mark, striking him solidly in the head and sending him reeling down the steps after his companions.

Decisive action had to be taken without delay if the carnage was to be ended, Carleton decided swiftly. But striking their colors was not it. The raw fact remained that if *Richard* surrendered, Jones would be the first to hang and he the second, an ignominious fate he had no intention of suffering. If he was destined to die, he would meet his end fighting to the last breath.

His chest ached at the thought. The vision of Elizabeth briefly filled his mind, blessedly safe now thousands of miles away at Thornlea. For a piercing moment he could see her cradling a small blanket-wrapped bundle to her breast, and anguish pierced his heart.

Lord Jesus, I take refuge in you. Spare us!

He sucked in a steadying breath, then strode to Jones's side. "We are sinking," he said tersely. "Our hull is essentially reduced to lacework, we've lost one of the pumps, and the crews working the other three are on the point of collapse."

He was interrupted by an urgent, hopeful voice that echoed through the din from *Serapis*. "Have you struck, sir? Do you strike?" It was Captain Pearson.

Livid, Jones stared at Carleton through narrowed eyes, then jerked around and brandished his fist at the enemy captain. "I may sink, but I'll be cursed if I strike!"

Carleton wrestled his rage into submission. "In that case, now might be an opportune time for us to try boarding again!" he shouted above the battle fray. He indicated the flames that licked upward along *Serapis*'s forecastle directly across from them. "If we're not all to drown, we'll have to take her and hope she still floats."

Jones jerked a nod and snapped, "See to it."

Carleton turned in time to see a large contingent of men flood through the hatch below into the ship's waist. The British prisoners, around a hundred in all, had evidently been released from the hold by *Richard*'s master at arms, who followed on their heels. All appeared dazed and greatly relieved despite the chaos they stepped into.

The threat they posed should they join forces with *Serapis* was immediately obvious. Could anything else possibly go wrong?

Carleton stifled a groan as he followed on Jones's heels to the head of the quarterdeck ladder, where his lieutenants already clustered at its base. Jones fixed the cowering men in an icy stare, a pistol in each hand. Wasting no words, he quickly persuaded them that their best chance of survival was to return to the hold and help work the pumps to prevent the ship's sinking. To Carleton's relief they meekly retreated below with the master at arms.

Crisis averted, Carleton ran down the ladder intending to assemble a boarding party. Before he could step onto the waist, however, he was arrested by Stowe's shout from the foretop high above.

"Enemy gatherin' to board!"

Is there no one on either of these ships who possesses the least fragment of common sense? Carleton fumed silently. He felt trapped in one long, protracted, recurring nightmare with no end in sight.

Then the familiar surge of battle fever swept through him, and he ran to gather every man he could lay hands on.

IN FULL BATTLE CRY, more than two dozen British sailors and Marines burst over the bulwark onto *Richard*'s waist. Brandishing cutlasses and pistols, they surged down the gangway to the base of the quarterdeck ladder in a furious assault only to be met by even fiercer resistance. Barring their way, Jones viciously wielded a pike, backed up by Carleton's cutlass and tomahawk and the bristling weaponry of First Lieutenant Richard Dale and every officer and crewman who could reach them.

The outnumbered enemy was no sooner thrust back to their own ship than *Alliance* again passed off *Serapis*'s stern and unleashed another indiscriminate broadside. It tore across both ships, filling the air with explosions, screams, and outraged oaths. In desperation Jones ordered lanterns to be hoisted aloft to larboard on the fore, main, and mizzen shrouds to indicate friend rather than foe.

After several agonizing moments *Alliance*'s barrage ceased. But by then Carleton distinctly felt the pace of *Richard*'s settling increase. Landais's assault had doubtless caused more destruction below the waterline.

Would this interminable night never end? he wondered. And what further disasters still lay in store before it finally did, whether in triumph or defeat?

Just as he noted another inferno climbing the tangled rigging on both ships, the concussion of gunfire suspended. Exhaustion dragged at his limbs as he sprang to help extinguish a conflagration on the quarterdeck.

With that fire under control, he straightened to look toward the ship's bow. And drew in a sharp breath.

The towering mainmast swayed dangerously, shot through at its base, with little more than shrouds, stays, and ratlines holding it erect. His gaze flew upward.

The maintop was ablaze.

He stumbled down the steps onto the waist, chest constricted in breathless horror, while the men manning it, Red Fox among them, emptied their water casks onto the flames to no avail. Tearing off jackets and shirts, they fought frantically to beat the fire down. Gratitude left Carleton weak kneed when they at last contained the firestorm. Red Fox's soot-streaked face appeared over the platform's edge, meeting his anxious gaze with a weary nod.

It was then that Carleton caught movement along the main yard from the corner of his eye. The long spar jutted out above *Serapis,* and one of the topmen was edging far out along its footropes. He carried a bucket, looped by its rope handle over one arm, in the same hand holding a smoldering slow match. He stopped, hooked his arm over the yard, and with his free hand began taking grenades from the bucket one by one, lighting them with the match, then dropping them onto the enemy's deck, where they bounced several feet and exploded with little effect.

As Carleton watched, transfixed, the man leaned as far out as he could, arm extended, and opened his hand. Gut clenched, Carleton followed the grenade's plummet downward. It vanished from his sight straight through a jagged break in the deck's planks.

There followed a moment of heart-stopping suspense. Then an enormous, blinding flash boiled upward through the hole, ripping the planking wide to all sides on a rapidly expanding wall of sound and flame beyond anything Carleton had ever witnessed. *Richard*'s violent pitch caused him to stagger and fall to his knees, eyes pressed shut, hands clapped over his ears as did everyone around him, while successive waves of fiery explosions resounded the length of *Serapis*'s lower gun deck, billowing clouds of smoke and shredded debris.

When the clamor at last diminished to an endurable level, he pushed to his feet and shoved into the mass of sailors and Marines clustered at the starboard weather rail, looking on in awe and horror. What he could see of the destruction aboard the enemy frigate was beyond description.

Serapis's mizzenmast canted to port at an alarming angle held up only by entangled yards and rigging. Great, jagged, charred holes rent her upper deck and the visible portions of her hull. Heartsick, he watched blackened, screaming men, clothing aflame, leap out of her shattered stern into the heaving sea.

It occurred to him then that *Destiny*'s final moments must have been similar. And the bitter taste of bile burned in his mouth.

IT WAS OVER WITH startling suddenness.

Carleton had just dragged himself up the quarterdeck steps, feeling as mentally and physically wasted as every one of *Richard*'s hollow-eyed crew obviously were. By now it must be nearing midnight, he reckoned, and fires had yet again blown across from *Serapis*. With their last dregs of energy both crews attacked blazes in single-minded desperation.

Wearily he headed for Jones, still hunched over the 9-pounder with the gunner preparing to fire another round into *Serapis*'s tottering mainmast. Hearing a shout from behind him, he swung to see Pearson yards away at his frigate's quarterdeck railing, his speaking horn to his lips.

"Sir," the captain cried, "I have struck! I ask for quarter!"

For an instant Carleton stood frozen, then he turned and rapidly closed the distance to Jones. Appearing equally worn and filthy from head to foot, the commodore straightened to look beyond Carleton to the enemy captain, appearing taken aback. Then, as though recollecting himself, he shouted to Pearson, "If you've struck, haul down your ensign!"

Together they watched Pearson walk stiffly to his ship's shattered taff-rail and tear down the huge red flag, ripping the frayed, shot-torn fabric loose from the nails that held it. The instant the flag fluttered down, Jones shouted for his crew to cease fire. Officers scurried across the decks to spread the command.

On *Serapis* Pearson's officers, after several moments of shocked dis-belief, reluctantly did the same. One by one the guns on both sides fell silent.

In short order a boarding party under Lieutenant Dale's command crossed to *Serapis* to take control of the ruined frigate. Carleton sent Red Fox and Stowe along to assist.

A short time later as *Richard*'s crew was engaged in cutting away the grappling lines and entangled rigging that held the two ships together, Lieutenant Dale escorted Pearson and his lieutenants onto *Richard*'s deck for the formal surrender. At that moment, with a resounding crash, *Serapis*'s canting mainmast toppled to port, dragging down with it the mizzen's splintered topmast. Both ships heaved violently on the impact's wake.

Once the sea settled, Pearson turned to Jones, eyes narrowed. Bowing with obvious resentment, he tendered his sword, saying curtly, "It pains me that I'm compelled to deliver up my sword to a man who may be said to fight with a noose around his neck."

Carleton clenched his jaw to stifle an oath. The glint in Dale's eyes told him that the lieutenant shared his emotions. Jones, however, appear-ed to take no exception to Pearson's slur that he was nothing more than a pirate.

"Sir, you've fought like a hero," he said in his normal mild tone as he accepted the sword. "I've no doubt your sovereign will reward you most amply for it."

Pearson's lips thinned. Scanning the destruction around him, he deman-ded, "From what country is your crew?"

"America—in the main," Jones murmured, considerably stretching the truth, Carleton thought wryly.

Pearson's crestfallen countenance appeared slightly to clear. "Then it's diamond cut diamond," he conceded in a patronizing tone, evidently taking comfort in the delusion that at least Americans were at heart Englishmen and that he had been spared the humiliation of yielding to either France or Spain.

While the rest of the British officers surrendered their side arms to Dale, Fanning, and the other American officers who by now clustered around them, Jones said, "We've all fought hard and well this night. Would you gentlemen do me the honor of joining me in my cabin for a glass of wine?"

As he moved to usher the British officers to the hatch, Carleton drew him aside. "There's considerable destruction below, particularly to your cabin, which took several broadsides," he cautioned in a low voice. "You might wish to conclude the business topside."

Doubtless suffering the aftereffects of battle's hectic frenzy, Jones directed a vague gaze around him as though seeing the wreckage for the first time. "I'm sure we'll manage," he said softly. "Join us if you will, sir."

He beckoned courteously to Pearson, who for a moment stared intently at Carleton before following Jones through the hatch, Carleton reluctantly trailing the officers. As he had warned, they were forced to navigate the lower gun deck to Jones's cabin through a scene of astonishing carnage and ruin.

The dead lay sprawled all around them. Giant timbers had been dangerously mangled by the dozens of 18-pound balls that had torn entirely through the ship. Only a splintered few still prevented the poop from fully collapsing into the commodore's cabin.

Tipping his head toward Carleton, Fanning, who had spent the entire battle in the maintop, indicated a cavernous hole in the upper deck. "You could drive clear through that one with a coach and six," he muttered, eyes wide with awe.

"That you could," Carleton answered grimly.

"What in tarnation is keeping this wreck afloat?"

Carleton raised his eyebrows. "The Almighty?"

Fanning gulped. "But how much longer?"

"Let's hope just long enough."

The destruction to Jones's elegant cabin was, if possible, even worse. He stopped just inside the door as though disoriented before ushering everyone inside. They had to shove debris aside to find space to stand.

After manhandling a splintered beam out of the way, Carleton turned to find Pearson studying him, eyes narrowed. "Who you are, sir?"

Making a point of not bowing, Carleton answered crisply, "Major General Jonathan Carleton at your service, sir."

For an instant Pearson stared at him, his expression blank. Then the color drained from his face, almost instantly succeeded by a rising tide of heat.

"*Ca-carleton?* The traitor?" he spluttered, uttering Carleton's name as though it was an obscenity. He looked Carleton's befouled form up and down with a sneer, then drew himself up and spat, "Well, I suppose there's no shame in losing to *two* notable pirates."

A number of responses occurred to Carleton. But mindful of all the remarks he had made during his lifetime that would better have been left unsaid, he contented himself with responding in deliberate, icy insolence, "Which one of us is a pirate, sir, depends entirely on one's perspective. Does it not?"

Chapter Four

ELIZABETH TOOK IN the Great Hall while basking in the warmth that radiated from the huge, flaming log crackling and popping in the enormous granite fireplace centered on the rear wall. Banks of tall mullioned windows several feet away on either hand offered a fine view of the terrace at the building's rear and the sweeping slope of lawn that descended to a picturesque stone bridge spanning the river to the forested far bank.

Overhead four immense wrought-iron chandeliers in the form of wheels hung from chains, their myriad lighted tapers casting a warm glow over the vast space. The ceiling rose two stories high, its thick plasterwork depicting thistles, unicorns, Saint Andrew, and the Carleton crest. The same decorations covered the underside of the wide second-story gallery that ran along the front and side walls. Accessible via the spiral stairways in the turrets on either side of the manor's main entrance, it connected the laird's chambers, which took up the entire second floor in the manor's short north wing, to the spacious guest chambers and her parents' rooms in the south wing.

A fireplace at each end of the Great Hall helped to hold cold drafts at bay, both, like the central hearth, large enough for a man to walk into. Through the wide doorway next to the south fireplace lay the large dining room decorated with matching elaborate ceilings and its own granite fireplace. A second door on its adjacent wall opened onto the manor's front entry passage and the drawing room, parlor, and music room beyond, which occupied the rest of the south wing's first floor. The north wing housed the library and Carleton's study, accessible along a passage that led to the terrace door at its end.

Elizabeth turned from the fireplace, her gaze drawn, as always, to the swirls, whorls, braids, and wide ribbons of weaponry that arrayed the Great Hall's walls as high as a tall man could reach. Polished muskets, rifles, bayonets, pistols, broadswords, pikes, halberds, axes, and targe shields glittered in the dancing firelight, a veritable arsenal ready to hand at a moment's notice.

The manor was a formidable fortress indeed, she mused, built of three courses of heavy limestone blocks, the interior walls finished with a thick layer of fine plaster, the exterior with a rougher mortar. It was a castle, in fact, clearly meant to intimidate any enemy—whether the Cherokee, who had raided through the area until forced to surrender their lands east of the Blue Ridge two years earlier, or the British.

The message could not have been proclaimed more defiantly. And to back it up, a ground-floor magazine cached impressive stores of gunpowder, bullet lead, flints, and cartouche boxes full of cartridges. A narrow spiral stairway secreted within the fireplace set into the sixteen-foot thick foundation wall that formed the Hall's southern end gave quick access to it.

She directed a veiled glance at her companion, Thornlea's steward, Alistair Durie, a dark-haired, slender man of medium height in his late thirties. "When I first met him, Jonathan implied that after Sheriffmuir Sir Harry threw over the role of a rebel for that of a sedate businessman. But judging from the home he built here in the wilderness, he was by no means a meek, subservient vassal to England's king. It's obvious he was fully prepared to defend his freedom against any enemy who might attempt to wrest it away."

Durie followed her gaze across the Hall. Comfortable wing chairs upholstered in clan tartan; deep leather couches; and walnut tables, chairs, cabinets, and shelves lent a welcoming aspect to their surroundings without diminishing the impression of wealth and power.

"As they say, 'A man's home is his castle,'" he replied dryly. With a wink he added, "And I must say, mistress, for all that ye be sassennach, ye couldna look more the part o' a laird's wife. On his return yer husband'll be pleased to see ye wear the arisaid."

She couldn't restrain a pleased smile. Her maid, Jemma, had arrayed her for dinner in the Scottish women's traditional dress. Jemma's mother, Sarah, now the manor's housekeeper, had fashioned it from a length of the Carleton clan's favored tartan of deep blue-grey, charcoal, black, and cream, its sett accented by a narrow crimson thread.

It was the first time Elizabeth had worn it, and she delighted in how the plaid draped over her shoulders, pinned with an antique silver plaid brooch. Held together by a loose sash around her waist, the fabric parted at the front to fall almost to her ankles over the cream-colored wool gown she wore beneath. Its style comfortably accommodated the thickening of her waist, and the finely woven Thornlea wool felt heather-soft, the colors perfectly enhancing her fair complexion and dark auburn hair.

"Thank you providing this lovely plaid."

He bowed. "It suits ye verra well, mistress. And as yer husband deeded the property to ye, Thornlea and everythin' that belongs to it is yers forby."

She returned his smile. "That's still hard for me to grasp."

She turned to gaze searchingly up at the large portrait that hung above the ornate marble mantelpiece, the blue-and-white Scottish saltire displayed boldly above. "Sir Harry looks to be quite a stern man. And a determined one."

"Ooch, he was that. But those o' us who had the privilege o' servin' him kent he had a tender heart."

She studied the craggy contours of Sir Harrison Carleton's face. Indeed the portraitist had hinted at a smile in the tilt of his subject's generous mouth, she noted, and in a subtle twinkle in sky-blue eyes lighter than Carleton's.

She canted her head, returning her gaze to Durie. She knew little about him other than that he had been a childless widower when he came to Thornlea from St. Andrews along the Firth of Forth. But in the short time she had known him, he had proven to be canny, judicious, and close mouthed, his reassuringly calm, steady demeanor quickly winning her trust.

"You worked for him for several years before his . . . death?"

" 'Afore he was murdered by the king's men, d'ye mean," Durie return-ed, his rich Scottish burr hardening. "Aye. The gen'l told ye what hap-pened?"

"He did."

Biting her lip, she moved to stand before the portrait on the wall to the hearth's right, Durie following. It portrayed a handsome, powerfully built man, in his mid thirties, she guessed, with noble features, sun-streaked light brown hair, and piercing hazel eyes that gazed out at the viewer with authority and challenge.

"I can't say that Lord Carleton and his elder brother look much alike. Of course, this portrait must have been painted when he was still a young man, while Sir Harry is considerably older in his."

Durie nodded. " 'Twas done no' a year 'afore we lost him. From what he told me, Lord Carleton's likeness was taken when he was a widower, not long 'afore he married Gen'l Carleton's mother."

She remained silent for a long moment, haunted by the memory of finding Carleton standing motionless before his father's portrait shortly before he had left to return to France. His expression had been so bleak then that a sharp pang had stabbed through her.

Hesitantly she said, "Jonathan told me that he always averted his face from his father's likeness, believing that Lord Carleton had sent him away because he held him unworthy to be his son. Now that he's learned the truth, he's much grieved by his hardness of heart."

" 'Twould be natural," Durie murmured, nodding. "Yet he oughtn't to be. How could a wee bairn understand the concerns o' a grown man till he was grown himself?"

Elizabeth glanced back at Sir Harry's portrait. "I don't see much of either of them in my husband."

"The three o' 'em had much the same build, far as I can tell. But I believe the gen'l takes after his mother the more."

"So her brother, le comte de Caledonne, maintains. Judging by how closely Jonathan resembles his uncle, I have to agree."

Durie frowned. "The gen'l was already gone in England when I took this position. I didna meet him until five years ago when he returned to take over control o' the estate and Sir Harry's business interests—'afore he was called to Boston as aide to Gen'l Gage."

"And a spy for General Washington."

Durie nodded. "He was verra cut up at the time, ye ken, yet he impressed me greatly." He turned to fully face her. "None'll dispute that yer husband's a braw man, one who inspires loyalty in those who serve him. And love as well. 'Tis a shame he's become a target o' the Royal Navy and lost so many o' his ships to the devils."

"It was to be expected considering all the havoc his privateers have wreaked on British shipping," she responded. "It's the loss of so many of his sailors that's the most painful for him."

"The fortunes o' war, alas."

She looked quickly away, one hand resting on her abdomen at her babe's sudden kick. Her gaze alighted on the large portrait to the left of the fireplace that she ever sought to avoid for the turmoil of emotions it evoked, yet was inevitably drawn to, as now.

Unlike them it delineated its subject at full length and close to full size, and more even than the other two, dominated the room. Instead of the others' more muted tones, its colors were richly vibrant. Surely it must have been painted at about the same time as the miniature of Carleton she possessed. For he appeared to be a young man of about twenty in the full bloom of early manhood.

Masterfully done, the painting portrayed him in a verdant landscape, tanned, with sunshine gleaming on his long pale-golden hair, worn loose and falling to his shoulders, windblown. His smile appeared mischievous, tinged with the supreme confidence of vigorous youth. Studying it now, however, she realized that the artist had depicted his eyes as more grey than blue, casting a troubling shadow in their depths.

Tall and muscular but more slender than he was now, the contours of his face still holding a hint of childhood's softness, he wore full Highland kit of white shirt and dark charcoal waistcoat and jacket with the *féileadh-mór,* or belted plaid, and gartered hose in clan tartan. A broad black leather belt from which hung a matching sporran; the dagger called the *sgian-dubh* tucked into the top of his stocking at his right knee; laced black leather brogues; and rakishly tilted blue bonnet trimmed with a ribbon cockade completed his attire.

On seeing it for the first time from across the Hall, she had drawn Carleton eagerly to it, but his jaw had hardened as he stared at his younger self. "That young man existed in another lifetime," he had said curtly, strangling her questions in her throat. "He'd only learned a little of the world and its ills, of betrayal and war. He's a stranger to me now."

"He's still a part of you," she had protested, stricken. "He always will be."

"As a shadow perhaps," he had responded gruffly.

"He has more substance than you realize," she had countered, believing it.

For a suspended moment he had searched her eyes, then had swung away.

Just to look up at his portrait now caused a deep ache in her chest, the blurring of her vision, the wrenching consciousness of his absence. A sharp longing for the solid physical reality of him overwhelmed her, for his strong arms enfolding her to his breast, his sweet kisses and endearments, the passion of their lovemaking.

Yet for all that she missed him so painfully, she took comfort in the settled confidence in each other they'd shared since their wedding: a deeper, more vital trust like a strong cord that would bind their hearts even beyond the grave. It was from this surety that she knew in her bones he prayed for her even now, entrusting her to God's keeping as she did for him.

She heard someone enter the wide double doors of the Hall behind them. Blinking back the tears that stung her eyes, she turned to see Red Fox's younger brother, Spotted Pony, and his wife, Rain Woman, enter with Laughing Otter. They were followed by Andrews with Blue Sky and Brown Bear, one of the leading Shawnee warriors, all arrayed in festive tribal garb.

"I can see why he'd be drawn to the Indians and cast his lot with 'em," Durie said shrewdly, nodding toward the group. "He descends from a long line o' fierce warriors, ye ken, from Norse raiders to Normans."

She fingered the antique brooch that pinned her plaid at the shoulder. "I hadn't thought of that, but you're right. Like the Highland clans, the Shawnee are implacable in defending their lands."

Looking away, he muttered, "And like for us Scots, in the end their cause will be lost."

"Surely not!" she protested.

He made no response, finally said gruffly, "I didna ken what to expect when he brought ye here out o' the blue this summer. 'Tis been my experience that ladies o' such beauty and grace such as ye are most oft lofty and ill-tempered w' those they consider beneath 'em. But none could be kinder than ye, whether to servants or those o' rank. Ye wield authority, aye, but gently. And considerin' all ye did in service o' our cause, 'tis a remarkable woman ye are indeed."

Taken aback, she met his earnest gaze. In the few months she had known him, Durie had always been astute and sparing with his words. He had never overstepped the bounds of one conscious that he held his place at his master's pleasure. Yet neither had he ever displayed any hint of subservience. What she read in his eyes was a reassuring forthright admiration and goodwill.

"Thank you, Alistair," she said softly. "I've come to lean heavily on your wise guidance, your faithfulness to your charge, and your friendship."

He bowed again. " 'Tis my great pleasure to serve ye, mistress."

Chapter Five

ANDREWS IDLY TWIRLED the stem of his wineglass between his fingers. His thoughts were occupied with the news he'd gleaned the previous day from Brigadier General Andrew Lewis at his estate outside the small town of Salem, six miles away on the other side of the Staunton River. When a footman leaned in to refill the empty glass, he lifted it, downed a long swallow, and set it back in its place.

"There's much about General Lewis that impresses me," he said thoughtfully.

He noted that around the long dining room table the Shawnee men and their wives stiffened and scowled. Clearly they were very far from forgetting Lewis's most famous accomplishment, Cornstalk's defeat at the Battle of Point Pleasant in 1774 during Lord Dunmore's War. And its far-reaching consequences for their nation, not the least of which had been the murder of the Shawnee's great sachem only two years ago at Fort Randolph on that very same Point.

Elizabeth apparently noted their reaction, too, for she hastily changed the subject. "You believe the information he shared is accurate?"

"I've no reason not to. He receives regular reports from the legislature and his contacts in the army. The charges of treason that forced him to retire a couple of years ago were for actions that are wide open to interpretation and were leveled by only a few officers. Washington esteems him, and he's served honorably as a member of Virginia's legislature and now as Indian commissioner."

The low fire crackling softly in the spacious dining room's fireplace dispelled the fall afternoon's chill. Andrews and Blue Sky were seated next to Elizabeth and her parents at the long table covered with a spotless linen cloth and set with fine silver, porcelain, and crystal.

Present along with the warriors and their wives were Colonel Isaiah Moghrab, commander of the Rangers' Second Regiment composed mainly of black troops, and his wife Sarah. They were flanked by his subordinates: tall, lean, muscular Major Apollos Matheson, whose coppery-brown complexion and the angles of his hawk-like visage reflected his mixed African and Cherokee blood; and Major Jeremiah Prince, a caramel-skinned, green-eyed black man of medium height with loosely curling brown hair.

Opposite at the table sat the Rangers' chaplain, Major James McLeod, with his wife Mary, whose slender figure had just begun to show evidence of her pregnancy. Colonel Matthew Farris, a lean, handsome, dark-haired Scot, commander of the Rangers' First Regiment; Carleton's aide, rugged Major Josiah Hutchinson; and Andrews' aide Captain Tom Spencer, a veteran of the Delaware Continentals, completed their company. The latter two, Elizabeth's fellow prisoners aboard the British prison ship *Erebus,* had been crucial to her survival.

" 'Tis a shame Washington had to abandon Stony Point back in July after all General Wayne's efforts to wrest it from the British," Farris growled, referring to a strategic peninsula jutting from the Hudson River's western shore. "Had we been able to hold it, we'd have controlled King's Ferry and the river practically to New York City."

"It'd been fittin' payback fer the British navy's raids 'long the coast and burnin' New Haven, Norwalk, and Fairfield back in May," muttered Hutchinson, who had been captain in a Connecticut regiment before being captured by the British.

"As long as the British control Verplanck's Point directly across the river, that's impossible," Andrews pointed out. "Washington no sooner left for West Point than the British threw that assault back, which gave Wayne no alternative but to withdraw from Stony Point. He did destroy as much of the British works there as possible—for all the good it did in the end."

"You think Washington bears any fault for the debacle?" asked Spencer, frowning. "Or Wayne?"

Andrews shook his head. "According to Lewis, things were well in hand when His Excellency left. And it appears Wayne did all he could for being outnumbered and outgunned. Since the British took the Point back, they've constructed extensive new defenses under an officer named Patrick Ferguson—captain, I believe."

Frowning, Andrews passed the dish of stewed collard greens to Anne. "His men call him the Bulldog," he continued. "According to the intelligence Lewis received, the works are quite impressive. Even so, Washington is champing at the bit to renew the assault, but his council of war is split straight down the middle as to whether gaining back the ground is worth the losses we'd take."

"So it remains a burr under His Excellency's saddle," Elizabeth put in. Slathering a generous helping of Salome's delicately pink mayhaw jelly on half of a feather-light biscuit, she savored a bite of the mingled tart-apple and sweet ripe-peach flavor.

Chuckling, Andrews exchanged a grin with Blue Sky. "There's always at least one to keep His Excellency exercised. The debate is apparently still simmering, though things remain relatively quiet at the moment. But you never know what tomorrow may bring, particularly now that Spain has finally allied with us and declared war on Britain."

"A positive development to be sure," Elizabeth returned. "But it still feels as if the war's ground to a standstill. In more than five years, what progress have we really made toward defeating the British? In spite of all the maneuvering on both sides, we're essentially still in the same place we were at the beginning."

Dr. Howard finished his serving of roasted sweet potatoes and leaned back in his chair, wiping his mouth with his serviette. "The French are helping a great deal by supplying us with vast quantities of goods, my dear, including arms and uniforms that we desperately need if the army's to continue the fight."

Farris helped himself to the last slice of tenderloin. "So far, at least," he growled. "But how much longer will they continue with no victory in sight?"

"Mind that the Dutch ha' also been generous in their support though they've held back from declarin' war on England," McLeod countered as the two footmen passed unobtrusively around the table, removing empty platters and plates and carrying them into the adjoining servery, where a stairway descended directly to the buttery and kitchens on the ground floor.

"As far as the French are concerned, it doesn't help that after failing miserably in the effort to wrest Newport from the British, d'Estaing abandoned our troops and sailed his fleet right back to the Caribbean last November," Elizabeth returned sharply, referring to French admiral Charles-Hector, le comte d'Estaing. "Or that with the French navy out of the way, the British were easily able to capture Savannah in December, not to mention that the militia offered hardly any resistance at all."

"Things might be looking up, however," Andrews broke in. "Shortly before we left Richfield, a courier arrived with news that d'Estaing's returning with twenty-five ships of the line. There's talk he'll combine his four thousand troops with General Lincoln's army down in Charlestown to lay siege to Savannah. He's got more than five thousand men, counting militia."

The officers around the table straightened, their attention momentarily distracted from the large, fragrant, apple compote one footmen carried in, followed by the other bearing the rich boiled-custard sauce. "Don't know anybody holds much confidence in Lincoln or d'Estaing no matter how many men they got," grumbled Matheson, exchanging a doubtful look with Prince.

As the footmen began to serve the dessert, Elizabeth noted absently that Matheson directed a sidelong glance at Jemma, who kept her gaze demurely fixed on her bowl.

"Then we'd better hope they surprise us," Andrews returned. "According to Washington's intelligence, the British believe the South to be a great loyalist haven. They're turning their attention to Virginia and the Carolinas now."

"They might just find out different if they venture into the Carolina backcountry," Farris drawled.

Andrews exchanged a knowing glance with the colonel before returning his attention to the others. "By the way, Lewis shared a bit of gossip you might find interesting. General Arnold's court-martial has been postponed yet again."

"Benedict Arnold?" Dr. Howard put down his spoon and turned to Elizabeth. "Wasn't he the hero of Saratoga, defeating General Burgoyne at the Battle of Bemis Heights?"

"The victory is counted to General Gates since he held the command, Papa. But Burgoyne would most likely have escaped had Arnold not ignored Gates's express order removing him from the battlefield."

"From what I've heard, Arnold still hasn't recovered from the wound he took in the leg and may ne'er," McLeod said. "The ball shattered the bone, but he wouldna hear o' it bein' amputated. He's been left crippled, yet he keeps petitionin' for another command."

"Why is he being court-martialed?" Anne demanded, puzzled.

Arnold had served as Philadelphia's military commander following the British withdrawal the previous year, McLeod explained. And credible charges were brought against him by Joseph Reed, a powerful local politician formerly an aide to Washington, that Arnold had used his position to profit from illegally buying and selling military goods.

"I heard he livin' might' high on the hog," Prince put in.

"What do ye expect o' one who married that loyalist woman, Peggy Shippen, that's been courted by the likes o' a British major," Hutchinson growled. "John André, I think his name is. Her father's a judge who did plenty o' business with the British while they occupied Philadelphia. Wouldn't be at all surprised if they waren't still in close contact."

Farris narrowed his eyes. "Rumor has it she holds considerable sway over ol' Benny."

"He made hisself stink to many of our senior officers for what sure looks like consortin' with the enemy," Isaiah noted with a snort.

Andrews swallowed the last bite of his pudding. "You know how ambitious and jealous Arnold is. That he's repeatedly been passed over for honors and a promotion in favor of those with less seniority grinds him. He's not about to forget it. And when Washington reprimanded him for his dealings in Philly—"

"If ye want to call it that." McLeod rolled his eyes.

"It hardly qualifies as a rebuke, but obviously it stung Arnold's delicate self-esteem," Andrews returned. "At any rate, he demanded a court-martial to clear his name. And I have a bad feeling that we'll all be better off if they find him guilty and send him packing."

ANDREWS LIGHTLY STROKED seven-month-old Snow Flower's soft, rounded cheek with the back of one finger, delighting in her delicate, dark features. She waved her arms and kicked her feet, cooing happily up at him.

"If my wife doesn't bless me a daughter next time," he teased, reluctantly handing the baby back to her mother, "I shall have to buy this one from you."

"She's a rare beauty indeed," McLeod agreed, bending over the child cradled in Rain Woman's arms. "And she already knows how to charm a man."

Rain Woman lifted her youngest to cuddled her against her neck, her cheek resting on the little girl's downy black hair. "My husband will not give her up, Golden Elk," she said, exchanging a proud smile with Spotted Pony. "Nor will her sister and brothers."

"You know how babies are made, my husband," Blue Sky said pointedly. Holding their own squirming nine-month-old in her arms, she regarded Andrews through narrowed eyes, one brow raised meaningfully. "If you wish for a daughter, you will have to give me one."

"Should she bear you another son, however, I think you will not complain," Laughing Otter returned with amusement, eliciting grins from the men. "At least you will have pleasure in the trying."

"None could complain at havin' such braw lads." McLeod said. "I'll no' care whether the Lord gives my Mary and me a son or a daughter in a few month's time, only that our child'll be healthy."

As the others murmured their agreement, Andrews took in his wife and baby, overcome with gratitude at how God had made his life entirely new since he had accompanied Carleton to America. When she returned his gaze with one beaming with love and devotion, his heart swelled. Indeed he had been blessed beyond all he had longed for, all he could ever have imagined.

They had just returned to their clustered cabins nestled among the trees that fringed a wide curve of the river's bank. On the other side of the valley road, two picturesque stone barns stood on the meadow surrounded by cattle, horses, and sheep grazing contentedly on the browning grass. The prospect was as peaceful as one could wish, Andrews thought. Deceptively so.

That summer he had taken the precaution of posting pickets well down the road in both directions outside the fortifications he had added in the spring to guard the valley's entrance. After the British attacks on Portsmouth and Suffolk back in May, he couldn't help wondering whether they might intrude even this far.

While they had been absent at the officers' dinner, Laughing Otter's daughters, Yellow Feather and Morning Dew, had supervised the youngest children. For a moment Andrews watched the little ones playing around the *msikahmiqui,* the long gable-roofed cabin serving as council house that dominated the clearing at the camp's center. Jimmy Douglas and Leads the Way ran shouting and laughing in happy abandon with the warriors' children and others belonging to the black troops and the estate's workers. All appeared to receive equal acceptance, none taking note of color and language.

Smiling, he mused that too often people focused on their differences instead of what they shared in common: that all were made in God's image, that God loved them equally, that Jesus had died and risen to make them all one.

He directed a surreptitious glance at McLeod, who had lost his first wife and two small children to an Indian attack on the frontier, wondering whether the sight brought renewed hurt and anger. But the major held his gaze with one that held no shadow.

" 'Tis God's grace alone that can truly redeem our past and reconcile us to one another," he said softly as though reading Andrews' thoughts.

Andrews nodded. "I'm learning the truth of that."

"Well, now," McLeod returned briskly. "I'd better take wee Jimmy to his mam so she can put him down for a nap. She'll have my head if our boy misbehaves tonight," he added dryly to the others' chuckles.

Andrews gave Blue Sky a meaningful look. "Our sons would benefit from a rest too." His mouth quirked when Little Elk let out a fretful cry as though in affirmation.

McLeod went to retrieve Jimmy, then took his leave, carrying the protesting boy, eyelids drooping and head nodding against his adoptive father's shoulder. The women rounded up the smallest children and led them back to their cabins, while Andrews lingered in the shade of a tall poplar with Spotted Pony and Brown Bear.

A short distance away a group of warriors recently returned from a hunt lounged idly in the trees' shade. Their numbers had noticeably dwindled over the long, idle months spent encamped in the Shenandoah Valley the past winter, when Washington had dispersed his cavalry units to find better forage. Lacking opportunity for battle and its consequent loot had discouraged many, but events on the western border had caused others to abandon the Long Knives altogether.

That spring several small parties had trickled away to the British or to move their families farther west, out of reach of the conflict. Only those from Black Hawk's clan along with a few others from their Kispokotha division and the Maquachake division of the Shawnee who were most closely allied with Carleton, the war chief White Eagle, remained with the Rangers now, along with a scattering from a few other tribes.

Before leaving for France in July, Carleton had urged all the men whose families were absent to bring them to Thornlea's mountain fastness, where they could be protected, fed, and cared for. The native camp had correspondingly expanded, but without increasing the warriors' ranks. In contrast, Isaiah's mostly black regiment continued to swell with the arrival of more freemen and escaped slaves, while numerous Irish, Scots, and Germans had swarmed to Farris's command.

Brown Bear followed Andrews' gaze and swept his arm toward the lounging warriors. "What good is it for us to continue fighting for the Long Knives when so many of those who joined with us in the beginning have turned their backs on us now?" he demanded bitterly. "How can we stand against the British when our own brothers ally with them or, thinking to live in peace, return to their homes while ours remain undefended?"

"Those who changed their allegiance were mostly from other nations," Andrews countered. "Only a few from our people returned home, even fewer to fight on the side of the British."

"Have not even our friends McKee, Elliott, and the Girtys, thrown off the Long Knives and gone over to the British?" Spotted Pony demanded. He referred to Alexander McKee; Matthew Elliott; and Simon, James, and George Girty, white traders with close connections to the native tribes who had previously served as intermediaries between them and the Americans.

For several moments they glumly discussed the unsuccessful siege Black Fish had laid against Boonesborough the previous September, leading a mixed force comprised mainly of Shawnee. It had cost the lives of many warriors, and the past spring Kentucky militia had attacked Chillicothe in reprisal, burning the town and crops in the fields. Although Black Fish and his warriors had driven them off in a determined defense, the great war chief of the Shawnee's Chillicothe division had been shot in the leg, and the festering wound had taken his life.

"You see what happened to our brother Cornstalk and our grand-father White Eyes when they tried to appease these Long Knives," Brown Bear said.

He went on to remind them that the powerful Lenape sachem White Eyes had given sanctuary to Cornstalk's sister, Nonhelema, and those of their Maquachake division who advocated for peace with the Long Knives as well as many other native Christians at his town in Ohio Territory's Muskingum Valley. A year earlier, after tireless negotiations, White Eyes had signed a treaty with the Americans at Fort Pitt that promised to establish a Lenape state with representatives to the American Congress, subject to Congress's approved. In return the Lenape agreed to serve as guides for the Americans when they passed through Ohio Territory to attack the British and their native allies.

Only months later, while serving as a guide and negotiator with an American expedition, White Eyes had died of smallpox—or so the Americans claimed. But his close associate, George Morgan, an American Indian agent and trader who had helped to negotiate the Fort Pitt treaty, maintained that the great sachem had been treacherously murdered by American militia. Enraged, the majority of Lenape had abandoned the Americans to fight on the side of the British.

Andrews exchanged a glum look with Spotted Pony. "In both cases it was militia soldiers who alone were responsible. But since none of their comrades would testify against them, they could not be held accountable. Is it not so among us also?"

"When White Eagle returned to us, you saw that it was as hard for him as for the rest of us to restrain his rage and encourage us to stay with the Long Knives," Spotted Pony returned, ignoring Andrews' question.

For a long moment Andrews remained silent. At last he said, "I also long to return home to live at peace with my wife and children. But will that be possible if the Americans win and we have opposed them or remained neutral? I cannot see any hope for our people apart from the path White Eagle calls us to walk, which Cornstalk trod and Nonhelema still does despite his murder."

"This is all that holds me here, my brother," Spotted Pony admitted. "We must urge our nation to do the same. But I fear that leaders will rise among our people who will persuade them to fight, and in the end we will either be utterly destroyed or driven far from our lands."

Chapter Six

CARLETON STARED through the window's thick, wavy panes, his attention only peripherally on his companions' conversation. Jones's muted voice and the hearty replies of Charles-Guillaume-Frédéric Dumas, French agent for the Americans, were all but drowned out by the lively clatter that filled the tavern wedged among the weathered buildings bordering Texel Island's crowded quays.

It was an hour before midday, 4 October, the day following their arrival after miraculously eluding the Royal Navy's pursuit. A stiff wind had dispelled the night fog, and he idly watched the bustling traffic of small pilot and supply ships that clogged the Reede van Texel, the main harbor at the town of Oudeschild on the island's eastern side. The largest of the West Frisian Islands, Texel served as the port for Amsterdam on the mainland, seventy-five miles farther along a narrow, winding channel through the United Provinces' Zuider Zee.

With little appetite for the steaming food set before him, he studied what was visible of the long lines of merchantmen, whalers, and warships anchored in the sea road beyond the white sand dunes at the harbor's entrance. Their draughts too great to enter the shallower waters, more than a hundred vessels bound to or from the Netherlands, France, Spain, Portugal, the Baltics, and East India anchored in the roadstead waiting for pilots, supplies, and favorable winds and seas. Jones's small squadron bobbed among them along with his prizes: a schooner taken during their raids along the

English coast; *Serapis;* and *Countess of Scarborough,* forced to surrender to *Pallas* in a fierce contest shortly before Pearson yielded to Jones.

"It's impossible to describe what I felt this morning to see those red and white lines with the blue square in its headquarter waving from a British warship!" Dumas enthused. "Monsieur Franklin will be most gratified to receive your report."

Carleton glanced over at Jones. Resplendent in his uniform of blue coat with white waistcoat and breeches, the commodore handed the Frenchman a thick packet of papers he had assiduously labored over ever since the battle.

"This should provide all the details he could wish." Disgruntled, Jones added, "I'd thought to run for Dunkirk, but your captains insisted we stick to the official plan in coming here."

"A good thing you did, sir, as the British sent eight ships of the line after you. But luckily they searched everywhere you were not. By the by, the accounts of your triumph have exploded across all of Europe and cemented your fame as the Terror of the British. I assure you that multitudes wait breathlessly to bow down and kiss your feet, Commodore, while the British are gnashing their teeth that you escaped them! The news that you were accompanied by the famous—or should I say infamous—Général Carleton, whose privateer fleet has decimated their shipping, adds even more fuel to their impotent fury," Dumas concluded in high good humor, nodding to Carleton.

Jones appeared gratified, but inwardly Carleton cringed. He'd realized that titbit of information had to leak out eventually, while at the same time cherishing the forlorn hope that he'd be able to remain in the shadows. To that end he'd dressed plainly for their transport to Texel: white shirt and carelessly tied cravat; worn, sea-stained grey coat, waistcoat, and breeches; unpolished boots; hair roughly finger-brushed back and secured with a black ribbon—efforts clearly to no avail.

It had been obvious from the moment they entered the tavern that they were both recognized; beaming nods and hearty greetings from the proprietor and his employees made that uncomfortably evident. As they were ushered to a table, Carleton had grimly noted the stares and gusts of whispers that followed in their wake, while pretending not to.

His rueful thoughts were interrupted by Jones, who motioned at Carleton's virtually untouched plate. "Cheer up and eat, man."

"At the moment food is the least of my concerns." Suppressing a growl of frustration, Carleton raised his tankard and downed the last swallow of *Skuumkoppe,* the locally brewed beer.

A plump, red-cheeked young woman garbed in colorful, mixed-print Dutch dress and ruffled white cap, wove through the crowded room carrying a foaming pitcher to refill each of their tankards. When Jones winked at her, she blushed prettily, returning his smile. But it was on Carleton that her coy gaze lingered, a fact he studiously ignored.

Jones's gaze followed her speculatively as she bustled away. Wrenching his attention back to his plate, he took another bite of steak.

"You're uncommonly morose for having taken part in defeating a British ship of the line and her escort in a fair fight just days ago, Carleton."

"If it had been up to Landais, we might not have."

As Carleton expected, Jones's face darkened. He had harped on what he considered the French captain's treachery the entire eight days they'd spent tacking through the North Sea to escape the pack of pursuing British hounds.

"Were it left to me, I'd haul him up on charges in front of a naval court. But I think it prudent to wait for Franklin's advice and approbation before taking any steps against the man," Jones conceded reluctantly.

After vanquishing *Serapis* Jones had lingered for a day and a half, making desperate attempts to save the mortally wounded *Bonhomme Richard,* while they drifted slowly east southeast away from the Yorkshire coast. But at last he had given in to the inevitable and ordered further efforts halted. They'd had to abandon personal possessions, including Jones's official papers.

Stowe, however, the wonder that he was, had managed to retrieve his own, Carleton's, and Red Fox's baggage, secured in a locker in the bow of the lower gun deck. The sturdy rawhide pouches had been soaked in seawater but were still intact, the contents merely wrinkled and damp along the edges and easily dried without serious damage.

By the time *Richard* slipped beneath the waves shortly before noon on 25 September, all the gunpowder and equipment that could be salvaged had been transferred to *Serapis,* sufficient repairs made for her to sail, and the ghastly toll of dead consigned to the sea, with the wounded and prisoners distributed among the other ships. They had cast off their sea anchors just as multiple racks of sails blossomed on the horizon, presumably the same vessels that hovered just within sight at the edge of the Netherlands's neutral waters.

A rustle of movement at the next table wrenched Carleton's attention back to his surroundings. A nearby diner had fixed them in his rapt scrutiny from the moment of their arrival, to the point of neglecting his meal. Suddenly surging to his feet, he pushed his way between the closely packed tables toward them.

"Commodore Jones, please excuse my interruption, but I must congratulate you on your astounding victory!" he gushed breathlessly on reaching them. "Your reputation is enhanced even more if that is possible. The whole world stands in awe of your victory!"

Jones thanked him softly, basking in the sun of the man's compliments, while Dumas looked on with barely suppressed amusement.

Carleton focused on his now cold food, but unhappily did not escape notice. The man eventually turned his ecstatic gaze on him.

"And you, sir, are you not the pirate Carleton whose exploits have equally transfixed us all?" he exclaimed joyfully. "Ah, that two such illustrious men would join forces to drive a stake into the very heart of the British lion, as it were! Our country is exceptionally honored that you've favored us with your presence—"

Carleton raised his eyes, leveling a stare at the would-be acolyte that caused him to stumble backward a step, face paling and effusions choking away.

"B-but I'll leave you to your dinner, my very dear gentlemen." He hurriedly bowed, then rushed off to pay his bill and hastily depart the tavern.

Carleton became aware that his companions observed him, Dumas with a speculative smile and Jones with a frown. "How do you do that?" the latter demanded querulously.

Carleton raised one eyebrow. "What?"

Jones waved his arm after the retreating man. "That. Freeze people with a look."

"It's an acquired talent," Carleton drawled, a deliberate edge of insolence to his tone.

Flushing, Jones returned an assessing look. "More likely born and bred, I'd think, in one of noble birth like you. Or perhaps it's simply a skill native to the *pirate* Carleton."

Carleton dropped his fork onto his plate with a clatter. "I beg your pardon," he said in an icy undertone, well aware of the alarmed glances turned on them from nearby tables. "For such a charge to come from *you* of all men—"

"I was only joking," Jones protested, hands raised, palms outward. "Nevertheless, I apologize if I offended you. Our nerves are all stretched at the moment. See here, I've had occasion over the past weeks to learn your quality, Carleton, and your able assistance was invaluable to our success."

Carleton accepted the graceful apology with a short nod before snapping, "Is this what everyone thinks of me—that I'm a mere pirate?"

"The exploits of both you and Commodore Jones have captured the public's imagination," Dumas reasoned. "You must understand, *mon général*, that the tales circulating of your appearance and actions during the battle cast you in a piratical light, which many consider highly romantic."

"*Romantic!* A curious description for a cold-blooded killer."

By now Carleton's ire had climbed to all but intolerable levels. He fought to hold his temper under tight rein but felt it rapidly slipping from his control. Privately he cursed his seemingly ungovernable propensity to thumb his nose at opponents at the worst moment.

"It's well known that I carry letters of marque from the United States Congress, if not also—" he began heatedly, only to stop himself in time from blurting out in his fury that he carried the same papers from Sartine, secretly provided in case unexpected opportunities arose—a fact known only to France's naval minister himself, Caledonne, Teissèdre—and Louis XVI.

Dumas regarded him intently. When Carleton remained frostily silent, he said, "I believe you hoped to find your captured ships and men, *général*. Have you made progress in that regard?"

Welcoming the change of subject, Carleton related tersely that he'd gleaned no information either from the prisoners Jones had taken during their raid along England's coast or from *Serapis*'s captured crewmen and officers. He'd intended to interview *Countess of Scarborough*'s crew that day but had instead sent Stowe, who was likely to have better luck in loosening tongues as he'd spent many years at sea laboring for the British Navy.

He didn't mention his servant's other assignment. Carleton was well aware that Amsterdam and her port crawled with the agents of a multitude of nations, including spies maintained by Sartine. In addition to gleaning news of his men, Carleton's most urgent concern was to make contact with one of the French naval minister's agents, an assignment for which Stowe was eminently equipped.

Dumas nodded thoughtfully. "Then I wish you better success in your endeavors."

Wondering whether Dumas had any inkling of the depths the word *endeavors* might imply, Carleton returned his attention to the scene outside the window.

Jones had paid their conversation scant attention. Slouched back in his chair, he selected a slice of one of the creamy island cheeses on the plate between them. He chewed it thoughtfully while surveying the buxom young women who bustled about the room carrying foaming pitchers of beer and plates piled with steaming victuals.

When another curvaceous, red-cheeked girl stopped to refill Carleton's tankard, Jones gave her a wink. She returned a smile before glancing deliberately at Carleton, who purposely gave no indication that he registered her inviting gaze. To her question he answered that he needed nothing further, and after a brief hesitation she hurried off.

Jones's gaze followed her. "Now, gentlemen, what more's needed when there's good food aplenty, than a comfortable bed and the company of the fair sex? And even better, the satisfaction of presenting two British warships to the prize court at Fort De Schans," he crowed, referring to the star-shaped fort protecting the harbor's sea road that also served as a naval court.

Carleton knifed into the remains of his lamb chop as though cutting an enemy's throat. At any other time he would have savored the tender meat, its flavor characteristically salty from the animals' pasturage on sea grass. But he could hardly choke the bite down and chased the morsel with another long swallow of beer, while wishing passionately for something much, much stronger. He paid as much attention to Jones's plans for having his three captured ships repaired as quickly as possible as he would have to the buzzing of a fly.

"As you know, sir, Dutch law requires commanders of foreign ships to present their government's authorization when making port in the United Provinces," Dumas cautioned. "You must understand that Britain will insist that, since you're not accredited by a recognized state, the States General must treat you as a pirate and return your prizes to their rightful owners. The Dutch will have to take their demand seriously."

"I plan to present my case at the Hague," Jones maintained loftily. "And I hope also to negotiate an exchange of my prisoners for my countrymen held by the British."

His companions' voices faded into the background. Morosely Carleton calculated that it would still be some while before Stowe returned —and then more than likely bearing none of the information Carleton sought. With nothing to occupy him, he felt too restless to sit idle at the inn where Stowe had arranged accommodations for their hopefully short stay on the island. He craved air and space.

After taking abrupt leave of Jones and Dumas, he lingered on the quay in the cold wind. Pulling his spyglass from his coat pocket, he intently surveyed the long, grey-misted line of ships anchored in the sea road outside the harbor. And the chain of sails beyond them, their tops intermittently revealed at the horizon by the sea's heaving waves.

Why the deuce is Louis always absent when I need him most?

Irritably he conceded that the charge was unjust. Teissèdre had known that the plan was for them to take refuge at Texel following their raids. Having no way of knowing exactly when or even whether they would arrive, however, he was highly unlikely to settle in and wait for them there like Dumas. And considering their arrival just the previous day, the news couldn't have reached Teissèdre yet if he was still in Paris.

Carleton turned away from the quay and began to walk with no destination in mind. It felt good to stretch his legs after weeks at sea bounded by a ship's narrow confines, and he breathed in deep lungfuls of the invigorating sea wind.

Through a thinly overcast sky the hazy sun bathed his surroundings in a pale golden glow. Within a short distance he passed beyond Oudeschild's warehouses, offices, shops, inns, and tidy cottages into open countryside. The sandy white beaches and dunes that fringed the island's coast on each side soon gave way to tidal inlets and salt marshes awash in the dusky purple blooms of sea lavender. Overhead, sea gulls and spoonbills dipped and rose in graceful flight.

The well-traveled road he wandered down pointed across the island's flat interior. Small farms with distinctively shaped sheep barns amid their fenced fields and pastures dotted the landscape on each side, herds of cattle and sheep grazing peacefully on the verdant, vividly green grass. Narrow creeks and canals overarched by graceful bridges wound across the land, numerous dikes and windmills scattered among them. Farther off he could see the roofs and spires of picturesque villages. The one directly ahead was larger, and he took it to be Den Burg, the island's main town.

The scene couldn't have been more charming, yet it only served to intensify the ache in his breast. He had cherished the desperate hope that he could recover *Destiny* by main force, rescue her surviving crew from British clutches, and return to Thornlea and Elizabeth before their baby was born. Indeed, along with Jones and every member of *Richard's* crew, he had done everything he was capable of to wreak destruction on the enemy. But now he couldn't help wondering whether he'd entirely deceived himself.

The approach of a donkey cart piled high with hay wrenched him back to his surroundings. He stepped to the side of the road to allow it passage and perfunctorily returned the friendly smiles and nods of the farmer and his wife. Then, standing still, he stared blankly after them.

All he'd accomplished on this ill-advised foray was to cement a reputation as a lawless pirate. Now that he was a husband and soon to be father, he found that he felt keenly the damage to his honor that could only reflect ill on his wife and children.

At that moment he wanted nothing more than to abandon this blasted port before another day dawned, escape that frenzy of British sharks circling at the sea's horizon, and get back to Thornlea with all possible haste.

Chapter Seven

RETURNING TO THE INN, Carleton cast himself upon the bed in the small, modestly furnished private room Stowe had engaged and stared at the ceiling. He knew from long experience that the turmoil besetting him was the common aftermath of battle's high excitement and frenzied action. But understanding did nothing to ease his mind, calm his spirit, and drive back the black despair that, as too often, threatened to drag him back into its suffocating depths.

A good part of it was the battle's ghastly toll. That the casualties aboard both *Richard* and *Serapis* had climbed to near fifty percent deeply appalled him. Yet he'd seen enough of war to hold no illusions on that score. It was his failure, in the face of that carnage, to achieve what he'd hoped that bore so heavily upon him now.

But it went deeper still than this.

The memory of that moment in Chateau Broussard's music room when he'd at last—at last!—hungrily clasped Elizabeth to his bosom after almost a year's separation of his own doing replayed before his eyes with accusing clarity and unutterable anguish. He'd wanted more than anything to heal the wounds he had so cruelly inflicted, believing it was the best for her, heart of his heart. But she would not raise her face to his gaze, her head bowed as though, if she looked up, she'd find him to be nothing more than fantasy or apparition.

Her fear had undone him utterly, piercing his heart to the core, constricting his chest so tightly it had hurt to breathe. In spite of it, yet again he'd left her, carrying their child this time, even though their lives were so inextricably intertwined that the doing of it fair ripped his soul asunder.

As so foolishly before, he had believed that he had no other choice. But had it been so indeed? Had he followed God's leading, or had his own blind willfulness driven him?

The two of them must surely have spent half of their acquaintance apart, and he felt this separation the most keenly. Had not Washington warned him of this very thing if they married while the war still continued? And now, with a depth of passion that consumed him, he yearned for his own country and hearthside, for Elizabeth in his arms, and soon for their own dear wee one cradled against his heart.

Yet amid the tumult of emotions he clung to the blessed comfort that the periods of deepest desperation had noticeably receded since he had learned the truth of his father's sending him away when he'd been hardly more than a babe himself. And most of all since he and Elizabeth had wed.

That their journey home to Thornlea had been safely accomplished despite his fears brought grounding as well. Several years had passed since he last bided there, and he had found himself unexpectedly overcome by an unsettling tide of memory and emotion. Telling Isaiah and Sarah the uncertain fate of their son, Pete, had added painfully to the deep wrenching. But at the same time, Elizabeth's joy at reunion with her parents and the opportunity to resume her work as a doctor had assured him that bringing her there had been the right decision. And Red Fox's insistence on returning to France with him and Stowe had provided an additional measure of surety, confirmed when they then re-crossed the ocean without harm.

"Our times are in your hands, Lord," he whispered, adding a plea for the Almighty's wisdom and guidance—and for a means of escape from British pursuers and a safe return to Thornlea.

He came abruptly upright at a sharp rap on the door. "Come!"

The door creaked partially open to reveal Stowe's stocky form. Middle-aged, with the thick neck, brawny arms, and bandy legs of a bulldog, he appeared as desperate a character as a true pirate, an impression enhanced by a livid, badly healed scar running from his left eye to his jaw.

Before he could speak, Carleton demanded, "Have you managed to make contact with any of the French agents crawling about this place?"

"Sent out feelers, sir, but heard nothin' back yet," Stowe responded. A wide grin puckered the left side of his face. "But I brung along some'un I wager ye'll want t'see."

Carleton rose from the bed just as Stowe moved out of the doorway. Allowing a black man to pass into the room, the servant closed the door behind him.

Almost as tall as Carleton, the stranger was gaunt and filthy, his ragged clothing barely covering his mahogany skin, curly beard and hair gown out in a wild tangle. It wasn't until he met Carleton's astonished gaze with a weary smile that recognition dawned, and a shock went through him.

"Pete!" He crossed the room in three long strides to grasp him by the shoulders, scanning his face closely. Once handsome and muscular, the young man appeared to have aged a decade, though his eyes still held the fire Carleton remembered. "It *is* you!"

Pete gave a short laugh. "What remains of me, leastwise."

"You were aboard *Countess?*"

Pete nodded. "Can't say I was thrilled when they threw me aboard a ship bound for the Baltics, but I've since revised my opinion."

"We might never have found you else." Carleton released him with reluctance. "I joined Jones's little jaunt in the hope I'd find some of *Destiny's* crew—or at least learn your fates. Do you know anything of the others who were captured?"

"No, sir," Pete answered, dropping his gaze from Carleton's. "We were all separated."

Carleton took a breath, chest clenching. He had to know, but could hardly speak the name. "Captain Eaden?"

Pete's face tightened, his hands fisting. "Hanged as a pirate. The lieutenants too. They threw their bodies into the sea without so much as reading the rites for the dead."

Carleton stared at him, staggered, before groping blindly to the nearest chair and sinking into it. From the moment he had heard of *Destiny*'s capture and the capture or destruction of the ships with her, he had told himself that the fate of their officers was settled. Inevitable. Unchangeable.

In spite of it, he had blindly clung to the hope that it would not be so.

The confirmation of his worst fear broke him utterly. Waves of grief, fury, anguish overtopped and washed him under, down into that dark pit that ever lay just below consciousness. Bent forward, elbows propped on his knees, he buried his face in his hands and wept.

Oh, God . . . . Oh, God!

By agonizing degrees he became aware that Pete gripped his shoulder, in his other hand held out a rag that appeared to once have been a handkerchief. He took the stained, frayed square of linen and mopped away his tears, fighting with difficulty back to a measure of composure. At length he straightened and lifted his gaze to Pete's brimming eyes, grateful to find no censure there.

"Dr. Lemaire?"

"He died caring for the wounded."

Carleton felt as though he'd taken another vicious punch to the gut. "The women?" he managed, teeth gritted.

"The ones who survived were rounded up and taken aboard one of their ships. You can guess their fate," Pete added, biting the words savagely off.

"Mademoiselle Glasière?"

"I didn't see her among the others." Pete shrugged and shook his head. "There was too much chaos at the end . . . "

Carleton sprang to his feet and caught him in a fierce embrace. "Thank God you survived! If I'd had to tell your parents you were lost—"

Pete snorted. "I'm just a black boy with a strong back, useful for tasks judged too menial for others."

Stepping back, Carleton fixed him in an intent gaze. "And that's what saved you."

"It did."

Turning abruptly away, Carleton paced across the room. The renewed conviction that war was a great evil weighed heavily on him. He had known from the first that vengeance bred but more and worse vengeance. He knew it more bitterly now.

They all knew. Yet here they were.

When men stubbornly pursued their own evil ends, what was the alternative? Would not refusing the battle only ensure that evil would prevail? Did not the Almighty's armies fight the Deceiver unseen in the heavens? Did God not also use human agency to accomplish his great purposes no matter how ignorant, flawed, and willful his chosen creatures?

Father, use me according to your perfect will, he prayed silently at last. *And let me never tread beyond the boundaries you set.*

Turning back to Pete, he briefly recounted the events of the past months, concluding, "I can't delay any longer, Pete. Even now it's doubtful I can return in time to be with Elizabeth when our child's born. But I must try. Now that you've been recovered and I know what happened to at least some of the others, I'll bend my efforts to find us a way out of here." He hesitated before asking, "What will you do now?"

Pete squared his shoulders, head high. "As long as you've a ship fit for battle, I'll return to the fight. Or if you're unable or unwilling to continue, I'll enlist in the Continental Navy under Commodore Jones or anyone else who'll have me."

"You'll always have a place with me, Pete. I'll never sit idle during this war, let the British do what they will. They'll have to kill me to stop me. But first you must come with me to Thornlea. You've gone through hell, and you need rest to restore your strength."

When Pete began to protest, Carleton said firmly, "There are three people who long to know that you're alive and well, to say nothing of all the others who are also greatly anxious for you. A report is not enough. They must see you with their own eyes and hold you in their arms."

Pete chewed his lip, then nodded. "You're right, of course. I've been gone so long I need to see them too. There's also a fellow prisoner I'd like to take along if that'd be all right. His name's Tommy Mersereau. He ran away from his home on Staten Island when he was a boy to serve aboard a merchant ship. It was captured by the British and the crew pressed into their service even though it was well before the war."

"Not an uncommon occurrence, unfortunately. We lost many ships and men to the Royal Navy's depredations."

"Tommy helped me stay alive when I'd given up all hope," Pete return-ed. "He's been used badly all these years. He's desperate to go home and learn whether his parents are still alive and whether they'll forgive him for leaving as he did."

"I've a feeling they will. Bring him to me."

Pete went to the door and admitted a slight man equally gaunt and rag-ged whom Carleton guessed to be in his mid twenties, although the deep lines that creased his weathered face made him look older. He stepped into the room hesitantly, clutching his cap in front of him and moving with a limp, head and shoulders hunched. He looked, Carleton thought, like a whipped dog.

"You're Thomas Mersereau?"

"That'd be my father, sir," the man said humbly, his voice reedy and weak. "I be called Tommy. Though I share his name, I be not worthy to be called by it."

"I doubt he'd agree with you."

For a long moment Tommy remained silent. Then he faltered, "Even if they still be living . . . and I could go home . . . they probably forgot me after all these years. I was a rebel as a boy. Chose to go my own way. But what I'd give to go back, just to learn whether they're well and happy!" He hazarded a fearful glance at Carleton.

"Pete vouched for you, and that's good enough for me. If you can bear an ocean voyage and the dangers we'll face, I'll take you to my estate in Virginia, God willing, and we'll send word to your parents."

It seemed as though a light broke over the young man's countenance then. He fixed Carleton in a gaze that held a tentative hope, too clearly an emotion he had long despaired of.

"Oh, sir," he said, voice catching, "if you'd do that fer one such as me, surely God'll bless ye fer it!"

CARLETON SET DOWN his pint of ale, all he could force down, while Red Fox, Stowe, Pete, and Tommy concentrated on devouring every morsel on their plates. The sight and smell of food still made his stomach roil.

Idly scanning the inn's dining room, he tensed at sight of a familiar rotund figure just then entering. He stood abruptly, tossing his serviette on the table.

"Excuse me."

His companions looked around to follow his gaze, but ignoring them, he strode swiftly toward the door, heedlessly pushing past the tables that crowded the half-filled room to grasp the Frenchman by the arm. He dragged him unceremoniously out into the narrow foyer.

He glanced at the two burly, roughly garbed men who casually hovered there, ignoring them as though they waited for someone else. Under his breath Teissèdre said, "Mine."

Carleton nodded. "Where've you been?"

Teissèdre blinked, regarding him with wounded virtue. "Coming to find you, of course," he replied, an edge of outraged dignity in his tone. "What did you think?"

Carleton scowled. "Don't tell me, as usual, that I'm a hard man to find. You knew very well where I'd be if we survived our little expedition. Why are you so late? Dumas was waiting for us when we got here."

Teissèdre's eyes narrowed. "I had . . . ah . . . pressing business to attend to before I could leave Paris."

"What business would that be? Something to do with Sartine? Louis the Sixteenth? My uncle?" When Teissèdre spread his hands noncommittally, his bland expression a study in duplicity, Carleton concluded dryly, "Ah. All three, then. And what was this business?"

"I am, alas, not at liberty to speak of the matter at present," Teissèdre returned self-righteously.

"Has it anything to do with me?" Carleton persisted.

Looking distinctly uncomfortable, the Frenchman remained silent.

Carleton suppressed a groan. "Why do I have the distinct impression that it does, and that I'm not going to be happy about it?"

"Not to worry. All will turn out for the best. In time."

This time Carleton did groan. "Dear Lord, spare me!"

A wolfish grin spread over Teissèdre's round face. "By the by, I received reports of the battle from one of my agents in England even before news of your raids reached the Continent. They included lurid details of your participation in the venture, as well as that the lot of you disappeared despite the entire Royal Navy's scouring the ocean for you. Knowing how the commodore likes to keep everyone guessing, I wasn't entirely sure you'd turn up here."

"We wouldn't have if our French captains hadn't insisted on sticking with the plan," Carleton conceded acidly. "But then, France did fund a very large portion of the scheme."

Just then a well-dressed middle-aged man entered the inn. Glancing at the four of them with interest, he brushed past to climb the stairs.

Teissèdre immediately led the way outside into the sunset's fading golden rays, his companions moving off a discreet distance. Hunching his shoulders against the icy wind blowing off the sea, he scanned their surroundings to make sure that no one was close enough to overhear them.

In an undertone he related that Sartine and Caledonne were developing a plan to recover *Destiny*. In the meantime, their spies in Portsmouth were keeping continuous watch on the progress of her overhaul and would transmit news of when she was to sail and her destination the moment they uncovered it.

Two couples approached, bound for the inn. Taking pity on Teissèdre's obvious discomfort in the cold, Carleton beckoned him back inside. With the agent's two men trailing nonchalantly, they quietly slipped upstairs to Carleton's room, leaving the men to guard the door.

They found Carleton's companions waiting inside. He motioned them to keep their seats before turning back to Teissèdre.

"I'm sure you understand that my most urgent concern is to return to Thornlea at the earliest instant. My wife is due to deliver our child in less than two months."

"Bah, that is no difficulty, *mon général*. I have arranged for you and your party to be whisked, in disguise, into Amsterdam, from where you will be taken by coach directly to L'Orient to sail immediately—"

"It'll take entirely too long to travel such a distance by land," Carleton snapped. "And considering how many British spies prowl Amsterdam's canals and alleys, we're likely to be discovered the instant we enter the city, if not before."

Teissèdre waved his objections airily away. "I'm well aware of the dangers. You're not to worry as I've arranged everything to perfection. *Naturellement* the utmost precautions will be taken to conceal your identity and mislead the British so as to avoid any interference."

Before Carleton could object, he abruptly changed the subject. "You might find it of interest that *Maiden of Rotterdam,* one of the Dutch East India's newest and fastest merchantmen, is preparing to leave from here, bound for Calcutta. Her cargo must be loaded by midnight for she sails promptly at dawn, you see. She and her escorts are heavily armed . . . against pirates."

Arms crossed, Carleton leaned his back against the wall and studied him suspiciously, his eyes narrowed. Red Fox and Tommy appeared puzzled, but Carleton noted that Stowe and Pete follwed their conversation with amused expressions.

When Teissèdre bent forward to lightly touch Carleton's arm, he returned his attention to his agent. "Ah, but I almost forgot. Caledonne wishes me to inform you that one of his squadrons will leave L'Orient tomorrow for the Caribbean. First they'll make a brief stop off Ushant," he added dismissively, as though it was a matter of no consequence.

Carleton straightened, a faint smile tugging at the corners of his mouth. "Then I assume you'll return tonight to accompany us to our transport."

"I'll bring the effects for your disguise."

As Teissèdre turned toward the door, Carleton clasped his arm, arresting him. "Louis . . . thank you. You've never failed me yet—though I was beginning to wonder if you were going to this time," he added wryly.

His smile as satisfied as a cat's, Teissèdre returned an elaborate bow. *"Serviteur, mon général."*

When he had gone, Red Fox said, "Why did you agree to this plan since it will take longer to cross France—"

"We ain't goin' by land," Stowe broke in, grinning.

Red Fox turned back to Carleton, shaking his head in bewilderment.

"Teissèdre's decoys are the ones who'll cross to Amsterdam and take a coach bound for L'Orient. Meanwhile we'll sail boldly out of this harbor at daybreak aboard a Dutch merchantman right under the noses of Eden's agents," Carleton added, William Eden being head of Britain's Secret Intelligence Service. "Our friendly merchantman will rendezvous with Caledonne's squadron off Ushant."

He pulled out his pocket watch. "We've not much time before Louis returns. If we're to board our tansport before midnight, we'd better pack our kit and be ready to leave the moment he gets here."

"What about notifying Jones?"

Carleton waved Pete's question away. "He's the last man I want to know what we're up to. As far as I'm concerned, everyone can think we've vanished into thin air."

Chapter Eight

ELIZABETH TURNED HER FACE to the keen wind, breathing in the tang of oak tannin and pine resin, decaying leaves and moist earth. On this late afternoon, Wednesday, 27 October, the sun hovered above the western ridge top, its pale rays gilding the trees' thinning but still brilliant canopies, the ground at their roots littered with leaf drift. The fields all along the valley lay fallow now, shorn of crops of wheat and oats, rye and maize bundled into sheaves to dry several weeks earlier. The harvesters' wagons moved among them now, collecting the bundles for threshing, after which the grain would be stored in large bins in the lower barns until ground into flour at the estate's grist mill.

Farris's and Isaiah's new light infantry companies moved across a nearby meadow, practicing drills and maneuvers in coordination. Formerly unmounted support troops, they had received additional training during the past winter to provide the Rangers greater flexibility in battle, but would be mounted when needed, as before. A short distance away along the lane, another hive of activity surrounded the row of newly finished buildings.

"The troops are moving into the new barracks Jon ordered to be built, I see," Dr. Howard said approvingly, following Elizabeth's gaze.

"In good time, too, with winter coming on," she responded.

A wave of emotion swept over her at the thought of Carleton's concern for the welfare and discipline of the men who served under him and his quick, decisive commands to rectify any lack. The same concern applied to his family as well. The more she gained glimpses into the recesses of his heart and mind, the more her own heart melted, and she felt her being intertwining ever more inextricably with his.

She had spent the early afternoon in the music room, practicing at the lovely pianoforte that had arrived at Thornlea a couple of weeks after Carleton had left for France. Unknown to her, he had arranged for it to be shipped from his import office in Baltimore.

She found much solace in playing it in his absence and had made a habit of spending an hour or two in practice each day. She missed the musical evenings they'd shared, first in Boston after her rescue, when Carleton had played the violin while she, her parents, and Abby sang. Then later at Passy, when she had accompanied him on the pianoforte while everyone present joined in singing.

She became aware that the sun had sunk below the ridge top, setting their surroundings in darker shadow. The air's chill deepened as well, and she rubbed her arms briskly beneath her cloak before drawing its folds more snuggly around her shoulders.

Her father offered her one arm and her mother his other. Feeling awkward and clumsy, Elizabeth gave careful heed to her steps as they meandered back along the lane. Passing through Thornlea's hawthorn-hedged gardens, they skirted the hospital and came around to the manor's front.

Anne paused outside the courtyard gate. Looking up at the building's façade, she exulted, "I never imagined you'd one day be the mistress of such a grand estate, Elizabeth! Have you decided yet what changes you're going to make? You do plan to redecorate, I assume."

Elizabeth frowned. "I don't know if I shall, Mama. For the most part I like everything as it is."

"It's too much of a man's lair."

Elizabeth laughed. "That it is, but then Sir Harry never married. It is Jonathan's childhood home . . . " She let the words trail off.

"And it needs a woman's touch. Jonathan did encourage you to make any changes you wanted."

"Now is not a good time, Mama. The war's dragging on, and with all of his merchantmen and privateers confined to safe ports for the time being . . . well, I simply can't justify spending money I don't need to."

"Your family's bound to continue growing," her father pointed out. "Making some modest investments in your home wouldn't be unwise."

"I suppose a bit of paint and fabric to brighten some of the rooms wouldn't cost too much." Elizabeth frowned. "Alistair keeps a store of goods for the manor's maintenance, and we've men enough to do the work. The nursery's already done, and a few other rooms might be freshened up a bit." She hesitated. "But I do want to leave the Great Hall as it is."

Suddenly everything seemed overwhelming. She rubbed one hand across the swell of her belly.

"It's too much to think of at present." Wistfully she added, "I hoped we'd have heard from Jonathan by now—"

When she broke off, her mother said briskly, "We will any day, dear, I'm sure. In the meantime I'll ask Alistair if he might send to Williamsburg for samples of the latest fabrics and furniture styles so that once the baby comes and you're all settled, we'll be able to make the desired changes."

"I'm sure you and Jon talked about names for the baby," Dr. Howard broke in as he ushered them into the courtyard, "but you've never told us what you were thinking."

Elizabeth brightened, glad for a distraction from her anxious thoughts. "If it's a girl, Jonathan very much wants to name her after his mother, with which I heartily agree. She'll be named Julianne Abigail Theresa. Should we ever have another girl, I want to name her Elizabeth Anne and call her Anne."

Her mother beamed. "What if it's a boy?"

"We agreed on Oliver Harrison Samuel, and we'll call him Harry. And I insisted on Jonathan Stuart Alexandre should we have a second son."

Clearly pleased, her father encircled her shoulders with his arm. "Excellent choices, my dear."

They stepped into the entrance hall, grateful for the warmth radiating from its small hearth after the chill outside. As always when she entered the manor, Elizabeth's gaze was first drawn overhead to the exquisite barrel-vaulted ceiling. Fashioned of bowed walnut planks, it extended along the broad passages to either side that gave access to the rest of the manor's main floor. The double doors in front of them that matched the massive exterior portal stood open to afford an expansive view into the Great Hall, deserted at this time of day.

After they handed their wraps to the footman, she turned to the butler, who greeted them with a bow and proffered the silver mail tray. It held two letters and a thicker packet bound with cord.

"The post rider delivered the packet while ye were on yer walk, mistress. The letters came soon after by separate couriers."

Elizabeth concealed her disappointment that there was still no letter from Carleton. "Thank you, Burns," she said, taking the packet, then cried in delight, "Oh, look—letters from Passy at last!

"And this one is for you, Mama," she added, extending the first letter to her mother. "It's from Mount Vernon, so I assume from Mrs. Washington, and direct by courier. Important news perhaps. You've struck up quite a correspondence."

Anne took it, beaming. "So we have. As I told you, she was quite familiar with Jonathan's exploits, of course, and then with yours too. She first wrote to offer her kindest felicitations on your wedding. Soon after you arrived I wrote her that you're expecting, so I imagine she's responding to the news. I'm finding her to be all one would expect in a great Southern lady, the very soul of grace and kindness. In fact, I believe she was the instigator of Caty Greene's writing me too," she added, referring to the vivacious young wife of Major General Nathanael Greene, Washington's most trusted officer.

"You've heard from several other officers' wives as well," Dr. Howard noted.

"A number of them appear to be great friends, and they've been very kind to include me in their correspondence. Mrs. Washington appears to take a great interest in the welfare of the officers' wives and families."

Burns indicated the second letter, addressed to Andrews. "This came from Colonel Byrd over at Salem, mistress. He indicated it's important, but I've been told the general took a detachment down to Big Lick."

He referred to the commander of the militia regiment based at the small town of Salem, six miles northwest of the valley beyond the Staunton River. The tiny hamlet of Big Lick lay along the river northeast of Thornlea where the Great Wagon Road forked. From there the main road continued southeast through the Carolinas to Augusta, Georgia, while its branch turned southwest into Tennessee territory, joined the Wilderness Road in Kentucky, and ended at the Ohio River.

Dr. Howard took the letter from the butler. "He meant to return before nightfall. I'll make sure he gets this."

Elizabeth directed Burns to have tea sent to the library, one of her favorite spaces. The spacious chamber with its tall bookcases, mullioned windows with graceful draperies in muted colors, comfortable sofas and chairs, and paintings of verdant Scottish landscapes had a cozy, welcoming atmosphere.

They settled in front of the fireplace where a low fire crackled. After the maid had delivered the tray and withdrawn, Elizabeth eagerly broke open the packet from Passy. She distributed letters from Abby, Tess, and Caledonne's daughter Cécile, while her mother poured the tea. For some moments they were all absorbed in reading as they sipped the fragrant brew, nibbled on tiny, delicate cakes, and exclaimed over each letter's contents before passing it to the others.

That Abby continued to excel at her studies and was clearly blooming in spite of greatly missing her parents and sister was a source of comfort, as was the assurance that Tess was happily settled with the Martieu-Broussards. The latter's affection and regard for Elizabeth and her family could not have been more warmly expressed, as were their concerns for

Elizabeth's welfare during her pregnancy and eagerness for news of the birth.

"Oh, how dearly I miss them all!" Elizabeth exclaimed at last.

Anne sighed. "What a happy stay we had with them last winter. If only there weren't an ocean between us and we could visit more often."

"Thankfully we'll have Abby back when she turns eighteen and finishes her studies." Dr. Howard fell silent for a moment before adding, "I wonder whether my sister will ever return or permanently settle in France."

"I wonder too," Elizabeth admitted. "She and Uncle Alexandre are completely devoted to each other and will not be parted."

"I can't imagine what drew them together!" her father returned sourly. "Alexandre's a powerful and handsome man who could have any woman he wanted at the snap of his fingers, and Tess has always seemed so set in her ways. Don't get me wrong. I love my sister dearly, but you have to admit she can be a trial to deal with."

"What are you saying?" Elizabeth demanded. "It must be because you're her brother that you're completely blind to her sweetness of character that drew Alexandre like a bee to honey."

Dr. Howard's eyebrows rose. "This is my sister we're talking about?"

"Samuel!"

Exchanging an outraged glance with her mother, Elizabeth narrowed her eyes and fixed her father in a pointed look. "Perhaps the two of you would get along more peaceably if you weren't so insufferable at times!"

"Me? Insufferable?"

"Only now and again, dear," Anne soothed, reaching to pat his arm. "Most of the time you're quite sunny and sweet."

"Well . . . I wouldn't go quite that far," he allowed, a sparkle coming into his eyes.

Anne leaned over to kiss his cheek. "Though you are growly at times, you're never so to me. You're the dearest of husbands."

He chuckled, good humor restored, and returned her kiss. Dismissing the subject, he said brusquely, "Well, at least we now know that Jon reached

L'Orient safely. Tess mentions that Alexandre sent word they arrived just as Jones was on the point of sailing, and Jon, Stowe, and Red Fox were able to board in time."

"We still haven't heard anything directly from Jonathan." Elizabeth set down her cup. "If he posted a letter as soon as they made port as he promised, we'd surely have received it before these."

"Tess writes that he did and that Alexandre personally arranged for its transport," Anne reminded her. "The ship may very well have been delayed on its return voyage. Then, too, it could have been lost at sea."

"Or captured by the British," Dr. Howard muttered.

None of them broached the subject of the disaster that would cause if any intelligence about Jones's mission could be gleaned from the letter's contents. Elizabeth assured herself that Carleton was never so careless, but even so, she felt ill at the prospect.

"Even if his letter finally reaches us, so much time has passed that we still won't know what's happened since . . . " Staring bleakly into the fire, she let the words trail off.

Anne had broken the seal on the letter from Mrs. Washington while they were talking. Scanning the page, she said, "Mrs. Washington asks that I convey her congratulations and well wishes for your confinement and delivery, Elizabeth. She also says that if you find it agreeable, she'd be delighted to correspond with you."

"I'll write her before the post rider comes by again."

Reading further, Anne exclaimed, "Listen to this! The General just received news that Commodore Jones prevailed in a fierce battle against one of Britain's newest frigates!" She quickly scanned down the page. "The battle took place somewhere off the coast of Yorkshire . . . Jones actually captured the ship and her escort —and at least one other vessel from raids they'd already made along England's coast."

Startled, Elizabeth abruptly pushed out of her chair. Staggering at her baby's sharp response, she gasped and pressed her hand tightly against her ribs, feeling momentarily faint and dizzy.

Her father was on his feet and at her side in an instant. "Are you all right, my dear?"

She caught her breath and waved him away before straightening cautiously. "Sometimes it feels as though there's a war going on inside me," she said with a rueful laugh.

Anne gave her a sharp look. "You were an exceedingly active baby too. It must run in the blood."

Elizabeth grimaced. "Does Mrs. Washington give any further details? Any reference to Jonathan?"

"Only that." Her mother handed her the letter.

Elizabeth studied the page, heart pounding. "Then we've no way to know whether he survived the battle—or the raids that led up to it, for that matter."

"We don't know that he didn't," Dr. Howard countered firmly.

Elizabeth gulped in air as she sank back into her seat, her father steadying her.

"I wonder whether he ever informed His Excellency that he was planning to enlist in Jones's scheme," Anne ventured, brow creased.

"Somehow, knowing Jon, I doubt it." Seeing the anxious glance Elizabeth exchanged with her mother, he added hastily, "Now, we can't let our fears overcome us when we know nothing as yet. No sense borrowing trouble. As our Lord reminded us, each day has enough of its own."

"AND WHAT AM I to do to occupy my time if you won't let me assist in the hospital anymore?" Elizabeth blurted out. Seated in front of the dining room fire at breakfast with her parents the next morning, she blinked back angry tears.

"Overseeing the management of such an establishment as this should occupy your time well enough."

Elizabeth rolled her eyes and pushed her plate away. "Oh, Papa, Alistair takes care of everything, and—"

"Concerning the overall management of the estate, yes. But you have the direction of the household staff, the kitchens, the—"

Elizabeth turned to her mother. "That's Sarah's responsibility as housekeeper. She manages every detail of running the manor so efficiently that I'm hardly needed. Besides, you're always available to offer any guidance that could possibly be wanted."

"And you are having a baby!"

"As women have since the beginning of time. Pregnancy is not an illness!"

Brows arched, her mother gave her a meaningful look.

"I'm well aware of the dangers, but I'm in perfect health."

"You've increased so much over the last month, dearest, that it's hard for you to stand long, let alone to bend over. Deny to me that you have terrible backaches. All the strain you're putting yourself under can't do you any good when the baby comes."

Soberly Dr. Howard added, "It's hardly been two years since we almost lost you, Beth. You were on your deathbed, but by God's grace you lived. Do I need to remind you how many months it took for you to recover? Do you think your mama and I want to live through that again?"

"You'll understand when you hold your own dear little one to your breast," Anne added, her voice trembling.

Elizabeth bent her head. "I know, but . . . " She stopped, then murmured, "When I keep busy, I don't worry so much about him."

Silence hung over the room. Her mother looked hastily away, but Elizabeth saw her dab her eyes with her handkerchief.

"Oh, very well!" she huffed, feigning exasperation even as she fought another flood of tears. She made a show of consulting the mantel clock. "It's getting late, and Alistair wanted me to go over the changes we talked about for the parlor and drawing room before the end of the day." Pushing awkwardly to her feet, she hurried from the room.

ELIZABETH DESCENDED the spiral staircase to the ground floor, clinging tightly to the railing, her body feeling heavy and unbalanced. Durie's spacious office was off the ground floor's main passage with an exterior door next to it that gave onto steps leading up to the courtyard.

The next hour of quiet consultation over colors and several pieces of furniture to be crafted for the parlor and drawing room did much to soothe Elizabeth's ruffled emotions. Afterward Durie accompanied her to the storeroom beneath the manor's main wing where fabrics woven by the estate's weavers were kept, to determine whether any suited. She chose several and directed a couple more to be woven in colors complimentary to the paint she'd chosen. Satisfied with her choices, she took her leave of the steward.

After a brief hesitation, instead of returning upstairs she popped into the warren of kitchens, pantry, buttery, stillroom, and storerooms that comprised the domain of Salome, her three daughters who served as assistant cooks, the kitchen maids, and the stillroom maid. There was no need for her to consult with them or give any directions, but she always received an enthusiastic welcome into the cheerful, fragrant space. As usual she was immediately set at the table and plied with tea, tastings of dishes in preparation, and happy conversation that lifted her spirits and kept at bay her worries and fears for Carleton, if only for a little while.

Chapter Nine

THE FOLLOWING DAY, lying on the high canopy bed, stripped to her shift and stockings, Elizabeth grimaced as Laughing Otter probed her abdomen, eliciting a sharp kick. Frowning, the Shawnee matron looked up to exchange a puzzled glance with Blue Sky, Mary McLeod, and Stowe's plump, pleasant-faced wife, Sweetgrass.

"I still feel but one." She hesitated before returning her gaze to Elizabeth's fully rounded abdomen. "And it seems smaller than I would expect for how large her belly is."

Her voice strained, Anne said, "Likely there's simply much water. It was that way for me with Abigail."

"The babe be turned as he should be," Sarah noted.

Blue Sky regarded Elizabeth doubtfully. "It may be she will give birth sooner than we think."

Elizabeth carefully counted backward, then shook her head. "Judging from my last monthly flow, it couldn't be full term until the end of next month."

Sweetgrass helped her to sit up, murmuring reassurances in her native tongue. Elizabeth swung her legs over the side of the bed, stood, and stepped into her shoes. The older Shawnee matron hovered as Jemma assisted her back into her petticoats and loose caracao, her girth no longer accommodating stays.

"A second one cannot always be felt," Rain Woman put in. "One might lie on top of the other."

Elizabeth saw her mother tense.

"Bringing one baby to birth is dangerous enough. But twins—"

Grasping her mother's hand, she squeezed it. "Mama, every time we've checked, there's only one as far as anyone can tell. There's no evidence whatever that I'm carrying twins. And even if I am, I'm young and strong—"

"My mother's twin was stillborn, and Grandmama lived not a fortnight after the birth. I never knew her. And Mama was never strong. She died when I was only twelve."

Elizabeth bit her lip, the memory of what Carleton's cousin, Caledonne's daughter Cécile, had related about the twins her mother had borne filtering into her mind. Of course, it was possible that any tendency toward twins ran on the side of his uncle's first wife and not on Carleton's maternal line. But the opposite was also possible, as well as that the tendency existed on both sides. Certainly twins were not uncommon in her own mother's family.

None of which necessarily meant anything for this pregnancy. Her head spun dizzily with questions and possibilities.

Sarah went to the table in the bartizan that extended from the chamber's northwest corner. The cozy space, offering a view from its diamond-paned windows toward the north and west across the river behind the manor, had become Elizabeth's favorite reading nook. Fetching a steaming teacup from the small table sitting next to a comfortable chair, Sarah brought it to Elizabeth.

"I make this raspberry leaf tea for you every day now, Miz Beth. It strengthen your womb for the birth."

The tension eased from Anne's features. "You made it for me, too, remember?" When Sarah smiled and nodded, Anne turned back to Elizabeth and said, "It eased my pains, and I'm certain it speeded the birth for both of you girls."

As Elizabeth drained the cup, Mary admonished, "It's best ye stay active and walk as much as ye can in the fresh air each day too. And don't be liftin' anything heavy, o' course."

Elizabeth smiled at her and Blue Sky. "Remember how you gave birth to your boys while we were at Bemis Heights?"

The two women exchanged affectionate looks. "And now my wee Jimmy and Leads the Way may as well be brothers," Mary said.

"And sons to both of us," Blue Sky added.

"Your time isn't so far off either," Anne noted, giving Mary an assessing look.

Rain Woman smirked. "The four of us fill this camp with babies. Next may be Laughing Otter."

She raised her hands in alarm. "My husband gives me enough! I help to deliver yours, and look forward to the day I have grandchildren by my sons and daughters."

All of them laughed except for Anne. Noting her anxious expression, Sarah gestured toward the Shawnee woman and said firmly, "I deliver many mothers and babies alive, and so have these. Whether twins or no, we bring them all through safe."

Laughing Otter gave her a respectful nod before turning to Anne. "Do not worry, but trust in the Great Father. He will keep Healer Woman and every child to come under his wings."

"And we will all pray mightily," Blue Sky said, with Rain Woman and Mary quickly agreeing. Sweetgrass nodded and smiled, too, even though Elizabeth knew she understood little of their conversation.

Anne's mouth tightened, and she turned away. "What does it say of my faith that Indian women should convict me of it?"

As the other women stiffened, Elizabeth protested sharply, "Mama, please!"

"Does not the One who created the red man as well as the white speak to both? Does he not love all his children alike?"

Elizabeth's mother flinched at Laughing Otter's quiet rebuke. "Forgive me," she said in a muffled voice. "It's hard to learn that one's long-held opinions are not always right."

Elizabeth placed her arm around her mother and leaned her head on her shoulder. "The Lord's teaching all of us new things. He'll help us to be better than we are if we let him."

Anne conceded a wry smile. "Slow though the process may be."

AFTER THE OTHER WOMEN had gone, Elizabeth and her mother crossed the alcove that opened onto the gallery from the bedchamber and passed through the door on its opposite end. The space occupying the short north wing's front, previously the laird's study, also connected to the bedchamber through the dressing room between the two. At Carleton's direction during his brief stay, it had been cleared to serve as a nursery, his study removed to the first floor.

Elizabeth had decided on a soft ripe pear yellow for the walls, which lent the chamber a fresh, cheerful atmosphere. A new rug in soft hues with figures of dancing animals covered the center of the floor's polished wood planks, and floor-length creamy gauze draperies admitted softly filtered light.

She lingered at one of the narrow windows that flanked the fireplace. Paying scant heed to her mother's happy chatter about the placement of cradle and dresser and other furnishings for her coming grandchild, she took in the view beyond the courtyard. The trees were almost completely denuded now, what little was left of their once brilliant foliage withered and brown, the web of their bare branches spectral against a background of darkly shadowed fir and pine.

Autumn was waning far more quickly than she wished. With every passing day the weather was becoming more uncertain, keen winds and early, hard frosts portending a harsh winter. And doubtless a perilous ocean crossing as well.

The nights were the hardest, when Carleton seemed the farthest from her, the least likely ever to return. At night, curled up in the bed they had shared too briefly, she ached to feel his arms cradling her, banishing all fear and worry about what the morrow might hold.

She felt his presence in every corner of the manor and its grounds as though he were there. Yet he was not. All around her she saw the evidence of his life before it had been so sharply and irrevocably upended. First unwillingly sent to England to Lord Carleton's deathbed only to arrive too late. This succeeded by an unplanned decade separated from all he held dear and wandering emotionally and spiritually. Only to return to face the painful aftermath of Sir Harry's death at the hands of British soldiers and, hard on its heels, the rising rebellion against England that had taken him to Boston as British General Thomas Gage's aide, while covertly a spy for the patriots and within a hairsbreadth of the gallows.

What had followed had torn away every expectation and hope for his life: the mission to forge an alliance between the native tribes and the patriots, his capture and enslavement by the Seneca and rescue by his old friends, the Shawnee. His adoption by Black Hawk and the aging sachem's subsequent murder by white settlers that had sparked a war Carleton had been forced to lead as the war chief White Eagle. Then his unwilling return to a life he had foresworn that forced him to live intractably torn between two hostile worlds—and those he loved on both sides.

Her own life had borne its share of tearing, beginning with her betrothal to the loyalist David Hutchins and the abuse that had deeply wounded her spirit, but had finally, thankfully, broken their engagement. That wrenching experience had sent her on a quest to prove her worth by serving as spy, courier, and smuggler for the rebels, dangerous missions kept secret even from her parents. And the greatest upending of all, when she and Carleton had met, and all that had happened as a result of that fateful encounter.

Both of them had been broken time and again. Yet little by little she was coming to understand that each rending had been necessary, for each had ripped away what hindered their faith and led them forward step by step into the true kinship God had made them for, with himself and with each other. She could not regret one moment of that journey. Yet as she looked into the vague shape of a dim, clouded future, she could not help wondering what it held for her.

Looking around at her surroundings she realized that despite the powerful maternal instincts her pregnancy aroused, behind those emotions lay an ache in her bones: an unsettling disassociation from the war's ebb and flow and the part she had played in it; a longing for the camaraderie she had enjoyed with her compatriots and the very excitement, even risks and ever-present danger, that had compelled and challenged her as nothing before or since.

Her body felt increasingly wearisome and ungainly; her back and feet pained her. With a pang she wondered whether she was now to be forever relegated to domestic concerns because she was a woman, doomed to sit on the sidelines while others engaged in this great endeavor to secure their nation's liberty. The thought made her chest clench.

Her arms ached to hold her babe and those to come, to embrace her husband in the passions of the marriage bed, to savor all the sweet charms of domestic bliss. But she couldn't help recognizing that God had not made her only for this, that something had been woven deep into her nature that drew her powerfully toward action, toward adventure, toward . . . some as yet unknown obedience for which her Maker had fitted her.

It was obvious that she could never again serve as a spy because of her dangerous role's exposure. But her training and skill as a doctor and the healing she often felt flowing through her hands to her patients remained. That she had a genuine calling to this ministry had become clear during her sojourn in France, and she would return to it as soon as possible after giving birth.

She had the distinct impression that more would be required of her, however. And the sense that when challenges arose it would not be possible for her to turn away.

✳ ✳ ✳

LATE THAT AFTERNOON, fingers trembling, Elizabeth broke the letter's wax seal. It did not bear the imprint of Carleton's signet, but the hand that had hastily scrawled its direction could not be mistaken.

Unfolding the single page, she scanned its contents, then returned to the top to read the brief note more slowly. She lingered hungrily on each word despite sensing that her parents watched with anxious impatience.

Dear Heart,

We arrived safely and immediately joined the endeavor, which will begin its course within the half hour. Your letters have been forwarded as directed, and I have only moments before I must entrust this to the courier.

Know how deeply I'm torn at leaving you. My only comfort is that you understand and that your dear ones are with you now.

I swear I'll make every effort to keep my promise. God willing it will be so. May our Father be merciful to us.

I can say nothing more than plead: Stay safe, stay well. Beloved light of my life, pray for us in the days to come, as I pray for you ever with all my heart and soul.

I love you so. God's mercy guard you until I hold you again in my arms.

He had neither dated nor signed it, and her throat tightened painfully even though she realized the necessity for the most extreme discretion. Unable to speak, she handed the letter to her father, who scrutinized it while her mother read over his shoulder.

He let out a breath. "Well, there's nothing here that could have offered any intelligence had it been intercepted."

"Jonathan's very careful about such things. From what I've observed, Uncle Alexandre taught him very well."

He looked up sharply to meet Elizabeth's gaze.

She returned a rueful smile. "Uncle Alexandre had the best of teachers himself: Sartine."

Slumping back in his chair, he muttered, "Well! That explains a considerable amount."

But not whether he still lives and will ever come home. The bleak thought caused Elizabeth's breast to clench.

Just then Andrews strode into the parlor. Livid, he brandished the letter he clenched in one hand.

"I just received news from General Lewis. Count d'Estaing launched an attack on Savannah on the ninth. Clinton drove both his and General Lincoln's forces off in a bloody battle. A fortnight ago, after dithering for more than week, d'Estaing loaded his men back on his ships and sailed off, while Lincoln high-tailed it back to Charlestown. Which he'd left unprotected in order to support d'Estaing, whose utter steadiness in the face of any little setback is so very well known!" He bit each word off sarcastically.

Dismayed, Elizabeth gasped, "Then there's no hope of our recapturing Savannah now?"

Andrews gave a curt nod. "The port's an excellent base from which the British can drive attacks all along our southern coast. And I'll warrant Clinton has a tempting target in his sights at the moment."

After a short silence, Dr. Howard guessed, "Charlestown? Well, thankfully Lincoln's returned to his command and—" He stopped abruptly and pressed his hand to his brow with a low groan.

Andrews returned a bitter smile. "My thought exactly."

Chapter Ten

JONATHAN, WHERE ARE YOU?

Stripped to her perspiration-soaked shift, moisture trickling down her flushed face and between her breasts, Elizabeth bent over on the birthing chair as another contraction seized her, gripping the arms until her fingernails dug into the wood. By now the pains were hardly more than a minute apart, and with each one she felt as though her belly and back were clamped unmercifully in a vise. The pressure forced a gasp from her, and she bit her lip until it bled, fighting a wave of panic.

Are you even alive? Have I lost you forever this time? Please, God—

It was Friday evening, 12 November. The contractions had kept her awake all the previous night. They had not been hard or frequent enough that she roused anyone, but by the morning when Jemma came to assist with her toilette, she was not able to conceal her discomfort. Her maid immediately ran to call her mother, Sarah.

Elizabeth's parents had come back back with them. Sarah sent for a tray to be brought up, and Elizabeth half-heartedly nibbled a few bites of shortbread, but drank the valerian tea gratefully for its pain relief and calming properties.

Soon thereafter the three Shawnee women arrived bringing Sweetgrass and Mary McLeod with them and banished her father from the room. Before leaving he had ordered them to call him if needed, then made sure all the draperies were drawn back and partially opened one window, warning sternly that the common practice of keeping the lying-in chamber dark and overly warm increased the risk that the mother would contract puerperal fever.

For the next hours, while the day waned, Elizabeth had paced the spacious chamber and up and down the gallery overlooking the Great Hall, leaning by turns on the arm of one or another of the women. Her water had broken an hour earlier, and Sarah had led her, legs trembling, to the sturdy birthing chair with arms and footrest that the woodshop craftsman had fashioned several weeks earlier. The Shawnee women had never seen such at thing and at first had regarded its U-shaped seat with its open center and front suspiciously before conceding nods of approval.

Laughing Otter bent over Blue Sky, who knelt in front of Elizabeth, her expression unreadable. Elizabeth lifted her weary gaze to meet the older woman's and read the same emotion in her eyes that gripped her.

Red Fox was with Carleton. And so was Stowe. No further news had yet reached Thornlea, and both Laughing Otter and Sweetgrass feared for their husbands' lives too.

Elizabeth reached for Laughing Otter's hand, clutching it so tightly that she winced. After what seemed an eternity, the contraction receded, and Elizabeth slumped back, panting.

"You're doing well, dearest," her mother assured from her other side. "Don't despair. He will come home—I promise you. Perhaps not yet today, but he will come."

"I so hoped—" Elizabeth broke off, tears starting.

"Hush. I know."

Elizabeth leaned forward again, feeling another agonizing contraction begin inexorably to build. *I will not scream. I will die first!* she admonished herself, teeth clenched, shamed by the memory of how Blue Sky had made no sound other than an occasional grunt during her labor for He Leads the Way while battle raged at Bemis Heights.

❋ ❋ ❋

Stowe and Red Fox trailing on his heels, Carleton strode through the double doors into the Great Hall to find Andrews, Dr. Howard, McLeod, and Spotted Pony on their feet in front of the roaring fire, staring in their direction. The servants had made the deuce of a fuss, and the commotion at the manor's entrance had no doubt alerted the men to his party's arrival. Nevertheless, Carleton had the vague impression that something was not quite as it should be for the entire lot of them appeared to be struck dumb.

Looking from one to the other, Carleton pried off his gloves, divested himself of hat and cloak, and cast the items onto the nearest chair. He couldn't blame the four men for gaping. Their arrival at that late hour was certainly unexpected, and his and his companions' appearance was disreputable, to say the least. The rough clothing they'd adopted to avoid attracting unwanted attention was windblown, dusty, and travel-stained from the long, fast journey, their boots dirty and scuffed, their hair disheveled.

He scowled at Andrews. "Isaiah's guards gave us the devil of a time before they'd allow us entry to my property. All because none of us knew the sign and countersign for the day."

Andrews folded his arms, smirking. "They were doing their duty then."

Carleton conceded a wry smile. "They were, and I'm gratified. If they'd let us through with any less objection, I'd have had them flogged on the spot. But all's well that ends well. Isaiah rescued us."

He turned to indicate the colonel, who just then stepped inside, wiping tears from his eyes with one hand. His other arm encircled the broad shoulders of his son, who looked himself again: beardless, hair neatly shorn, fully clothed in garments that fit his tall, muscular frame.

"Pete!" Andrews, McLeod, and Dr. Howard exclaimed in unison. They rushed to grasp the young man's hand and pound him on the back.

"Thank God Jon found you!" McLeod exclaimed.

"No one's praising the Lord more than I," Pete answered gruffly, but with a wide grin.

"How—where—"

"That's a tale for another time, Samuel." Carleton abruptly stilled, the four men's presence there at such a late hour beginning to sink in. "What are all of you doing here at this time of night?" he demanded, eyes narrowing. "And where's my wife? She's well and hasn't been delivered as yet, I hope." With growing apprehension, he noted the doctor's hesitation and the look that passed between him and the other men.

"Well . . . as to that, you're quite fortuitously come," Dr. Howard temporized.

His heartiness felt distinctly forced. At Carleton's frown the doctor raised his hands as though to ward him off.

"There's nothing to worry about, Jon. She's as well as can be expected. The women are all with her, and . . . "

Half turning to follow Dr. Howard's apprehensive glance toward the gallery, Carleton momentarily froze. Then he strode away in the direction of the entrance hall and the stairs. Only to be blocked by Spotted Pony and Red Fox.

"You know the women will not allow a man to enter at such a time."

"Then perdition take them! I'm her husband and the father—"

"And you are Shawnee," Red Fox reminded him dryly, placing a restraining hand on Carleton's shoulder, his fingers digging into the muscle with painful pressure.

"You know they're right, Jon," Andrews confirmed with a rueful laugh from across the Hall. "They'll throw you out." Soberly he added, "And that will only distress Beth."

For a long moment Carleton's gaze locked with the two warriors'. Knowing that Andrews was right, he at last swallowed hard and turned back, frustration and fear churning in his gut.

✳ ✳ ✳

Elizabeth felt a gentle hand rub her back and looked up dully at Sarah. "Don't fight the pain, Miz Beth. Let it come and it be easier."

When her contraction began to recede, Sarah held the glass of wine in which columbine leaf had been steeped to her lips again. Trembling, Elizabeth swallowed the decoction, praying that its reputation for ensuring a speedy delivery was well founded.

Blue Sky reached between Elizabeth's thighs, then looked up, smiling. "I feel the top of his head. It will not be much longer, but you must push harder with each pain."

"I can't!" Elizabeth snapped. The cry left her lips before she could bite it back, and she instantly felt ashamed.

She heard Rain Woman's footfalls approaching from the direction of the fireplace. "You can, Healer Woman," she urged, bending over Eliza-beth. "Have you not helped other women give birth?"

Elizabeth gave a weak nod. Indeed she was well familiar with the moment when the laboring mother felt entirely overcome, as she did now.

"One is not so brave on the other side of this agony," she gasped.

Rain Woman responded with a sympathetic chuckle. "We have all endured it, and we stand beside you now. You will forget the pain when your baby is in your arms."

Sweetgrass came to kneel at Elizabeth's side and gently caressed her belly, murmuring indistinguishable, but comforting words.

Gathering all her remaining resolve, groaning, Elizabeth forced herself to bear down as the pain mounted. When at last it eased, she flung one arm toward the flames crackling in the fireplace.

"It's unbearably hot in here! I can't breathe! Mama, why did you close the window when Papa said it should stay open?"

"Night air is unhealthy," Anne objected.

Elizabeth could only interpret Laughing Otter's forceful exclamation in Shawnee as "Nonsense." She strode across the chamber and flung the window wide, returning a fierce frown to Anne's adamant objections.

"It is not good for the mother to give birth where there is no fresh air, nor is it good for her baby. We should have built a birthing hut as we intended," she muttered as she stalked back to Elizabeth.

"Regardless of your traditions, my daughter is not going to give birth in a stick hut!"

The three native women rolled their eyes, but Elizabeth could give no heed. A tendril of fresh air cooled her brow, drawing a sigh of relief before a sharp contraction once more enveloped her. There was little space at all between them now. As one began to recede the next immediately gripped her so that she had no time to relax or even to draw a breath.

"Your pacing isn't likely to speed things along, Jon," Dr. Howard growled.

Carleton arrested halfway across the great hall and turned to regard his father-in-law with equal exasperation. "Thank you for disillusioning me."

He'd lost track of how often he had flung himself into a chair only to spring to his feet shortly thereafter and resume pacing. No matter that he was far beyond bone weary, he simply could not settle.

Sprawled in a chair half asleep, Andrews pushed himself up, chuckling. "If you'll remember, I had a raging battle to divert me at the birth of my first."

"Unfortunately we haven't an enemy at hand, Charles. At any rate, I'd rather not begin an attack at this particular moment."

"I wasn't so lucky with the second either," Andrews allowed with a grimace.

"Nay, nor was I with the bairns my first wife gave me," McLeod noted softly. "And with my Mary carryin' our first, I'll be lookin' forward to the same predicament afore long."

Carleton's gaze sharpened. "Then I wish you joy, James. And many more to come."

Spotted Pony exchanged an amused look with his brother. "Men are useless in such circumstances. It is a matter best left in the hands of the women."

"Ah, yes," Carleton countered dryly. "That makes the waiting so much easier." Transferring his gaze upward to the gallery, he muttered, "How long can Beth bear this?"

"She's receiving all the care one could want. She'll make it through."

Despite Dr. Howard's outward confidence, it felt as though he spoke more to reassure himself than Carleton. For what seemed the thousandth time—though he doubted much more than an hour had passed—he strode out to the staircase and contemplated the steps as though if he only stared at them long enough one of the women would descend to announce Elizabeth's safe delivery and their child's health.

When no one appeared, he turned back in frustration, only to see Jemma approaching from the direction of the stairs leading to the kitchen. She carried a pail of steaming water in one hand and clutched a bundle of towels in her other arm. The moment she caught sight of him she jerked to a halt.

"Oh, sir, you've come!"

He went to her. "I've brought your brother."

The words were hardly out of his mouth when Isaiah and Pete stepped out into the entry hall. Jemma's mouth dropped open.

"Pete!" She set down her pail with a thump that sloshed hot water onto the hem of her gown and apron, dropped the towels onto a nearby table, and flew to Pete's arms.

"What's happening? How's Beth—our baby—" It was impossible for Carleton to make his anxious queries heard over her happy exclamations and her brother's and father's explanations.

After a moment Jemma cried out, "Mama!" Extricating herself from Pete's embrace, she caught up her burdens, then ran up the stairs and out of sight, leaving Carleton standing there, staring helplessly after her.

✳ ✳ ✳

"She's exhausted," Elizabeth heard her mother say worriedly as she gently brushed the sweat-soaked hair back from Elizabeth's brow.

"The first always take longer," Sarah answered, sounding as though she was at a great distance, "but she be doing well."

Elizabeth paid scant attention to the women's voices, her entire focus on the misery of her weary, laboring body. All else, even, mercifully, the anguished longing for Carleton, had muted into a distant haze.

She roused when Jemma burst into the room. Her maid carried a pail of water and a bundle of clean towels to the fireplace almost at a run and when she had disposed of them whirled to face her mother.

"General Carleton's come! Oh, Mama, he brought Pete! He's well—he's whole! Papa's with him."

Crying out, Sarah clamped her hands over her mouth, tears starting to her eyes. When she hesitated, looking from Elizabeth to the open door, Anne shooed both her and Jemma off.

"Go! Stay with them. We'll take care of everything here."

Elizabeth had never seen Sarah so undone. Laughing and crying at the same time, she fled from the room with her daughter on her heels.

Again Elizabeth doubled over. "Please—Jonathan!" The breathless plea came out in a croak.

"Your son is coming! Push hard!" Blue Sky commanded her.

Teeth gritted, Elizabeth obeyed with a guttural groan, at last felt the infant slip from her in a warm, sticky flow. The contraction abated, and she slumped against the back of the chair, felt her mother's arms slip around her shoulders.

"You have a daughter!" Blue Sky announced in surprise, then began to laugh.

Faint and shaky, Elizabeth watched anxiously while her adoptive sister quickly cleared the infant's mouth. Relief and intense joy washed over her as the babe's chest suddenly expanded in a gulping breath. Her skin's bluish tinge gave way to a delicate pink, then to an angry red as she vigorously and inconsolably protested the indignity of her birth.

All of them were laughing then. Blue Sky placed the babe into Elizabeth's trembling arms. She cradled her squirming daughter, slippery from her birth, to her breast, so weak she feared she would drop her.

"Julianne," she whispered, hungrily taking in every perfect detail of her newborn. "Welcome, my dear one."

When she kissed the small, creased brow, the infant stilled, fixing her in an unfocused gaze. Elizabeth was unaware of the umbilical cord being tied off and cut, the afterbirth being delivered, the other women's chatter. All her attention focused on her babe's face.

At last, reluctantly, hardly able to hold up her head, she surrendered the tiny girl to Mary, who wrapped her in a soft towel. When Sweetgrass gently wiped away streaks of blood and waxy white vernix from the baby's face with the fabric's edge, she let out a tremulous wail that quickly gave way to loud cries and quavering sobs.

"This one will grow to be a warrior woman like Nonhelema!" Rain Woman declared, laughing.

"Let me hold her!"

Mary relinquished the small bundle to Anne, who rocked her granddaughter in her arms, crooning, "Hush, dearest. Oh, how sweet you are!"

Mary turned back to Elizabeth. "She's so beautiful!"

"Please . . . Jonathan—"

A sudden sharp contraction seized Elizabeth before she could say more, and she pressed her hand to her belly in alarm.

Laughing Otter immediately knelt again and ran her hands along the contours of Elizabeth abdomen. "There is another who has not turned."

Elizabeth gasped, then groaned as a succeeding pain bore over her. Frowning in concentration, Laughing Otter massaged her belly for several moments. At last Elizabeth startled, feeling the babe flip.

"He is ready to be born now," Laughing Otter said approvingly, and the tension that had stilled the rest of the women eased.

Blue Sky quickly resumed her place, with Mary kneeling at Elizabeth's side to support her, while Anne stood behind, clutching her new granddaughter, her face ashen. "Dear God, have mercy!" she cried.

For Elizabeth the next minutes were a blur. She felt as though she fought against the merciless current of a raging river with no certainty that she would make it to the other side. At last she felt a gush of warmth leaving her body on a wrenching pain harder than the rest, gave a weak, guttural cry, and slumped, feeling the second babe slip free.

"A son!" Blue Sky announced triumphantly.

When Blue Sky handed the boy to Rain Woman to swath, Elizabeth saw that he was heavily smeared with blood, that he did not move. She fought weakly to pull away from Mary's restraining arms and reach for him though her own arms felt heavy as lead.

"Stay still!" Mary commanded urgently.

Distantly Elizabeth heard her friend's murmured prayers. She was suddenly cold as death, nauseated and shaking, black spots blooming and receding before her eyes, the last of her strength rapidly seeping away. Mary and Sweetgrass cradled her while Laughing Otter gently but firmly massaged her flaccid belly.

"I'm s-so c-cold," she managed to whisper through chattering teeth.

She was only vaguely conscious that Blue Sky and Laughing Otter lowered her onto the folded blankets Rain Woman hastily laid on the floor in front of the chair, of someone hurriedly winding thick layers of soft toweling around her loins, of a wool blanket, heavenly warm from the fire, being wrapped snugly around her. Someone banged the window sash down, the sound strangely muffled. Her daughter's cries muted, but still she heard no sound from her son.

Her mother's chalk-white face hovered over her. Sliding one arm under Elizabeth's shoulders, holding a glass of red fluid in the other hand, she raised her and commanded urgently, "Drink this!"

Earlier Elizabeth had taken a draught of the tincture of Shepherd's Purse mixed with lichwort and juniper spirits that Sarah had prepared in case of hemorrhage. When her mother pressed the glass against her lips now, she convulsively swallowed its bitter contents, half choking.

She became aware of the warm, metallic odor of blood, wondered dimly whether she was dying. Her surroundings receded, darkness beckoning her, yet oddly she felt no fear at all.

Oh, blessed warmth and absence of pain! How inexpressibly wonderful to lie still, to feel light as air and allow herself to drift . . . .

As from a great distance she heard voices praying over her and sensed an urgent bustle in the room, felt herself being gently handled. Bending over her, Blue Sky wiped her face with a damp cloth and whispered words Elizabeth could not make out.

Jonathan . . .

The awareness of an inexorable tide flowing from her body intruded then, and she sank gratefully into darkness.

THE FIRE BURNED LOW, night well advanced, when Anne appeared suddenly at the upper gallery's balustrade, face ashen. Chest constricting sharply, Carleton sprang from his seat.

"Jonathan! Samuel!" She beckoned urgently to them.

The others were all on their feet now, too, but Carleton paid them no heed, was hardly aware that Elizabeth's father followed close on his heels as he crossed the Hall and charged up the stairs, a terrible fear settling deep into his soul.

He came into the chamber, in several swift steps stood beside her prone form, aware of nothing else.

"She's bleeding badly!" A sob muffled Anne's voice.

He dropped to his knees, supporting himself with one hand on either side of her head, his heart seizing at the sight of her face entirely drained of color. He leaned to press a light kiss to her clammy forehead.

"Beth," he murmured raggedly, "I'm here. Stay with me, dear heart."

Her eyelids fluttered, and she angled her head slightly toward him but appeared otherwise insensible. He had only a vague awareness of the women clustered close by, of Dr. Howard kneeling on one side, Anne on his other, a muted whimper in the background like a kitten's faint mew. All his being centered on that beloved face.

Pushing back, he laid one hand on Elizabeth's head, the other on her abdomen, felt the babe's absence. "Dear Jesus, if it be your good pleasure, I beg you, please heal my dear wife!" he whispered in anguish. "Don't take her from me, Lord! As you did for the woman who touched the hem of your garment, please stanch her hemorrhage."

Chapter Eleven

ONE MOMENT SHE FELT life rapidly ebbing. The next, the flow from her womb ceased. By degrees warmth began to trickle back into her limbs even as a deep and blessed peace settled over her weary body.

"Dear one . . . soul of my soul . . ."

The tender plea of that beloved voice drew her back from the gaping void. With great effort she forced her eyes open and managed a tremulous smile. She took brief note of her parents and the women anxiously gathered around before focusing on his face.

"I am well, dearest. The bleeding has stopped." She had only strength to mouth the words.

He drew in a breath and let it out, tears spilling, bent over her until his forehead touched hers. "Father, I thank you with all my heart. Your grace is beyond my deserving." He found her mouth and kissed her, his touch light as a feather.

Everyone in the room was smiling now, uttering soft exclamations of relief and praise. An outraged wail in the background jerked her back to full awareness. When Carleton pushed back to his haunches and looked toward the sound, she realized that she had not heard her boy cry even once nor seen him move, and a piercing fear stabbed through her.

"My son!" She struggled weakly to push upright.

Blue Sky sat down cross-legged beside her and with Anne gently pressed her back against the blankets. "You must lie very still until we are certain the bleeding will not start again, Healer Woman," she admonished firmly, adding with a smile, "Mary has him. He is awake and well. A quiet one he is, but strong like a warrior."

"We have a son?"

"Your daughter came first," Anne returned as she stood up, appearing almost giddy with relief. "Your son took us all by surprise."

Thunderstruck, Carleton scrambled to his feet. "Two?"

"One of each."

Directing a mischievous glance at her astounded husband, Anne crossed the room to the fireplace, where Mary and Rain Woman were gently rubbing both babies with fragrant, lavender-steeped oil of lanolin. They wrapped the smaller of the two, and Anne carried Carleton's crying daughter to him.

Dr. Howard beamed, his chest puffed out. "Didn't I tell you I suspected as much?"

"A lad and a lass!" When Carleton took the squalling infant into his arms, she quieted to shuddering sobs, and he gazed down in wonder at her tiny, rosy, cherub face through blurred eyes. "Ah, my Father, you anoint my head with oil. My cup runs over!"

Dr. Howard leaned over Carleton's arm to stroke the baby's cheek, his smile broad. Then as Anne carried his grandson to him, he clapped Carleton on the back, and exclaimed, "I believe you've friends downstairs who are anxiously waiting to hear the happy news."

"Twins! Had I known, I'd have been even more out of my mind with worry than I already was."

"Then I'm glad you didn't," she returned, smiling so sweetly up at Carleton that he would have caught her and their son into his embrace had he not been holding Julianne and fearful of crushing all of them.

He and Dr. Howard had carried the twins downstairs to show them off to the waiting men and receive their hearty congratulations and blessings. While they were gone the women bathed Elizabeth and slipped a clean shift on her, taking care not to jostle her unduly. By then Carleton and her father had returned. After being assured that there was no more bleeding now than natural, Carleton had scooped her up and carried her to the bed as tenderly as though she were herself a babe.

She appeared to have regained a small degree of strength. But though she seemed determined not to show it, she was still worrisomely weak. The dark shadows beneath her eyes troubled her father as much as it did him, Carleton noted anxiously.

He sat in a chair pulled to the bedside, still astounded, holding his daughter, while Elizabeth lay partially propped up against a couple of pillows, wrapped in warm blankets.

Her parents hovered over them. "How are you feeling?" Dr. Howard asked brusquely.

"Better," she murmured. "As though a great weight has been lifted."

"Actually, it has been," Carleton said dryly, pleased when a smile lit her drawn face.

Transferring her gaze to her nursing son, she beamed down at him. "Hello, Harrison. Our own dear, sweet Harry." She looked up, laughing softly. "All these months I've longed to see our babe, not knowing we were in for a surprise."

"A happy one," Carleton returned, his voice hoarse.

The boy nursed for only a few moments before his eyes drooped and his head rolled to one side, his pursed lips momentarily still making sucking movements. Gently she folded back his wrappings as she had the girl's earlier. He jerked his arms and legs at being unwrapped, but unlike his sister only snuffled and grunted. After a moment he frowned up at his mother intently as though studying her features while they all marveled at the perfection of his tiny body.

Elizabeth gave him up to her father, and Carleton transferred their daughter to her. Their eyes met, and he saw moisture glimmering in hers even as tears stung his own.

Dr. Howard reluctantly surrendered the boy to Carleton. Carefully he lifted the infant to his shoulder and patted and rubbed his back while Anne helped Elizabeth to settled their girl at her other breast.

"He is a handsome lad—though it's possible I might be biased."

"Nonsense!" Anne exclaimed. "He's the most handsome of babes. And no one could deny that he takes after you. He's most certainly his father's son."

"Thankfully he's a quiet one, unlike our equally beautiful but very vocal daughter. I fear for what that characteristic portends for her future," Elizabeth added drolly, drawing everyone's chuckles.

Each was quite distinct from the other, Carleton reflected, smiling, not only in appearance, but already in personality. Although second born, Harry was the larger of the two and more sturdily formed, with the fuzz of hair covering his head as light as tow, now mostly concealed beneath a tiny embroidered gauze cap. Julianne was also fair, with delicate features that owed much to her mother, though her abundant hair gleamed red-gold in the firelight, wisps curling around the lower edge of her matching cap.

Harry appeared to be content cradled securely in Carleton's arms, already sound asleep. Finished nursing, Julianne fussed and struggled against her swaddling, but calmed when Elizabeth lifted her to her shoulder.

Elizabeth met his gaze, and he saw that her heart swelled with the same emotions as his. Gratitude welled up, so intense that he felt a physical ache.

Oh, Lord, what grace is this that through many dangers and trials you've kept us safe and brought us to one another's arms again! And our babes—how can we ever doubt your good will for us? And yet in our human weakness, we too often do. Oh, help Thou our unbelief!

✱ ✱ ✱

THE CHAMBER WAS FINALLY quiet. But in spite of a deep, sapping weariness, Elizabeth did not wish to sleep, wanted to hold onto this moment of wonder as long as possible.

The tall case clock below in the Great Hall had struck the half hour after eleven shortly before. The babes' clouts and pilches had been changed, and they had been snugly swaddled and tucked into the large cradle near the banked fire. For the moment, at least, they slept contentedly, cuddled together as they had been in the womb.

The chamber had been tidied and aired, the bloody cloths and other detritus of the birthing carried away, and the others had all withdrawn for a few hours of sleep. Laughing Otter's daughters, Yellow Feather and Morning Dew, were bedded down in the nursery with the connecting doors open through the dressing room so they could tend to the babies and bring them to Elizabeth as needed.

At Elizabeth's insistence Carleton stripped and drew on a nightshirt, then slipped gingerly into the bed as though fearing to unsettle her. She laid her head on his chest, and he gently curved his arm under her shoulders.

Sensing his reluctance, she lifted her head to scrutinize his shadowed face. "Is something wrong?"

He raised himself carefully to bend over her and brushed the damp, curling strands of hair back from her face. The worry in his gaze sent a pang through her.

"Beth, I don't want to move you any more than necessary. I'm afraid the bleeding might start again."

"I need you to hold me, kiss me," she said, by now so weary she could hardly speak above a whisper. "I need to know you're really here. I've been so terrified all these months that—" Her voice choked.

Still he hesitated. Shifting to wind her arms around his neck, she drew him hungrily to her. When she raised her face insistently to his, he brushed her lips lightly with his . . . and then tucked her body close against him with infinite gentleness and covered her face with kisses of such urgency that she entirely forgot her exhaustion. She buried her fingers in his hair and held onto him, consumed by the irrational fear that if she let go he would again dissolve into the ether as he had so often in her dreams.

For long moments she was conscious of nothing beyond his arms safely enclosing her, his mouth seeking hers, the beating of their hearts like two wild birds bursting from a cruel captivity. They were both trembling when he released her and lay back, facing her on the pillow.

"I didn't hurt you?"

"Dearest, your absence is the worst hurt I could ever feel." She smiled tremulously at him. "I'm well now you're here. Truly. I can't describe what I felt when they told me that you'd come home. I feared so that you . . . wouldn't."

He let out a shaky breath. "It's only by God's grace that I have."

His muttered response caused her to search his eyes. "Mrs. Washington wrote that she'd received word from the General of Jones defeating a British warship in a great victory."

He nodded, rasped, "Dear God, I thought we were lost, that I'd never see you again, or our babe—babes," he corrected with a muffled laugh.

She regarded him searchingly. "Was it so very bad?"

He glanced away, but not before she caught the darkness that shadowed his eyes. "Worse, if possible, even than that night I snatched you from *Erebus*. So many men dead on both sides—" He stopped as though finding it impossible to go on.

"Mrs. Washington gave no details of what happened," she prompted, afraid to hear the truth of it, yet needing to. When he did not respond, she said gently, "I've seen battle, too, heart of my heart. I can imagine—"

"No you can't," he cut her off curtly. "That night is beyond imagining."

He did not meet her gaze, staring into the shadows, his face blank of any expression. But when she took his hand and pressed it, she received answering pressure in return.

"What I *have* seen haunts me still."

"It'll haunt us until the day we die. Men were not made to kill other men."

"No. And yet we do . . . that our children may live free."

She could feel a tremor go through him. Lifting her hand, he pressed it to his lips.

"It might help if you confided in someone."

He fixed her in a weary look. "Have you? Really? Even in me?"

Stricken, she hesitated, then reluctantly shook her head, throat painfully tight.

"Jones is a madman," he said then with a harsh laugh. "I'm not easily daunted, yet even I'd given us up. But, bless him, if it hadn't been for his obstinate refusal to surrender, I'd not be here. The worst of it reminded me quite vividly why I decided as a youth not to pursue a naval career. Waging war on solid ground is one thing. Engaging in battle on an uncertain, fickle sea is another matter altogether.

"The same thought struck me in New York Harbor, too, while we fought to wrest you from that foul hulk." He turned his head, his gaze piercing her. "But I'd freely give my life and everything I possess to save you from danger. And our children."

"And the men who depend on you," she murmured, stroking his cheek.

He remained silent, anguish tightening his features. After a moment he made a quick, dismissive gesture and glanced toward the cradle standing in the fire's faint glow.

"This I'll ever hold in memory. Our children. And you."

She nestled her head on his shoulder and wrapped her arm across his waist, wishing with all her being that she could heal the wounds—both his and hers—added to other wounds before them and still more before those. And more yet to come. But there was only One who could make shattered hearts whole again. She had to believe that in his mercy the Father would. And that what they suffered was not without meaning.

"All I wanted was make it back to you, dear heart." Gently he kissed her temple, his breath warm against the fine curls. As though it was an assurance he clung to above all else, he whispered, "And I did. And you came through your own trial. Praise God for his unfailing faithfulness."

IN SPITE OF HIS WEARINESS Carleton could only doze by short spells, jerking awake at the slightest noise or movement. A couple of times Sarah had left her newly reunited family and stolen in to tend to Elizabeth. Hearing the babies fuss, Yellow Feather had slipped into the room to bring them to the bed so Elizabeth could nurse them. Each time she immediately fell back into an exhausted sleep.

Sometime toward morning, after Morning Dew changed the twins' clouts, Carleton motioned her to bring them to him instead of returning them to the cradle. When she withdrew he settled the infants between him and Elizabeth and gently kissed each tiny, perfect face. She turned toward him and opened her eyes, giving him and their little ones a drowsy smile before drifting off to sleep again.

As he held his little family close, he had a distinct impression that Lord Carleton, Sir Harry, and Black Hawk, too, hovered near, smiling down at them. And his heart swelled with a fiercely possessive surge of pride, joy, and love far beyond any emotion he had ever felt, until it seemed as though his chest must burst from it.

By degrees the scene seemed to shift into shadow, however, until he stood in this same chamber at Sir Harry's knee, a young boy of eight. In memory he clearly heard Sir Harry's voice, unyielding as steel: *Ne'er let down your guard, laddie. For if ye do, sure as death an enemy'll creep in when ye least expect it and wrest everythin' ye love from your arms.*

A deathly chill settled into his heart. All thought of sleep fled, and until first light he kept watch while Elizabeth and their wee ones slept unaware, the silent vow of his heart that should any put out a hand to do them harm, they'd not live to see another day.

Chapter Twelve

" 'L O, CHILDREN ARE an heritage o' the Lord: And the fruit of the womb is his reward.' "

Although Elizabeth was still weak and wan, a happy warmth spread through her at midmorning the next day as McLeod's resonant Scottish burr filled the hushed room.

" 'As arrows are in the hand of a mighty man: So are children o' the youth. Happy is the man that hath his quiver full o' them.' "

Cradling her daughter, Elizabeth sat in a chair at the bedside, dressed in a pretty russet bedgown and matching sprigged petticoat, her curly hair pinned back and topped with a small lace-trimmed white lawn cap. Carleton stood next to her, their swaddled son in his arms, while McLeod faced them, Bible in hand. Her parents, all the women who had attended her labor, Durie, Andrews, the two Shawnee warriors, Carleton's and Andrews' aides, and Isaiah and Farris all ranged around the laird's chamber, along with as many servants as could squeeze into the space, every face reflecting a solemn joy.

McLeod paused to share a smile with Mary before continuing, " 'Thy wife shall be as a fruitful vine by the sides of thine house: Thy children like olive plants round about thy table. Behold, that thus shall the man be blessed that feareth the Lord.' "

Head bowed, he prayed, a murmured "Amen" from those gathered softly affirming the blessing.

Yellow Feather and Morning Dew whisked the twins away to the nursery. Red Fox, and Spotted Pony along with Isaiah, Farris, and the two aides soon withdrew to return to their duties. The servants followed, everyone tendering warm congratulations to Carleton and Elizabeth before filtering quietly out of the chamber in a muted stir.

Those remaining found seats on the chairs brought in earlier along with a table and trays laden with small, matching silver cups, glasses, and a bottle of the estate's finest brandy. In moments Salome returned carrying a large silver pitcher, accompanied by two kitchen maids. While the cook and maids distributed cups filled with traditional Scottish caudle to the women, Carleton poured generous portions of brandy into glasses for the men.

Durie proposed a toast to the newborns, and the others joined in with hearty well wishes. Elizabeth savored the custard-like drink of milk, eggs, and gruel fortified with spiced wine, its bracing warmth radiating through her body.

Carleton raised his glass to Salome and bowed, before taking a sip of the brandy. "I've been away so long I'd forgotten about the caudle." Turning to Elizabeth, he explained, "In Scotland it's not only served to new mothers and their female attendants and visitors, but everyone also drinks it at Beltane. Though then it's made a tad stronger."

"That's putting it mildly," Dr. Howard said, his expression rueful.

Elizabeth gave Carleton a questioning look. "Beltane?"

"The Gaelic May Day festival."

"We arrived here at the end of April just as preparations were being made," Anne put in. "Alistair and James told us all about the tradition. We thoroughly enjoyed the bonfire, food, music, and dancing. The fairy stories, however—" she raised one shoulder "—well, they're charming, but quite fanciful."

Carleton exchanged amused glances with his steward and chaplain. Noting Elizabeth's and the Shawnee women's puzzled expressions, McLeod explained that Là Bealltainn was one of the four Gaelic festivals that inaugurated each season, the others being Samhain on 1 November; Imbolc, 1 February; and Lughnasadh, 1 August. Beltane marked the beginning of summer when the cattle were driven out to pasture.

" 'Tis an auld tradition that our Scots and Irish servants insist on," Durie allowed. He went on to explain that fertility rites for humans, animals, and crops were observed, but the most important feature was the ancient fire ritual. Cattle were driven between two fires on their way to pasture to protect them from both natural and spiritual forces by appeasing invisible beings believed to be spirits, fairies, ancestors, or, by some accounts, gods and goddesses.

"They're called *aos sí* in Irish mythology and *daoine sìth* by us Scots," Carleton broke in. "It means people of the mounds. They're believed to be most active at Beltane and Samhain. Various legends have them either living far across the western sea in underground fairy mounds or inhabiting an invisible world outside our physical one and walking unseen among humans to do either good or harm."

"And you believe in these myths, Jonathan?" Elizabeth teased.

He grinned. "I assure you that Sir Harry made sure I was properly schooled in the gospel—though as a lad I found the festival to be great fun, as any young boy would."

"These legends sound much like our ancestors' vain beliefs," Laughing Otter noted, exchanging frowning glances with Rain Woman and Blue Sky.

" 'Tis nothing more than pagan superstition," McLeod grumbled, shaking his head. "As wi' your people, some o' ours still hold to such to this day, even among those who outwardly claim Christ."

"Then we must testify to them of our one true hope," Blue Sky responded firmly.

AFTER EVERYONE HAD GONE except Elizabeth's parents and McLeod, they discussed plans for the twin's churching on Sunday a week in the chapel. With arrangements agreed on, McLeod took his leave.

Carleton remembered suddenly that in his rush to reach Thornlea he'd neglected to send a report of the battle to Washington the moment Caledonne's squadron docked at Jamestown, as he'd intended. It occurred to him that he'd also forgotten the letters from Passy that Caledonne had delivered to him.

Hastily he fetched the letters from his pack. They spent some minutes reading and exclaiming over the latest news from Tess, Abby, and the Martieu-Broussards and their eager demands for news about Elizabeth's giving birth.

They were interrupted when Morning Dew and Yellow Feather brought the twins in from the nursery, Elizabeth's parents the first to claim them. After several minutes of being passed between the four of them, little Julianne set up a wail, as was becoming expected, though Harry made only an occasional mild protest.

Beaming, Anne surrendered her granddaughter to Elizabeth and gathered the letters. "I'll answer these directly and share our happy news!"

Dr. Howard checked his pocket watch and started to his feet. Handing Harry over to Carleton, he said, "Here it's almost dinner time, and I'm forgetting my duties. I wanted to look in at the hospital this morning and check on Mersereau again. Traveling all the way from France didn't do him any good, Jon. His weakness concerns me."

"As it does me," Carleton said, rocking his son gently in his arms. "I made sure Tommy was well attended throughout our voyage, and he seemed to be improving. I'm afraid the ride here from Jamestown was hard on him, but we didn't dare tarry."

Dr. Howard nodded. "Well, I suspect what he needs most is rest and nourishment. Come along, my dear," he said to Anne. "I'm sure you're eager to get to those letters."

"Tommy Mersereau?" Elizabeth demanded as soon as they had gone.

Carleton returned a questioning look. "Yes. He's an American who was impressed by the British while serving on one of our merchantman. He and Pete became friends aboard *Serapis*'s escort, which we also took as prize." When Elizabeth stared at him, open-mouthed, he frowned. "You know him?"

"I know of him. When Aunt Tess and I were staying in New York, I encountered his parents on Staten Island while spying out Lord Howe's newly arrived fleet," she explained, referring to Admiral Lord Richard Howe, at that time naval commander on the British North American station.

"You crossed to Staten Island while Howe's fleet occupied the harbor?" Carleton held up his free hand to forestall her reply. "Of course you did. How could I have imagined you wouldn't?"

"Why wouldn't I? You've gone far more dangerous places."

"But I'm a—" He broke abruptly off.

She glared at him. "What? A man? And I'm a mere woman incapable of such exploits?"

Carleton cuddled his son against his chest, the boy's head tucked under his chin. "Be warned, Harry," he soothed. "When you're grown you must never imply by look, word, or deed that a lady is incapable in any way of doing everything you can do—and more."

At that Julianne suddenly arched back and began to wail desolately. "Oh, my darling girl," Elizabeth cooed, "so young, yet already you apprehend the travails you must suffer at the hands of men."

She countered Carleton's scowl with an arch look. Mirth danced in his eyes, however, and although she returned a fierce frown, it was a losing battle. When he burst into laughter, she could contain her own merriment no longer. Each time they gained control long enough to take a breath, their eyes met again, and laughter bubbled up once more, while Julianne screamed as though she was being pinched.

It was some moments before they finally sobered enough that Elizabeth could comfort their daughter. Carefully avoiding Carleton's smug smile, she settled into the wing chair ensconced in the bartizan. Unpinning the top of her bedgown, she loosed the ties on her shift. When she cradled Julianne to her breast, the child quieted and began to suckle contentedly.

"As I was saying," Elizabeth continued, "Tommy's father was already keeping watch on the British in the hope he could smuggle intelligence to General Washington, so naturally I offered my services. He and his wife told me about their son who had disappeared some years earlier after having run away to sea. They'd heard nothing of Tommy's fate in all those years and were understandably heartsick," she told Carleton.

"His health is broken, and he fears they won't welcome him home."

"Oh, Jonathan, they grieved greatly for him! I can't tell you how dearly they longed to hold him in their arms, and I can't imagine their hearts have changed in the years since."

He nodded. "It's as I thought. The journey here was quite hard on him, however, and he'll not be fit to travel for some time. I'll send a messenger directly to his parents and have them brought here if they'll come."

They exchanged babies, and she settled to nurse Harry. "I'm so thankful you also found Pete alive and well! Did you gain any news of *Destiny* and the rest of your crews? What of Eaden, Dr. Lemaire, and Marie?"

He related what he had learned of his officers and sailors, the surviving women, and *Destiny*'s location and plans to recapture her. Her own grief was evident as she listened.

He fell silent and for a long moment stared into space. At last, his voice rough, he said, "I can do nothing for the others. I know that. And yet somehow, in my heart, it feels as though I've abandoned them. I can only hope that in rescuing Pete and Tommy I've in some measure, at least, redeemed the loss of the rest."

✳ ✳ ✳

AND YET THE LOSS of all those others, and particularly of Eaden, continued to gnaw at Carleton. The following day, glossing over the most unsettling details, he dictated a brief report of the battle to Hutchinson, who made copies and dispatched them to Washington; General Lewis; and Virginia's governor, Thomas Jefferson. That dreaded task completed, Carleton busied himself as necessary with the business of his command while spending as much time as possible with Elizabeth and the twins.

A couple of nights later, troubled and unable to sleep, feeling restless and as though he had neglected to do something he wasn't yet sure of, he slipped out of bed, careful not to wake Elizabeth. Easing the chamber door closed behind him, he paused at the gallery's balustrade, uncertain.

Below, the Great Hall lay awash in shadow, its only illumination the dying glow of the banked coals on the hearths and the moonlight streaming through the tall windows. At last an unidentifiable longing drew him down the stairs and across the broad space.

He arrested before the shadowed portrait of Lord Carleton, knowing suddenly what it was that drew him. Staring up at the image, for a long moment he fixed his father's face in a searching look, then reached tentatively to touch the painted surface. He leaned forward until his brow rested lightly against it.

"Forgive me for judging you harshly," he whispered, chest painfully clenched. "You were right in making the sacrifice you did to keep me safe, and I'm thankful for it. Truly. The life I have is due to your care. Despite my misunderstanding and anger, all these years I ever longed for your love, your approval. To know I had it unreservedly even when I least merited it . . . "

He gulped in a ragged breath before continuing, "Your example has taught me what it is to be a man. A father. And I swear I'll do my best to live up to it. Oh, Papa . . . I love you."

Sensing movement beside him, he turned blindly to find Elizabeth there. To his gratitude she didn't speak but simply enfolded him in her arms. He clung to her, his cheek pressed to the crown of her head.

"I'm glad you've made peace with your father—the real man, not the ghost you thought you knew," she murmured at length.

He cleared his throat and nodded. "There's someone else I need to make peace with," he admitted gruffly.

At her questioning look, he drew her to his own portrait and studied it earnestly for some moments. At length he said softly, "You didn't know—couldn't have known then in your youthful arrogance—how the Father watched over your steps . . . and does to this day, despite my wanderings."

Looking heavenward, his arm tightening around Elizabeth's shoulders, he added, "But I do know it now, Father. And though in my weakness I'll doubtless often fall short in the days left to me, I thank you for always calling me back home to you."

Chapter Thirteen

ELIZABETH SAT ON the camp chair beside the patient's cot as Carleton helped him to sit up.

Placing a pillow behind his back, Dr. Howard said, "The last few days I've had him sitting up and even walking as much as he could bear."

She smiled and fixed the young man in a searching look. "How are you feeling today, Tommy?"

He looked anxiously from her to Carleton, then back. "I'm some improved, ma'am."

She had been eager to finally meet Tommy to determine what progress he was making and what could be done to reunite him and his parents. A little more than a week had passed since the twins' birth. Thankfully neither of her parents approved the month-long lying-in after giving birth that women of the higher classes typically observed. So after several days of rest and adjustment to new routines, she had begun to resume her normal activities as she could without tiring unduly. As she expected, her strength was steadily returning.

"You're looking better than the last time I stopped by, Tommy," Carleton approved. "My wife has been eager to meet you."

Tommy regarded her questioningly. "The general told me you . . . you know my parents."

She nodded. "I helped them transmit intelligence they gathered to

General Washington in New York until the British took the city. They told me about you."

Hope and fear vied on his features. "T-they were well?" he stuttered.

"As well as they could be for dearly missing their son who had run off to sea," she gently chided. "They were grieved that they'd heard nothing of you in all those years."

Tears came into his eyes, and he swallowed. Looking away, he said gruffly, "Surely they'd not welcome back such a son as me after—" He broke off when she took his hand and squeezed it.

"I came to know your parents well, Tommy. They'd more than welcome your return. The best thing you can do for them—the thing they long for the most—is to have you home with them again."

Carleton gently gripped Tommy's shoulder as tears coursed down his cheeks. After some discussion, Carleton related that he had already sent a letter to the Mersereaus by a courier, who would arrange with one of the army's spies at New York to smuggle it through the British lines.

"It'll take some time for it to reach them, and then for their response to come back to us. Until it does, you'll stay with us here."

"I expect within the week you'll be well enough to stay up and move around during the daytime," Dr. Howard interjected. "We'll see how you get along. Once you're strong enough we'll move you into the barracks. But mind that you eat as much as you can. Your body needs sound nourishment and exercise more than anything else."

"Yes, sir!" Tommy said, a smile breaking over his face.

ON THE MORNING OF Sunday, 21 November, Carleton stood in the chapel at the baptismal font with Elizabeth and her parents. He could hardly keep his gaze from her.

She wore a lovely robe à la anglaise. The supple Chinese silk brocade striped in soft shades of sage, jonquil, and cream enhanced her complexion and dark curls, and the bodice with its fitted, lace-trimmed elbow-length sleeves and graceful fall of petticoats set her figure to advantage. Other than the slight thickening of her waist that still remained from her pregnancy, there was little evidence that she had given birth less than a fortnight ago.

He wore full uniform, as did those of his officers in attendance. As the twins' godparents, Andrews and Blue Sky stood beside them facing McLeod. Mary, Red Fox, Spotted Pony, and their families, and Isaiah, Sarah and Jemma, Farris, Hutchinson, Spencer, and Durie surrounded them.

With inexpressible emotion, feeling a blessed joy hovering over them all, Carleton surrendered his daughter, and, in turn, Elizabeth their son, to McLeod, who baptized the babies and proclaimed their names: Julianne Abigail Theresa, and Oliver Harrison Samuel.

The following evening Elizabeth and her parents stood with Carleton again, this time outside the council house, warmed by a roaring bonfire. The large assembly of warriors, Rangers, the estate's servants, and their families spilled across the meadow and along the road.

This time he had donned the regalia of a notable war chief: shirt of finely woven blue-grey wool over fringed buckskin leggings, with richly quilled and beaded moccasins. A striped trade blanket draped one shoulder, and painted bands of crimson, white, and blue crossed his face. Silver armlets clasped his muscular upper arms over his shirtsleeves, a knife in a quilled sheath hung at his neck, and his roached hair was adorned with three snowy white eagle feathers. Andrews and all the warriors were garbed in their finest garments and silver adornments as well, the women also arrayed in festal garb.

Late in the afternoon Blue Sky, Laughing Otter, and Rain Woman had come to the manor to prepare Elizabeth and the twins for the night's celebration. She had related to Carleton how her mother had watched with barely suppressed astonishment and disapproval while they arrayed her in a green wool jacket ornamented with quillwork, a blue stroud, knee-length skirt, and red leggings, all covered with numerous intricately wrought silver brooches. Ornate silver earrings dangled from her ears, and a round daub of red paint colored each cheek, while more silver brooches studded the red cloth band that wrapped her hair at the back of her head. Once finished, the women had removed the twins' tiny caps and wrapped them snugly in small, finely woven, striped wool blankets.

To Elizabeth's astonishment, her father had done no more than shake his head and heave a sigh when they had all come downstairs. Neither of her parents had given voice to their objections and now watched the proceedings with carefully controlled emotions—but with interest, it seemed to both Carleton and Elizabeth. He reflected with humble gratitude on the great change their attitudes had undergone since that shattering scene after Elizabeth's rescue from the British, when he had given her up in despair.

The boisterous assembly quieted when the drums began their rhythmic low throb. Carleton returned his attention to Red Fox, who lifted their swaddled daughter to the dark heavens. Julianne let out a wavering cry and, smiling broadly, he announced, "Little sister, you are named She Thunders!"

Her cry gave way to an indignant wail. A gale of laughter went up from the crowd, punctuated by the renewed beating of the drums, applause, and shouts of approval.

As the drums silenced and the clamor died down, he returned the baby to Elizabeth and turned to Carleton, who handed over their son. When Red Fox held the boy up, he made no protest, his gaze fixed on the flickering firelight.

"Your name is Still Waters, little brother."

The announcement met with equal approval, the drums echoing the throng's applause.

"The names seem extraordinarily prescient," Dr. Howard noted with a smirk, to Elizabeth's and Carleton's laughing agreement.

"Still Waters," Elizabeth murmured when she sobered. "It reminds me of the psalm: 'He leads me beside the still waters.' "

Red Fox returned her smile with a meaningful one. "And so it will be, my sister. Your son will grow to be a peacemaker between our peoples. And your daughter also—though more vocally."

A lavish banquet followed, succeeded by dancing in the flickering light of numerous fires, the cool wind mingling the pulse of drums and hiss of rattles with the lyrical notes of pipe and fiddle. At length Elizabeth tired. She and her parents returned to the manor taking the babies, with Yellow Feather and Morning Dew, by now a fixture in the nursery, happily accompanying them.

That afternoon Carleton and Andrews had met with their leading warriors to address concerns about developments in the war over the past months. In February on the northwest frontier, Colonel George Rogers Clark had captured Fort Sackville at Vincennes and taken British Governor Henry Hamilton prisoner. It was a thorn in the side of the warriors that because Governor Henry had authorized and funded Clark's campaign, Virginia now claimed the entire territory, calling it Illinois County.

General John Sullivan's attacks laying waste to a wide swath of Iroquois lands in the north that summer had caused greater outrage, however. Sullivan had indiscriminately massacred men, women, and children and put homes and crops to the torch, leaving the survivors destitute and with no choice but to seek refuge among the British at Niagara for the winter.

Despite his own anger, Red Fox reminded his warriors that Washington had sent Sullivan in order to put a stop to the relentless war that Thayendanegea, also known as Joseph Brant, had driven against white settlers in the Mohawk Valley and elsewhere who supported the Americans in the war with Britain. The British-allied principal war chief of the Iroquois had also commanded the Indian forces that committed atrocities in the Battle of Oriskany two years earlier and had gone on to destroy the town and fort at Cherry Valley in New York, killing indiscriminately there as well. Since then Brant had spread destruction and fear far and wide.

"White Eagle and I fully share your anger," Andrews said finally. "But if we let unreasoning emotions drive us, we will only lead our own people to destruction as Thayendanegea is doing."

His heart torn, as he knew Andrews' was, Carleton looked around at the men who regarded them with anger, and yet with trust. "Golden Elk is right. We must choose battles that we have hope of winning if our people are to survive and live free."

He spoke firmly. And yet deep inside he could not help wondering whether the path they counseled would not ultimately prove as futile as declaring all-out war.

As the assembled company began to disperse late that evening, Carleton turned to Red Fox. "Everything is prepared for your journey?"

Red Fox nodded. "We leave for Grey Cloud's Town at daybreak. And we will be careful to avoid white settlements."

"How many men go with you?" Andrews asked.

"Only three others," Spotted Pony replied. "Brown Bear will stay to command those who remain."

"It is well that you leave now," Carleton approved. "The wind grows colder and the frost thicker each morning. I fear the winter snows will come early."

Red Fox gave Carleton a brooding look. "I'm eager to learn whether our clansmen's hearts have changed even more since the last runner reached us."

"As am I. The word he brought was not good."

"We will distribute the food and gifts you send and make a good report to any who will listen. But I fear it will be difficult to persuade more men to join us now. Our people will demand assurance that the Long Knives will do justice and keep their promises to us. They have not so far, and added to Cornstalk's murder, Clark's and Sullivan's raids do not offer hope for the future."

Carleton stared into the darkness, his jaw hardening. "They do not."

"Our clan will rejoice at news of your children's birth, brother," Spotted Pony said, clasping Carleton's shoulder. "But they are eager to see your face and Golden Elk's again." He cast a significant glance toward Andrews.

When Andrews turned a hopeful gaze on Carleton, he conceded, "It's been far too long since we walked among them, and our hearts yearn to see them as well. For now, assure them that I will send Golden Elk with Blue Sky and their children as soon as I can spare him. I also will come when I am able and will bring Healer Woman and our children too."

A sharp pang went through him as he spoke, a deep ache to return to his people and to the wilderness that ever beckoned him. And the longing to bring Elizabeth and their children with him to establish them also in the world that held such a powerful claim on his soul. But his heart sank at the foreboding that many moons would yet pass before he would embrace his Shawnee kin again.

Chapter Fourteen

ELIZABETH PLACED A SMALL candle in a tin holder at the center of the mountain-laurel-and-pine garland draping the windowsill. She cast a quick glance across the shadowed terrace outside. The wind gusted flurries of snow against the manor's walls, and intermittent spates of sleet pecked the windowpanes. Temperatures continued to fall, but inside the fires cheerfully crackling on the Great Hall's three hearths radiated welcome warmth.

It was late afternoon on Christmas Eve, Friday, 24 December. The previous day a large party of the manor's residents and servants and Carleton's officers, all warmly bundled, had trooped into the woods surrounding the manor to gather an abundance of fragrant pine, laurel, holly, and magnolia boughs along with ivy and mistletoe. By now a host of artfully arranged garlands, swags, and wreaths trimmed with bayberry candles and the antique ornaments Elizabeth and her mother had plundered from the attics lent the massive space a festive air that extended throughout the entire manor and brightened officers' and employees' cabins as well.

The leavings carried away and floors swept, most of the servants had scattered to their normal duties a short time earlier. Durie, then Andrews and Blue Sky and the McLeods had taken their leave soon thereafter along with the rest of the officers.

Elizabeth turned to survey the results of their efforts. Her mother stood in front of the south hearth trimming the last mantelpiece garland with red brocade ribbon and pinecones from the baskets Morning Dew and Yellow Feather held. Carleton and her father had abandoned the work to lounge in front of the fire with the twins. At the Hall's center, the last of the workers were folding the tall ladders after securing swags of laurel branches interwoven with holly and ivy around the outer bands of the enormous chandeliers and hanging a large bunch of mistletoe from each one.

Crossing to her mother, Elizabeth passed one of the older workers on his way out carrying a ladder. "Thank you for all your hard work, Alfred. The Hall looks marvelous!"

He grinned. " 'Tis many a year since Twelve Days be kept at Thornlea, mistress. Warms the heart t' see all the bustle and cheer again."

"Did Sir Harry celebrate Christmas?"

"Indeed he did. Could be no one loved the season more. 'Tis good t' see ye and the gen'l bringin' back the old ways. We all be thankful that ye and yer parents came along, and now the wee bairns. Ooch, we'll ha' us a grand celebration again." Smiling broadly, he tugged his forelock and, whistling under his breath, followed his mates out.

McLeod was to hold a service early the next morning in the festively decorated chapel. And later a number of the militia officers and their wives from the surrounding area would join their family and Carleton's officers and families to dine and dance well into the evening, while troops, warriors, and employees enjoyed their own festivities.

Already delectable scents wafted up from the kitchens, where Salome and her maids were at work preparing the next day's groaning board. Elizabeth and her mother had taken inventory of the array of meats, fish, mincemeat pies, brandied peaches, fruitcakes, and plum puddings being readied. Nor would the traditional English wassail bowl, eggnog, ale, port, a spiced-wine punch, Madeira, and other wines be lacking. The sheer volume of food and drink made Elizabeth's head swim.

She directed an affectionate glance at Carleton, who slouched at ease on the sofa. Their girl lay across his knees clutching one of his fingers in her tiny fist, excitedly kicking her legs against her long white linen slip when he jiggled his hand playfully back and forth. At the same time he held Harry against his shoulder on his other arm, their boy bobbing unsteadily back to gaze wonderingly up into his father's face. She smiled as Carleton carefully shifted his position until his son's head rested on his shoulder again.

Her mother dropped the much diminished roll of ribbon into Morning Dew's basket and the two maidens headed for the sofa, drawn to the twins, as usual. Indicating Elizabeth's arisaid, Anne said, "The plaid fits you exceptionally well now you've almost got your figure back."

Carleton glanced toward them, one eyebrow raised. *"Bhiodh tu nas bòidhche às aonais, a ghràidh,"* he drawled, looking Elizabeth meaningfully up and down. *"Cho brèagha ris á bhan-dia Diana."*

Narrowing her eyes, she replied tartly, "You've obviously been spending too much time with Alistair, James, and Matthew. The Gaelic appears to be coming back to you."

He grinned. "I've no' had anyone t' speak it wi' fer sae long that I've fair lost the tongue. But one ne'er forgets entirely."

"And what exactly did you say?"

His suggestive smile caused her face to heat. "I'll tell you later, dearest. In private."

"Before long you'll be speaking Shawnee with a Scots burr," she huffed.

He threw back his head, laughing. Flailing her arms and legs, Julianne set up a doleful howl.

He hastily laid Harry across his knees and lifted the tiny girl to his shoulder in a deft movement, forestalling the two maidens who hovered anxiously. As soon as Julianne was settled, he freed one hand to tuck Harry closer against him, then reached up again to gently rub Julianne's back. She buried her head against his neck and subsided into hiccups, while Harry happily cooed at Yellow Feather.

When Carleton looked up, Elizabeth met his gaze with a smirk before resuming her conversation with her mother. "I credit nursing the twins and being up and about as much is prudent, Mama. I've all my energy back and have never felt better."

"You've been very good about not overdoing," Dr. Howard approved.

Anne smiled at the two men. "I've never seen any man take so happily to fatherhood—except your father, of course."

Elizabeth followed her mother to the chairs that bracketed the sofa, and they settled opposite her father. "Abby and I couldn't have asked for kinder or more attentive parents. I'm determined that our children shall benefit from your example."

"I think Harry and Julianne are extraordinarily brilliant already," Carleton interjected smugly.

"Of course they are, dearest. How could they not be? After all, we're their parents."

"They also happen to be the loveliest creatures on the face of the earth," Anne said proudly.

Carleton frowned. "Close. But that distinction still belongs to their mother."

"I'll not argue that. I've always thought my wife even more beautiful than our daughters, which is saying a considerable amount." Dr. Howard beamed at Anne, drawing her blush and a warm look.

He shoved out of his chair and appropriated Julianne. Cradling her in his arms, he crooned, "You certainly inherited your mama's and grandmama's beauty, my love. Not to mention their amiability."

Julianne focused on her grandfather's face, then hers crumpled, her lower lip quivering. Eyes squeezed shut, fat tears rolling down her cheeks, she began to screech.

"What's the matter now, sweeting?" he chided. "You were perfectly pleased to let me hold you earlier."

Elizabeth came over and looked doubtfully down at her daughter. "Perhaps *amiable* wasn't exactly the right word."

"It is for *my* son," Carleton pointed out, patting Harry's back as the baby mouthed his cheek, liberally baptizing it with drool.

"Well, *your* daughter appears to have inherited *your* temper."

Carleton regarded Elizabeth with a look of mild outrage as he settled Harry back on his lap and wiped the baby's face and his own with his handkerchief. "We certainly wouldn't want to discuss *your* temper now, would we, my darling?"

Hearing snickers from her parents, Elizabeth directed a glare at the offenders before returning her attention to Carleton, arms folded. Over Julianne's wails she said haughtily, "I can't conceive how anyone could possibly contrive to be more amiable than I."

Carleton guffawed. Grinning, he chucked Harry under the chin, eliciting happy grunts.

"Another maxim you'll want to pay strict attention to, my lad, is never to imply to any lady that she might just possibly be out of temper."

"Now, children, stop fussing!" Dr. Howard growled playfully.

Anne rolled her eyes and came to take Julianne from him. "I'll warrant she's hungry—and she definitely needs to have her clout changed!" she exclaimed, her expression turning to alarm as she felt her granddaughter's pilch. "Oh, you poor dear, you've been inexcusably neglected!" She frowned at Harry. "And most likely your brother is in the same state."

Grimacing, Carleton hastily lifted the boy off his lap. "I do believe you're right."

Morning Dew and Yellow Feather immediately claimed the babies with a possessive air.

"I'll be up as soon as I've set things right here," Elizabeth called after them, fixing Carleton in a narrowed look. The two maidens flashed smiles back her as they headed up the stairs with their charges.

Anne watched them go thoughtfully. "I have to admit that it's terribly convenient having those two girls as nursery maids. They're so good with the twins. I can't imagine how we'd ever manage without them."

"They are a godsend," Dr. Howard admitted.

Carleton raised an eyebrow. "You and Red Fox seem to be forging somewhat of a friendship. At least I often see you with your heads together."

Dr. Howard shrugged. "He's an interesting man, and I enjoy debating issues with him. I have to say I'm impressed by his knowledge and understanding of a surprising number of subjects."

He paused for some moments before adding gruffly, "I've come to realize that when you get to know them, people are just people no matter their color or race. Some have a good heart, some not."

"Amen to that," Carleton seconded. Directing a glance at Elizabeth, that caused her to blush, he murmured, *"Nollaig Chridhheil, mo chridhe."*

"Merry Christmas to yourself," she replied saucily, looking him up and down with a sultry look that had him wanting to snatch her into his arms and sweep her off to their bed. Despite the worry that nagged at him, it required considerable willpower to banish the impulse.

Elizabeth turned to see Burns enter the Hall followed by a chapped and windblown stranger in Continental uniform whom he ushered to Carleton.

"Sir, Lieutenant Mayfield just arrived from Morristown." The butler quietly withdrew as Carleton pushed to his feet to return the lieutenant's salute.

"All's well at headquarters?"

"As well as it can be, sir." The slender young officer proffered a sealed letter. "General Washington sent me to deliver this message into your hands."

Carleton took it, frowning.

"He's summoning you to Morristown."

He gave Elizabeth a rueful look as he broke open the letter's seal. Unfolding the page, he scanned it, while Mayfield took in the Great Hall and its decorations, wide-eyed.

"Surely His Excellency won't expect you to leave with the holidays upon us or to travel all that distance in this weather!" Anne exclaimed.

"We're talking about the commander in chief of the army," Dr. Howard pointed out dryly.

Elizabeth chewed her lip. "What does he say?"

"He offers his and Mrs. Washington's felicities on the twins' safe birth, of course," Carleton answered, looking up. "And he wants me and Charles at headquarters as soon as possible."

Elizabeth's heart contracted even though she had known when Carleton sent his first report to his commander after his return that a summons would inevitably come. "How soon must you go?"

Carleton glanced at Mayfield, who shrugged. "Weather's beastly up north, general—the worst I've ever seen this early in the season. We've had one blizzard after another, and it's cold enough to freeze—" At Carleton's sharp look, he wryly amended, "a heavily bundled man into an ice statue."

"It's been unusually cold here as well, though not as bad as that."

"You can't make many miles a day traveling, sir. It's been all but impossible to bring in provisions for the army at times, too—worse even than at Valley Forge. I left camp the end of last month, right after His Excellency received your report, and at times was forced to hole up for days along the way. Didn't help that I wasn't given good directions to get here," he grumbled.

"His Excellency won't expect us immediately then," Carleton said briskly. "You deserve a few days' rest, Mayfield, and at any rate it'll take some time for us to prepare for such a long journey in harsh weather."

Mayfield drew in a lingering breath of the Hall's fragrant air, then grinned. "That'd be wise, sir."

Carleton called for Burns and directed him to see to the lieutenant's accommodations and provide him a hot meal. Bowing, the butler ushered Mayfield out of the Hall.

Carleton turned back to the others. "Considering the weather, no one can fault us as long as we reach Morristown by the end of next month.

We'll leave the day after New Year's, which should give us sufficient time even in the worst circumstances."

It was better than Elizabeth had expected. Thinking of all Mrs. Washington and the other officers' wives suffered, she resolved to meet each coming separation without complaint.

Taking his arm, she put on a cheerful expression and smiled up at him. "Then we'll enjoy the holiday with happy hearts, dearest, and deal with tomorrow when it comes." Another thought intruded, and her face fell. "Oh, but this means you'll miss our first wedding anniversary! January twenty-nine is hardly more than a month away. You couldn't possibly return in time."

Carleton let out a groan. "The General isn't likely to give us a pass even for that since so many other officers are making similar sacrifices."

Disappointment creased her parents' brows as well. After a moment, however, Anne brightened.

"Then we'll have the celebration before you leave! There'll be a grand banquet for all the officers, with dancing here in the Hall—"

"My troops and warriors must have a feast and dance as well, and also the servants," Carleton broke in, smiling. "All of Thornlea will join in the festivities."

Elizabeth clasped her hands in delight. "We'll have it on New Year's Eve!"

When the others gave their hearty approval, Elizabeth and her mother bustled off, gleefully exchanging ideas for entertainments and menus.

"It's the perfect solution, Jon, one that will keep our ladies happily occupied for the next sennight," Dr. Howard observed as Carleton shook his head, chuckling.

Chapter Fifteen

"**I** APOLOGIZE FOR OUR tardiness, Your Excellency. Lieutenant Mayfield had the devil of a time reaching Thornlea, and—"

"I commend you for making it through under these conditions," General George Washington cut Carleton off, waving his apology away. Now in his forty-seventh year, the commander of the Continental Army was an imposing figure in his dark blue uniform coat with gold epaulets on each shoulder, buff-colored facings and cuffs, waistcoat, and breeches.

"Since making camp here we have enjoyed all the close acquaintance with nor'easters one could possibly wish for," he went on wryly. "If I had known another would blow in before you could reach us, I would not have sent for you. Indeed, I was beginning to wonder whether we would ever see Mayfield again, much less the two of you."

"It's a miracle we arrived this soon," Andrews interjected with a laugh.

Following the grand celebration of Carleton and Elizabeth's anniversary, he, Andrews, and their servants had left Thornlea in the early-morning darkness of 2 January 1780, Lieutenant Mayfield serving as guide. They had not traveled very far north along the Great Wagon Road when they rode into a monstrous nor'easter that worsened the farther they went, devouring the landscape and bedeviling them with brutal temperatures and wave after wave of knifing winds and dizzily swirling snow.

The certainty quickly sank into Carleton's bones that it would be two months at best before he would hold Elizabeth and their children again.

Long weeks during which the weather would undoubtedly make correspondence difficult, if not impossible, and anything might happen. Nor had it helped to see Andrews suffer equally at leaving his own small family. Thankfully Mayfield had proven to be a congenial companion who kept them distracted with lively conversation.

The farther north they went, however, the fewer miles they were able to cover each day. Though heavily bundled and wrapped in bearskins, their horses swathed in blankets, they were forced to seek refuge at an inn or private house as soon as daylight began to fade and the temperature to plummet. At the storm's height, they had no choice but to remain where they were for a couple of days, frustrated and questioning whether they ought not to turn back. Even the lieutenant's cheerfulness had at last been daunted.

The storm finally abated on 7 January, six days after they left Thornlea. But intense cold, freezing winds, and clouded skies continued. They were so often blocked by roads chest high in snow, with drifts above their heads, that they began to despair of reaching their destination before the spring thaw. During the nights' vacant hours, as at his worst times, Carleton sank into a black and seemingly bottomless pit, only to rise the next morning and unwillingly drag himself into the saddle oppressed by an unwelcome sense of duty.

At last, shortly before noon that Wednesday, 26 January, they had finally pushed through to Arnold's Tavern in Morristown, New Jersey, where Carleton secured the last room available. Stowe and Briggs remained behind to sort out their baggage, while Mayfield escorted them to the Ford mansion where Washington made his headquarters. Carleton and Andrews had been admitted to the mansion's parlor, which they found crammed with tables and all the detritus belonging to five aides-de-camp.

They barely had time to shake the snow from their hats, remove their gloves and scarves, and shed the greatcoats they wore over their buckskins before Washington's longtime aide Colonel Tench Tilghman ushered them across the wide hallway to the private study Washington had appropriated for his office.

Washington now motioned them to take seats and settled back into the chair behind his writing table. Carleton slouched into a chair in front of the fireplace next to Andrews, basking in its radiating heat.

While they exchanged pleasantries, Washington asking after Elizabeth and the twins and Andrews' family, Carleton glanced idly around him. The room was nicely appointed, though cluttered by the addition of another larger table surrounded by chairs and awash in papers, pens and inkwells, books, and rolled-up maps.

"It appears you've improved your accommodations over our earlier encampment here," he observed.

Washington stretched back in his chair. "It is better than Arnold's Tavern but still far from ideal."

Mrs. Washington found the house too cramped, draughty, and ill-equipped, he related ruefully. Although the mansion had eight rooms in addition to the kitchen wing, the upstairs chambers had been unfinished when they moved in. The space was hardly adequate when he and his wife, five aides-de-camp, and eighteen servants were forced to share it with the mansion's owner, Mrs. Ford, her four children, and her servants.

That guards and visiting dignitaries often had to be housed added to the chaos. He'd had two of the upstairs rooms finished at public expense and a stable built and was also having a log kitchen and cabin built to accommodate the Fords and some members of his staff to alleviate the worst of the crowding. Carleton and Andrews listened with amused sympathy and offered their condolences.

Washington quickly dismissed the issue. Noting that Carleton had offered only a brief accounting of the battle with *Serapis* in his report on his return home, the General prompted him for details. Reluctantly Carleton complied, only referring to the carnage in passing and couching his descriptions of Jones's and the French officers' actions in as diplomatic terms as possible. He was relieved when a rap at the door interrupted him.

At Washington's bidding James McHenry, a young Irishman who served without rank as one of his aides, strode inside. "Pardon me, sir, but General Arnold just delivered this," McHenry said as he crossed the room to hand over a letter. "He insists it's a matter o' some urgency."

Arnold's concerns are always a priority—to him, at least, Carleton ruminated, meeting Andrews' sidelong glance with a smirk.

McHenry turned to nod at them. "Gen'l Carleton. Gen'l Andrews. 'Tis good to have ye back after so long a time. Ye've been missed."

"That's good to know," Carleton drawled lazily. "It may give us some leverage."

Scowling, Washington raised his eyes from Arnold's letter.

"Or not," Andrews noted dryly.

Conceding a faint smile, Washington returned his attention to the page he'd been scanning. Carleton studied him, noting with concern that their commander's hair had begun to thin and that grey strands increasingly threaded the auburn strands. The creases that lined his face had also deepened since they last met, though his piercing blue eyes remained keen and his bearing militarily erect.

When he looked up, Andrews asked, "How did Arnold fare in his court-martial? I presume it has concluded by now."

Washington sighed. "As of Friday. The board vindicated him on all charges except a couple of minor ones, which leaves me with the distasteful task of issuing a formal reprimand. Unfortunately Arnold is inclined to take even a mild rebuke as a mortal wound, as persons of such passions are wont to do."

Inclined? Carleton raised his eyebrows but managed to keep control of his tongue.

"He gave a very affectin' summation," McHenry put in, his expression supremely innocent.

Under his breath Carleton muttered to Andrews, "I can imagine."

Washington folded the letter and laid it on the writing table. "He asks for a private interview. Undoubtedly he means to press his suit for a new

command, and I would like to oblige him. He has done us outstanding service, as you are both well aware. Despite the slights he has received from Congress, he has made great personal sacrifices for our cause. We cannot afford to lose an officer of his quality."

"He's a highly effective battle commander," Carleton agreed.

Washington turned to McHenry. "I don't suppose any shipments arrived this morning."

The aide's face fell. "I'm afraid not, yer Excellency. The roads are exceedin' bad once you get out o' town, and—"

"Our situation has been exceedingly bad ever since we encamped here almost two months ago," Washington broke in, his voice steely. "This country suffers its soldiers, which are employed in the defense of everything that is precious to humankind, to perish for want of food. Despite all my pleading, Congress and the states appear to believe an army can live on air—which we may have to make shift to do since we are provided with an abundance of it!" he exclaimed as a gust of wind rattled the house.

Carleton would have laughed had the matter not been so serious. After advising McHenry to set up an appointment with Arnold the following day, Washington dismissed him.

"Unless food is delivered within the next day or two, the men are going to starve," Washington said bitterly after the aide withdrew. "The forests hereabout provide more than enough wood for shelter and fire. It is warm clothing, shoes, weapons, money to pay the troops, but most of all food that are lacking."

"Is the army indeed in such dire straits again, sir?" Carleton asked.

Washington scrubbed one hand over his face. "We have never experienced a like extremity at any period of the war, not even at Valley Forge. On paper I have sixteen thousand men at my command. Today's returns show thirty-six hundred. We are daily on the verge of mutiny, nor can I blame the men. I fear I will be forced to disband the army if we do not receive adequate stores of food within a fortnight."

Carleton listened, dismayed, as Washington explained that the soldiers were being issued half or less of the daily allowance of food. Game had almost disappeared from the surrounding forests, and at times the men went without bread or meat altogether until they were so desperate that they ate boiled shoe leather or the bark of trees and even consumed dogs and other stray animals.

"But there are farms all over this area," Andrews protested. "Can you not buy or confiscate what's needed?"

The harvest had been poor because of drought, and the farmers had families to feed, Washington explained with frustration. In many cases their situation was nearly as bad as the army's. They were also cultivating fewer acres because Continental currency, which was all the army could offer for goods, was essentially worthless. To make things worse, the severe weather hampered transportation of any supplies they did manage to acquire.

"I am loath to anger our farmers by confiscating their grain and cattle," Washington concluded unhappily. "It will turn the populace against us just as it turned them against the British. But if I am to keep my men from starving, I will soon be forced to."

Carleton gave him a sympathetic look. "I'd have brought along some of my cattle if I'd known and the weather hadn't been so foul that it would have taken us another month to drive them all the way up here—if they could have made it at all. But my Rangers are rapidly consuming my herds even though we're carefully rationing meat. There's also been little game in our vicinity for some weeks now, and I've had to send detachments far and wide to find better hunting."

Washington shoved his fingers through his hair. "You have done more than enough, Jon. This is not your concern. I depend on you to maintain your Rangers, especially now with the British turning their attention to the South."

He rubbed his chin thoughtfully, a faraway look coming into his eyes. "Another frustration is that this abominable weather has handed us the perfect opportunity for an attack. According to our intelligence the Hudson has frozen so solid from the Paulus Hook ferry to Cortlandt Street in New York City that both the residents and the British use it as a thoroughfare to Brooklyn and Staten Island. We received reports that provisions and stores are daily brought over on sleighs at a point where the river is two-thousand-yards wide—and the British even transport artillery across!"

Andrews let out a short laugh. "If what we endured on the way north is any indication, I can easily believe it."

Washington directed a narrowed glance through the window. "This is the perfect opportunity to launch an attack across the ice bridge directly into the heart of the city!" His shoulders slumped. "But as my staff keeps reminding me, the army is in no shape for battle."

"We passed drifts on our way here that towered over our heads, and many roads are impassable," Carleton cautioned. "Believe me, sir, moving men and equipment any distance is going to be impossible until a thaw."

"At which point the roads will turn into bogs," Andrews contributed cheerfully.

Washington scowled. "Thank you for that heartening observation, general."

Andrews returned a cheeky grin.

Pleading the press of business, Washington informed them that all general officers were to meet the following afternoon, and that he expected Carleton to give a detailed report on the clash between *Bonhomme Richard* and *Serapis*. He also invited them to a dance organized by Mrs. Washington and several of the other officers' wives for that same evening.

Carleton's stomach clenched, but he swallowed a vehement protest at reporting, yet again, on the battle, this time to unwillingly stoke the officers' glee at Jones's bloody victory. Instead he contented himself with blandly tendering his and Andrews' acceptance of the invitation to the ball before the two of them took their leave.

Another chorus of coughs and sneezes greeted them as they entered the parlor to reclaim their greatcoats and other accoutrements. "I beg your pardon," Carleton said politely to the aides crowded together in the room. "I was under the impression that this was the corps' office, but it appears we've blundered into the hospital."

Andrews guffawed as four of the men looked around to scowl at them.

"Very funny, general," muttered Lieutenant Colonel Alexander Hamilton before dipping his pen into an inkwell and returning his attention to the page in front of him.

Tilghman hastily pushed away from the farthest table, grabbed Carleton's and Andrews' outerwear piled on the one adjacent, and came to meet them. "Quite the comedian, isn't he, Andrews?" he said, tipping his head in Carleton's direction.

Carleton grinned. Over another round of coughs, he said, "I thought you could use a bit of levity to brighten your day."

"You certainly were a font of hilarity while we were blundering through that endless nor'easter, Jon," Andrews countered dryly.

Tilghman suppressed a laugh. "I'm sure you had a quite entertaining trip. We were all astounded when you rode up this morning. We'd given you up to the storm gods."

"To our eternal gratitude, they did finally spit us out," Carleton drawled as he and Andrews settled their greatcoats around their shoulders and wrapped scarves around their necks.

After they pulled on their gloves and took their hats, Tilghman escorted them out to the front door. He would have their horses sent around from the stable directly, he told them, and reminded them of the meeting the following afternoon.

"By the way, your man Teissèdre arrived earlier in the week—on his way south from Boston," he informed Carleton. "He intended to visit with our Frenchies while waiting for the weather to clear. When he learned that you were expected by the end of the month, he told me he'd stay on a few more days. I understand he's taken a room at Arnold's Tavern."

An unsettled feeling tightened Carleton's chest, but he kept his expression masked while thanking Tilghman. He led the way outside into the icy wind, pretending not to register Andrews' amused gaze.

They paused at the top of the wide stairs to look out across the broad, tree-shaded lawn buried beneath a deep mantle of snow. One of the largest houses in town, the white clapboard Georgian-style mansion occupied a commanding prominence south of the Whippany River on Morristown's east end.

"It seems strange that Louis happened to show up here just days before we arrived," Andrews ventured.

Carleton narrowed his eyes. "Regardless of what he told Tilghman, I can't help wondering what he's really up to. The man's never done anything casually or at whim during our acquaintance. My guess is he was headed to Thornlea to discover my plans and decided to stop here on the way to see whether he might sniff out additional intelligence for my uncle and Sartine."

"Kill two birds with one stone, then."

"I've never known Louis to waste an opportunity." Carleton led the way down the steps.

Just then an officer rode up, heavily bundled against the cold, with a thick scarf wrapped around his wind-reddened face. He dismounted as a groom came around the end of the house leading Carleton's and Andrews' horses. When they took their mount's reins, the groom hurried to take charge of the newly arrived officer's horse and led the animal away.

As the man turned toward them, Carleton regarded him with a shock of recognition. He had noticeably aged and was thinner since the last time they had met, but his face and figure remained unmistakable.

"Josh!"

"I thought I recognized you," Andrews echoed, grinning.

Brigadier General Joshua Stern, commander of a Massachusetts brigade who was also Anne Howard's brother and Elizabeth's uncle, pulled the scarf loose from around his neck and strode to them, his square, genial face wreathed in a broad smile. Shaking hands, they exchanged hearty greetings.

Cocking one eye at Carleton, the stocky officer doffed his hat and ran his fingers through his curly grey hair. "You're a sight for sore eyes!" he exclaimed, planting his hat firmly back on his head. "Charles told me you'd embarked on an adventure with Commodore Jones, and the reports I heard bordered on the fantastic. You'll have to fill me in on the details."

"You're in luck. I've been commanded to give a detailed report at tomorrow's meeting."

Stern brightened. "Well then, how are Beth and your twins? Jane was ecstatic when she received Anne's letter, and she's been champing at the bit for a visit ever since."

"They're doing very well. Is Jane here with you?"

Stern shook his head. "If you've met with the General, you know our situation. I thought it better for her to stay at home where there's food enough, a warm house, and our children and grandchildren nearby to look out for her."

They talked for some moments more before yielding to the freezing wind. Clapping their gloved hands together to warm them and pulling their scarves up around their faces, they agreed to meet for dinner at Stern's quarters the following day and parted company.

Chapter Sixteen

C ARLETON AND ANDREWS navigated the three-quarters of a mile into
town along Elizabethtown Pike with their horses at a walk, the road-
way only cleared to a narrow track edged by staggeringly high, ice-
crusted snowbanks. Carleton's thoughts drifted back to the winter of
1777, when the army had first made camp there following the victories at
Trenton and Princeton. Then also they had suffered through a harsh winter, which the current one, nevertheless, already threatened to eclipse.

It had been that same winter that Elizabeth had found him among
the Shawnee and brought him back to rejoin Washington in the war
against Britain . . . Hastily he wrenched his thoughts away from that
treacherous territory and back to his present circumstances.

The peaceful village of Morristown, New Jersey, lay at the foot of
Thimble Mountain. It consisted of perhaps 250 residents, with around
fifty houses in addition to a church, courthouse, tavern, and several shops.
A center of farming, mining, and logging, it once offered the army convenient access to many needed supplies, badly depleted now.

It also provided a triple defense against the British at New York City.
The Watchung Mountains' long parallel ridges, their narrow gorges bordered by marshlands, stretched southwest to northeast from the Raritan
River to New Jersey's northern boundary, effectively protecting the town's
approaches as well as the army's lines of communication with New England and with Congress in Philadelphia.

Carleton and Andrews soon drew to a halt in front of Jacob Arnold's expansive three-story tavern on Morristown's Green. The establishment was a popular meeting place for both the town's residents and travelers. After turning their horses over to their servants, they headed up the tavern's steps.

Just as they reached its top, General Benedict Arnold pushed open the door and stepped outside. He arrested at sight of them, his hard expression easing.

After they had dispensed with greetings Carleton said, "We heard that you were acquitted a few days ago at your court-martial."

"Not fully," Arnold replied testily, his pale grey eyes cold, his tone laden with resentment. "The board directed that I be reprimanded on two minor counts—and for what offense? Nothing even worthy of mention!"

He leaned on his cane, favoring his left leg. His swarthy complexion was unnaturally pale, undoubtedly due to extended confinement while waiting for his shattered thigh bone to heal, Carleton surmised, an injury suffered two years earlier during the battle at Bemis Heights. Against Arnold's high, sloping forehead, prominent nose, and black hair, the pallor caused him to appear even more morose than usual.

"If you can believe it," he went on, tightlipped, "I was accused of abusing my power while military governor of Philadelphia for my own personal financial gain—conduct unworthy of an officer and a patriot! You know I've devoted my time, my fortune, and my own person to my country in this war. I've gained no little reputation and acquired the favorable opinion of those whose approbation is an honor to gain. Indeed, if it had not been for me, we'd not have triumphed at Saratoga!"

"We were sorry to hear that your wound was so severe."

Arnold brandished his cane at Andrews. "I've become a cripple in service to my country, but I'll spare you a description of how greatly I've suffered these past two years. And when the army found itself in dire straits and His Excellency was forced to flee through New Jersey to find refuge across the Delaware with his few men, *I* was not the one who basked in the sunshine of his favor while at the same time treating him with the greatest disrespect by vilifying his character to others behind his back and even considering going over to the enemy!"

Arnold's malicious reference to rumors that Joseph Reed, a former aide to Washington who had led the attack against Arnold, had himself contemplated committing treason during the dark fall of 1776 took Carleton aback. He met Andrews' meaningful gaze with a veiled one but held his tongue.

Arnold seemed not to notice. "At least it's over. I've always enjoyed His Excellency's gracious support, thank God, and I have hopes that he'll see no reason to issue a reprimand. I'm owed a command, and regardless of what anyone says, my leg has healed sufficiently that I expect no further delay in assigning me one."

After Arnold had taken his leave, Carleton watched him cautiously navigate the steps and limp away. "Methinks the man doth protest too much. Was there something furtive in his manner or is it just my imagination?"

"He does seem a tad off," Andrews returned. "More than ordinarily, that is."

"I can't quite put my finger on what it is about Bennie that puts me on guard. His constant preening and whining is annoying, but otherwise there's little to fault him on. No one can dispute that he does have a talent for leading soldiers in battle. But I get the impression that there's more going on behind that façade than one might suspect."

"My sense is that he believes the rules don't apply to him, that everything he chooses to do is justified and he bears no fault in anything."

"An attitude that might lead to actions most men would consider indefensible," Carleton said thoughtfully, leading the way into the tavern. "Perhaps the charges against him were justified after all."

✳ ✳ ✳

THEY FOUND TEISSÈDRE in the taproom. At sight of them, the Frenchman sprang to his feet, beaming.

After greeting them heartily, he exclaimed, "I was told the two of you might show up. As long as I was waylaid here by the storms, I thought I might as well wait around for a few more days in hopes that you would. I've some business to conduct with you," he added, turning to Carleton.

"How convenient that of all the places in the world, you just happened to arrive here in time to meet us," Carleton noted dryly.

Teissèdre gave a wolfish smile. "*Notre Dieu* works in mysterious ways."

Frowning, Carleton beckoned to the proprietor, who hurried over. In moments he had arranged for use of the private parlor and ordered luncheon. Seated at the parlor table before a crackling fire with his long legs stretched out in front of him and his head propped against the high back of his chair, he regarded Teissèdre through narrowed eyes.

"I hear you've been visiting with your fellow countrymen while you waited for us to appear. Did you glean any useful information you'd be willing to share? I've been rather preoccupied with other concerns these past weeks, as you might imagine."

Teissèdre shrugged noncommittally. "I doubt I've learned anything that won't be covered at your meeting tomorrow."

Carleton smiled. "So you know about that. And doubtless also every subject to be discussed and decision to be made."

His expression pained, Teissèdre waved the comment away before brightening. "By the by, you have my sincerest felicitations on the birth of your twins."

They were interrupted by a couple of maids, who entered bringing their meal. While they devoured the food set before them, Teissèdre inquired about the welfare of Andrews' family. He then proceeded to ply Carleton with questions about the twins' birth, Elizabeth's and her parents' health and the Rangers, which Carleton answered with barely suppressed frustration.

Finally the Frenchman retrieved a small bag from his coat pocket and slid it across the table to Carleton. "Your manager at Boston entrusted me with a portion of your profits to convey to you. In case you need coin."

Carleton weighed the pouch in his hand before slipping it into his pocket. "Thank you. I'll put it to good use. You've more for Durie, I presume?"

Teissèdre conceded a gracious nod. "I'm bound directly to Thornlea after leaving here."

"The question is how much longer I'll have any income from my business when both my merchantmen and my privateers are confined to port."

Teissèdre glanced hastily away. Before Carleton could question him, however, he drew a small book from another pocket. Laying it open on the table, he began to read off the details of Carleton's various accounts.

The sums were disastrous all around. Expenses were higher than income, which had declined to essentially nil. Only to be expected with his ships sidelined. Remembering his discussions with Durie about Thornlea's resources being stretched to support the Rangers, Carleton stifled a groan.

"What's the situation with my fleet? With *Destiny?* I assume my uncle has a plan to counter British attacks on my privateers. If I'm to avoid bankruptcy, I need every ship back in action sooner rather than later. Has he found a captain with the experience and skills to command my fleet as he promised?"

Teissèdre considered him speculatively. "As a matter of fact, he has."

"What are the man's qualifications? Le comte is satisfied that he's committed to wreaking every possible destruction on British shipping? How soon can he take command?"

Teissèdre held up his hands to ward off the staccato fire of questions. "You do know that your uncle promised la comtesse that he would retire from the navy once this war is ended?"

Carleton dismissed the subject impatiently. "Tess mentioned something to that effect."

"Then you may be interested to know that he's decided to take leave from his duties, at least for the time being, with a view toward full retirement by next spring."

"To do what? The war couldn't possibly end so soon, and he's not one to sit around twiddling his thumbs." An amusing thought struck Carleton. Exchanging a glance with Andrews, he laughed. "Perhaps he's considering taking over command of my tiny fleet—"

"Two dozen ships do not comprise a *tiny* fleet."

Sobering, Carleton stared at him. "As you well know, that number has significantly diminished, thanks to our British friends."

Teissèdre spread his hands. "There are still countries that have smaller navies."

Carleton narrowed his eyes. "My privateers are converted merchantmen, and the rest of my ships *are* merchantmen—which you also know."

Patiently Teissèdre pointed out, "Your privateers already carried armaments equal to any respectable ship of the line before le comte bolstered them so that they've become floating engines of death. And your remaining merchantmen can as easily be converted—"

Carleton's gut clenched, suspicion rapidly becoming unwelcome certainty. "Surely you're not implying that he actually proposes to throw up his career in the French Royal Navy in order to commandeer my fleet."

"Mmm, *propose* is not the word I'd necessarily choose."

Carleton moved to shove out of his chair, then sank back into it. "He's *decided?*"

Teissèdre continued with admirable innocence, "It was la comtesse's proposal that your uncle could be of assistance to you in the difficulties you've recently encountered—"

"When has he not been of assistance to me, even when I've not request-ed or wanted it?" Carleton growled. "Do you mean to say that *Tess* urged him to place himself in even greater danger than he already is, and my uncle blithely agreed?"

Teissèdre crossed his arms, one hand cradling his chin. Carleton glan-ced from him to Andrews, who was listening with every evidence of sup-pressed merriment and no indication of intervening, and back.

"Let's say that there were mutual discussions about the possibilities," Teissèdre went on, carefully couching his words. "And in consultation with the king—"

"The *king?*" Carleton exploded. Springing to his feet, he paced across the room. "*Louis Seize* approved this mad scheme?" He broke off abruptly, then in sudden comprehension snapped, "This is the pressing business that delayed your arrival at Texel!"

Teissèdre raised his shoulders in an expressive Gallic shrug. "Possibly. You have to admit that there are certain advantages to both Caledonne and the crown if—"

"Oh, indeed!" Carleton fumed, hands clenched. Returning to his chair, he flung himself into it, drained his ale, and slammed the empty mug back onto the table.

"Caledonne has always held the preposterous belief that the use of warships is to make war. He's long chafed at the restrictions the king and France's naval establishment impose to ensure that their precious ships remain unscathed."

"Building and outfitting a warship is ruinously expensive," Teissèdre pointed out.

"You think I'm not aware of that? And that with my uncle using *my* ships to distract the enemy, France only gains, while risking nothing?"

"That's not entirely true. Our navy does provide protection for you American privateers."

"And now—at my expense—le comte will be free to sail blithely off and smash things up as he pleases without regard to the consequences!"

Teissèdre cocked one eye at Carleton. "That was not your intent when you converted so many of your merchantmen to privateers? Or when you joined up with your Commodore Jones?"

Carleton closed his eyes, fighting to rein in his temper. *"Touché,"* he muttered grudgingly.

"Smashing things up appears to run in the family," Teissèdre noted, a glint in his eyes. "But you do have Caledonne's word that he'll return your ships—"

"If any are left!"

"—at the end of the war along with all prize monies collected," Teissèdre finished, unruffled.

Carleton glared at Andrews, who instantly erased the expression of high amusement from his face and sat back in his chair, hands raised palms out and lips pressed together in a firm line.

Carleton swung back to Teissèdre. "And in the meantime he'll convert all my merchantmen to privateers so I'll have no income from them." He bit off each word.

"You have none from them now," the Frenchman pointed out reasonably, "and that is not likely to change as long as the British admiralty remains determined to sink or capture every vessel you have afloat. But not to worry. Le marquis de Martieu-Broussard will make sure you're supplied with ready cash."

"On loan." Impatiently waving away the bitter comment, Carleton demanded, "How much involvement did Sartine have in this scheme?"

"He did sit in on the meeting," Teissèdre returned, his face as innocent as a babe's. "In an advisory capacity."

"Advisory capacity!" Again springing to his feet, Carleton strode across the room, turned on his heel, and marched back. "Am I to take it that my ships are to become yet another tool in Sartine's and my uncle's intelligence networks?"

"It might be possible that any intelligence gathered could be shared between friends—for mutual benefit." The Frenchman dismissed the issue as of no account.

"Possible? How about certain? I've had my suspicions, as I'm sure you're aware, but just how involved with Sartine are you really, Louis?"

"Bah! Let's just say we're . . . acquaintances."

Carleton gave a short, bitter laugh. When he had first employed Teissèdre at Caledonne's urging he had suspected that the Frenchman had a finger in more than one *tarte*. Even considering that Carleton by now knew many of his suspicions to be actual fact, he couldn't help feeling that their discussion had lost its anchor in the solid ground of reality and soared into the realms of fantasy.

"Of course, you had no hand in this discussion."

"I might have contributed an occasional ray of illumination."

"I'd be astonished if you hadn't."

"Shall I assume that you approve of this 'scheme', as you call it?"

"Do I have a choice?"

"It is to your advantage, *mon général.* You must admit there's no one more qualified for the task than your uncle. And while he pursues your vendetta with the British Royal Navy, you're free to return to your duties under His Excellency General Washington—and to your lovely bride and children."

There was no denying that despite the threat to his income and conscience the arrangement was to Carleton's advantage, though that did nothing to cool his ire. If anything, it fueled it, regardless that the gratitude he'd felt when Caledonne had rescued him and his squadron from British clutches on his voyage to France to claim Elizabeth little more than a year earlier caused a twinge of conscience. Not that he was about to concede that information to Teissèdre.

Carleton waved one hand airily. "By all means then. Let him take my privateers, my merchantmen, all of their proceeds, and Thornlea to boot if it pleases him."

"A generous offer."

"I didn't mean that literally!'

"So I assumed."

"Since they *are* my ships, may I ask what role you're to have?"

"No more than usual, of course," Teissèdre returned loftily.

Which allows you unlimited latitude, Carleton reflected. Forcing a wholly insincere smile, he said, "Of course. Why did I bother to ask?"

He couldn't help laughing at the irony of it all. Considering that he'd never been one to shy from risk, however, why the devil should he now try to hold back the wind? Nevertheless, the prospect rankled.

After Teissèdre had gone, he rounded on Andrews. "Well, weren't you a great help?"

"I wasn't about to step into the midst of that row." Andrews grinned. "Are all of your discussions with Louis as entertaining? If so, I'll have to sit in on more of them."

"Not . . . always." Carleton muttered.

Andrews studied him thoughtfully. "You know as well as I that Louis is right, Jon. It's the logical solution. Who better to command your fleet than Caledonne, especially as he's willing to set his own career aside to do it?"

"That's the worst part. No. I take that back. Being used—again—as a cog in the French intelligence machine is worse."

"What in the world happened all those years ago to put you so on edge?"

Carleton waved his question away. "You don't want to know. I survived. That's all that matters."

Andrews let out an exasperated sigh. "Then putting that issue aside, if you ask me—and I know you haven't, but as your friend I'm telling you anyway—the real trouble is that you're locked in an unwitting but fierce competition for dominance with your uncle."

Carleton scowled but on second thought conceded with some rue, "I wouldn't call it exactly . . . unwitting."

Andrews rolled his eyes. "Well, if you mean to save your business and thereby your income, I'd counsel laying aside your pride and your concerns about French machinations and being grateful that God put a man like Caledonne—and Louis as well—into your path. Maybe even Sartine. There's a cost to everything, but the truth is that they're as useful to you as you are to them. Besides, your uncle does love you and ultimately has your best interests at heart. You know he'll do his best for you."

Carleton winced. "I hate it when you're right."

Andrews returned a smug smile.

After a moment of frustrated silence Carleton said abruptly, "I promise I'll try to make peace with Louis."

Andrews snorted. "It might be advisable to first make peace with yourself."

Chapter Seventeen

"I T'S PETE WHO DESERVES your thanks," Elizabeth said to the middle-aged farmer who stood beside her at the drawing room's fire. "If he hadn't brought your son to my husband, he wouldn't be here."

Thomas Mersereau grasped Pete's hand. "I can't thank ye enough fer takin' care o' my boy," he said in a choked voice. "If ye hadn't, his mother and I might never have seen him again nor learned his fate. Indeed he might not be alive."

"He took care of me after I was captured even though he'd suffered greatly at the hands of the British sir," Pete replied. "I'd never have left him behind."

The Mersereaus had arrived half an hour earlier on the cold, blustery Friday afternoon of 4 February. Elizabeth would never forget that reunion. Oh, the tears at first sight of one another, the passionate embraces and whispered endearments, the trembling touch of hands, searching looks and beaming smiles! She had not been able to hold back her own tears, nor could any of those watching.

His eyes bright with moisture, Mersereau shifted from one foot to the other as he drank in the sight of his plump wife seated on the couch with their son. She held the young man's hands tightly, her brimming eyes fixed on his face and joy shining on her softly rounded features, while tears spilled down Tommy's cheeks as well.

Dr. Howard stepped out of Anne's way as she moved around the tea table to help Sarah and Jemma arrange the feast Salome had sent up. "I admit I was very concerned when I first examined Tommy after General Carleton brought him to us. His health was entirely broken, and the voyage so far across the ocean was hard on him though he did receive good care aboard ship." Dr. Howard put his arm around Elizabeth's shoulders. "But my daughter and I have been able to do him some good. And as you see, he's well on the way to a complete recovery."

The young man's transformation over the past months was indeed remarkable, Elizabeth thought, greatly pleased. He no longer appeared a broken, hopeless man older than his twenty-five years. Indeed his vigor had been restored, his countenance was brighter, and his tears reflected unshadowed joy and gratitude. The son who had been lost was found, healed, and restored to his rightful place, she reflected, a lump forming in her throat.

"I can't tell ye how grateful Marie and I be to both o' ye fer all ye did fer him." Clearing his throat, Mersereau bobbed his head at Elizabeth. "It was more'n kind o' yer husband to bring him here. He even sent coin fer our journey with his letter." He broke off, then exclaimed, "And to think that the boy we called Joseph is actually the wife o' one o' Washington's generals!"

Elizabeth laughed merrily. "Well, I wasn't at the time." She tipped her head. "What you and Marie told me about Tommy that night you found me on Staten Island came to my mind often thereafter."

Heat stained Mersereau's cheeks. "Ah, now don't remind me o' how I near strangled ye."

"There is that," she teased, then sobered. "Because of that encounter I continued to pray for the two of you and Tommy even after we lost contact. And, you see, the Lord heard and answered in his good time."

Mersereau nodded. "He did that, indeed."

"You didn't have any trouble passing through the lines?"

Mersereau gave Dr. Howard a wink. "We told the authorities our son down in Virginie was ailing bad. I figure when we go back we'll tell 'em we brought him home to tend."

A maid bustled in carrying a steaming kettle, and Anne called everyone to the table. When they had settled with cups of hot tea and plates generously filled, a hum of conversation filled the room. Tommy answered his parents' eager questions about the years he had been absent, though with an occasional hesitation that caused Elizabeth to suspect he passed over the worst of his trials. Even so it was evident how greatly his sufferings pained them.

To her own parents' questions, the Mersereaus explained how they had met Elizabeth on Staten Island and her role in transmitting intelligence to Washington during the summer of 1776. Tom related their forays into the British camp with relish, to Elizabeth's discomfort and her parents' openmouthed astonishment.

He and Marie had continued to relay intelligence to Washington ever since then through a contact Elizabeth's cousin Caleb Stern provided after she secretly left New York to find Carleton among the Shawnee. Caleb had served Elizabeth and her Aunt Tess ostensibly as a butler, a role in which capacity he had been free to assist the two women in spying on the British.

As he listened Tommy brightened. "When we get home, I'm goin' to join ye in gatherin' intelligence," he said eagerly to his parents. "And maybe I'll have a hand in freein' other prisoners, as was done fer me."

LATER IN THE NURSERY, after their guests had been settled for the night and while Elizabeth nursed Julianne, her mother glanced up from rocking sleepy, sated Harry. "I don't think I need to tell you what your father and I felt to learn all you were involved in, thankfully without our knowledge. I'll simply say how relieved we are that that foolishness is done with—and I'm sure you are too, dear. It gratifies me to no end to see my eldest so well set up in her proper role as wife and mother at last. There's no greater fulfillment than cuddling one's own babes in the peace of a secure home."

Smiling, Elizabeth looked down as Julianne sagged in her arms, her eyes drifting shut and her tiny fist falling slack from where she had clutched the edge of Elizabeth's bodice. She bent to kiss her daughter's softly flushed brow.

"I wouldn't trade this for the world, Mama. I'm quite content." Warmth filled her at her mother's approving nod.

Indeed she was content. Those dangerous escapades were lost to her now, a part of her youth never to be regained. Her marriage, her children were grounding her in ways she hadn't expected. Teaching her to take into account the effects of her actions and pray for God's wisdom when before she had too often run impulsively ahead, guided by her own faulty understanding.

She resolved to focus on the goodness of the life the Father's loving hand provided, for it overflowed with all the dearest desires of her heart. The lasting joys she now possessed, not only of husband, home, and children but also of equally fulfilling work as a doctor, were sweeter far and more precious than the excitement her former adventures ever offered.

And yet . . . she found herself stifling an inward sigh. Despite the passage of time, the memory of the perils she had navigated in service of her country still reawakened the thrill that had coursed through her veins with each feat of reckless daring. And with it an undeniable pang of longing no matter how sternly she reminded herself of the ache for home and children that had possessed her heart back then.

Resolutely she thrust the beckoning memories away. She would face new challenges in the coming years, she reminded herself. So much lay ahead that she could not see now.

Her thoughts turned to Carleton. She had awakened at first light that morn. On parting the curtains to look out upon the shadowed, snowy scene, she had beheld the expanse of winter sky above the ridges cast in the deep smoky blue of his eyes.

She had dreamt of him as she did often when missing his arms around her and the warmth of his lean, muscled body against hers. And sharp pain, heart-deep, lanced through her breast.

He had been gone for a month, and they had received no word as to whether he and his party had arrived safely at Morristown. Repeated storms had swept the valley since his leaving, and the weather was certainly even worse farther north. It was unlikely a message would reach Thornlea for some while yet, much less would it be possible for him and his party to soon return.

No matter how she assured herself of his safety and busied herself with her daily responsibilities, however, a shadow of worry constantly hovered at the back of her mind as always with each parting.

ANOTHER STORM DESCENDED on the valley a couple of days later. Though this one was milder than the ones that preceded it, Elizabeth and her parents insisted that the Mersereaus delay their departure.

At last the days turned sunny, with pale blue skies scattered with fair-weather clouds. Rivulets of snowmelt began to trickle, then to cascade in miniature waterfalls at multiple points along the mountains' flanks, while the Mersereau's visit lengthened into a fortnight. Finally, with temperatures hovering above freezing and Tommy anxious to return home to reunite with his sisters and their families, they took their leave.

After seeing them off with embraces, tears, and well wishes, Elizabeth's parents went back inside the manor while she lingered on the drive outside the courtyard, watching until the carriage rounded the road's bend. It had no sooner passed out of sight beyond a cluster of pines than three riders emerged, headed toward the manor.

The rotund figure and bald pate of the man in the lead seemed familiar. Suddenly Elizabeth's heart leaped. When he and his companions drew to a halt in front of the courtyard gates, she ran to them, causing their mud-splattered horses to dance nervously on the graveled drive while they endeavored to dismount.

"Stand back, madame!" Teissèdre exclaimed in alarm.

"Louis!" The moment he regained his balance she threw her arms around his shoulders, laughing. "You're the last person I expected!"

He gently disentangled himself from her embrace and bowed with great dignity. "Bah! But you are looking very well, madame." Straightening, he swept the manor with a keen glance, one eyebrow arched. "This place appears unchanged since I accompanied your husband here in the fall of 1774 after Sir Harry's death. Except for the military presence," he added dryly as a detail of Rangers rode by on the way to relieve Colonel Farris's pickets outside the valley's mouth, each man respectfully touching his fingers to his helmet in passing.

She wrapped her shawl more tightly around her shoulders and took in Teissèdre's travel-stained appearance and that of the two roughly garbed men with him, who bowed, one taking the reins of Teissèdre's horse. The small party had clearly ridden far and fast.

Before she could speak, two grooms approached from the stables to lead the horses away. She directed them to make sure accommodations were arranged for Teissèdre's servants.

After the men led the horses off, she turned back to the Frenchman. "Have you any news of Jonathan?"

He smiled broadly. "I left him and General Andrews at Morristown a fortnight ago—in perfect health, if I may say so. They arrived only a couple of days earlier and send their greetings." His brow contracted in a pained look as he added, "General Carleton wished me to convey to you his abiding love."

She beamed at him. "How soon—"

"He feared it would be at least the end of this month before they could get away."

A pang of disappointment cut through her, but before she could question him further, he continued, "I'd have been here sooner had I not suffered the misfortune of encountering yet another storm along the way. *Mère de Dieu,* your country has been besieged this winter! Thankfully I wasn't delayed overlong."

She took his arm, shivering, and led him into the courtyard, where the butler waited at the head of the steps. "It's freezing out here! Come inside and warm yourself. We've more than enough time for you to share all your news before dinner."

TEISSÈDRE HAD LITTLE to say as far as any substantial news related to the war was concerned. At least, he wasn't sharing everything he knew, she concluded with considerable frustration.

On entering the manor he had first insisted that the babies be brought for his inspection. Predictably Julianne wailed, while Harry was all toothless smiles and giggles. Never daunted, Teissèdre offered his hearty congratulations and proclaimed them the most superior of infants.

At dinner he regaled Elizabeth; her parents; Durie; and Isaiah and Farris, who shared command of the Rangers in Carleton and Andrews' absence, with descriptions of the bleak conditions at the Morristown camp. Mrs. Washington and the other officers' wives were wonders, doing everything possible to succor the ill and bring cheer to the soldiers, he assured them.

Elizabeth remembered with dismay how the army had suffered during the previous Morristown encampment three years earlier as well as at Valley Forge the following winter. Her spirits sank at thought of what the soldiers must be enduring in even more bitter weather, with food and other provisions at times nonexistent for days.

Over the course of that afternoon and early evening, she, her father, and the two colonels plied Teissèdre with questions about the ongoing negotiations with France for increased military aid, the war at sea, and plans for the coming summer campaign, subjects that held their most urgent interest. Their questions were met with broad generalities when not by noncommittal smiles, shrugs, or pleas of ignorance. The colonels finally made their excuses and left.

It took all of Elizabeth's patience to pretend that she believed the canny Frenchman. From what Carleton had told her about his agent, she knew full well that he had ferreted out every scrap of intelligence to be had at Morristown down to the vaguest rumor. By the time the evening ended, she was dangerously close to snatching a large antique vase off the drawing room mantelpiece and smashing it over his bald head.

Teissèdre interrupted her exasperated musings, the glint in his eyes assuring her that he sensed her ire. "I must leave the day after tomorrow, as early in the morning as possible. General Carleton directed me to bring young Moghrab with me on my return to France. I assume you know that he's anxious for a new assignment, and I'm certain Caledonne will accommodate him. You might wish to alert him and his family tonight so he can make preparations."

Elizabeth's breath caught, and she started to her feet. "I'll go tell them at once." She hesitated for a moment, meeting the Frenchman's steady gaze with a sad one. "We all knew Pete was determined to return to service, of course. It's been a joy to have him with us for this long, but . . . it seems like no time at all."

TWO DAYS LATER Elizabeth stood with her parents, Isaiah, Sarah, and Jemma on the graveled drive outside the manor's courtyard, shivering in dawn's tentative light. Well bundled against the cold, they waited while Pete cinched his saddlebags behind his mount's saddle, with Teissèdre and his servants holding their horses closely curbed, clearly impatient to be gone.

Finally the tall, lean young man came over to them. He embraced each of Elizabeth's parents before reaching for Elizabeth.

She held onto him tightly, murmuring, "Stay safe, Pete. God go with you." Beneath his reluctance she felt the tension in his muscles, the suppressed eagerness to meet what lay ahead.

He cleared his throat as he released her. "And with you," he said huskily.

"I be proud o' you, son," Isaiah said, voice choked. He took Pete's hand and shook it.

For some moments Pete clung to him, his mother, and sister as they exchanged whispered farewells and endearments. "Come back to us safe," Sarah said finally, voice trembling.

"I will, Ma. God willing."

At last, they let him go. As he swung into the saddle, Isaiah dashed away the moisture trickling down his cheeks with the back of one hand. Sarah and Jemma leaned into each other's arms, dabbing at their eyes with the hem of their aprons.

The small group stood forlornly together, watching as, with many backward looks and waves good-by, Pete urged his mount down the road after Teissèdre and his servants to the bend, where they rode past the trees and out of view.

Chapter Eighteen

HE FELT A TREMOR go through her as he trailed feather-light kisses across the bridge of her nose, her eyes, along her cheekbone to the tender flesh below her ear, then down along her jaw. When he found her mouth, she melted into him, returning his kisses hungrily, stealing his breath and wrenching a muted groan from him.

"I've missed you dreadfully," she murmured.

He'd sworn he'd not give in. But the alluring scent of her, the supple feel of her body pressed against his aroused a tide of desire that he was hard pressed to wrestle into submission. Because of the twins' birth, they had not made love since he had returned to France in mid July the previous year. By now he wanted her so badly that his body ached with it.

Taking a shaky breath, he pulled away to take her in. Her sweet face was rosy with his kisses, loosened curls trailing from beneath the edges of her cap. Her expressive eyes brimmed with a love that came far too close to dismantling every one of his carefully constructed defenses.

"Every second since I left has been torture, dear heart," he returned huskily. "All I could think of was you and our wee ones. I was on the verge of going stark, raving mad by the time we finally got away."

He bit back the fervent endearments that sprang to his lips in the wake of his admission. Clearly it was going to be even harder to keep his distance than he'd insisted to himself it would be. But somehow, for her

welfare, he had to maintain his guard by main force of will while never causing her to doubt his love.

"By the time Louis arrived I'd begun to fear you'd be snowed in at
Morristown for the entire winter," she returned, eyes sparkling with laughter.

He forced a smile. "He did make it here then?"

"Not a moment too soon!" she answered, thankfully appearing not to
sense his inner turmoil. "We'd heard the weather was even worse up north
than here. I was afraid you must have ended up frozen into a snowbank
and wouldn't be found until the spring thaw!"

"We questioned our sanity every moment until we finally made it
through," he answered with a rueful laugh.

It was a cold, blustery afternoon, Tuesday, 7 March. While Andrews
and his servant headed down the path to the warriors' camp on their arrival,
Carleton had tossed Devil's reins to Stowe and wasted no time heading
for the manor's front door.

Elizabeth had run into his arms the moment he set foot inside the
entrance hall, leaving him hardly enough time to toss his snow-frosted
hat and bearskin to Burns. He barely registered that her parents offered
smiling, but brief, greetings before they and the servants vanished from
sight, leaving them alone by the small hearth where the crackling fire
melted away the chill that had settled into his bones during the punishing
journey. Forgetting all else, he had immediately drawn her into his arms,
feeling as though he had been parched and starving since leaving her.

All he wanted was to see their babes, and then scoop Elizabeth up
and bear her to their bed with no further delay . . .

He wrenched his thoughts back from the edge of that that dangerous pitfall. Gently extricating himself from her arms, he stepped back,
pretending not to register the slight frown that creased her brow and the
question in her eyes.

"How are Harry and Julianne doing? They must surely be full grown
by now."

A smile dimpled her cheeks at his teasing tone. "It seems as though every day they're changing and learning new things. You won't believe how big they've grown."

"And how much I've missed," he said, looking away.

"But you're home now. Come along!"

Their hands clasped, fingers entwined, he eagerly followed her into the Great Hall, where the two Shawnee maidens were playing with the twins on a blanket laid in front of the main fireplace, while Elizabeth's parents relaxed on the leather couch facing it. When he entered the two young women rose to greet him, then quietly slipped out of the room.

The next hour provided a welcome distraction from the dilemma that had been nagging at him from the moment he had left Morristown anticipating their reunion. Ensconced on the sofa he held Harry in the crook of his arm, balanced on his knee. That both held their heads up steadily now and responded alertly to those around them delighted him. And to his amazement, when he had knelt to pick Harry up, his boy roll-ed over onto his back effortlessly, babbling as he reached for him.

Elizabeth came to stand beside Carleton, cradling Julianne. "He goes happily to everyone, but I do believe he remembers you."

"I think you're right." Carleton chucked Harry under the chin, smiling as the boy giggled, his arms waving and legs kicking in excitement, his eager gaze fixed on Carleton's face. "You've learned to roll over, my lad! Well done!"

Anne laughed. "He's very proud of himself too."

"Julianne hasn't quite accomplished the task yet," Dr. Howard put in, his chest noticeably swelling, "but I wager she'll manage it within the week."

Carleton could feel his own chest expanding as he looked from one child to the other. Happily their swaddlings had been discarded, and both were clothed in pretty, ruffled white linen dresses that afforded them free use of their limbs.

Despite his dress, however, there was no question that Harry was most definitely a boy. Sturdily built, he had put on noticeably more length and weight than his sister and appeared to be a bright, happy lad.

Carleton looked up to smile at his girl. She was all femininity, a bundle of soft, sweet curves and delicate coloring as fragile as a porcelain doll.

He knew it to be a deceptive appearance. From birth she had demonstrated a determined will that would not be tamed by harsh methods. Only a firm and loving hand could guide her to maturity as the woman God had designed her to be, he reflected, adding a quick prayer that the Almighty would equip him and Elizabeth for the task.

At the moment, however, Julianne appeared chastened as she looked doubtfully down at him from her mother's arms. Wide-eyed, chin and lips trembling, tears starting, she whimpered and turned away, burrowing her head into the curve of Elizabeth's neck.

"Surely you haven't forgotten me so soon, Julianne," he protested.

Elizabeth gently patted her daughter's back. "Sweeting, you've nothing to be afraid of. Your papa may be big and fearsome, but he adores you and would never do you any hurt."

Carleton frowned. "Fearsome?"

She looked him up and down, taking in his height; the breadth of his shoulders; and his lean, muscular form with a deliberation that suffused his entire body with heat. "As you pointed out yourself, my love, you are quite a bit larger than she is."

"You're looking very well yourself for a harried mother of twins," he drawled before he could stop himself.

She returned a smile that despite his resolve caused his pulse to quicken. "Harried? Don't be silly. There are so many people tripping over one another to carry our babies about that I hardly get to touch them except when they demand to be nursed."

"That's all too true!" Anne agreed. "If everyone keeps spoiling them, they'll soon be intolerable to live with."

"You're the main culprit, my dear," Dr. Howard said, a twinkle in his eyes.

Anne gave him a cross look, obviously feigned. "It's a poor thing if a grandmother can't spoil her grandchildren," she returned, illogically contradicting herself and causing Elizabeth and Carleton to burst into laughter.

Elizabeth bent to set Julianne into the crook of Carleton's free arm. The little girl squalled and made every effort to cling to her mother, who pulled gently out of her grip.

Before Carleton could try to comfort her, Harry leaned forward to pat his sister, burbling several indistinguishable syllables in what could only be described as a soothing tone. She gulped down a sob, lower lip trembling, and focused on her brother's face. He kicked his feet against hers, and she quickly joined in, giggling as Harry bounced up and down, crowing and waving his arms. Carleton glanced up to meet Elizabeth's amused gaze with raised eyebrows.

"Harry seems to have taken it as his responsibility to calm his sister whenever she's upset. He's gotten very good at it."

Chuckling, Carleton reached around to tickle Julianne under the chin. She immediately whimpered and pulled away.

He bent to kiss her brow. This time, to his surprise she pressed into him and tilted her head to peer up through the veil of her lashes, frowns alternating with fleeting smiles. When he tickled her again, she squealed and squirmed away from his hand while returning a coy look that completely captured his heart.

After relinquishing Harry to Elizabeth, he gently stroked Julianne's cheek, marveling at the silken softness of his tiny girl's skin. Appearing fascinated, she studied him, mouth half open, and after a brief hesitation suddenly reached up, bouncing and babbling excitedly as she batted at his face. She tried to grasp his nose, and when he turned his head away, laughing, she grabbed a fistful of his hair and jerked the long strands free from the ribbon that held it back.

Hearing protesting grunts followed by louder objections voiced in distinct syllables, he looked up while carefully disentangling Julianne's fingers from his hair. Harry was leaning down from Elizabeth's arms, reaching for him.

"You're jealous because your sister is getting all the attention, aren't you, Harry?" Elizabeth cooed.

Carleton held back a happy sigh. What he felt holding these little persons who were his and Elizabeth's very own was indescribable.

Suddenly he found himself wishing violently that he could stop time from moving onward. Already he felt the hours slipping from his grasp like iridescent beads of quicksilver. And yet at the same time he longed to know the man and the woman they would one day grow to be.

He met Elizabeth's understanding gaze, feeling the sting of tears and the weight of his responsibility to protect the ones he loved so dearly from any harm.

And the impossibility of it.

THE MCLEODS JOINED them soon after Elizabeth nursed the twins and Morning Dew and Yellow Feather bore them back upstairs to the nursery. A fortnight earlier Mary had given birth to Aileana, a delicate fair-haired cherub of a lass who, it was clear, owned not only her mother's and father's hearts, but also that of her half-brother, Jimmy, who hovered over her like a wee guardian angel. A placid babe, she made no complaint as she was passed from arm to arm to receive everyone's ardent admiration.

They were interrupted when Andrews and Blue Sky, who bubbled over with joy at her husband's return, were ushered inside with their children. Leads the Way burst exuberantly into the Hall ahead of them to run to Jimmy, while Andrews clasped the hand of fifteen-month-old Little Elk, who followed his older brother as quickly as his short legs could carry him.

"He's walking so well now!" Anne exclaimed before corralling the two older boys and admonishing them on their behavior.

Carleton and Elizabeth exchanged smiles as Jimmy and Leads the Way happily settled beside Anne on the couch, to all appearances undaunted. Not for long, however. As soon as Elizabeth summoned the two Shawnee maidens to carry Aileana and Little Elk off to the nursery, the two boys gleefully jumped off the couch and raced after them.

Elizabeth's mother shook her head. "Soon Daniel will be running after the older boys," she sighed, using Little Elk's English name as always. "I'm beginning to wonder if they'll ever be tamed."

"They'll grow up soon enough," Carleton returned. "In the meantime, let them run and burn off some of their energy. They are boys, after all, and I well remember how difficult I found it to sit still when I was little."

"Quite right," Dr. Howard agreed with a firm nod. "It doesn't spoil boys to allow them to run now and again. In fact they'll be much more agreeable to settling down when required."

Carleton captured Elizabeth's hand and drew her down on the settee beside him, resting his arm along its back to encircle her shoulders. "There's nothing sweeter in life than a house filled with family and good friends and a nursery full of children," he said expansively, returning Elizabeth's affectionate look.

The Father's blessed us with two healthy children, and Beth suffered no lasting harm, he reasoned, feeling that his heart would burst with happiness. *We've been given more than enough joy to be content.*

In the years following his youthful profligacy, he reminded himself, he had successfully kept physical passion in check. He had only to do so again.

The trouble with his plan was that it evaporated the instant Elizabeth leaned into him, as she did now, her head so sweetly resting on his shoulder as though she had been made to rest right there, next to his heart. He found himself wondering whether, now that he had known the deep, exclusive intimacy of what it meant to be one flesh with his dearest earthly love, he could keep the desperate ache for that bond at bay. At least until she was past childbearing.

For that matter, could she? For she made no secret that she desired him as passionately as he did her. And he feared that would be his downfall.

HE TOOK REFUGE in insisting Elizabeth and her parents relate all that had happened during his and Andrews' absence. In turn the two of them described their trip and stay at Morristown.

"The week before we left we took advantage of a break in the weather to ride over to the Hudson River with General Greene to see the improvements made to the fortifications at Stony and Verplanck's points since we retook them from the British last fall," Andrews volunteered. "We decided that as long as we'd come that far we might as well sail upriver to take a look at Fort Putnam's defenses."

Leaning eagerly forward, Carleton said, "The fort sits on the Hudson's west bank, and the fortifications that surround it are unmatched on this continent, terraced all the way up to the top of the highest crag, which is quite steep. It's well garrisoned, with many redoubts and cannon commanding the river and the plain on its far bank. At the hill's base, where the river narrows in a tight S curve, a great chain is laid between the banks to bar ships from further passage. It'd be well nigh impossible for the British to seize the fort. The only way I can imagine it could be taken is by treachery."

With dusk gathering, the footmen entered to light candles and torches to dispel the deepening shadows. Salome had prepared a lavish early supper for the travelers, and everyone moved into the dining room. While they ate, the conversation turned to the army's dire situation, especially with the devaluation of Continental currency, due largely to the British flooding the country with counterfeit bills.

Dr. Howard shook his head. "It's unjustifiable that our soldiers are reduced to such want because the very people for whose liberty they're fighting can't be bothered to provide them sustenance!"

"According to Louis, Sartine's spies reported that the British Army faces a similar crisis," Carleton responded. "England's citizenry and many members of Parliament no longer share George the Third's determination to keep these former colonies within the empire. The war has cost them lost trade and increased their national debt."

"How much longer can they continue then?" McLeod demanded.

Andrews shrugged. "Washington insists that Britain will be forced to the negotiating table if we win the naval war. So the Marquis de Lafayette is back in France trying to persuade Vergennes to send us another fleet and additional troops." He referred to France's foreign minister, Charles Gravier, le comte de Vergennes.

"Well, d'Estaing didn't exactly distinguish himself at Savannah, did he now?" Elizabeth said sharply.

"Nor did Gen'l Lincoln," McLeod observed. "I wager it'll not be long afore Clinton tests his mettle at Charlestown."

"There's a gloomy prospect, James." Andrews quipped, looking deflated. A suitably dour silence settled over the table.

Carleton slouched back in his chair, arms crossed. "You might be interested to know that a large fleet of warships and troop carriers left New York Harbor at the end of December. Bound south."

Elizabeth raised her eyebrows. "Louis never mentioned that. Is there any intelligence as to their destination?"

"We know Clinton and Cornwallis were aboard, so the only destination that makes sense is Charlestown," Andrews put in. "They're not needed in the Caribbean, and we can be certain they're not headed to England."

Everyone around the table exchanged concerned glances.

"The fleet hasn't been seen or heard from since putting to sea," Carleton noted. "After delivering Pete to York, Louis planned to head south into the Carolinas to see whether they turn up there."

Dr. Howard snickered. "Considering all the nor'easters that have torn through this winter, it might be a long time before they reappear."

"I hope we'll be that lucky," Carleton said. "I suggested to His Excellency that it might be advisable to send more men and materiel to Lincoln, but he has little of either to spare and is understandably reluctant to weaken his own forces."

"He also places a great deal more confidence in Lincoln's abilities than I would."

Carleton directed a narrowed glance at Andrews. "There's nothing we can do since our assignment—at least for now—is Virginia's defense. But Louis promised to alert us as soon as Clinton's fleet appears on the horizon. If it does."

Andrews hesitated before saying, "Red Fox and Spotted Pony should return soon. I'm anxious to know what's developing on our western borders."

Carleton snorted. "Nothing good, I'm sure."

Following a light supper the McLeods left to take their sleepy children back to their cabin. The others found seats in front of the fire in the Great Hall, Elizabeth again settling at Carleton's side on the sofa.

Sprawled next to Blue Sky on the settee, Andrews cocked one eye at Carleton. "Do you intend to tell them or will I have to?"

Avoiding Elizabeth's bemused gaze, Carleton focused his scowl on Andrews. When he returned a determined look, Carleton threw up his hands in resignation.

"Caledonne is taking leave from the navy," he growled.

The announcement was met with stunned silence. At last Dr. Howard ventured, "You can't be serious."

"Oh, he is," Andrews put in with undisguised glee.

Heaving a sigh, Carleton gave a terse summary of his uncle's plans to commandeer his fleet, including Teissèdre's claim that the impetus had come from Tess.

Openmouthed, Elizabeth stared at Carleton. "*Excuse me?* This plan was suggested by *Aunt Tess?*" she exclaimed, voice scaling upward.

"My sister?" Dr. Howard echoed, plainly astonished. "And you believe that?"

Carleton shrugged. "I've no idea what to believe. It's true my uncle's talents and abilities have never been used as he deserves. The French naval establishment learned early on in his career that if it came to a fight and they gave him his head, some of France's precious ships would end up being wrecked. My uncle's taking over my fleet serves their ends while relieving them of any responsibility and expense."

Elizabeth regarded him with outrage. "So they'll stand back and allow Uncle Alexandre to use your ships to fight Britain for them. You'll effectively be financing a part of France's naval war and Uncle Alexandre's ambitions, allowing both to benefit at your expense."

"Mmm . . . that's essentially the substance of it."

"*Essentially?*"

He gave a harsh laugh. "Entirely then."

Chapter Nineteen

A FEW DAYS LATER Carleton and Andrews met with their officers,
Dr. Howard and McLeod included, to detail developments in the
war that had been discussed during meetings at Morristown. Prime
among them was the circulation of counterfeit Continental currency by
the British, with the resulting devaluation that had forced Congress to
replace the old paper currency with new, and hopefully more secure, Continental bills.

Although thankfully that debacle did not affect him to any great
degree, Carleton explained, the discouraging reality was that other factors
were making it increasingly harder for him to maintain the division. His
import business and investments that provided the foreign specie funding
the Rangers had, of course, been severely curtailed due to Caledonne's commandeering his entire fleet to wage war against the Royal Navy on France's
behalf.

Added to that, the large portion of food and other goods produced
on the estate that had formerly been sold at profit were now needed to
sustain the Rangers. And the little excess remaining after their needs and
those of the manor staff were provided for could only be sold locally for
valueless Continental currency.

After their meeting broke up, Carleton went with Dr. Howard to
seek out Elizabeth and her mother along with Durie and Sarah to
explain the strictures they would face—temporarily, he hoped. With his

income hemorrhaging, he had no choice but to hold spending in check for the foreseeable future, he emphasized glumly.

The announcement did not come as any great surprise after the news of Caledonne's plans. Carleton was gratified that not only did everyone he spoke with assure him of their cooperation, but they immediately began consulting with each other and those under their supervision about measures that could be put into place. But in a private discussion, he confided to Elizabeth his concerns about the uncertain future they faced.

"We'll weather this storm, dearest," she assured him. "Mama and I will work with Alistair and Sarah to reduce our expenses as much as possible. And your men will do their own part. They're well aware they've not suffered as the army and the militias have, and they'll stand by you through hard times."

Her steadfast confidence heartened him. Despite worries that continued to nag at him, he determined to keep moving forward as he felt guided and trust that God would provide all they truly needed to sustain them.

It did not escape Carleton's notice that Elizabeth listened with rapt attention to discussions of political issues and developments in the war. The realization of how divorced she must feel from the heady adventures in which she had formerly engaged struck him forcefully.

He consequently made a point of entrusting her with detailed intelligence that he confided in no one else other than Andrews. She was a highly experienced and daring spy, after all, with considerable knowledge of military and intelligence operations from the very beginning of the war. It pleased him deeply that she soaked up every scrap of information from intelligence transmitted by Washington's spies operating in New York City to developments in the wider war and prospects for the upcoming campaign.

This soon included Teissèdre's report from Charlestown, South Carolina, which arrived not long thereafter outlining the progress the British were making in their march on that city. For Clinton's vanished fleet had finally reappeared, landing on the southern coast so badly battered by storms that they had been forced to sacrifice all their horses to Neptune while at sea.

Carleton had also confided his disheartening private meeting with Washington at Morristown in which he questioned Sullivan's brutal campaign that had decimated the Iroquois towns. He understood his commander's reasoning, he told Elizabeth, and could not deny the necessity to protect the white settlers in the area and stop the savage warfare the Mohawk war chief Thayendanegea had unleashed.

In that Sullivan had succeeded, but Carleton warned Washington that the peace that had been imposed was only temporary. By leaving the Iroquois destitute, without food, clothing, and housing for the winter, the campaign had cemented the Iroquois' allegiance to the British. And it had irreparably damaged relations with the Shawnee and other native nations who had suffered similar attacks by the militias, thus making them implacable enemies of the Americans. But Washington had shrugged off Carleton's counsel, and the divide between them on this issue had become unbridgeable.

To his gratification the astute insights Elizabeth offered challenged and broadened his own perceptions and strengthened his determination to follow the course he had set out on. This deepening oneness of spirit was what he had longed for most in marriage. To discover daily how fully the two of them possessed that now made the doubts and separations of the preceding years worth the struggles they had endured.

Before they married Elizabeth had been frank with him about her woeful lack of domestic skills—and, clearly, her lack of interest in such matters. Which bothered him not in the least, as he had assured her. At Thornlea she had a full staff at her disposal. Having her mother and Sarah in residence as well eliminated any lingering worry that she might be overwhelmed by the management of such a large estate.

What mattered infinitely more to him was that along with being intelligent, high spirited, and ready for any adventure, she was also a devoted, tender, attentive, and loving wife, mother, and doctor. Watching her with the twins filled him with emotions beyond his power to express. And seeing how her skillful work in the hospital and concern for her patients fulfilled a deep need in her to heal the sick and wounded knit his heart to her even more.

At the same time, however, the most intimate part of their life together was becoming harder to manage by the day. On his return he had quickly realized that whenever he was in any proximity to her, his resolve to hold this issue at bay teetered on the brink of collapse.

His excuses, whether voiced or implied, were not only hurting her deeply, but now even causing her to doubt his love. Nothing could have pierced his heart with greater agony than the tearful, wounded look she gave him one night in bed when he returned her passionate kisses with restraint, then pulled away, turned his back to her, and pretended to fall asleep. Only to lie wide awake for hours, his body aching for hers.

He had no idea how he was going to be able to shore up his crumbling defenses much longer. But the possible consequences if he were to give in to her loving enticements tormented him past bearing.

ELIZABETH TRAILED SLOWLY from the hospital back to the manor, her emotions tangled into a painful knot in her breast. She was grateful that Rain Woman was assisting today, for it had been impossible for her to conceal her distraction. At last her father had gently suggested that she spend the rest of the day with the twins, evidently assuming that motherly concerns occupied her mind.

Indeed they often did, though most of the time she was able to set them temporarily aside, confident that her babies couldn't be more lovingly tended in her absence. At the moment, however, other concerns were uppermost in her mind.

She let out a deep sigh. How could she communicate to her parents the nagging worry that plagued her when all her tender wiles had failed miserably to draw Carleton into confiding what troubled him? Truthfully, it was not an issue she felt comfortable discussing with them.

She was at a loss to understand why he continued to treat her with the same sweet affection each day as though nothing was wrong, but as soon as she began to give in to passion, he inexplicably pulled away. Even when she clearly felt the intensity of his desire for her.

It was as though her husband had returned to Thornlea without quite returning . . . to *her*.

Pondering whether Blue Sky might be able to offer some insight, she entered the manor and handed cloak and scarf to the footman. As she began to ascend the tower's spiral stairway to the upper gallery, she met Jemma coming down.

"You're back early today!" the young woman exclaimed in surprise, glancing over her shoulder at Elizabeth as she turned to retreat upstairs. "Do you want to change now? It's hardly more than an hour until dinner. Which gown would you like?"

It was then that the perfect solution to her dilemma struck Elizabeth along with the memory of Carleton alluding to it on Christmas Eve. And she laughed.

He had no one else to blame. It was entirely his own fault.

He'd forgotten, in fact, the costume of the Roman goddess Diana that Elizabeth had worn to a masked ball in Paris. Which, at his insistence, she had modeled for him in private after his arrival at Passy. And which he now guiltily remembered teasing her about in a veiled reference at Christmas.

She was taking her revenge.

She stood seductively at arm's length, the glowing light cast by the fire on the shadowed chamber's hearth revealing every alluring, sensuous curve of her slender body through the tissue-thin lustrine of the sleeve-less Roman stola. He remembered all too well that he had expressly forbidden her to discard it and its accoutrements, certain that he would want her to wear it for him again after they were wed. And never imagining that he might have cause to curse his stupidity, as he did now.

Mouth dry, he took her in, unable to wrench his gaze away. She might as well have worn nothing at all, for the supple, iridescent fabric clung intimately to her contours as though wet through, shimmering from silver to gold with her slightest movement. Her glossy curls had been artfully arranged to crown her head, the dark strands sparking deep red and gold highlights in the fire's light.

Two braided golden cords, held in place by a wide golden sash at her slender waist, crisscrossed the loosely draped bodice's front to emphasize her bosom before passing over her shoulders and again crossing in the back. Composed of irregular, fluttering layers that gave the effect of constant motion, the floor-length skirt fell to her feet, angling upward on one side to expose her slim calves, wrapped to the knees with the thongs that secured the delicately wrought Roman-style silver sandals cradling her bare feet.

He closed his eyes, not daring to continue the inventory. The rich, spicy-sweet fragrance of her filled his senses to overflowing, arousing him so intensely that he despaired altogether of holding on to the rapidly fraying fragments of his self-control.

That evening, after she had retreated upstairs for the night, he had dismissed Stowe and lingered for some time in desultory conversation with Dr. Howard and Durie until he was certain she must be asleep. Then he had gone quietly upstairs, slipped into their chamber, and shut the door, making as little sound as possible.

And turned. And sucked in a sharp breath.

He stood stiffly motionless now, back against the closed door, tried to turn his face away as she placed her hands lightly on his chest, their touch burning through the fine linen of his shirt. But it was impossible to drag his gaze from her.

Swallowing, he said, "It's late and you need your rest. Julianne and Harry will have you up—"

She pressed her body against his and slid her hands up to his shoulders, searing heat following their movement. "They rarely awaken in the night anymore," she murmured. "I've missed you terribly, Jonathan. I've hardly seen you these past few days—"

"Beth . . . don't—" he pled huskily.

"But it's been months since we've made love—"

"We've . . . other things to concern us now."

For a moment she gazed up at him, her lovely face shadowed, lips slightly parted, eyes wide with hurt. Then she dropped her hands and bent her head.

"Oh. You mean . . . now that I've given you children you no longer find me desirable."

"No—never think that!" He tipped her face up so her sorrowful gaze met his. "You're the most desirable woman this side of Eden. There's no one on the face of the earth I could adore more than I do you, dearest wife. And the fact that you're the mother of my children only causes me to love you the more."

"Then why do you keep pushing me away?"

She was trembling, her cry so brokenhearted that it entirely upended him. He caught her into his arms meaning only to assure her of his love. But feeling her body against his, he was instantly lost. He covered her face with kisses, trailed more down her throat to the silken valley between her breasts, feeling her unrestrained response, the catch of her breath as he slid one hand down the curve of her back to the swell of her hips—

He hastily tore his hands from her and wrenched away. As though demon-pursued, he strode into the bartizan and stared through one window's diamond panes into the night's blackness, limbs shaking. Before his eyes the panes reflected her dear face, ashen, framed by her sweat-slicked hair at that moment he had knelt over her, lying on the floor just after giving birth. Again the thick metallic tang of her life's blood rapidly draining away clogged his nostrils, the odor all too familiar from battle-field and ship.

By degrees the vision muted into the haunting image of her body lying motionless on the bed at Roxbury after he had rescued her from the British and brought her back to Boston. Only to come so terrify-ingly close to losing her to the grave after all.

He could not bear that anguish again! It had been hard enough to endure before they had wed. Now it would utterly break him for the wife of his heart to be wrenched out of his arms forever and to see his little ones lose their mother as he had.

"Have I no say in this matter?"

He rounded on her. "You're not being fair!"

"Not fair? I . . . I don't understand . . . "

"It isn't fair to *you!* We can't do this—"

"Why? I'm your wife. Aren't we to be one flesh?"

He swallowed hard. "If I were to be irresponsible and—"

"IRRESPONSIBLE? How is it irresponsible for a husband and wife to share the bonds God provided for them?" Elizabeth caught her breath, under-standing suddenly dawning. "You're afraid."

She watched as he paced back across the chamber to the fireplace. Raking his fingers through his hair, he turned his back to her, braced his hands on the mantel, the hard muscles of his broad shoulders and back rippling under his shirt's fabric as he stared down into the flames.

"I *am* afraid, Beth. Afraid that the next time you'll be taken from me forever."

"You could as easily be taken from me."

"I know, but . . . " He drew in a shaky breath. "Twice I've watched as you hovered so near to death. Twice I've come within a breath of losing you! The thought that I might get you with child again so soon—especially if it were to be twins—"

"I'm completely recovered, dearest. Sarah, Laughing Otter, and all the other women assured me that I'm not likely to conceive as long as I'm nursing. And twins are rare. There's little chance of it happening again."

"I have a hard time trusting those odds!" he rasped.

"I don't want a barren relationship physically or otherwise," she burst out. "Do you?"

She saw his shoulders rise and fall in a sigh. "No . . . but that's only one aspect of marriage."

"A precious one."

He turned to fix her in a tortured gaze. "My responsibility as your husband is to protect you. Beth, all I want is to hold you close all my life. I want to keep you and our children with me always."

"And I want to do the same for you. But we can't! Every day we have to take some kind of risk."

"We can choose the risks we're willing to take!"

She pressed her eyes closed and let out a breath before again meeting his troubled gaze. Well did she understand his fear. With spring's advent he would inevitably lead his Rangers again into battle, and she would be left behind to endure her own fear and dread.

Yet she knew surely that if the deep bond between them was to remain strong and sweet as God meant it to be, both of them needed the intimacy of the marriage bed. The sharing of overwelling emotions. Of whispered endearments and loving, passionate touch. The deepening oneness of body and mind, heart and soul.

Tears stinging her eyes, she said tremulously, "I told you on our wedding night that I didn't want to waste another moment of the rest of our lives. I meant it and mean it still. Our days are written in God's book, and we're promised that not one of them will fail. He alone determines our end, and we must live each day as he chooses.

"You more than anyone know that life isn't safe—at least not *real* life. And no matter how long or short our lives are, I want to live them to the fullest, with joy and passion! Jonathan, I want to trust the Lord with our days, not holding anything back ever. I want us to live real life together for as long as God gives us, come what may."

Before she finished, he had crossed the room to capture her in his arms and kiss away the tears that trickled down her cheeks. "My fearless little Oriole," he murmured brokenly, "this is why I love you so."

He slid his hands with seductive slowness down her shoulders and back, delicious tingles following the heat of his touch as the shimmering silk fell away. She led him to the hearth, and pulling the quilted cover from the bed, he spread it before the fire and laid her on it, drew her to him then, and buried his face in the curve of her shoulder.

She felt the warmth of his breath against her neck as he whispered huskily, "Ah, Beth! You're the heart and soul of our home, the keeper of its flame. And I'll ever cherish you above all women."

HE GAVE WAY to the tide of desire then, kindling hers like flame to dry tinder while the night hours fled away unheeded.

Near dawn he awoke with her curled sweetly in his arms, her back to him. He pressed his lips lightly against her bare shoulder, careful not to wake her, gratitude and fear gripping him in equal measure.

A deep tenderness overwhelmed his soul for this woman, this help-meet and mother of his children with whom the Father had blessed him. He could deny her nothing for he knew she'd ask nothing of him in return that was impure or unrighteous or against the Almighty's will for them. With all that was in him he adored her.

Your will, not mine, Father, he prayed, heart aching so painfully he could hardly breathe. *Your will, not mine. But, ah, dearest Lord, in your mercy let your will be for our lives together to be long!*

Chapter Twenty

BY EARLY APRIL winter had eased its grip on the mountain valley. Only a few patches of snow still clung in the most sheltered swales along the ridges' flanks. In the valley's lower reaches tentative new buds in soft hues of green and muted shades of red lightly misted trees and bushes. Cattle, sheep, and horses eagerly grazed on the lush emerald grasses spreading across the meadows.

Twilight wrapped the valley in shadow on Monday, the third, when another of Teissèdre's couriers rode up to the manor. Carleton met the man at the courtyard gate and, after taking the letter he carried, dismissed him to find a meal and a bed in the barracks before heading back south in the morning.

His gut clenching, Carleton snapped the wax seal and unfolded the pages, quickly scanned the Frenchman's grim report that Clinton was inexorably closing in on Charlestown. He refolded the pages and began to turn, intending to go inside to his study to peruse it more closely. But hearing the sound of hoofbeats, he arrested and turned back.

A small party of riders garbed in Indian dress approached up the road at a slow walk, Red Fox and Spotted Pony in the lead. As they drew to a halt in front of him, Carleton's heart sank to see that they had brought not a single new recruit with them. It was enough bad news for the day, and after a brief conference he waved the weary men off to their cabins and families.

Everyone was gathering around the fire pits outside their cabins for breakfast the following morning when he and Elizabeth carried the twins to the warriors' camp. Yellow Feather and Morning Dew, no longer needed to tend the babies at the manor overnight, ran out of Laughing Otter's cabin and immediately took possession of them. In the company of several other maidens they happily bore them off with Blue Sky's and Rain Woman's youngest.

"Well, that's the last we'll see of them until they're hungry," Elizabeth said brightly as she joined Laughing Otter and the two other women at the fire.

Carleton found a seat with Andrews, Red Fox, and Spotted Pony. "You're complaining?" he teased, to which she returned a laugh.

Blue Sky affectionately drew Elizabeth down to sit beside her on one of the blanket-covered logs around the fire circle. "We need not worry about our children, for they have many clan mothers and sisters to watch over them."

"And grandmothers to spoil them by feeding them treats," Elizabeth retorted.

Smirking, Rain Woman handed out steaming corn cakes baked on the hot stones edging the fire pit, while Laughing Otter distributed pottery bowls filled with steaming bear-meat stew.

When they had finished their meal, the men pulled out pipes and tobacco. For a time they sat in silence, the grey tendrils rising from their pipes to drift into the fire's smoke and twine upward into the cloudy sky.

At length Carleton began to question Red Fox and Spotted Pony about the situation on the western frontier. It was as he had feared. Not only were the Shawnee towns overrun by former American colonial agents such as Alexander McKee, Matthew Elliot, and the Girty brothers, who had deserted to the British, but also by British Rangers and French Canadien militia and traders. Local Mingo and Lenape, Wyandot, even Pottawatomie, Ottawa, and Ojibwa warriors from the Great Lakes crowded the region as well, traveling through the area on their way to raid settlements along the Kentucky and Virginia frontiers.

After distributing great quantities of weapons, food, and other needed goods, Red Fox told them, the agents and traders boasted in long speeches about Britain's invincibility and reminded the people of the Long Knives' most recent atrocities. They went so far as to advise the sachems and war chiefs on strategies for waging war against the Americans.

The overwhelming majority of warriors from all the Shawnee divisions and those of the surrounding nations were by now firmly allied with the British, Spotted Pony, related grimly. These included almost all the Maquachake, Piqua, and their own Kispokotha division, factions from which had formerly followed Cornstalk and his sister Nonhelema in holding to neutrality or fighting on the side of the Americans. The towns of Chillicothe and Piqua had been rebuilt in new locations and along with other major towns were raising palisades to repel Long Knife attacks.

Red Fox reminded them that since many of the British and Canadiens had traded with the Shawnee and other native nations for years, many taking wives from among their women, they had become trusted intermediaries with the British. Their influence would be all but impossible to break.

When the two men finished their report, a glum silence settled over the gathering. The women silently carried off pots, bowls, and spoons to wash later, then returned to their seats.

"What of our clan?" Andrews asked.

Spotted Pony's face hardened. "A number of the young men speak of going over to the British."

"Blue Crane holds our sisters firmly to keeping out of the fight," Red Fox said, referring to the women's peace chief of Black Hawk's clan. "Before we left some were speaking of moving farther west before the corn planting festival. If they do, the men will follow."

Shoulders slumping, Carleton drew in a breath and blew it out. "Then they may be gone by now. How does our fellowship?"

Spotted Pony dropped a branch on the fire's seething embers and stirred them to life. "Several have withdrawn over this matter, but we pray for their return." Naming the Oneida disciple of the missionary Samuel Kirkland who had come with his family to live at Grey Cloud's Town two years earlier, he added, "Walk on Water preaches the Word of Jesus with great power and encourages our brothers and sisters to stand firm in the faith in spite of opposition in our clan and tribe."

"Blue Crane was baptized, as were others of the women who came to faith because of her strong testimony," Red Fox added.

Carleton brightened as did the women, who had been listening silently to their discussion.

"What of my father? Has he come back to the faith?" Andrews asked anxiously.

Red Fox directed a frowning glance at his brother before saying slowly, "He shows no interest in doing so, though Walk on Water often speaks kindly with him. We fear the shaman Loud Thunder draws him toward the British, though Grey Cloud speaks nothing of it. Blue Crane stands fiercely against both, and it is a matter of deep grief for your mother."

Andrews covered his face with his hands. After a moment he rubbed his eyes and looked up.

"The Great Father is more powerful than any other," he said, as Blue Sky grasped his hand. "We will continue to pray."

A thought struck Carleton. "What of the Moravian believers? Since they refuse to engage in war, they incur the wrath of both sides. I fear for their safety."

Spotted Pony related that the tribes allied with the British blamed the Moravians for hindering their efforts to persuade the western tribes to join the war and also accused them of providing intelligence to the commander at Fort Pitt. They considered the Indian believers, who were primarily Lenape, to be traitors. The Moravians had been forced to abandon several settlements because the war parties constantly traveling through their towns on raids threatened to destroy them.

Carleton pondered this information for several moments before describing his futile discussion with Washington on the effects of Sullivan's and Clark's campaigns. "I'll send a report to him of this news right away," he concluded grimly. "Perhaps it will enlighten his thinking on these matters."

Red Fox shook his head, his expression hard. "Both sides, the British and the Long Knives, look only to what benefits them. They make treaties with us as long as they can use us for their own advantage, but when we resist, they put our towns to the torch."

Eyes narrowed, Spotted Pony knocked the smoking tobacco from his pipe into the fire. "When they are done with us, they will cast us aside like a bone from which they have stripped all the flesh."

"I'm afraid you're right, brother." Bitterness laced Andrews' words.

Carleton gave them a keen look. "As long as we keep that in mind, it may be that we can find a way to use them to *our* advantage."

THE FOLLOWING MORNING dawned fine and clear and brought with it yet another thorny issue Carleton had feared would arise, but hoped he would not be forced to address.

After breakfast he joined Farris' troops for an hour of target practice with carbine and pistol. Then he went with Andrews to practice maneuvers with Isaiah's mounted troops, Red Fox's warriors divided between them. The two troops opposed each other as they charged across the meadows toward the valley entrance. The invigorating exercise demanded much hard riding and clashing of sabres, while he and Andrews shouted commands and encouragement, and impressed Carleton with his men's fearlessness and ever increasing skill.

Gradually, however, he became aware of an acrimonious undercurrent between Isaiah and Andrews, which became more evident as they rode back to the barracks, windblown and sweating. After Isaiah dismissed his troops, Carleton ordered him and Andrews to accompany him into the common room of the nearest building, deserted at that time of day, the fire's embers banked in the hearth. The two men settled at opposite ends of the bench on one side of the table, while Carleton took a chair across from them.

Slouched back, arms crossed and one ankle propped across the other knee, he fixed the two men in a questioning gaze, eyebrows raised. For some moments a taut silence filled the room as they avoided his gaze and each others'.

"Do you want to tell me about it?" he finally asked when neither volunteered to speak.

As though the words were being dragged out of him against his will, Andrews said, "I went down to check in with Isaiah's pickets before daybreak. They'd just stopped two black youths who had run away from a plantation a few miles beyond Salem and were pleading for the men to hide them."

Carleton straightened, groaning inwardly. His policy was to enlist any willing, able-bodied black men into Isaiah's regiment without asking questions. But he had been concerned from the first that escaped slaves might be drawn to Thornlea seeking sanctuary or passage north because of them.

That his Rangers included Blacks and Indians and that both he and Andrews had been adopted into the Shawnee tribe alone ensured hostility from many of the army's officers and even more so from the militias. That he had also freed the slaves inherited from his uncle was outright treachery in the eyes of those who profited from that evil institution, and he held no doubts that whenever slaves in the area escaped, he would inevitably be the first to be implicated.

"What happened?" he asked, suppressing a sigh.

Andrews bent forward, elbows on his knees, head supported in his hands. "A posse of armed slave hunters wasn't a quarter mile down the road with hounds howling. There wasn't any possibility of hiding the boys, not with hounds on their scent, and the men were on us in minutes, demanding that we turn the runaways over. There wasn't anything else I could do—"

His face contorted with rage, Isaiah sprang to his feet, and strode toward the door.

"Sit down, colonel!"

At Carleton's icy command Isaiah came to a halt, shaking. For a tense moment he stared at the door, wanting to rip it from its hinges and cast it, crashing, out of his way. It took herculean effort for him to swing around and return to his seat.

"Ever since we come here I see the way slaves travelin' with their mastahs up and down the river road look hopeful at us, with our uniforms and weapons—" Isaiah stopped abruptly, emotion clogging his throat.

"Charles did the right thing."

"The right thing? Handin' those young boys back to—"

"Isaiah, I had no choice!" Andrews cried, sitting up, his expression anguished.

"Those slave hunters take hold o' those boys like they animals! They insult me and my men and look us up and down as if we on the block before they demand papers proving we all free. You know what they do to runaways when they catch 'em?"

He could see Carleton's mouth tighten, the muscles of his jaw hardening though he answered evenly, "Our assignment is not to free slaves, but to defend Virginia against British incursion. We can't do that if we turn the local planters and militias against us."

Breathing hard, Isaiah made a dismissive gesture. "So we shed our blood to keep these high and mighty white folk free, but when one o' their slaves come to us desperate for freedom, we turn our backs 'cause their skin be black?" he demanded hotly.

Carleton met his smoldering gaze with a level one. "My orders would be the same if they were Shawnee. Or white."

Isaiah knew the truth of that and could find no answer even in his fury. Again a tense silence settled over the room.

At last Carleton said, "I'm not saying that we must refuse to help runaways, only that we can never be seen to do so."

"Those boys been sold away from their mama when their ol' mastah die, and their new one be a mean, hard man. They be scared—"

"What would have happened if Charles had refused to hand them over? Or—if there had been any possibility of hiding them—he had denied that they were here and refused to allow those men to search the grounds? They followed the boys' track right to this valley."

"They'd have all the evidence needed to bring legal action against us for violating Virginia law," Andrews pointed out grimly.

Again Isaiah sprang to his feet, fighting for breath. "I stand on that block when I be five year old after they rip me out o' my mama's arms. She be screamin' and cryin' 'cause they sell her off away from me, and her new owner strike her and drag her away. There be nothin' I can do for her or for me. And then I look out over those white men lookin' at me like dogs slaverin' after a lamb, while they call out bids for my body. What I feel no man can describe!"

He stared into the air. "I be one o' the lucky ones who manage to get away one day, spend fourteen year with the Lenape before I find my way to Boston. And you know what happen with Sarah. Thank God Dr. Howard agree to buy her away from bein' sold to men who want more from her than her labor."

He could see the agony in Carleton's eyes as he gave a curt nod. "I know how hard it is, Isaiah," he returned, voice brittle. "I also experienced what it is to be a slave—not as long as you did but long enough to know I want no man ever to suffer such violation. That's why I freed my slaves. That's why I fight for my people's freedom too.

"But if we're to do any good, for now all of us must do everything in our power to convince those who come looking that this division does not harbor runaways," he continued with visible effort. "We cannot allow our emotions to jeopardize our ability to see those we can help through to freedom by vainly trying to save those whose cause is irretrievably lost."

Isaiah's tension slowly eased. He swallowed hard, finally jerked his head in assent, though it took all his willpower to do so.

He resumed his seat. "After what happen this mornin', my men lose faith in your promise to keep us free when this war be over. Several even talk 'bout joinin' up with Colonel Tye up there in Jersey."

He referred to the feared and respected commander of a loyalist partisan band composed of fellow escaped slaves. Well paid by the British, Colonel Tye was renowned for attacking and plundering the homes of patriots, striking suddenly, then disappearing just as quickly among the swamps, rivers, and inlets of New Jersey's Monmouth County.

Carleton stiffened. "It's your responsibility to maintain your troops' discipline, colonel. I believe I've proven sufficiently that I keep my word, and I'll not brook desertion."

Spreading his hands, Isaiah demanded, "How you goin' to do that when you tol' us a while back you losin' so much money you may not be able to keep this division together?"

Carleton smiled thinly. "I have rich relatives."

Andrews smirked, but Isaiah rolled his eyes and sank back in his chair, shaking his head.

Sobering, Carleton conceded, "That certainly doesn't mean I can expect them to fully fund my Rangers for as long as this war may yet last. But my cousin's husband, le marquis de Martieu-Broussard, is highly placed in France's ministry of finance. In our last correspondence Eugène assured me that I'll receive due consideration from the French government for 'lending' my ships to their war efforts. I plan to set aside enough from their compensation to ensure that all those serving under me will be provided for as needed after the war. You'll have to persuade your men of that. Explain the situation to them, and afterward I'll meet with anyone who still has concerns."

Partially mollified, Isaiah regarded him suspiciously. "You talk about helping some through to freedom. What you got in mind?"

CARLETON LEANED BACK in his chair and stroked his chin thoughtfully. "There's a sizeable community of free blacks at City Point near Petersburg, upriver from Jamestown. In fact, according to what Salome and Rufus told me while I was here last July, a number of my former slaves now live there. And if I remember correctly, Hopewell Meeting House is also in the vicinity. Quakers officially oppose slavery, though not all of their members adhere to those strictures. But runaways could be transported from here to City Point within a few days, and I'll wager there'll be at least a few helpful folks willing to offer refuge and arrange safe removal north."

"We'd have to find some way to conceal those we afford refuge until they can be safely transported," Andrews pointed out. "If we can manage that—"

"I've something in mind, but I'll have to think about the issue of dealing with slave hunters' hounds. That complicates matters."

Andrews frowned. "The question is whether any local slaves bent on escape will try to seek refuge with us after this morning's disaster. The news of what happened is likely to spread fast, and it'll discourage further attempts."

"But the boys see how much me and my men hate to give 'em up. Charles too," Isaiah added, grudgingly nodding to Andrews. "Sooner or later somebody try again, maybe come over the ridge."

"That might be possible, but it'd be a challenge for anyone unfamiliar with the terrain to find a path," Carleton broke in, frowning. "The slopes on both sides are formidable, scaling them dangerous. But I suppose you'd better set a picket across the river to keep an eye out for any who try it and succeed."

"Me and my men'll do whatever needed," Isaiah said quickly.

"It's imperative we figure out a plan before someone else shows up." Carleton's gaze hardened. "However, let me be perfectly clear on this: I'll personally impose harsh penalties on any of my troops who go so far as to solicit slaves to escape. If they were to fail in the attempt or we were forced to give them up, as today, the consequences for them and for everyone in this valley will be on my head. I won't allow that."

Isaiah exchanged a charged look with Andrews, who turned to Carleton and said quickly, "We understand completely. I'll make sure it doesn't happen."

"Then let me talk to Beth and her parents," Carleton said briskly. "Alistair too. They'll have to know what's going on, and I'm certain they'll want to be involved in some way. In the meantime, Isaiah, get Sarah's and Jemma's thoughts. We need to confer with Rufus and Salome, too, since they stay in touch with friends at City Point. But as to everyone else, only those who have to be involved can ever know of the matter. And hopefully no more runaways will show up on our doorstep until we've come up with a workable plan."

Pushing out of his chair, Isaiah and Andrews following, he dismissed them.

Isaiah lingered after Andrews had gone. "The way those slave hunters look at me and my men this mornin' and demand our free papers got me thinkin'," he said abruptly. "What if some white folk decide we be fair game to put in chains and sell?"

"Not everyone in this country holds slaves or approves of it."

"Sure a lot down here in the South who do," Isaiah shot back.

"You and your men are armed," Carleton returned, fixing him in a hard gaze. "As Continental troopers you have the right to use your weapons to defend yourselves against any enemy who threatens you. And I order you to do so."

"We kill or even threaten anybody with guns and there be a mob out to lynch us! Ain't no law gonna stop 'em."

Taken aback by Isaiah's vehemence, Carleton massaged his brow, knowing he was right and hating it.

"You only one man. How can you protect us from all them out there who want us slaves or dead? Even some o' Farris's troopers not happy to be servin' with black men and consider us beneath 'em,"

"Charles and I are on your side, and there are many others among my Rangers and in this country who abhor slavery. You must keep in mind that our charge is not to protect slaveholders and slave states, but to defend America. This nation belongs to all of us regardless of those who don't see it that way. Our Declaration of Independence states that all men are created equal."

"Words!"

"Yes, words," Carleton countered earnestly. "When true words are written down, they hold a power that reaches through the ages. You can destroy the document, but men will still remember and pass it on and hope.

"By those words slavery cannot stand no matter how hard some fight to keep it. Though it may take a long time and we may not see it in our lifetimes, Isaiah, those who are born after us will see it. The day will come when everything is set right—our God assured us of it. Until then we must never give up."

Seeing the emotions that passed over the black man's face, Carleton said softly, "Don't give up, my friend."

Isaiah nodded. "Not possible. But it sting like fire to watch my people suffer and know there be nothin' I can do to free 'em."

Carleton turned to look out the window where a cluster of the older youths, native, black, and white, raced across the nearest meadow in a vigorous game of stickball. "I know," he said gruffly. When he turned back to Isaiah, he read understanding in his gaze.

Coming to a decision, he said, "I promise you I'll not take your regiment farther into the South except in case of extreme urgency, and then only with your full agreement. If we're ordered into the Carolinas, I'll commit Farris's regiment to action there, while you remain stationed here to protect our camp and supplies. But should the British invade Virginia again, which is likely, I'll have to commit our entire division."

Isaiah considered this for a long moment, carefully guarding his expression. Finally he touched his fingers to his brow in salute and took his leave.

Chapter Twenty-one

O N A MILD MORNING toward the end of April, to Elizabeth's delight Carleton finally set aside time to take her on the long-promised tour of the upper valley. He even ordered Salome to prepare a picnic basket.

She took leave from her duties at the hospital and forced down as much breakfast as excitement would allow. After nursing the twins and turning them over to the Shawnee maidens, she hurried into the bedchamber, where Carleton and her mother waited, to change into riding gear.

He insisted she put on a pair of his breeches, snugly cinched at the waist so she could ride astride. They were comically loose, the legs hanging to her ankles. In spite of her mother's disapproving looks, she laughed at her reflection in the mirror, undeterred, while Carleton grinned.

"I'll have a couple of pairs made to fit you properly," he told her with a wink. "Riding and hiking in these mountains wearing skirts is not at all practical."

Beaming, she donned riding coat, gloves, and boots in a flash and ran after him downstairs and outside, where two grooms waited in the courtyard with their charges. They had brought out Devil and the horse Carleton had given her from his herd, to her immense delight.

The sleek two-year-old mare reminded her of Night Mare, her beloved mount lost to the British when she was captured on the way back from Saratoga. Although this mare sported a small, white, crescent-shaped blaze, her coat was an otherwise unbroken gleaming black. She was as trim, neat, and fast as her namesake, for Elizabeth had immediately christened her in Night Mare's honor and made a pet of her. She rode the mare as often as she could find time.

They quickly sprang into the saddle and urged their mounts forward, riding abreast at a trot. The road was still muddy in places from a heavy rainfall a few days earlier. Today, however, a soft breeze still tinged with winter's keen edge drove a scattering of fair-weather clouds across the heavens' high blue arc overhead, sending rippling bands of shadow and sunlight across forest and meadow.

The earliest blooms spilled in clusters of color and fragrance in sheltered gardens, and redbuds cast their purpled hue among the surrounding trees' green-misted boughs. The moist soil of a nearby vegetable plot had been dug up, and a couple of servants moved along the rows, sowing peas. At beds farther along several men were raking away last year's decayed leavings in preparation for cultivation.

They urged their mounts to a trot past the barracks. Nearby a mounted troop practiced maneuvers on the broad parade ground. A crackle of carbine and pistol fire echoed from one of the light infantry companies on the target-practice range.

Farther along they passed the warriors' camp. Most of the men absent on a hunt, the younger children gleefully at play. The women and older maidens were busy preparing the fields surrounding the clustered cabins for planting.

They urged their mounts to a canter. The occasional, distant lowing of cattle and barking of dogs reached them from the tree-dotted pastures they passed.

Little more than a mile beyond the estate's last outbuildings, the road narrowed and turned rocky, deeply rutted by runoff from the previous month's snowmelt and recent rains. They were forced to rein their horses to a walk. Ahead of them herds of cattle, horses, and sheep grazed peacefully among scattered trees along the river's broad bends.

Following its course, they detoured around the gristmill built along a mill race diverted from the river. The sluice gate remained closed, stilling the large vertical wooden paddle wheel at the weathered clapboard building's side.

Elizabeth noted the land's gradual rise, the high, densely wooded ridges looming ever closer on either side as the valley narrowed toward its end. Here pigs foraged among the trees, scuttling off into the undergrowth, grunting, at their approach. A short distance farther they passed the sawmills, also standing idle, situated on the opposite riverbank where logs could be floated down to them.

The track they followed passed into dense stands of pine, hemlock, and fir, interspersed with enormous oaks and hickories. At length, with the sun high overhead, Carleton dismounted in a sun-dappled clearing, motioning her to do the same. After hobbling the horses where they could graze on the lush grass, he took the basket and led her to a sheltered nook under the trees, where they spread their picnic.

They did not linger long, for Elizabeth was eager to explore. After devouring the feast Salome had packed, they left the horses contentedly grazing and continued afoot.

He grasped her hand to steady her as they detoured around windfalls and rockslides and clambered carefully over and around boulders. Her gratitude for the breeches he had insisted she wear increased the farther they pressed toward the massive western ridge's intersection with the towering bulk of the eastern ridge. Looking up through the trees, she saw that the latter now held the sun's full radiance while the lower reaches of the western ridge lay in cool shadow.

She had just begun to note a muffled roar ahead of them when they passed around the cliff's jutting shoulder. The deafening thunder of water brought her to an abrupt halt at Carleton's side. She gasped and clutched his arm in astonishment, mouth falling open, while he looked down at her, pleased at her reaction.

The view that spread before them was far more than she had envisioned and fair took her breath away. Just below the jointure of the two mountains, a crystal stream trickled from a seam in the rock layers high above. Mist-veiled and wreathed in shifting rainbows cast by sunbeams dancing through the overhanging branches, it cascaded downward across several massive, jagged ledges from which more water poured to dramatically broaden its column until it crashed, frothing, into the wide pool below. Here was the river's head, the water spilling from the basin at its lower end into the bed it had carved into soil and stone for centuries, finally winding out of sight behind a towering stand of black locust trees.

"Thorn Falls," he said, indicating the scene with a sweep of his arm. "The pool is also fed by a spring. The falls dwindle to a trickle in midsummer when the weather turns dry, but this spring and several others down the valley keep the river flowing year round."

She looked up to meet his gaze with a mischievous one. "Can we climb to the top?"

He bent to brush a kiss across her lips. "I was hoping you'd want to. But there's another place I want to show you first."

He took her hand and guided her along the pool's bank to its opposite side, weaving through the pines that bordered it, the hissing thunder of falling water muting all other sound. Through the trees to their left she glimpsed the eastern ridge's ancient rock wall, a behemoth powerfully upthrust through the earth eons ago. When she looked down again to mind her steps, she realized that they followed what must once have been a narrow path, its outline now barely noticeable beneath a thick layer of pine needles.

They emerged suddenly from beneath the trees, the falling water cascading into the pool directly in front of them, so close that she shivered in the the cold mist-drift. Carleton stopped and drew her close to his side, his arm around her shoulders.

She followed his gaze, after a moment making out what she guessed to be an irregular cleft in the mountain's flank, discernable only as a darker shadow inside the rushing falls' near edge. All but obscured by the veil of mist that shrouded the thundering column of water, it was so heavily cloaked by thick, weathered vines that unless one stood exactly where they were standing and knew it was there, it remained invisible.

She directed a questioning look at Carleton. Smiling, he slid his hand to the small of her back and urged her forward onto a broad, moss-covered rock ledge that extended behind the curtain of falling water. Excitement growing, she led the way past the edge of the cascade.

He held aside a mass of drooping vines and stepped with her into what she first thought to be a cave or tunnel. In the faint light she sensed more than saw that the ceiling rose high above their heads. Cautiously they felt their way through the dim interior until they stepped into brighter light.

A few feet forward, and she looked back over her shoulder, realizing that they had passed through a cleft riven by the tremendous force that had thrust up underlying layers of rock to form the mountain ranges enclosing Thornlea Valley. Where the two ridges joined it had left a bridge of stone, its entrance equally obscured on both sides by rank growth.

He urged her from shadow into bright sunlight, and she looked around with wonder as they moved forward. The glen angled toward the west, she saw, widening into a sheltered meadow dotted with trees.

"Are you getting tired?" When she shook her head, Carleton cast an assessing glance toward the lowering sun, still well above the western ridge-line. "It's about a mile to the end, and we haven't time to walk all the way if we're to get back before sunset. But there's a pass over the mountain that can be crossed on horseback. It's also well concealed by heavy growth, which makes this place a great hideout."

"It's magical!"

"I've always thought so."

"Does it belong to Thornlea?"

"Yes, but not the land beyond it. Come look at this."

He beckoned her to follow, and within a short distance they passed around the valley's bend. What looked to be a stone barn loomed before them set amid spindly, tangled weeds with a network of gnarled vines twining across its walls.

Exclaiming in delight she followed him inside through its wide entrance, stepping carefully over fallen, rotted planks that appeared to be the remains of once sturdy double doors. She paused to look about her, shivering in the gloom. The structure was surprisingly spacious, darkly shadowed and chill inside. And obviously quite old.

It must have been built long before Thornlea Manor, she reckoned. The back of the roof and the hayloft beneath had caved in, but the thick stone walls with a small window high up on either side still provided fine shelter.

"I thought you might like this place."

She could hear the smile in his voice. Before she could turn, he wrapped his arms around her from behind and drew her against him with his chin resting on the top of her head.

"It looks very old," she said almost in a whisper, feeling strangely awed.

"It is. There's a stone foundation of what was probably a house somewhere nearby. It's so buried beneath the overgrowth now that when I came here a few days ago it took some searching before I found it."

She turned to look up at him. "This seems quite an odd place for a house and barn. Who do you think built them, and why here when there's so much open land in Thorn Valley?"

He shrugged. "All I know is that it was here when Sir Harry bought the property and that the roof was still intact then. I wouldn't be surprised if some digging turned up the foundations of other buildings too. Over the years I've collected pottery sherds and the rusted remnants of a few iron tools, but also a number of arrowheads and stone tools. Apparently Indians camped here before white men invaded the area."

"One of the earliest settlers must have built this then."

He nodded. "They were likely seeking a place that could easily be fortified against attack by natives and is difficult to find. I discovered the cleft behind the falls purely by chance when I was perhaps ten or eleven. When

I told Sir Harry, he already knew all about it, of course. He impressed on me that it was to be a secret between the two of us—and his steward, naturally. No one else was to know, especially the slaves. They were forbidden the uplands anyway except for those who cut timber and rounded up pigs for slaughter. I couldn't even tell the boys who were my playmates."

"Sir Harry let you play with the slave boys?" she asked, surprised.

"Oh yes, when their work was done. He had no objections at all to my having close relationships with the house slaves and their children, as he did too. That's common on plantations."

Averting his face, he said softly, "I was good friends with several of the boys. But he found out that I often helped them with their work so we could run off to play, and he put a stop to it at once. As we grew older we spent less and less time together until our worlds were entirely separate."

Troubled, she took his hand. Glancing down at her, he forced a smile.

"I loved to play here, even alone. This barn was by turns a castle, a frontier fort, an Egyptian pyramid or Roman palace, or any other place my imagination conjured up."

"I can see why," she returned cheerfully. "Does the valley have a name?"

"Sir Harry simply referred to it as the back valley," he answered. "It seemed a haunted place to me, and I privately settled on calling it Valley of the Ancestors. Would you like to give it a better name?"

She smile up at him. "Valley of the Ancestors feels just right. It'll be our own name for it."

Returning her smile, he bent to kiss her, and she melted into his arms. For some moments all other thoughts evaporated.

At length he loosened his embrace with a sigh. Straightening, he cast a speculative glance at their surroundings and said dryly, "I suppose that storm a few nights ago left the place too sodden for us to comport ourselves in a scandalous manner."

She blushed but couldn't stifle a regretful laugh. "Sadly so. I'm afraid our dishabille would give us away and draw highly disapproving looks from everyone we encountered on our return. Though we are married, even our small community has its strictures."

He grinned. "Then we'll just have to control ourselves somehow until tonight at the approved time and place."

Sharing their mirth, they went back outside, Elizabeth leaning on Carleton's arm. "Does anyone else know about this?"

"Alistair does, of course. He knows every detail of the estate. And naturally Red Fox, Spotted Pony, and our warriors discovered it within a few days after the Rangers camped here, and they showed it to Charles. Now you know too."

When he bent to kiss her, she drew back and gave him a reproachful look. Before she could chide him, however, he explained, "I wanted to surprise you with it personally and see whether it delights you as much as it did me when I first found it. And this is the first time the weather's allowed for such an adventure since the twins were born."

"I am delighted! If I'm ever in need of a hiding place, I'll know where to go."

Meeting his gaze, she continued thoughtfully, "You know, we could conceal escaping slaves here by using the far pass to smuggle them in, then away to City Point once safe transport is arranged. From this side, just getting through the uplands to reach the falls is difficult enough, and finding the valley's entrance when you don't know it's there would be well nigh impossible. It's unlikely anyone searching for runaways would ever discover it."

"That's what I was thinking," he returned with a smile.

His discussions with her, her parents, and Durie after the incident with the runaways had resulted in eager agreement that whenever the opportunity arose to help fugitive slaves, they would do whatever was possible. The Howards had acquaintances in Boston who owned slaves, a practice they had viewed with disapproval. But now after seeing how widespread and entrenched the institution was in the South, Elizabeth and her parents had come to unalterably oppose it. Even Anne, who worried about flouting Virginia law, could not bear the thought of turning away anyone in need.

"If you approve, I'll have Isaiah assign a detail to repair that roof," Carleton said, "but we'll have to keep the work secret from anyone who doesn't need to be involved."

"The fewer people who know about our efforts, the better—only those who can be trusted," she agreed. "I can't help thinking the Lord provided this safe haven long in advance for this work."

She smiled up at him, again becoming aware of the distant rush of the falls that reached them from the other side of the ridge. "Now what about our climb?"

"This way."

He led her back toward the bridge to where a winding stairway appeared to be roughly carved into the western ridge's stone layers. As they drew closer, she saw that the steps were natural, not manmade. The large, gnarled roots of the trees growing along the slope held back hard dirt and layers of jutting rock to form rough footholds that defined an irregular path up the cliff face.

"This leads to just above the falls and a view out over the valley that's spectacular."

She needed no urging to mount the first step and begin to climb, grasping the trunks of sturdy saplings and bushes along the ascent to pull herself upward, while he followed close on her heels. She was breathless by the time they emerged onto a shallow, timbered swale linking the two ridges, whose crests rose yet higher on either side, crowned with massive pines.

Below their feet, steps away, water gushed out from between the weathered rocks of the cliff face. Fascinated, she followed its downward course, breath held, his arm around her shoulders steadying her.

At last she lifted her gaze to look out over the valley. The heavily timbered upland gradually descended and widened as it receded to the north. Farther off it gave way to tree-dotted, greening meadows and pastureland

and fallow fields that flung across the valley like a subtly hued quilt, its blocks defined by meandering dry-stacked stone walls and split-rail fences.

Beyond lay Thornlea's outbuildings, the various camps, and the roofs and chimneys of the manor that were visible between the surrounding trees. Through it all wound the river's wide, silvery ribbon, tracing down the valley's misty reaches out of sight to its mouth, where it escaped its confines on its way to the Staunton River.

"To think that this is our home!" she exclaimed, a thrill going through her. "I never imagined I'd live in such an enchanted place."

When he didn't answer, she looked up at him, chewing her lip. "Mama told me that she and Papa are thinking seriously about moving here with us permanently—if you've no objection."

He returned a warm smile. "Why would I? I love your parents and want you and our children to always have them near, especially when I need to be gone."

Her heart near to bursting, she turned to take in the scene again. "It delights me more than I can say to have Thornlea as a refuge for us and our family and a haven for you always to return to."

He remained silent for so long that she directed a questioning look at him. He took her in his arms, regarding her earnestly.

"Thornlea is yours to do with as you wish, freely."

She tiptoed to slip her arms around his neck and kiss him. "It's ours together, dearest, and we'll do with it what we together decide."

Her words clearly pleased him, though he cautioned gruffly, "This war is not yet won, nor can we see what this world will look like when it is. That may influence any decisions we make."

Gazing into the depths of his deep blue-grey eyes, she perceived no cloud there, only his unshadowed love. And yet she had the sense that something deep in his heart remained unspoken.

Chapter Twenty-two

H E WAS NOT QUITE what she had expected, Elizabeth reflected as she studied Patrick Henry from her seat beside her mother.

He wore his customary dress of formal black suit and tie wig, while Carleton and her father were both in uniform. With them stood General Andrew Lewis, a tall, powerfully built man imposing in appearance despite his sixty years and plain riding garb. Having arrived only an hour earlier, he listened to their discussion with an inscrutable expression while taking little part in it.

It was Saturday, 6 May, and they had settled on the manor's rear terrace to enjoy the mild breeze and fair weather. From meadow to mountainside trees spread full crowns to the sun in every hue of fresh green. Dogwood, black locust, and hawthorn perfumed the air with froths of fragrant blooms as did Thornlea's overflowing flower gardens. The day was warm enough that Elizabeth and her mother had put on new spring gowns of fine lawn, Elizabeth's a shade of apple green that particularly pleased her, her mother a flattering robin's egg blue.

Standing at the balustrade, the great orator was deep in an animated discussion with Carleton and her father about the right to freedom of conscience for Baptists, Quakers, Lutherans, Presbyterians, and other dissenters from Virginia's established Anglican Church. His father had been staunchly Anglican, Henry was telling them. He had grown up in that church and remained in it. His mother had been raised Presbyterian, however, and as a child he had often accompanied her to their worship services, where the ministers' fiery preaching had profoundly influenced him.

"This great nation was founded by Christians on the gospel of Jesus Christ alone, not on 'religion,' " Henry said forcefully. "Those who hold to different doctrines as a matter of personal conviction must be afforded the same freedom of worship as Anglicans. That our established church here in Virginia goes so far as to arrest and imprison dissenters is an outrage."

"I can't say I've devoted much thought to the issue," Dr. Howard said thoughtfully, arms folded, frowning as he stroked his chin with one hand, "but I certainly can't argue with your reasoning."

"I've never believed that any government has the right to establish one religion over another," Carleton put in. "After all, didn't the majority of those who first came to this country from Europe and England do so because they wanted the right to worship God as their consciences convicted them?"

Henry nodded triumphantly. "Exactly so."

Elizabeth exchanged a smiling glance with her mother. Henry was renowned as a highly successful lawyer from Virginia's backwoods and a fiery orator who commanded his audiences with both passion and reason. One of Virginia's delegates to the first and second Continental conresses, he regularly served as a representative in the state's House of Delegates. And having retired after four terms as her first governor barely a year earlier, he had been promptly elected to the House again.

She had never imagined that he would be so genuinely amiable and mild in person. Attended only by his black servant, he had arrived at twilight the previous evening after riding all the way from Leatherwood, his recently acquired home in the county named for him, some fifty miles southeast of Thornlea. From the moment Carleton introduced them, Henry had put her and her parents at ease with his unassuming manner, wit, and good humor.

A pleasant supper had given way to a friendly, but fierce, violin contest between Henry and Carleton, fingers and bows flying across the strings so rapidly that both were left breathless and laughing as their audience vigorously applauded and declared them evenly matched. By the end of the evening Elizabeth had felt that this longtime friend of Carleton's was truly a dear friend of her own, a sentiment her parents clearly shared.

To their disappointment, Henry planned to leave for Richmond early the next morning, already late for the first session of Virginia's House of Delegates, scheduled to begin the next day. The state capital had recently moved to the town, fifty miles up the James River from Williamsburg, a location deemed more secure from British attack and more convenient to Virginia's burgeoning western settlements. Lewis, recently appointed to the governor's executive council, had arranged to meet Henry at Thornlea and travel with him. But a recurring illness that often afflicted Henry had forced both men to delay their trip.

Listening to the men's discussion with only partial attention, Elizabeth found the appearance of the renowned orator, lawyer, and politician as magnetic as his manner. Henry's profile had a Roman cast, with a long, straight nose and high forehead and cheekbones. She had heard he was a keen judge of men's character, and she could believe it. His eyes, blue-grey like Carleton's, appeared almost black beneath thick, bushy eyebrows, and their gaze seemed to her to pierce to one's soul.

From their conversation the previous evening she had learned that Henry's father had emigrated from Aberdeenshire, Scotland. Like Carleton's, Henry's ancestors had been Normans who accompanied William the Conqueror to England. His family line included many notable orators and educators, with influential relations residing in England, Ireland, and the Scottish Highlands, as well as in America.

At forty-three, Henry was a couple of inches shorter than Carleton, equally lean, but slightly stoop-shouldered, with a tanned, weathered countenance. Early failure as a small shopkeeper, and then a farmer during his youth had led to his true calling. On the strength of his quick grasp of the law he had earned a license as an attorney after a stunning mere two weeks of study.

Equal success had followed in politics, where Henry's oratorical skills had swiftly raised him to the ranks of the most influential men in the colonial House of Burgesses. He had been highly instrumental as well in the removal of Royal Governor Lord Dunmore from office and in advocacy for the nation's independence.

What drew her attention to the man most, however, was Henry's strong, harmonious voice. Carleton had told her that he could easily make himself heard up to half a mile away, and that much of his success lay in an instinctive ability to modulate his voice in such a way as to strike a deep chord in the hearer. It now drew her attention back to the men's conversation, which had flowed into other channels during her reverie.

"You know I've always treated my slaves with kindness and lenity, Jon," Henry was saying patiently.

"Just before I was captured by the Seneca," Carleton returned, his voice hard, "a wise man, now the colonel in command of my black regiment, told me that no man owned by another is treated well. I soon had occasion to learn the bitter truth of that statement."

Henry gripped Carleton's shoulder. "I'm sorry that you suffered such ill treatment, Jon, but thank God you were delivered from it! And I applaud you for freeing your slaves. You've done the right thing. I'll not justify the lamentable evil of slavery any more than Tom Jefferson and some others of our acquaintance. Tom's pursued reforms to slavery, in fact, to the extent of invoking Natural Law before the Bar. He made the point that everyone comes into the world with a right to his own person given by the author of Nature and that personal liberty is necessary for men's sustenance.

"But, alas, those of us who own large estates cannot maintain them and support our families without slave labor. White indentures are of no practical use to us since they're as susceptible as everyone else to the heat, agues, and malignant fevers that plague the tidewater regions here and in the Carolinas during the sickly season. The native populations have also been weakened by the sickness, and with their new Southern strategy the British are suffering the effects too. Only West Africans are resistant."

When Carleton opened his mouth to respond, Henry released his grip and held up his hand to stop him. "A couple of years ago our legislature passed a law ending any further importation of slaves into Virginia. It's our hope that we'll reach the point at which we can finally abolish the institution altogether, as over time their numbers diminish."

"Yet children will continue to be born to your slaves, Pat," Carleton pointed out. "How many will you be able to maintain before it becomes necessary to make them, like their parents, a commodity to be bought and sold?"

"We must teach our children to abhor the practice so they'll end it."

Dr. Howard shook his head, echoing the disappointment that stabbed through Elizabeth. "Actions speak more loudly than words. It's from what we do, not what we say, that our children take their example."

"I'm convicted of that more than ever now, Papa," Elizabeth broke in, thinking of her own little ones.

Henry sighed. "Unfortunately, I'm afraid it's the best we can do until the hearts of men change."

Feeling deflated, Elizabeth chided herself for expecting more from Henry. Despite all that was admirable in him, despite all the good he had accomplished and yet would, he was still a mortal man, thus imperfect and, in some matters, blind.

Indeed that was true of every human being, she mused. One erred greatly by making an idol of any person, for inevitably every one would fail those high expectations. Only the Creator of all flesh could claim perfection. Meeting Carleton's grave gaze, she saw that he was thinking the same thing.

"I must chide you for not bringing your dear wife along, Patrick," her mother said, changing the subject and dispelling the growing tension. "We'd have loved to have her stay with us while you're at Richmond."

Henry had remarried in 1777, several years after his first wife's death, taking as his bride then twenty-year-old Dorothea Dandridge. The beautiful granddaughter of former Governor Alexander Spotswood and daughter of Colonel Nathaniel West Dandridge, she was also a cousin of Martha Washington.

"Or, if she preferred, it would have been no trouble at all for us to arrange for her safe travel back to Leatherwood whenever desired," Dr. Howard interjected.

Lewis slanted a sly sidelong glance at Carleton. "Did you know that before her marriage Mrs. Henry was once courted by your good friend Commodore Jones?"

The others scoffed, but Carleton turned an expectant gaze on Henry, eyebrows raised.

Chuckling, he raised his hands. "It's true, though, as you might imagine, Dolly's family quickly put an end to that relationship—to my great benefit a few years later. She assured me that she was never tempted."

"Wise lady," Carleton noted dryly.

Henry turned back to Elizabeth's parents. "I know Dolly would have been very agreeable to coming if she hadn't just given birth to our youngest in January. She has the care of our older daughter and the six I brought to our marriage to concern her as well, although thankfully the oldest two are fully grown."

"Bring them all," Carleton urged. "The more, the merrier, as far as we're concerned."

Henry's expression brightened. "It might be more practical to arrange for you to visit us at Leatherwood when I return from the legislature. You've only two little ones to manage, and they'll be several months older by then. You'll find we're situated quite pleasantly, though we can't quite rival Thornlea."

"We'd love to," Carleton responded. "From what I remember from hunting in that area some years ago, it's beautiful country."

Interrupted by a footman announcing Andrews' arrival with Blue Sky, they all went inside into the Great Hall. Like Carleton, Andrews wore uniform, while Blue Sky was arrayed in her finest native dress. Carleton had no sooner introduced them than the butler called the assembly to dinner.

Smiling, Henry offered his arm to Elizabeth with a bow, while Lewis did the same to Anne, and, to Elizabeth's happy surprise, her father escorted Blue Sky. As they moved toward the dining room, Carleton gave Andrews a questioning look.

"They were just behind us—" Andrews began, looking back over his shoulder.

At that moment Red Fox, Spotted Pony, and their wives, were ushered inside. And as everyone turned toward them, Elizabeth could distinctly feel the temperature in the expansive space plummet.

FIGHTING A RISING ALARM, Elizabeth reassured herself that both Henry and Lewis had been informed that Carleton's leading warriors would join them for dinner to report on the situation along the western frontier. It was to be expected that they and their women would wear their finest garments for such an occasion. And like Blue Sky, Laughing Otter and Rain Woman had adorned their clothing with numerous intricately wrought silver brooches, painted spots of red paint on their cheeks, and dressed their hair with feathers and yet more brooches.

That their husbands chose to appear at table armed and arrayed in their finest—and distinctly warlike—garb was another matter altogether. Silver armlets ornamented the two warrior's upper arms, emphasizing their bulging muscles. A knife in a beaded sheath dangled from each neck, and a tomahawk hung from each belt. Their hair was freshly shaven along the sides and roached, while bold bands of black and red paint crossed their faces.

Elizabeth caught her breath and glanced anxiously toward Carleton. He regarded his cousins calmly, a faint smile tugging at the corners of his mouth as though they had taken him by a bit of surprise as well. Her parents were quite obviously shocked, while Henry's expression remained unreadable.

Lewis's face had darkened, however, tensing into even sterner lines as, trailed by the women, Red Fox and Spotted Pony strode toward them, their countenances hard, stance stiff and on guard. A deeply suspicious, even hostile fire glinted in their dark eyes.

It struck Elizabeth forcefully that Lewis had accompanied Washington in 1754 on the doomed expedition to capture Fort Duquesne, which had ended in ignominious defeat by a French force bolstered by Indians and sparked the French and Indian War. Both Lewis and Washington had afterward served in Braddock's expedition that was ambushed by Indians allied with the French and destroyed.

Lewis had not been present at the disastrous battle that won Washington fame. He had, however, gone on to earn an independent command in the Virginia Regiment, with orders to punish the Shawnee raiding the frontier. Although his Sandy Creek expedition had ended in failure, foiled by weather and faulty logistical support, almost a third of his force had been Cherokee—no more a propitious sign for their meeting today than was their great sachem Cornstalk's death at the hands of Virginia militiamen.

As though unaware of the ominous atmosphere, Carleton stepped forward to present the two warriors to his guests, making introductions in an easy gracious manner. But neither of the brothers reached to clasp hands with the men they obviously held to be adversaries.

The moment hung suspended while Carleton waited with apparent patience. Elizabeth noted, however, that his eyes were slightly narrowed, his steady gaze fixed on his cousins as though daring them to break the peace of his home.

In the end it was Henry who broke the spell by extending his hand to each brother in turn and smiling warmly as they reluctantly took it. "It is good to see you, my brothers. White Eagle speaks highly of you, and it's long been my desire to meet personally with you. Allow me to convey my anger and sorrow at the injustice done to your great leader Cornstalk and his companions. He was our greatest friend of your nation, a highly valued and trusted ally, and we deeply feel his loss."

Red Fox's mouth tightened, but before he could speak, to Elizabeth's surprise Lewis's expression eased, and he also reached to clasp the warriors' hands. "I share Governor Henry's anger at Cornstalk's death," he allowed gruffly. "During the battle at Point Pleasant almost six years ago, he fought with a skill and bravery that won the admiration of me and my men. We could hear him calling out orders to his warriors as any general would."

"We were at his side," Red Fox broke in stiffly.

Lewis inclined his head. "No soldiers could have fought with greater courage and skill than you and your men did under his leadership. I personally held Cornstalk in great respect and regret that he met such a cruel end at Fort Randolph on that same Point."

"Words come easily, but when they are not honored they are of as much use as clay pots thrown to the ground," Spotted Pony said, his tone laden with a contempt that again brought the color to Lewis's face as he took a step back.

"We hear you, my brother," Henry said earnestly. "And I assure you that I made every effort to bring those responsible for that unspeakable deed to justice. But the murderers were never identified even though I offered a substantial reward for witnesses to come forward. Even those who abhorred what their comrades had done refused to testify against them, thus my hands were tied."

Red Fox scowled. "This outrage is great enough. But when added to Clark's and Sullivan's raids and countless others before them, can it be a matter of wonder that our people ally with the British in ever greater numbers?"

Henry frowned. "It's my personal belief that the men responsible for Cornstalk's murder are, in fact, Tories who stir up strife between us to prevent the backcountry militias from joining Washington's army."

"Our dinner waits, gentlemen," Carleton intervened smoothly. "After we eat, we'll meet with my warriors at their camp, and Red Fox and Spotted Pony will acquaint you fully on the situation among the tribes on our western borders."

He directed a pointed glance at his cousins. "It is my desire that we first share good food and respectful fellowship so that we may discern one another's hearts more clearly." Beckoning to Burns, he added quietly, "To this end, I'll allow no weapons at my table."

Both men clamped their mouths shut and reluctantly surrendered their weapons to the butler, who bowed and whisked them away. Then, with their wives following regally, the two men stalked after Carleton as he led the way into the dining room.

CARLETON HELD HIS SILENCE as he sat with the others around Spotted Pony's fire circle. He listened to the discussion between his warriors, Henry, and Lewis with a certain amount of grim satisfaction. But although the warriors' vehemence was making an impression, the two men gave little ground.

Henry had begun with an approving nod to Andrews and Blue Sky, who was holding Little Elk while the other children played. He had long been of the opinion that the only permanent remedy for the hostility between Whites and Indians was intermarriage, he had noted. Ties of blood provided common interests and affections as nothing else could.

Red Fox and Spotted Pony had shrugged that observation off, returning coolly that the Shawnee, along with many other native nations, had a long history of adopting captives and intermarrying with other peoples, who were then accepted into their clans and nations as their own. The conversation had devolved from there, the worst, in Carleton's view, being that Andrews joined in, expressing his opinions as hotly as the rest.

Henry pointed out that, fearing settlers would make further unwaranted attacks on the Indians, he had offered a reward for Cornstalk's murderers. He had gone so far as to appoint two men, one of them Lewis, to meet with the Shawnee, the Lenape, and other tribes at Fort Pitt the previous summer. The Shawnee refused to treat with them, however, instead laying siege to Ft. Randolph. And although with the aid of Cornstalk's own sister, Nonhelema, they had been driven away, they had then moved on to attack other settlements. When again repulsed, the war party had gone on to massacre the settlers in Pennsylvania's Wyoming Valley.

"What more could I have done?" he questioned. "You Shawnee, as all the native tribes, must be held responsible for your own behavior."

"So must you Long Knives," Spotted Pony responded darkly.

Biting his tongue, Carleton let the dialog play out as it would. In the end his waning hopes for some small measure of rapprochement was entirely disappointed, the tension between the two sides remaining unrelieved.

After Henry and Lewis headed back to the manor, Red Fox grudgingly admitted as much. "That did not go well, brother."

"An understatement if I ever heard one," Andrews said in disgust.

Carleton let out a sigh of frustration. "I understand your feelings, my brothers. You well know that I fully share them. But nothing can be gained by refusing to even consider the other side of a matter. Now another opportunity has been lost to make friends who might do us some good, and I fear it's our people, not the Long Knives, who will suffer the most bitter consequences."

Chapter Twenty-three

EARLY IN THE MORNING a week later, Elizabeth pushed aside her plate and rose from her chair as Henry entered the dining room.

Indicating that he should take a seat, she went to the large sideboard crowded with steaming chafing dishes, poured a cup of coffee, and brought it to him at the table.

Smiling, he thanked her before taking a sip. She sat beside him and studied him intently for a moment before briefly laying her hand on his forehead.

Satisfied, she said, "You've improved a great deal. The fever hasn't returned, which is a good sign. You slept well?"

"Very well, thank you."

"No more headaches or chills?"

He shook his head. "I believe this miserable malady has passed for the moment, thanks to you and your father." He took another sip from his cup and set it down. "I apologize for causing so much trouble."

"You've been the best of patients," she countered. "Jonathan told us that you suffer from the intermittent fever and ague that's common along our southern coast. It's a good thing you were here when you fell ill so we could begin treatment immediately."

Chuckling, Henry agreed.

"An Italian physician, Giovanni Maria Lancisi, maintains that the disease is spread by the mosquitoes that are prevalent in in swampy areas.

He recommended draining marshes and swamps to eliminate them. If there are any such areas at Leatherwood, it would be advisable to drain them to prevent other members of your household from contracting the fever."

Thanking her, Henry promised to notify his overseer about the matter. "Now, I've tarried too long," he added. "I really must leave for Richmond tomorrow."

When it had become apparent that Henry was too ill to travel, General Lewis had left for Richmond alone at the beginning of the previous week to attend to pressing business of the Executive Council. Knowing that legislative matters weighed heavily on Henry's mind as well, she regarded him with concern.

"We'll see what Papa has to say. It wouldn't do for you to fall ill again somewhere along the road."

Before he could respond, Carleton strode into the room. He greeted Henry heartily and bent to give Elizabeth a quick kiss on the cheek.

Straightening, he said, "What, no food for our recovering patient?"

"I wanted to see how Patrick is feeling today first," Elizabeth remonstrated. "He's much better, and I was just about to fill a plate for him." She took in Carleton's buckskins and windblown appearance. "Wherever you've been, it appears to have been a fast ride."

Carleton pulled off the woven headband that held back his long hair and absently combed the tangled strands back with his fingers. "Devil needed a good run, and it's such a fine morning that I thought I'd ride down to the pickets at the valley's entrance. Everything's quiet," he added sharing a significant look with her as he shoved the headband into the pouch hanging from his belt.

He drew a sealed letter from it and extended it to Henry. "My messenger returned from Leatherwood just as I rode in."

Brightening, Henry took it and broke the seal. "Thank you again for advising Dolly of my illness," he said as he eagerly scanned the page.

"She needed to know." Motioning to Elizabeth to remain seated, Carleton went to the sideboard and loaded a plate with steaming portions of ham, potatoes, eggs, and toast from the chafing dishes.

"Dolly directs me to thank all of you for your thoughtful message and for caring for me," Henry said, looking up, as Carleton set the plate in front of him. "Happily she and the children are all doing well."

"I hope we'll be able to meet them soon," Elizabeth said.

Carleton returned to the sideboard to fill a plate for her and another for himself, while she came to pour coffee for both of them. "If you're serious about leaving tomorrow and traveling so far, Pat, you'd better eat up," Carleton said. "Build up your strength for the journey."

"My pleasure," Henry responded with a twinkle in his eyes. He spread quince marmalade from a crock on the table onto his toast, one eye cocked at Carleton. "Have you decided to come with me?"

Carleton delivered Elizabeth's plate as she sat down, took the cup she offered, and sat across from her and Henry. "As I don't think it wise for you to ride all that way alone, I'll see you safely delivered to Richmond."

Henry sliced his ham. "You do know that everyone in the legislature will be eager to hear from you. Especially Tom," he added before taking a bite.

Carleton swallowed a forkful of crisply browned potatoes, wiped his mouth on his serviette, and shook his head. "There's not much I can tell them that they don't already know. Besides, I can't spare the time. I'll need to return straightaway." Dismissing the matter, he dug into his eggs.

When Henry directed a questioning glance at Elizabeth, she said firmly, "In any case, Papa will decide whether it's wise for you to leave tomorrow or rest for another day or two. He's at the hospital, and we'll speak with him after we finish our breakfast."

✳ ✳ ✳

As it happened, Henry's health remained stable. With Dr. Howard's approval, the two men and their servants rode away early the following morning, carrying with them a quantity of Peruvian fever tree bark in case Henry's symptoms returned.

A thin overcast blown in on a hot, desultory wind from the coast muted the sun high overhead on Friday, 19 May, when they passed between the steep hills that ringed Richmond. They drew their mounts to a halt in front of the substantial but unimpressive building that housed the state's new capital.

Carleton vividly remembered the scene that had taken place five years earlier, not long after his return to the colonies from England. Brief weeks before the clash between British Regulars and American militia at Lexington and Concord—into which he and Andrew had unwillingly been dragged—the two of them had sat in a pew in one of the town's churches while Henry, in a moment of high drama, warned Virginia's legislators that war with Britain was about to begin.

They entered the chamber where the House of Delegates was meeting in time for Henry to immediately take his seat—and the reins of leadership in that body. Enthusiastically welcomed by all, he plunged headlong into legislative matters, while Carleton went with Stowe and Henry's black body servant to stable their horses and leave their baggage at the lodgings Lewis had secured for them. Carleton then returned as promised, fully intending to remain in the background as much as possible until he could slip out of town—a vain hope, it quickly became apparent.

As soon as Henry saw him reenter the chamber, he broke from a discussion with Richard Henry Lee and other leading members of the House to introduce Carleton to them and to a number of other delegates who passed by. Among them was Henry's brother-in-law Colonel William Campbell.

Everyone was well acquainted with Carleton's exploits, an inauspicious sign. Inevitably, making every effort to repress his exasperation, he reluctantly gave in to demands that he speak before the gathered House and Executive Council the following day.

Accordingly, the next afternoon he stood at the head of the packed chamber, sweltering in full uniform despite every window being thrown open to the sluggish, muggy air that infrequently stirred. A few delegates went so far as to throw off their coats, but the majority doggedly endured the heat and humidity, only acknowledging their discomfort by occasionally mopping the dripping perspiration from their flushed faces with damp handkerchiefs.

Carleton presented a detailed report of his meetings with Washington at Morristown; the army's want of every necessity; continuing French, Dutch, and Spanish aid in the war; and the expectation of a French fleet soon appearing. He concluded by outlining the deteriorating situation on the western frontier and its causes, which he painted in such unsparing detail that many of the members shifted uncomfortably in their seats.

The clamor that followed dragged out the session from one hour to more than two. His patience steadily eroding, he answered questions and comments with all the diplomacy he was capable of, including details of his meetings with Louis XVI and Vergennes in Paris and, once again, the battle at Flamborough Head and his impressions of John Paul Jones. Inwardly he cursed his decision to ever set foot in the town.

Not satisfied, the members of the executive council then pressed him with questions about his privateers, Caledonne, and what he knew about the operation of French and British spies, to which he responded with evasive answers he hoped were plausible enough to satisfy them. At length, in a tone that raised Carleton's hackles, one of the delegates from the southern counties brought up the subject of his enlisting black troops and Indians in his Rangers.

Evenly, but with an edge of steel in his voice, he answered, "I have always believed that all men are created equal and are endowed by their

Creator with the unalienable right to life, liberty, and the pursuit of happiness."

He noted that a scattering of men across the chamber conceded a smile, whether ironic or rueful, as he quoted the nation's Declaration of Independence back to them. In the front row Henry regarded Carleton over his spectacles, eyebrows raised.

"Let it be noted," he said mildly, "that free Blacks who hold manumission papers are enlisted into our Virginia Regiment."

Carleton made a graceful half bow. "So I've heard, to my pleasure, Mr. Henry. As an officer of the Continental Army, I don't believe in wasting manpower that can be put to effective use in securing our nation's independence. I've also found that my Blacks and Indians consistently rank among my best troops."

A caustic voice reached him from the back of the room. "You're certain that all your Blacks are indeed free men?"

"I am," Carleton answered, reflecting with satisfaction that all former slaves under his command were from the northern states and were now, in fact, free because he had made them so.

No.

He turned his gaze beyond the rows of tables and chairs that crowded the sun-washed chamber to a small cluster of enslaved black servants waiting just inside the door for their masters' summons, all emotion carefully erased from their faces. God had made them free and had merely used him to restore some of them to their proper place, he reminded himself. A deep humility washed over him, and a greater pleasure. Keeping his own expression masked, he returned his attention to the assembly.

Many of the delegates appeared somewhat less than convinced, but little more was said thereafter. With the session finally adjourned, he made to leave, wanting nothing more than to immediately quit that place for the road home.

To his dismay a swarm of delegates impeded his path, jostling to press yet more questions. Amazingly, however, several expressed their appreciation for his service and the report he had presented. At last he stepped out into the passage, relieved, only to have Henry pull him aside to meet his companion—Thomas Jefferson, Carleton guessed from what he'd heard of the man.

Handsome and slender, Jefferson was about Henry's height and, Carleton reckoned, close to his own age. Sandy hair and freckles, an unlined brow and long straight nose distinguished Virginia's young governor. Direct grey eyes revealed nothing of his thoughts, however, a match for his reserved manner.

Carleton had noticed him slipping inside the chamber to slouch into a chair at its back, the last to enter before the session began. Displaying little sign of interest in the proceedings, he had made no comment nor asked any questions. Now he fixed Carleton in a piercing gaze while Henry introduced them. They exchanged bows.

"I'm guessing you're as eager to escape this political bog as I am," Jefferson said, a faint smile lifting the corners of his mouth.

"Am I that transparent?"

"Only to one who shares the sentiment."

"Tom much prefers wielding a pen to oratory," Henry observed.

"I'm happy to leave that office to you, Pat," Jefferson responded equably.

Carleton had heard that after qualifying as an attorney Jefferson had been elected as a representative to Virginia's House of Burgesses before the colonies had broken away from royal rule. In 1775, as one of a number of Burgesses opposed to Britain's harsh policies that included Henry and Washington, he had been named a delegate to the second Continental Congress. Regarded its silent member, he had written the first draft of the Declaration of Independence. After receiving the rank of colonel in his county's militia, he had been elected to the newly formed Virginia House of Delegates and a year ago had succeeded Henry as governor.

Jefferson noticed Lewis pushing through the exiting throng and beckoned him to join them. Leading the way down the passage, he ushered them into a smaller chamber at its end that evidently served as his office and closed the door behind them.

The room was sparely furnished, a large desk in front of the window strewn with papers and books, a couple of tall bookshelves half-filled with more books, and several upholstered chairs. A silver tray on which sat a full decanter and a cluster of glasses topped a small cabinet.

When all were seated with a glass of bourbon in hand, Jefferson said to Carleton, "You've given us much to consider, general. Thank you for bearing with our contentious members."

Carleton returned a bland smile. "I've had considerable experience in battle."

Jefferson and Henry exchanged glances, mouths quirked, while Lewis studiously considered the amber fluid he swirled in his glass.

"The session did rather give the impression of armed combat, didn't it?" Henry remarked, a twinkle in his eyes. "If not ambush."

"You think I didn't expect their reaction?" The men's chuckles eased Carleton's tension, and he allowed himself to relax.

"You certainly made an impression."

Noting the irony that tinged Jefferson's tone, Carleton said, "That wasn't my intent. I'd rather motivate our delegates to take action."

Henry nodded approval. "That's always been my aim in speaking."

"I'll never forget the speech you gave before the House in this same town five years ago. You set our countrymen on the path to independence, me included, though few of us fully realized it at the time."

"A few of us had designs on it even then."

"It's been a long road," Jefferson put in with a sigh. "God willing, we'll make it to the end."

"Give me liberty or give me death," Carleton quoted Henry's speech dryly. "If the army doesn't receive provisions quickly, the latter may yet be our fate. The men were on the point of mutiny when I left Morristown and may well have done it by now. I know you sent Washington all the supplies you had at hand while governor, Pat. You kept us going, and everyone was grateful for it."

Turning to Jefferson, he continued, "We need everything you can spare now if His Excellency is not to be forced into disbanding the army. The men are literally starving."

He pretended not to note that Jefferson stiffened, his lips tightening and his color rising. "We do as much as we can for Virginia's regiment, but our militias are in equally dire straits, as General Lewis can testify."

Lewis looked up, his expression glum. "You've never seen such an ill-looking, scarecrow, rag-tag body of men as the great majority of our militias, Carleton, not even the Continentals. They've hardly any ammunition for the few worn-out muskets and rifles they've collected between them."

Over the next half hour they discussed the thorny military issues confronting them, leaving Carleton less than encouraged

At last Jefferson said, "Your assessment of the situation on the frontier particularly interests me, general. Over the years I've become personally acquainted with a number of Indians, among them the Cherokee chief Ontasseté—you may know of him."

When Carleton acknowledged that he did, Jefferson continued, "He used to stop by my estate at Shadwell on his way to Williamsburg to trade, and we became good friends. We had many frank conversations about the native people's situation, and I assure you I'm not unsympathetic to their plight. Indeed I greatly respect men such as Ontasseté who are open to reason. But as to those who continue their depredations along our frontiers, particularly the Shawnee, our first obligation is to protect our own settlers who are suffering intolerably from their attacks."

Carleton wrestled his ire under control. When he began to speak Jefferson raised his hand to forestall him.

"I'll be as frank with you as Ontasseté always was with me," he continued grimly. "As long as the Ohio Shawnee maintain their allegiance to the British and continue to raid our border settlements, they leave us no alternative. We're making every effort to turn the other tribes against them, but failing that, the only recourse left us will be to drive them from their lands, even if it becomes necessary to eliminate all of them to do so. You'd do well to transmit that message to the people you call your kin."

Carleton heard him out, careful to show no emotion. For several moments the only sound in the room was the muted ticking of the ornate clock on one of the bookcases, the distant murmur of voices and closing of a door as delegates drifted off to congregate in the local taverns. Lewis's face had hardened, and Henry glanced from Jefferson to Carleton, frowning.

Finally Carleton allowed a faint smile and inclined his head. "You may be sure of it."

Their discussion at an end, Henry led the way outside onto the building's front steps, Carleton and Lewis following. It was by now late in the sweltering afternoon, the sun declining in the west, where a dark band of clouds was rising on the wind.

"As hard as it is to hear, I'm afraid Tom's right," Henry said. "I sincerely hope the Indians can be brought to end this bloodshed and make peace. But our meeting with your warriors didn't leave me feeling very hopeful on that score."

"If they won't see reason, we have to put our own people's welfare first," Lewis growled, directing a significant look at Carleton.

Squinting into the red light of the lowering sun, Carleton stared across the clustered trees and rooftops of the town and its surrounding hills. "Indeed we must," he agreed thoughtfully.

Chapter Twenty-four

"GENERAL CARLETON has returned, madam," Burns announced as Carleton followed the butler into the Great Hall, Stowe trailing.

His gaze first found Elizabeth, who stood at the Hall's center, bouncing Harry in her arms. She was surrounded by her parents; Morning Dew, who held Julianne; and Yellow Feather. With a start he saw that Teissèdre stood with them, looking as windblown, dusty, and trail-stained as he was.

"Thank God you're here, Jon!" Dr. Howard exclaimed.

It struck Carleton then that Elizabeth and her parents appeared unnaturally pale, as though they had undergone some shock, and his gut clenched. He had barely time to exchange glances with Elizabeth, however, before Harry squealed, squirming in her arms and reaching for him, while Julianne fussed and did the same.

He crossed the Hall quickly to take Harry and lightly kiss Elizabeth on the lips, propriety be hanged. Morning Dew relinquished Julianne, sobbing inconsolably by now, to his free arm. Heart swelling despite a nagging foreboding, he held both babies close to his heart, one on each arm, as they burrowed into him, babbling happily. He kissed each small brow, thinking that surely they'd grown in just the week and a half he'd been gone.

"I'm so glad you're home," Elizabeth murmured, her face upturned to his.

Reluctantly he relinquished the twins to Yellow Feather and Morning Dew, who bore them quickly off upstairs, their objections echoing across the Hall. Ignoring the others he drew Elizabeth into his arms and gave her another kiss for good measure, lingering this time, aware that her parents looked discreetly away, smiling. Only Teissèdre's taut expression did not change.

Finally releasing Elizabeth, he rounded on his agent. "When did you get here?"

"Not half an hour since." The Frenchman pulled out a handkerchief, mopped his glistening face and bald pate, and tugged down his rumpled shirt, reminding Carleton of his own disordered state.

"Charles should be here shortly," Dr. Howard intervened. "I sent for him at once, but he was out with a detail. Josiah and James are on their way, and—"

He was interrupted by Carleton's aide, who just then strode into the room followed closely by McLeod, with Spencer, Isaiah, Farris, Red Fox, and Spotted Pony on their heels. Directing Burns to have wine and whatever else was on hand sent up for their refreshment, Carleton motioned to everyone to find a seat. He took one on the sofa directly across from Teissèdre, drawing Elizabeth down beside him, while Anne perched nervously on her other side.

"What's gone wrong? Charlestown?"

Teissèdre nodded, his expression glum. Hearing the mansion's front door open and bang shut, Carleton waited while Andrews hurried inside and, after apprehensively scanning all the faces turned to him, pulled a chair next to the sofa and sat.

"Lincoln surrendered the city to Clinton a fortnight ago," the Frenchman explained. "Casualties were relatively light, but more than five thousand men—both Continental soldiers and militia—were taken prisoner, denied the honors of war.

"Your Southern Army has essentially ceased to exist," he concluded wearily.

Carleton had expected the city's fall, but the confirmation struck him like a punch in the gut, made worse by the capture of almost the entire Southern Army. His spirits sank further while Teissèdre related that Lincoln and his senior officers were paroled until exchanged for British officers held by the Americans. Militia and civilian combatants also had been released on parole, but all the Continental soldiers had been consigned to prison hulks.

Aware that Elizabeth flinched and paled even more at hearing the latter, Carleton slipped his arm protectively around her shoulders.

"So our Southern Department is left without a commander and an army," he said hoarsely, briefly pressing his eyes shut and scrubbing his free hand over his face. "Why the deuce didn't Lincoln abandon that accursed place while it was still possible? No matter how many cities the British take, as long as we've an army in the field they have to reckon with us at an unsustainable cost of men and money."

"A wise policy," Teissèdre agreed, "as Washington has proven time and again. But your Congress insisted that the city must be saved, and—"

"Then let *them* man the fortifications!"

Teissèdre rubbed his chin thoughtfully. "An interesting proposition. However, Charlestown's leaders advised Lincoln that should he attempt to abandon them, they'd throw open the city's gates to Clinton, essentially handing his entire force over to the enemy."

"I'd have cast the entire lot into the gaol, removed every soldier I had from there, and let Clinton have that nest of vipers!" Carleton fumed.

"Bah! Lincoln's hardly the man for the job, though to give credit where due he did manage to send some of your Continentals and South Carolina militia forces out of the city before it was entirely cut off. The irony is that, with the last avenue of escape sealed and the British bombardment beginning to smash up their precious town, those same city leaders began to cry for Lincoln to negotiate favorable terms of surrender on their behalf."

Carleton gave a harsh laugh. "With Clinton holding all the cards? Good luck to them."

Teissèdre conceded a rueful smile. "Alas, fortune failed them."

Springing to his feet, Carleton paced across the Hall and back. "If I were superstitious, I'd count the rumors that reached Richmond just before I left to be a portent of this disaster and possibly more yet to come."

Everyone fixed him in puzzled looks that changed to confusion, and then astonishment as he recounted reports brought to Williamsburg by travelers from the north of a strange darkness that had gripped the New England states a week earlier. A dirty yellow tinge had reddened the sun for several days, while the skies remained clear and cold temperatures settled over the region.

In the early morning hours of 19 May, clouds and thundershowers blew in on a southwest wind, and a foreboding darkness progressively spread across the land. Birds began their evening songs, finally fell silent and retreated to their nests. Chickens sought their roosts, cows their barns, and frogs began peeping.

So deep was the gloom that travel became difficult. Reports that Judgment Day was at hand flew from town to town.

"Well, all's not gloom and doom, Jon," Andrews broke in when the others' amazed exclamations subsided. He pulled a packet of papers from his pocket, which he handed to Carleton. "A messenger arrived from Washington yesterday with this."

Carleton unfolded the report and began to scan it, while Andrews explained, "According to the courier, Lafayette returned from France a fortnight ago. His negotiations were successful, and le Comte de Rochambeau is on his way to Newport with six ships of the line and an army of six thousand men."

"Things are bound to take a turn for the better regardles of Charlestown's fall."

Carleton looked up from the reports to meet Elizabeth's hopeful gaze. "I hope you're right, dearest. But the British now hold two ports on our southern shores to which they can deliver soldiers and materiel. Savannah gives them free access to Georgia, Charlestown to the Carolinas, and sooner or later they'll turn their attention north." He beckoned to Stowe and sent him to retrieve a map of the Carolinas from his study.

Questioned by Andrews as to how he had come by his intelligence, Teissèdre explained that before Charlestown's surrender he had linked up with Colonel Buford on the city's outskirts. Carleton remembered Abraham Buford from a long discussion they'd had at Morristown. A fellow Virginian, the thirty-three-year-old colonel had been assigned to take the Third Virginia Regiment south to Charlestown.

Arriving too late to help oppose the British assault, Buford had been ordered to fall all the way back to Hillsborough, North Carolina, within roughly forty miles of Virginia's southern border. Teissèdre had also learned that Clinton planned to return to New York as soon as Charlestown and its vicinity were fully secured, leaving General Lord Charles Cornwallis behind to subdue the rest of the state. And, in fact, Cornwallis was already marching toward Camden with a substantial force, which would place him on a direct route to Charlotte, North Carolina.

Carleton exchanged a look with Elizabeth, whose expression reflected his own concern.

Before she could speak, Anne said fearfully, "How long can it take them to subdue North Carolina? And then they'll have us in their sights!"

Dr. Howard frowned. "I suspect the British won't find quite as much loyalty to the king in the Carolinas as they suppose. From what I've heard, there's considerable rebel sentiment in the backcountry settlements."

"I believe you're right," Andrews agreed gloomily. "But much of the backcountry is very poor, full of swamps, settled by Scots-Irish and German immigrants. I doubt their ability to raise, equip, and maintain militia that can stand against the British. With what's left of our Southern Army in complete disarray and scattered who knows where, any militia they can raise will be entirely on their own, at least until Congress assigns a new commander and reinforcements can be brought in. And we all know how well provisioned our army is."

Hutchinson pointed out hopefully that the French would bring with them at least some supplies for the American Army—when they finally arrived. It remained to be seen how deeply the British could penetrate into the Carolinas and beyond in the meantime, McLeod countered with a scowl.

British Army's politics might just work in the Americans' favor, Teissèdre speculated. The British government had little confidence in Clinton, and he in turn had become suspicious of Cornwallis's ambitions. It didn't help that since being passed over for the command in Clinton's favor, Cornwallis had informed Clinton that he didn't wish to share responsibility for the decisions his commander made and had withdrawn his counsel, confining himself to his assigned duties.

Best of all, Clinton had issued a proclamation that all those paroled must swear allegiance to the crown and serve whenever called on to maintain His Majesty's government in South Carolina. That should effectively turn many of those whose allegiance was waffling against the British.

Carleton listened silently to the ensuing discussion in which the others shared their opinions, concerns, and speculations. "How long will you stay, Louis?" he cut them off at last.

"I'm bound for France and must leave in the morning. It's necessary for Caledonne to know of these developments as quickly as possible."

"And Sartine," Carleton noted dryly, to which Teissèdre merely shrugged.

Turning to Hutchinson, Carleton directed him to write a detailed summary of Teissèdre's intelligence with Spencer's help. The two aides were then to make four fair copies, one for Carleton and the other three for him to add comments and sign, these to be sent by courier the following day to Governor Jefferson, Henry, and Washington.

"Add that Charles and I will leave for the Southern Army's headquarters at Salisbury, North Carolina, within a couple of days," he concluded.

"We'll take at least one troop?" Andrews broke in quickly.

Carleton directed an assessing glance from Isaiah to Farris. After ordering the latter to prepare his best cavalry troop for the journey and Red

Fox his warriors, he added the aides, McLeod, and Dr. Howard to their company.

"We'll want tents, extra weapons, ammunition, food, and any other supplies needed for at least a fortnight and the wagons to carry them," he told the aides. "With the situation in the Carolinas changing fast, I can't guarantee where we'll end up, but in any case there'll be little, if any, forage available along the way at this time of year. Take that into account.

"And be prepared as well to weather the devil's own heat," he concluded wryly. "If you consider it hot here in the mountains, you'll think you've stumbled into Hades itself if we end up venturing into the Carolina lowlands."

After spending as much time as possible with the twins, he and Elizabeth clung to each other with greater passion that night, each dreading the uncertainties, dangers, and separations that faced them in the months to come. Sleep evaded them, and they rose before daybreak the next morning to find Teissèdre already gone.

Chapter Twenty-five

S UN-BLINDED, CARLETON stepped through the open door into the
Southern Army's headquarters and came to an abrupt halt, vaguely
registering that Andrews and Farris almost collided with him from
behind. The shadowed shape of a man blocked his path, evidently on his
way out.

It was late afternoon on Tuesday, 30 May. In spite of doors and windows flung wide, it was even more wiltingly hot inside the house if that
was possible. Not a breath of wind stirred to provide relief. Carleton reckoned it would scorch them if it did.

He pulled off his helmet, as did his companions, and swiped the
trickling sweat from his brow with the back of his free hand. As his sight
adjusted to the dimmer light, he registered that the face of the man in
front of him was deeply weathered with hawk-like features and piercing
eyes. And a scowl. He grudgingly moved back to allow Carleton and his
companions entry, his black manservant sidestepping behind him.

Carleton eyed the man's worn blue regimental coat with its scarlet-
facings and the jaunty cock's feather tucked into his hatband. In turn, the
officer looked down his long, aquiline nose, eyebrows raised as he took
in the three of them from their blond-horsehair-crested green leather helmets to their knee-length black boots.

He doffed his hat and favored them with a stiff bow, which they
duly returned. "Thomas Sumter at your service, sirs, formerly lieutenant

colonel commandin' South Carolina's Second Regiment o' Riflemen,"
he announced in a gruff voice. "And you are—" He waited expectantly.

Carleton exchanged an amused glance with Andrews before introducing himself and his companions.

"Carleton?" Sumter exclaimed. "Imagine that. For a moment I thought
Tarleton must'a caught up with me, but he'd be green jacketed. Don't
believe I've heard o' you."

"I can't say I've heard of you either," Carleton returned with exaggerated politeness.

They were interrupted by a tall, handsome man Carleton guessed to
be in his mid twenties. Elegant in appearance and movement, with a
noble bearing and commanding presence, he emerged from a nearby
room and strode over to them. Saluting Carleton and his officers, he
introduced himself as Major William Richardson Davie and welcomed
them warmly, his cultured accent tinged with a faint Scottish burr.

Turning to Sumter with a smile, he said good-naturedly, "Not heard
of General Carleton, Tom? Why, he and his Rangers and privateers have
made themselves famous—or infamous, dependin' on whether you're
patriot or Loyalist. You can't have missed the newspaper articles detailin'
all the excitement. He was with Commodore Jones when he raided the
English coast last fall and captured one of His Majesty's newest frigates."

Sumter again scanned Carleton from head to foot, his gaze speculative. "Why, so he was!" he crowed. "And now the great hero's deigned to
favor us with his presence. We'll be all agog to see what exploits you've
in store for us down here in the backcountry, general."

There was an edge to Sumter's pronouncement that his hearty tone
and smile didn't conceal. It turned Carleton cold, and he felt Andrews
and Farris stiffen beside him.

"I'm sorry to disappoint you, sir, but I haven't any 'exploits' planned
—not for the Carolinas at least," he drawled, his tone freezing.

He deliberately turned to face Davie. "I had a man with Buford who
brought me a report on Charlestown's fall a few days ago. I've come to

gather intelligence for General Washington on what Clinton is currently up to and to determine what, if any, resistance is being mounted by the Carolina militias and whatever remains of our Southern Army."

As he was speaking, Davie and Sumter glanced through the open door at the scene outside, squinting against the blinding sunlight at the clusters of Rangers, warriors, and horses languishing in any spot of shade they could find on the sun-baked, tree-dotted green across the street. Carleton followed their gaze, noting that the company of ragged, gaunt militia soldiers who had loitered there when his detachment rode in now mingled with his troopers, gesturing toward his detail's laden wagons.

They had traveled the dusty, rutted Great Wagon Road 150 miles down from Big Lick, through the Maggoty Gap, then along the eastern edge of the Blue Ridge and across the North Carolina border to Salisbury. The center of the local judicial and militia district, the small town occupied the intersection of ancient Indian trading paths in the state's Central Piedmont.

The farther south they had gone, the more the road had been clogged with travelers. Most were headed north with wagons crowded with household goods, some driving livestock ahead of them—running from the northward sweep of Clinton's army, they learned on questioning some of the passersby.

"We can make good use of any supplies you're able to spare, gentlemen, particularly food," Davie said hopefully. "Harvest is a good ways off, and pickin's hereabouts are mighty slim."

"We're traveling light, with only enough provisions for our journey here and back," Andrews intervened quickly.

Movement outside caught Carleton's attention. McLeod and Dr. Howard had broken away from the detachment and were striding toward the house, their expressions strained. On entering they hastily saluted the other officers before drawing Carleton, Andrews, and Farris aside.

Without preamble McLeod said in an undertone, "The militia are pleadin' for food. They say it's been days since they've had anythin' at all to eat, and then there was little of it."

"The men's appearance backs up the claim," Dr. Howard vouched, his concern evident.

Carleton directed a glance at Andrews, whose shoulders slumped in resignation. Turning back to the two men, Carleton said quietly, "Give them as much as we can spare."

"Just mind the distance we have to travel back as we'll not be able to replace any shortage," Farris cautioned.

"No ammunition or weapons," Carleton added firmly.

Dr. Howard hesitated. "One has a festering wound on his leg that needs to be looked after. And a couple are sick with fever."

"Do what you can for them, of course, Samuel."

Both men saluted and hurried back outside.

Sumter watched the proceedings with apparent indifference, but Davie's expression softened. "Thank you, general. Both our militia and Continentals are in dire want of food, clothin', arms, and ammunition, and we've nothin' to give them."

Briskly he continued, "Come into the office where we can talk privately. We'll fill you in on everythin' we know about what Clinton's up to. Hopefully your report will move General Washington to send us reinforcements, supplies—and a more effective commander for this department."

He ushered Carleton and his officers into the spacious room from which he had emerged. Appearing originally to have been a parlor, it now served as an office. Sumter motioned to his servant to wait outside and sauntered after them.

"As far as reinforcements are concerned," Carleton told them, "His Excellency sent two brigades south a little more than a month ago—the Maryland and Delaware lines. They're our most experienced, battle-hardened troops, and with General De Kalb in command they'll stand up against anything the British can throw at them."

In Carleton's opinion Major General Jean De Kalb, another of the many French officers serving in the Continental Army, was one of Congress's happier recruits.

"We've had no word of them yet," Davie said, frowning, as they gathered around a large table strewn with paperwork and maps.

"The fact that there were no supplies available to provision his brigades might have something to do with that," Farris noted caustically.

Sumter tossed his hat onto a chair in disgust. "If they're dependin' on civilians to feed 'em 'long the way, they've starved by now!"

"As to a commander of our Southern Army, De Kalb will temporarily hold command—if he can only get here—and he's certainly up to the task," Andrews said, adding glumly, "But Congress must appoint a permanent commander as you know."

"His Excellency recommended General Greene, who's the best choice, as far as we're concerned," Carleton put in. "Unfortunately General Gates has many supporters among the delegates. We're afraid he's likely to get the appointment because of his role at Saratoga, despite the fact that General Arnold was most responsible for that victory."

Davie unrolled a map of the Carolinas. "As much as I respect our representatives, military decisions ought to be left to the military."

"We couldn't agree more," Farris muttered.

Davie dismissed the subject with a shrug. "Our intelligence indicates Clinton sent Cornwallis north to pacify the country and establish strongholds." Bending over the map, he indicated the locations he referred to. "Last we heard two weeks ago he crossed the Santee River at Lenud's Ferry, here, on his way to Camden, up here. That's the same road General Buford took ten days earlier carryin' Governor Rutledge and some members of his council with him."

"It's Tarleton I'm concerned with right now," Sumter broke in, referring to Lieutenant Colonel Banastre Tarleton. Pulling out a handkerchief,

he mopped the sweat from his face. "I was with my family at our summer home in the Santee River's High Hills when Charlestown fell. Two
days ago my son raced home from a neighbor's to warn us that Tarleton
was hightailin' it in our direction with near three hundred men. Appears
Cornwallis sent him on ahead to intercept Buford."

"With Buford having a ten-day lead?" Carleton questioned. "And in
this heat?"

"Tarleton has a reputation for drivin' men and horses hard when
he's on the hunt," Davie returned, expression and tone grim.

"I didn't wait for him to stop by my place to introduce hisself and
explain how he got there so fast," Sumter continued dismissively. "Thought
I'd come on up here instead and apply for authorization to raise militia
to fight him."

"That name's familiar," Andrews mused. "Wasn't Tarleton with the
patrol that captured General Charles Lee back in '76?"

Farris nodded. "I believe you're right."

"Wouldn't know 'bout that, but he's makin' quite a name for hisself
as commander o' the British Legion. Some call 'em Tarleton's Raiders.
They're provincials, trained and paid by the British, and all tricked out in
green. A company o' the Seventeenth Light Dragoons is ridin' with 'em
for good measure, lookin' as purty in their scarlet coats as redbirds in a
holly bush."

"Well, then, here's hoping the stars align for us to meet up with our
old regiment!" Andrews exclaimed, giving Carleton a significant look. "I
wouldn't mind getting a shot at them." When Sumter and Davie appeared
startled, Andrews explained that he and Carleton had served with the
17th at Boston when the war began.

Sumter's eyes narrowed. "Tarleton and Carleton. It'll sure be inter-
estin' to see what comes o' a match 'tween the two o' you."

"I wouldn't give you odds on that happening anytime soon," Carleton snapped. "For one thing, we've no authorization for any action in
the Carolinas."

"That may change," Davie countered. "If Tarleton was nearin' Tom's place two days ago, then he's got to be close to catchin' up with Buford, if he hasn't already." He put his finger on the border between North and South Carolina. "They couldn't be too far from the Waxhaws, which means they'd be maybe eighty miles south of us right about now. Fast as Tarleton's travelin' . . . " He shook his head, letting the comment hang on the heavy air.

Carleton exchanged sober glances with his officers.

"I decided not to sit around wonderin' what Clinton's next move is goin' to be, so I raised a company of cavalry to operate hereabouts. Tom's proposin' to do the same down south across here—" Davie pointed out the respective areas on the map.

"After layin' 'round home the past couple o' years, I figure I might as well see what I can do to pull a knot in Clinton's tail," Sumter broke in, giving a short laugh.

Davie gave an approving nod. "There are many other partisan troops formin' throughout the Carolinas as well, some Tory, but more patriot."

"The British are convinced the South is a hotbed of loyalist sympathy," Andrews said gleefully, "but I'll wager they're going to find out they've waded into a snake pit."

Sumter snickered. "You're right 'bout that. Goin' to be a mean fight in the Carolinas, and it'll take men who're mean to fight it. Backcountry down here's full o' desperate men—liars, cheaters, murderers, and worse."

I wonder which kind you are, Carleton thought as Sumter continued.

"Plenty o' families are divided right down the middle in their loyalties. It'll be like wrestling wild hawgs in a swamp, no holds barred and pardon never asked or offered. There's bound to be bloodlettin' like you never seen."

A profound silence greeted his words. Davie appeared to be sunk in thought, but after a moment he looked up and studied Carleton speculatively.

"Since De Kalb and his brigades are nowhere in sight, any chance y'all can stay a few days in case Tarleton lands on our doorstep?"

"As I said, we've no authorization for any action in the Carolinas. I didn't bring enough men or supplies for full-scale battle."

Even as Carleton spoke, however, he was rapidly calculating distances, travel times, and possibilities. Buford was headed to Hillsborough, roughly ninety miles northeast, and judging from what he'd just learned about Tarleton, it was guaranteed that he would stay hot on Buford's heels until he cornered him. If they hadn't connected yet, they might well do so in Salisbury's vicinity.

He weighed the odds, avoiding Andrews' and Farris's intent gazes. With his warriors and Rangers, he had around a hundred men on hand, plus Davie's cavalry troop for backup. That was still significantly short of the detachment Tarleton was reported to have.

That was without taking into account Buford's column, which had outnumbered Tarleton's when Buford began his retreat. But if he and Tarleton had already clashed . . .

Evidently reading his thoughts, Andrews drew him aside. "Admit it," he said in an undertone. "You're as hot for this contest as I am."

"That may be so, Charles," Carleton conceded, "but we've no idea where either Tarleton or Buford are, whether they've met up, or what happened if they did. Cornwallis is moving on Camden, which puts him on the road to Charlotte, with Virginia undoubtedly his ultimate goal. I don't want to get mired in a useless action here when we're assigned to Virginia's defense. If Buford's column happened to be put out of action, we'd be badly outnumbered, and I'm not picking a fight we can't win."

A PRIVATE CONVERSATION with Davie later left Carleton even more favoribly impressed with the man. A couple of years earlier, when Charlestown had faced the threat of a British attack that never came, Davie had taken brief leave from studying law at Salisbury to serve in the North

Carolina militia. The previous spring he had again left his studies to help raise a local cavalry troop, which was attached to General Casimir Pułaski's legion to halt a British advance toward Charlestown following Savannah's fall. Promoted to major and commanding a cavalry brigade, Davie had led a charge against British forces at Stono Ferry outside the city, where he suffered a serious wound and narrowly escaped capture. Afterward he had returned to Salisbury to complete his legal studies during his convalescence and obtained a license to practice law before raising another troop of cavalry that spring.

That night in the oppressive heat Carleton's detachment camped in the open air with pickets posted well out in all directions. He got little sleep, pondering further lengthy, inconclusive discussions with Davie, Sumter, several other local officers, and his own about the current situation and their next move.

Davie's modest demeanor, quiet resolution, and obvious competence greatly impressed Carleton. In the minus column, none of the other officers in the area that they met with did. Sumter especially rubbed Carleton the wrong way, reminding him of nothing so much as the strutting, crowing gamecocks inordinately popular in the South for their bloody fights, the feather in his hat heightening the comparison. Still, Carleton mused, if the man possessed a cock's spirit, he might prove to be a valuable asset if it came to a lopsided fight.

In the end he might as well have slept soundly. Shortly after he downed a meager breakfast the next morning, two pickets escorted one of Buford's soldiers into camp. The sergeant's bloodied, disheveled state and wild-eyed, lathered horse testified to a hard-fought battle and a swift, unsparing ride.

It was as Davie had speculated. Tarleton's Legion had caught up with the Third Virginia at the Waxhaws just south of the North Carolina border a couple of days earlier, the sergeant gasped out as Sumter and Davie came running. The two officers had to push their way through the crowd of Rangers and warriors jostling for position to hear him describe how Tarleton had pressed an immediate, savage assault against Buford's larger force.

"They drove through our rear guard like it warn't there. Fer some danged reason we was formed up in a single line and ordered to hold our fire till the enemy was so close we only had time fer one volley!" he spat out, fury mingled with anguish.

Although their fire had cut down many of the enemy's men and horses, the loyalist dragoons had literally ridden the Virginians down, obliterating their line, the sergeant continued. Casualties had mounted so rapidly that Buford had called for quarter, a plea to which Tarleton's Legion had responded by brutally hacking their countrymen to death with their sabres and bayoneting the fallen for good measure. Buford had finally managed to draw off his few surviving soldiers and escape, bringing Governor Rutledge and his council members with them.

Sickened, Carleton reflected on Sumter's comments about the divided loyalties within families and between friends in the Carolina backcountry unleashing widespread bloodletting. It was certain that as the news of this massacre spread, Sumter's prophesy would be fulfilled.

Haltingly, the sergeant related that during their flight word had reached them that Tarleton had sent a detachment to Sumter's home while on his way to intercept Buford. Finding Sumter absent, Tarleton's men had looted the house and burned it to the ground, thankfully sparing his wife, children, and slaves. At this news Sumter's knees would have buckled had Davie not gripped his shoulder to steady him.

The sergeant was quickly offered a seat and a cup of rum. Dr. Howard took inventory of his injuries and, after determining that they were not life-threatening, had one of his surgeon's mates clean and bind the man's wounds. More drink, then food and questions were pressed on him.

"Buford sent me on ahead," he mumbled between mouthfuls, his whole frame trembling. "He'n the rest ain't far behind."

✹ ✹ ✹

Within a half hour the first outriders straggled into the town. They were soon followed by Buford himself, then Governor Rutledge and his council. On their heels came the mauled remnant of the Third Virginia line. Uniforms ragged, filthy, and soaked with blood and sweat, they sagged in the saddle, most of them wounded, many badly.

"He had what—three hundred fifty men?" Andrews said hoarsely. "There can't be more than a quarter of them left!"

Heart clenching, Carleton noted that the rage boiling through him also played across the faces of his officers and troopers. Only his warriors' expressions remained impassive.

As Buford and his companions dismounted, Davie and Sumter hurried over to them. Carleton ordered McLeod and Dr. Howard to see to the needs of Buford's men, then went with Andrews and Farris to join the other officers.

Buford exchanged salutes with Davie and Sumter. His face drawn and weary, he expressed his relief at reaching Salisbury. A smile bloomed across his face when he turned to see Carleton and his companions.

He clasped their hands in turn, then said to Carleton, "I thought I recognized your Rangers when we rode up. Thank God you're here—I've never seen a more welcome sight!"

"Is Tarleton behind you?"

Buford pulled off his hat and ran his fingers through his sweat-drenched hair. "He didn't pursue. Must've figured he'd done enough damage to put us out of action," he concluded bitterly.

"He did what he was sent to do and most likely headed back toward Camden to rejoin Cornwallis," Davie said.

Carleton nodded in agreement. "Your sergeant told us what happened."

The colonel's face fell. "It was a massacre, pure and simple. There's no other word for it. After watching Tarleton cut apart General Huger's command at Monck's Corner, I should have known—"

"No self-recriminations, Abe. There's no justification for butchery."

Buford swallowed and nodded, not meeting Carleton's gaze. "I'm determined to learn from it," he said gruffly. "I'll be better prepared next time."

"You will be," Andrews returned firmly as the others murmured their agreement.

Chapter Twenty-six

ELIZABETH KNELT IN FRONT of the young couple huddled on stools in Blue Sky's cabin, shaking with exhaustion and fear. Their arms and legs bore scratches and bruises, and damp, muddy hems and several rents marred their ragged clothing. Their flight had clearly been long and taxing.

The slender young woman held her baby protectively against her shoulder, her dark brow creased with worry. When Elizabeth reached for him, she glanced fearfully at her husband. At his cautious nod, she relinquished the little boy.

Elizabeth settled him against her shoulder and gently rubbed his back to quiet his fussing. Looking up into their anxious faces, she said, "You're safe now, and we'll do our very best to keep you so."

"Thankee, mistress," the young mother answered, ducking her head.

Marah, the middle-aged black woman who had smuggled the little family into the valley overnight, grasped her hand and squeezed it reassuringly. Elizabeth smiled to see the young woman's tension ease as she looked wonderingly from Sarah and Jemma to Blue Sky, Rain Woman, Laughing Otter, and Sweetgrass, who clustered around them.

The man swallowed and stared at the floor. "Marah say you hide us till she can carry us to freedom."

"Izzy's mastah mean to sell him away down South—"

Elizabeth hastily raised one hand to stop her. "Don't tell us your real names or where you came from. The less any of us know, the better." Inspiration struck, and she added, "We'll call you Mary and Joseph."

The two exchanged tentative smiles, then sobered. "I live on the plantation neighborin' his," Mary explained, her low voice hitching. "We only see each other now and again though we be married. Can't bear thought of our baby never knowin' his pappy."

"Runnin' away our only hope of bein' together," Joseph volunteered.

"You got nothin' to worry 'bout," Sarah assured them. "Ain't nobody goin' to find the place where we hide you."

The baby's fussing gave way to a wail, and Elizabeth handed him back to his mother. Mary loosened her bodice and shift, and cradling him to her breast, pulled her shawl around him as he began eagerly to nurse.

It had been nearing noon on Tuesday, 6 June, when Rufus slipped into the hospital and stopped just inside the door. Noting his grave expression and that he clenched his hat with both hands in front of him, Elizabeth had quickly finished her round of patients, then led him outside.

"They come over the west ridge and walk right up to the pickets Colonel Moghrab set along the far side o' the river," he had confided. "They took 'em to Blue Sky's cabin like they was told, makin' sure nobody see anythin'."

Elizabeth's mouth had dropped open. "General Carleton told me that passing over these mountains is well nigh impossible."

"Seem like there be a pass nobody know 'bout 'cept the woman who brung 'em, name o' Marah," Rufus had returned, frowning. "Says she used to be a slave here years ago. Sarah and Jemma helpin' Salome put together food, an' Durie and your mother be gatherin' other needful supplies."

Elizabeth had immediately sent Rufus to help her mother and Durie. Acting as though nothing out of the ordinary was afoot, she had turned over the hospital's supervision to Captain Lawton and returned to the manor.

The kitchens had been a hive of activity with dinner's final preparations underway, while at the same time Salome and her maids were filling baskets of food with Sarah's and Jemma's help. Anne, Durie, and Rufus had soon joined them, bringing blankets and parcels of other necessities for the runaways' indefinite stay.

They had slipped outside through the kitchen's back door, Rufus carrying the heavier food baskets, while Elizabeth, Sarah, and Jemma divided the rest between them. Quickly skirting the hospital, they hurried down the road, screened by trees and shrubbery from view of the troops, whom Isaiah was keeping out of the way, and reached the warriors' cabins at the encampment's far end unnoticed.

When the baby had finished nursing, his father cuddled him while Mary straightened her shift and pinned her bodice back in place. They startled when a double knock sounded on the cabin's back door, Elizabeth rose, the others pushing to their feet with her.

"That's Rufus's signal that he has everything stowed in the canoes," Elizabeth assured the fugitives. "The sooner we get you safely hidden, the better."

Marah nodded. "I brung 'em the long way round through a pasture full o' cattle, then woods and up a creek, back down 'nother and 'crost shallows over the river afore we made our way to the path up the mountain. Figured to cover our route best as we could. But no use to sit 'round when somebody might come lookin' bringin' hounds."

The older woman's care in planning her mission impressed Elizabeth. She explained that all the warriors from the camp were gone with Carleton's detachment. The other women and the older girls were at work in the fields at the meadow's far side, Laughing Otter added, and she had made sure that the boys and younger children were at play near them. No one would ever know that Marah's small party had passed through the valley.

With the baby secured in his sling across his mother's back, and making sure they were not observed, the women escorted the little family down the bank behind the cabin. Several large canoes were tethered amid the reeds that grew thickly along the river's broad curve below. Rufus waited by one filled with supplies, and after Elizabeth, Jemma, and Sweetgrass were settled in it, climbed in with them. The other Shawnee women helped Sarah, Marah, and the young couple into a second vessel, then joined them. With everyone except Mary, who held her baby, wielding paddles they quickly pushed off into the river's stream.

They paddled rapidly upriver, keeping to the slower water along the bank as they passed through the uplands to the falls. After securing the canoes at the pond's edge, they shepherded their charges to the vine-shrouded cleft behind the falling water, carrying the parcels and baskets of provisions with them.

When they emerged into the hidden valley, Marah's and her charges' eyes widened even more. The three of them took in their surroundings with exclamations of wonder echoed by Sarah, Jemma, and the Shawnee women, who until now had only heard descriptions of the valley.

When Elizabeth told them that there was an equally hidden pass at the valley's far end, much easier to negotiate than the treacherous climb over the ridge, Marah let out a low, rumbling chuckle. "That goin' to make comin' an' goin' a whole lot easier—and hopefully trackin' runaways a whole lot harder!"

"General Carleton and I thought so," Elizabeth agreed with satisfaction. "He never found a navigable pass over these ridges, so the path you found must be difficult to navigate, to say the least." When Marah and the young couple admitted that it was, Elizabeth asked how Marah had discovered it.

Marah explained that after experiencing ill treatment while in bondage and witnessing the unmerciful punishment of fellow slaves far beyond anything that could be deserved, she had determined to run away. Before she could attempt it, however, she had been sold to Sir Harry.

He had turned out to be kind and reasonable, unlike her old master, but the fact remained that she was still a slave, her life and future subject to another's control. So she had begun slipping away away at night to surreptitiously scout the mountains for a way of escape.

" 'Course, I had to have moonlight to see by, and I couldn't be caught goin' out or comin' back," she said. "So it took a number o' years to find it, and I almost give up."

But then one night she followed a steep, rocky path that ascended the western ridge, she continued. At the top she found a narrow gap shrouded in trees and invisible from below. Although the way down the opposite slope had been equally treacherous, she managed to climb down to the lowlands along the Staunton River. There she fell to her knees and praised God.

It was under the Almighty's protective hand that she had found her way to City Point. She had married a free black man, and over the years had given birth to five children, all now grown.

"In all your searching you never found the entrance to this valley," Elizabeth marveled.

Marah let out a rueful sigh. "Sure wish I had. I could'a followed my heart's callin' a lot sooner. But it was too far to these uplands for me to make it up here and back in one night. I was only able to search out the ridges closest to the manor."

"None o' the other slaves ever talked about it?" Sarah questioned.

Marah shook her head. "I guess if they'd known, they would'a tried to get away. But only ones allowed to come into these uplands was those on work details, and they was watched over real strict by the overseer."

From the day of her escape she had been consumed by the longing to help free her people who groaned under bondage, she told them. During her escape she had taken careful note of the route over the mountain and had never forgotten it. And over the years she had maintained secret contact with acquaintances at Thornlea and other plantations in the area.

Several years earlier, on learning that Sir Harry's son had freed all his slaves, that sense of calling had sprung to life again. Then the previous summer she had heard that Carleton had returned to Thornlea, and it had burst into a flame that would not be quenched.

By then her husband had died, she confided to Elizabeth and the others, tears welling into her eyes. And when Carleton's servant and aide turned up at City Point secretly scouting for people willing to shelter escaping slaves and help them on their way north to freedom, she had known that the Lord had brought her all that way over all those years for his own inscrutable purposes.

Murmurs of praise punctuated her account, everyone brushing away tears. The young couple clung to her, thanking her with choked voices for her faithfulness to God's call.

They had been walking slowly down the valley's gentle curve, carrying their burdens and pausing now and then to listen intently as Marah related her story. A few more steps brought the old barn into sight, and they stopped, Elizabeth taking in the scene with renewed wonder.

Two sturdy new doors closed the barn's wide entrance, testifying to the efforts of Isaiah's troops assigned to repair the building. A short distance in front of these was a fire circle ringed with stones, and dry firewood was stacked under the barn's eaves along one side.

The men had also scythed the meadows' tangled, overgrown grasses across the narrow valley's upper half. Long windrows of sun-baked dried hay filled the valley with its sweet, heady fragrance, and nearby the broken foundation of what apparently had been a house lay exposed, the stones fallen from its walls scattered across the ground around it.

Rufus and Joseph pushed the barn doors open. Gratefully they and the women stepped out of the day's heat into the cool, dim space sheltered within the thick stone walls. Sunlight slanted in through the high windows, revealing that Isaiah's detail had been at work there too.

Just inside the door stood an iron kettle with a tripod lying beside it, which Rufus immediately carried out and set up over the fire circle. At the building's rear new rafters topped with freshly split shingles replaced the caved-in roof, and the hayloft was fully restored and stocked with hay.

Beneath it they found rude, but serviceable, table and chairs that the troops had constructed.

"This be a dream!" the young man exclaimed.

Everyone happily agreed. The women and Rufus went to work stowing baskets and parcels, then helped Marah and the couple spread mounds of hay below the hayloft, across which they spread blankets to make comfortable beds.

When the fugitives' immediate needs were taken care of, Elizabeth assured them that Rufus would check on them the next day and show Marah the way through the lower pass. At last Elizabeth and her companions reluctantly left their new charges and returned to the larger valley and to the duties that beckoned.

"This is a military encampment," Carleton said through gritted teeth, "a Continental camp, not militia, which means it's well guarded. As you can see by these gates and fortifications. No civilian enters here without my approval or that of General Andrews." He inclined his head toward Andrews, who drew his mount up beside him.

The roughly clad middle-aged man's fingers tightened over his musket, suspicion and defiance narrowing his eyes as he glanced from the two generals to his equally rough-looking younger companion. "Wagons go in and out o' here all the time—"

"Delivering goods needed for our men and the estate's establishment and carrying the estate's products to buyers," Andrews put in, to all appearances thoroughly enjoying the confrontation. "They're not smuggling slaves, if that's what you're implying."

The two men's eyes narrowed. Carleton took it that they harbored doubts as to the truthfulness of that statement.

After allowing Buford's exhausted men a day of rest and medical care, Carleton's detachment had taken four days to escort the broken regiment the ninety miles from Salisbury to the state's capital at Hillsborough, as dirty and disagreeable a hole as Carleton had ever seen. North Carolina's Board of War had its headquarters there, however, and goods collected from the vicinity for the army were stored there as well. It had consequently been crawling with Continental officers organizing wagon trains and forwarding troops south.

On their arrival they received the discouraging intelligence that British forces had swept across South Carolina. In addition to Savannah and Charlestown, they now occupied other important towns along the coast as well as strongholds in the north, west, and south. These included Camden on the direct road to Charlotte, North Carolina; and Augusta, just across the Savannah River in Georgia.

Following discussions with his officers and Buford, Carleton had turned over to the colonel as much of the ammunition, extra weapons, and food his detachment could possibly spare as well as all their tents and a wagon. Then, pushing hard, he led his detachment north, reaching the picket post at the entrance to Thornlea Valley only to face the tense dispute between the sentries and the two slave hunters.

Weary and famished from the long, unsparing ride back on quarter rations and anxious to end the discussion, Carleton enquired, "How long ago did these runaways disappear?"

"Three days ago," came the surly answer.

Carleton gestured toward the pack of panting dogs that wove restlessly around the men and their horses. "Did your hounds track them here?"

The younger man's mouth tightened to a thin line, but he grudgingly shook his head. "Ev'body knows ye freed yer slaves, and—"

"What business is that of yours?" Carleton cut him stiffly off. "They were my property to do with as I wished."

"Ye're one o' them abolitionists, I 'spect." The older man sent a stream of spittle into the dirt dangerously close to Devil's hoof. The stallion laid back his ears and sidestepped, eyes rolling.

Carleton tightened the reins in his right hand and stroked the animal's neck with the other, gently bringing him back under control.

"We heard ye employ them Irish and Highland Scotch—and even worse, Injuns! Sure don't put a good face on things." The younger man uttered the terms like curses.

Silence greeted this pronouncement. Over the course of several seconds, both men's faces tightened as the realization sank in that the tall, sun-bronzed, muscular, blond-haired, grey-eyed mounted Scot blocking their way fixed them in a coldly assessing stare that boded no good. That his carbine rested across his thighs, a sabre hung from his shoulder belt, with holstered pistols on each side of his saddle's pommel, and that he was backed up by an equally armed and grim-faced subordinate general along with several other officers, who now eased their horses forward, hands on weapons, appeared to cause a good measure of discomfort as well.

Neither did they find any reassurance in the large detachment of fully accoutered cavalrymen, and especially the Indian warriors they glanced uneasily toward, whose warlike appearance would have inspired terror in the hearts of men much braver than themselves. To say nothing of the sizeable detail of Farris's light infantry that was guarding the entrance to the valley that day, none of whom showed any inclination to give ground.

"As I said, *no one* enters here without prior approval," Carleton said softly, his tone and level gaze lethal.

"I kin see that," the older man returned in a hasty attempt at conciliation, "but they could'a come in o'er the ridge."

"I've never found any pass over these ridges," Carleton snapped, his patience at an end, "and I assure you I've explored these grounds extensively over the years. You have my personal guarantee that the fugitives you're seeking are not in this valley. Nor will any ever be, so you needn't bother returning on other occasions. Anything else?"

Evidntly there wasn't for the two men whistled to their hounds and reined their horses around, their countenances livid with anger as they galloped off.

Good humor restored, Carleton watched them thoughtfully until they disappeared from sight around a bend in the road. Then he glanced from Andrews to Dr. Howard, who rode up beside them.

"You don't suppose they might have the right of things, do you?"

Dr. Howard frowned, but his mouth twitched as though he fought to suppress a smirk. "I don't see how they could. As you pointed out, runaways are never harbored in Thornlea Valley."

Carleton reined Devil around. "I don't know about you, but I'm starving. Let's get these men fed and ourselves into the bargain."

"And find out what our wives have been up to," Andrews muttered, rubbing his chin.

"I have a feeling there's been mischief afoot, but I really don't want to hear the details," Carleton answered. "After all, I can't be held accountable for what I don't know, can I?"

Guffawing, they returned the pickets' salutes and urged their horses through the gates, past the guard's hut, and down the valley road. After them thundered the rest of the detachment, everyone suddenly in high good spirits.

Chapter Twenty-seven

THE GLASS EXPLODED against the hot firebricks at the back of the study's fireplace, Carleton's bitter curse echoing the impact. Elizabeth gasped and flinched away as glittering, knife-sharp shards flew across the granite hearth and amber liquid vaporized with a harsh sizzle on the seething logs.

Standing on her grandmother's lap, Julianne collapsed into her arms, screaming. Harry, who had been clutching his grandfather's hands while staggering across the carpet with clumsy steps, immediately plopped onto the floor, adding his wails to his sister's. Yellow Feather sprang from her knees in front of the boy, snatched him up, and sought refuge beside Elizabeth's mother on the sofa, Morning Dew scurrying after her.

"Jonathan! Your language!" Anne gathered the two maidens in her arms with their heads on her shoulders and the twins sheltered between them.

Carleton rounded to find himself the focus of the women's wide-eyed, reproachful gazes. His babies turned terrified glances on him before burying their faces against their grandmother's breast. Even ten-month-old Aileana clutched her mother, her face scrunched in alarm.

Dr. Howard, Isaiah, Farris, and McLeod stared at him in astonishment, mouths agape. Red Fox and Spotted Pony had stiffened as well, eyes narrowing. Only Andrews appeared more amused than surprised.

"Excuse me," Carleton muttered grudgingly, too furious to repent. That Andrews returned a smirk to his glare only fueled his outrage.

"Sorry, Jon," Andrews snickered. "It's just that you so rarely give in to a fit of temper."

"I dare say you won't be laughing at this news!" Carleton growled, biting off each word as he brandished the crumpled pages clenched in his fist.

Having regained her composure, Elizabeth sidled up to him and extracted the papers from his hand as she murmured soothingly, "Dearest, what could possibly be worse than Lincoln's losing Charlestown only to be followed by General Gates' debacle at Camden, and now Cornwallis's occupation of Charlotte? All in hardly more than three months."

It was mid afternoon on Thursday, 5 October. The previous evening Carleton and a detachment including all the officers in the room except Isaiah had returned from Hillsborough, where South Carolina's governor, John Rutledge, had established his government in exile. It was the most recent of several forays Carleton had made over the summer and early fall to gather intelligence, and they had arrived at the town only to learn that a couple of days earlier Cornwallis had crossed the border into North Carolina. Despite stiff militia resistance, he had occupied the tiny village of Charlotte, a little over 130 miles southwest of Hillsborough.

He folded his arms and scowled down at Elizabeth. She appeared more than usually lovely that day in a shimmering gown of russet silk taffeta shot through with gold that enhanced her slender figure, creamy skin, and gleaming dark auburn curls. Ordinarily he would have sunk into the alluring depths of her gold-flecked brown eyes with no thought other than kissing her. And . . .

At the moment, however, he was too enraged for even such an agreeable distraction.

While she scanned the report a plump young housemaid slipped into the room, dustpan, broom, and rags in hand, no doubt drawn by the crash of glass and his oath. She took in the scene before favoring him with a longsuffering glance. Then she crossed to the fireplace, got down on her knees, and began to sop up the splattered whisky that the arc of the glass's trajectory had flung across the floor.

"Don't bother with it, Fiona," he said gruffly. "I made the mess, and I'll clean it up."

"Nay, sir, ye won't," she replied saucily. Rising, she grasped the broom and began to sweep up the glass shards. " 'Tis my job ta do it. But next time ye decide ta hurl glassware 'crost the room, ye might give fair warnin'. The crash gave me a bit of a fright."

He briefly pressed his eyes shut, took a breath, and blew it out. "Aye. I'll do that."

Grinning, she finished her work efficiently. As other footfalls approached down the passage she slipped back out of the room, mouth pursed and eyes dancing.

"Everythin' be all right?" he could hear Sarah question softly.

"Ah, just the laird havin' a fit, tha's all. I cleant it up." Fiona's amused retort faded down the passage with the two women's retreating footfalls.

Carleton sighed and returned his attention to Elizabeth, who looked up to meet his gaze with an appalled one, the color drained from her face. Teeth gritted, he wrenched his attention back to the latest disaster at hand.

Swinging around to the others, he said savagely, "I'm sure all of you remember that General Arnold was appointed to command Fort Putnam back in August. Well, the traitor wasted no time taking advantage of the confidence Washington placed in him by plotting to hand over the fortress —and thus the entire Hudson Valley—to Clinton! Worst of all, he made his escape to the British just as the report of his treachery came into Washington's hands." Perverse satisfaction filled him to see Andrews' mouth drop and every face in the room blanch.

A short time earlier, following their weekly officer's dinner, the junior officers had scattered to their duties, followed by the Shawnee women, while the rest of the company had gathered in Carleton's study. Within minutes their good-humored conversation had been interrupted by the arrival of an express courier sent by Washington.

Elizabeth stared down at the papers she held and read slowly, " 'Whom can we trust now?' "

When she offered Carleton the report, he could see tears welling into her eyes at the evidence of the General's despair. He took the papers and her hand, which he kissed, tamping down his ire as best he could.

"I'm sorry, dear heart," he murmured, meaning it this time. "I didn't mean to frighten you and the children."

She forced a smile and tiptoed to kiss his cheek before hurrying over to her mother. The babies reached for her, Julianne pleading, "Ma-Ma-Ma, Ma-Ma!"

"Why don't you and the girls take the twins out for a walk, Mama?" she suggested brightly, smoothing their hair back from the twins' tiny flushed faces. "It's a glorious day, and you know how they love an airng. Blue Sky and Mary might like to go with you," she added, darting a quick glance at the two women, who immediately came to her side.

Feeling a stab of guilt, Carleton came to kiss his tiny son and daughter, but they pulled away, lips quivering, blinking back tears and refusing to look at him.

With an indignant glance in his direction, Anne shepherded her charges out of the hall to retrieve their wrappings and head outside into the golden autumn afternoon. They had no sooner than vanished out the door when rage again clenched his gut.

Dr. Howard and Elizabeth settled on the sofa, and the others found seats. "Why don't you read the report to us, Jon?" Dr. Howard suggested.

He did, though he found it necessary to pause several times to rein in his temper and stifle furious profanities.

On Saturday, 23 September, three Westchester militiamen had intercepted a man in civilian dress crossing the contested Neutral Ground separating British and American lines near Tarrytown, New York. Mistaking the soldiers for Hessian troops, he had identified himself as a British officer, to which they replied that they were Americans. He then hastily claimed that his name was John Anderson and proffered a pass signed by General Arnold. Suspicious, they searched him and found hidden in his stockings detailed plans of Fort Putnam along with an inventory of the fortress's artillery and personnel.

At that point the soldiers had taken Anderson to the commander of the Americans' advanced posts, who inexplicably sent him back to Arnold under guard while forwarding the suspicious papers to General Washington. Major Benjamin Tallmadge, the head of Washington's spy network, had arrived not long thereafter. On hearing what had happened, Tallmadge persuaded the post commander to have Anderson brought back and to send Arnold a message instead, informing him of the man's arrest.

On his return "Anderson" revealed himself to be Major John André, General Clinton's adjutant general and the head of the British general's spies. By then, however, Arnold had received the message that André had been captured and the betraying papers he carried forwarded to Washington.

Through sheer bravado Arnold managed to escape to New York mere hours before Washington arrived at his headquarters, where the packet of papers revealing his treachery was delivered into his hands. Washington had immediately bolstered the fort's security and was holding André for execution in spite of Clinton's desperate negotiations to exchange him for any American prisoner of equal rank—other than Arnold himself, of course.

"If he was captured in enemy territory in civilian dress, then by law he should hang," Farris said in a steely voice when Carleton laid the message aside.

"He was. And he will, God willing."

Carleton reached for Elizabeth's hand, and when she rose he drew her shawl more snugly around her shoulders before taking her hand on his arm. "We all need fresh air," he said, giving her a strained smile. "Let's go out on the terrace where we can breathe."

✳ ✳ ✳

OUTSIDE, THE BREEZE was cool, the sun offering little warmth as it lowered toward the top of the forested ridge. Its pale rays cast long shadows down the mountain's flank, where the trees were beginning to flare into autumn's brilliance, and across the turbulent river to the flowerbeds edging the terrace, now denuded of their blooms.

Elizabeth perched on the balustrade while Carleton prowled restlessly up and down. The others found chairs, except for Red Fox and Spotted Pony. The two tall warriors leaned against the balustrade near Elizabeth, drawing on their pipes, lit at the fire before they came outside. The fragrant smoke curled briefly upward to be carried away on the wind.

"Obviously Arnold agreed with you that Fort Putnam could only be captured by treachery, Jon." Andrews shook his head, his expression forlorn. "I confess I never trusted him, but neither did I believe the man capable of such brazen betrayal."

Isaiah shrugged. "What you expect when he marry a Tory's daughter?"

Dr. Howard rubbed his chin thoughtfully. "There were rather malicious rumors about Arnold's infatuation with Peggy Shippen back when they married, especially as she'd been romantically involved with André during the British occupation."

"Well, it appears likely that the two were the conduit through which Arnold sold his services to General Clinton." Elizabeth brightened. "But the plot was foiled before he could take possession of the fort."

"Thank God for that!" Carleton exclaimed. "And that Washington immediately put General Greene in command of the fort. But it occurs to me to wonder where Tallmadge's spies were. A plot this complex requires considerable time and effort to arrange, which inevitably leaves a trail. There's obviously a gaping hole in our spy networks if Clinton failed to capture our most vaunted fortification due to nothing more than pure chance!"

"Ye think Clinton'll offer Arnold a command now he's defected, in spite o' the plot's failure?" McLeod asked soberly.

Carleton paced down the terrace and back, hands clasped behind him. "I can't imagine they won't, James. He's more than proven his effectiveness as a battle commander. And he knows everything about our military establishment: our personnel, our strategies, our plans, our weaknesses."

"But who would trust him?" Andrews burst out. "Even those who benefit from treason are bound to view the traitor with contempt. If he betrayed us, what's to prevent him betraying them if they disappoint his ambitions? He'll be persona non grata on both sides. I'd certainly want nothing to do with him."

"Whatever Arnold may do from this point forward, that his plot failed is enormous," Elizabeth pointed out. "I have to believe there's a higher power working behind what seems at the moment to be a great calamity."

Andrews regarded her with disbelief. "Well, I pray that this is the absolute nadir of our cause, because if something worse is on the way, we're finished! Coming on the heels of losing Charlestown, Camden, and now Charlotte as well, this betrayal is an unmitigated disaster.

"Our Southern Army was decimated yet again at Camden," he continued hotly, "all lost in one hour of combat because the great 'Hero of Saratoga'—who'd just taken command of an unfamiliar army cobbled together from Continentals and militia who'd never even maneuvered together!—ignored his officers' advice and marched his starving troops through a hostile wasteland all the way to Camden! It took them so long that Cornwallis had time to bring up his army to reinforce the outpost, yet still the man attacked! No wonder they all dropped everything and ran at the first sight of British bayonets!"

"It was bad enough, Charles, but not so bad as all that," Farris scoffed. "The Delaware Line held their ground with the North Carolina militia at their side. Tarleton's charge into their rear is what broke them—

understandably so—but they still retreated in good order. And so did the Maryland Line."

"We still suffered over two thousand casualties, Matt," Carleton responded grimly. "And what did Gates do? The coward abandoned the field and his army on the fastest horse he could find and hightailed it two hundred miles to Hillsborough in three days. Contrast that to De Kalb, who was severely wounded in the battle and died a British prisoner."

Dr. Howard's face darkened. "If there's any justice, Gates's military career is at an end."

"Whate'er happened to the Granny Gates we knew who couldna be bothered to stir?" McLeod demanded, his expression morose.

Red Fox removed the pipe stem from his mouth and noted shrewdly, "He wished to prove he deserved his fine reputation as a battle commander."

Carleton folded his arms and regarded his cousin with a faint smile. "I wouldn't be the least surprised if the honor Gates received for Saratoga instead of Arnold had much to do with that traitor's defection."

Spotted Pony, standing closest to Elizabeth, muttered under his breath in the Shawnee tongue, "It is good that we fight alongside these Long Knives so we may learn their weaknesses and use them to our advantage."

Impulsively she laid her hand over the one he braced on the balustrade's ledge beside her. Glancing around, he held her gaze with one that sent a shiver down her back.

When she quickly pulled her hand back, his expression softened and he gave her a smile that was both reassuring and unsettling. She drew in a quick breath and transferred her attention to Carleton, who, she saw, observed their byplay.

"Are we not all men and brothers?" he asked in the same language. "Are our people not as divided as the Long Knives?"

"Remove the log from your own eye," Andrews quoted wryly, "that you may see clearly to pluck the sliver from your brother's eye."

The others all appeared bemused, not understanding what they said. "Maybe now Congress let Washington appoint Gen'l Greene commander in the South," Isaiah put in, resuming their conversation to approving nods and murmurs of agreement.

"It's possible this is God's leading." The words were out of Elizabeth's mouth almost before she realized she'd said them aloud. "I'm reminded of Gideon."

"Gideon?" Carleton tipped his head, considering. "You mean how he raised an army to fight the Midianites and Amalekites?"

She nodded. "To prevent Israel from boasting that their own power had gained the victory, God told him to send away those who were afraid and those who knelt to drink water. Gideon ended up with only three hundred men to fight an army that was as numerous as locusts and had as many camels as sand on the seashore."

"And you think something like that might be what's happening now? The Lord's giving the boot to those who are unequal to the task or unworthy—"

"Not necessarily. Perhaps, like Arnold, some are outstanding leaders and fighters. I don't think whether they're the best or the worst is the point."

"I agree wi' ye, Elizabeth. There's a higher power at work in all o' this," McLeod mused. "It's when our circumstances seem the darkest that we need to trust our Maker the more."

"Easy to say, James," Carleton returned. "It's considerably harder to do when you've been smashed in the face and you're lying on the ground with the devil's foot on your neck."

"Seems to me that's just the time to admit ye aren't goin' to be able to defeat the auld dragon on yer own," McLeod countered.

"Well, that's the position we're in," Carleton conceded with a rueful laugh. He slouched onto a nearby chair, stretched out his legs, and turned an intent look on Elizabeth. "So . . . some who surrendered at Charlestown or fled the battlefield at Camden might have been among those who stood fast as long as possible at Charlotte—with much of the credit going to Colonel Davie's firmness, God bless him."

"It does appear to me that the Lord is clearing out officers who've been a hindrance to our cause and is raising up those who have courage, energy, and will to stand fast against the enemy."

They spent some time discussing the intelligence Carleton had gleaned during the past three months. As Sumter had predicted, the fierce irregular war rapidly expanding across South Carolina increasingly consisted of mean, bloody clashes between patriot militias and Tory and British forces.

Recently promoted to colonel, Davie had led a number of daring raids throughout the summer, more than living up to Carleton's estimation. He had narrowly missed the battle at Camden, but instead of retreating north after Gates and the remnants of the American Army, he had pushed south toward Camden to recover supply wagons and gather intelligence on Cornwallis's movements.

On 26 September during the Battle of Charlotte, Davie had fearlessly led his 150 militia horsemen against Cornwallis's army of more than 2,000 professional soldiers, skillfully deploying his troops to repulse three charges of Tarleton's British Legion cavalry and only withdrawing when enemy infantry threatened to turn his right flank. By the next day his own cavalry had grown to a formidable force of 300, which he set to patrolling Charlotte's outskirts, driving off British foraging parties and intercepting messengers. For now his command was the only unbroken corps standing between the British and what was left of the Continental forces.

Sumter had also justified Carleton's assessment. He had defeated the British in an encounter in August, only to be routed by Tarleton in the middle of the night less than a fortnight thereafter. Neglecting to set out pickets to guard against a surprise attack, Sumter had been forced to flee half dressed astride an unsaddled horse.

Patrick Henry had not been idle either, despite being forced to return home from Richmond in June due to the recurrence of his illness. While recovering he had helped to recruit volunteers to fight Tory bands raiding the area. He had declined to act as their commander but had ridden with them on patrols, and their efforts to drive off raiders had met with such success that they had been able to disband the previous month.

Most intriguing to Carleton, however, was Colonel Francis Marion, a Continental officer who had served under Lincoln at Charlestown but escaped the city before its surrender. Commanding a small, tightly knit, highly mobile company of militia, he had offered his services to Gates on his march to Camden. Unimpressed, Gates had sent him off to take command of a newly raised militia unit in South Carolina that had bolstered Marion's band by 200 men.

Since then Marion had driven off a British guard at Murray's Ferry, freed over a hundred Continentals captured by the British, and defeated British Regulars at Sumter's abandoned plantation. Two weeks after that action and sixty miles away, he then ambushed a large Tory regiment in the swamps of the Little Pee Dee River.

Frustrated by numerous failed attempts to capture the elusive patriot leader, Cornwallis had sent out one of his officers to prevent Marion from hounding his march north to Charlotte. But instead of flushing Marion out of his haunts, the officer's brutal seventy-mile-wide campaign of burning and hanging had driven a flood of embittered volunteers into Marion's camp.

Adding insult to injury, two days following Cornwallis's occupation of Charlotte, Marion engaged Tory militia at Black Mingo Creek, sent them fleeing to the far side of the Santee River, and carried off the weapons, ammunition, baggage, and horses they left behind. As after every encounter, Marion and his men then vanished back into the mists of South Carolina's swamps.

"I'd like to meet the man and get a sense of his mettle," Carleton said. "His men seem to be exceptionally loyal to him personally, perhaps because, unlike Sumter, he doesn't act on impulse but with careful deliberation."

Carleton went on to tell them that shortly before his detachment left Hillsborough, reports had filtered in that a large body of Over Mountain Men was on the move south from the Watauga settlements west of the Blue Ridge. Mostly Scots-Irish, these hard-bitten, independent-minded frontiersmen led by highly respected local leaders such as Isaac Shelby and Jon Sevier had settled on land leased from the Cherokee on the border between Virginia and North Carolina.

They had heard about Charlotte's fall and that the Bulldog, Patrick Ferguson, recently promoted to major, had crossed into North Carolina in early September. He had been delegated to organize Tory militia and recruit troops for his provincial Regulars, the American Volunteers, while moving parallel with Cornwallis's main force to protect the British Army's left flank. Rumors held that Ferguson was camped at Gilbert Town, and the Over Mountain Men meant to intercept him there to prevent his reinforcing Cornwallis at Charlotte roughly 55 miles to the east.

Confident that the Carolina militias along with the Over Mountain Men should be able to contain any further movement north by Cornwallis for the time being, Carleton had hurried home. Early that morning he had sent out messages summoning the local militia commanders to a meeting in order to share the intelligence he had gained and determine their battle readiness should the threat to Virginia increase.

"There are still many who remain loyal against all odds and aren't giving up the battle," Elizabeth pointed out. "I don't believe the Lord is finished with us yet. We simply need to continue seeking his guidance, and then follow it."

"There's the rub: understanding what we're being led to do and doing it," Andrews broke in. "In my experience obedience doesn't always guarantee success according to human standards. God may have a different purpose in mind than we do. And if we lose this war . . . " He let the words trail off.

Red Fox turned to gaze out across the river at the shadowed ridge that loomed high above them. "In that case we will return to our clan and nation.

It may be that the British will heed their promise to keep settlers out of our lands."

Elizabeth directed an apprehensive glance toward her father. He studied the warrior, his expression shuttered but his lips pressed together in a hard line.

SPOTTED PONY'S MUTTERED remark and Red Fox's sober comment haunted Elizabeth during the coming days. They reflected their concern over the most recent developments on the western frontier, she knew. But the repeated debacles in the war against Britain did nothing to strengthen the Americans' ties with their remaining Indian allies. She could only hope that the shocking treason and defection of one of Washington's most effective officers had not delivered a fatal blow.

Reports had filtered in to Thornlea over the summer that in June a mixed force from Detroit composed of British soldiers and Shawnee, Lenape, and Wyandot warriors had struck far south into Kentucky. They were commanded by British officer Henry Bird and accompanied by McKee, Elliott, and the Girty brothers. Capturing several fortified settlements, they had seized more than three hundred prisoners.

The Shawnee had gone on to raid settlements throughout the Ohio Valley, driving the Americans out of Fort Randolph, the scene of Cornstalk's brutal murder, and effectively closing off the river to American traffic. Intelligence gleaned from British reports indicated that every day their Indian allies brought scalps to Detroit.

Reprisals had not been long in coming, however. General Clark had invaded Shawnee country with a thousand men. To prevent the capture of Chillicothe, established in a new location after its previous destruction, the Shawnee had burned it down and made a valiant stand at Piqua on the Mad River. Clark's soldiers had bombarded the packed council house with cannon, killed their elderly hiding in the cornfields, and set their crops to the torch. They had even gone so far as to plunder goods and scalps from the burial grounds. When winter came, Elizabeth mourned, the Shawnee would have no choice but to turn to the British for sustenance.

It was a pattern that seemed set in stone. Time and again Carleton had been proven right: To pursue the same failed strategy over and over hoping that it would at last succeed was madness. But what other strategy was there? Repeated negotiation and treaties had also failed. White settlers stubbornly continued to flood onto native lands, sparking bloody resistance they met with equally bloody reprisals in a conflict the tribes could never win.

In private talks, Carleton confided that, like the various tribes they belonged to, his warriors and their women were increasingly turning against the Americans. Little held them other than their strong personal allegiance to him.

Spotted Pony openly questioned why they should continue to fight for the Americans. Red Fox said little, but Carleton could tell that he also wavered. Even Andrews, in his concern for his wife and children, expressed a bitter cynicism on the subject. The women, however, continued to hold firmly to the Shawnee's peace faction led by Nonhelema.

Carleton also seemed outwardly unshaken in his course, settled on faithfully following such wisdom as was given him by God in the matter. But Elizabeth sensed keenly that deep inside him a festering anger continued to eat away like a slow but certain acid.

Chapter Twenty-eight

AT LAST, ON WEDNESDAY, 18 October, on the heels of gale-force winds and drenching thunderstorms that turned roads into sucking bogs and rivers into raging torrents, welcome news flooded into Thornlea. A bedraggled messenger brought a report from North Carolina militia general William Lee Davidson, which began, "Ferguson, the great partisan, has miscarried."

Early in the month the large force of Over Mountain Men, swelled along the way by Sumter's horsemen and Virginia militia commanded by Colonel William Campbell, had caught up with Major Patrick Ferguson's 1,100 American Volunteers a short distance south of the border between the two Carolinas at a place called King's Mountain.

A mere day's march west of Cornwallis's army at Charlotte, Ferguson had decided to make camp late on 6 October atop one of the many rocky, forested hills in the region, a position he deemed impregnable. A spy quickly alerted the Over Mountain Men to his location, and although exhausted by their rapid pursuit, they immediately sent out every rider fit to continue— nine hundred mounted men in all.

The pack of lean, rawboned mountain men rode hard in a steady rain through that night and the following morning. Reaching the mountain in early afternoon, they immediately surrounded the ridge and attacked like hungry wolves on the hunt, hollering their chilling war cries and catching Ferguson's regiment by complete surprise.

By agreement the separate militia detachments fought independently under their own commanders but in concert with the others. They used the rugged terrain to their advantage, pressing up the hill through trees and over boulders and forcing Ferguson's Tories to fire downhill so they often overshot their marks. Although the defenders' repeated, desperate bayonet charges drove the patriots back into the woods, every time they pulled back to oppose another party of mountain men advancing up the opposite side of the hill, those who had retreated fiercely returned to the attack.

While his regiment's casualties rapidly mounted, Ferguson had ridden back and forth across the hilltop, blowing his silver whistle to redirect his men from one side of the hill to another, wherever the threat was greatest. Inevitably, however, Shelby, Sevier, and Campbell pressed to the crest at Ferguson's rear and drove his soldiers back into their camp. With the Carolina regiments swarming toward the top at the opposite side, Ferguson's troops began to lay down their arms.

Ferguson had not been so faint hearted. Swinging his sword, he hacked down any white flags his men raised, finally gathered his officers and attempted to break through the Over Mountain Men's lines. Even when cut down by a volley and dragged by his horse, Ferguson shot and killed the officer who demanded his surrender. He was then immediately shot dead by the surrounding soldiers. The battle had lasted hardly an hour.

"I'll give Ferguson his due," Carleton said, looking up from the report, stony faced. "Whatever his faults, he was a brave soldier."

The courier nodded, his expression grim. "Accordin' to accounts that reached us at Hillsborough, the Tories' calls for quarter were answered with demands to give 'em Buford's play. A second flag had to be sent out, and even then it took all of Campbell's and Shelby's efforts to stop the slaughter. The men plundered Ferguson's camp and the dead, and left the injured and dyin' Tories cryin' on the battlefield that night. Next day the captives who could be moved were herded off for fear Cornwallis might be sendin' reinforcements."

The Over Mountain Men's casualties had amounted to a fraction of the roughly 300 men killed and 150 wounded that Ferguson's regiment suffered. The courier went on to soberly describe the harsh treatment inflicted on the more than 650 prisoners who had been marched north.

As Carleton heard the man out, he reflected that Sumter's claim that the backcountry would be engulfed in a bitter blood feud within families and between neighbors was indeed being fully vindicated. As was the certainty that Tarleton's bloody quarter wreaked on Buford at the Waxhaws was very far from being forgotten or forgiven. And this was only the beginning, with no end in sight.

Two days later another report reached Thornlea: Ferguson's defeat and the destruction of his loyalist regiment had forced Cornwallis to withdraw from Charlotte to Camden, South Carolina. And Davie's cavalry had harried him relentlessly all the way.

The most heartening news of all followed: Congress had confirmed General Nathanael Greene as commander of the Southern Army.

At that Carleton swept Elizabeth into his arms, exulting, "At last we have a commander who'll actually do something!"

She laughed with him, but then sobered. "I suspect Greene will have a long, hard road of it scraping together enough men, materiel, and supplies to rebuild the Southern Army, to say nothing of dealing with those contentious militia commanders. But I have a feeling that now this war has an assured and victorious end, no matter what struggles might yet lie ahead of us."

THE WEEK FOLLOWING this welcome news, an express rider arrived carrying an urgent message from Governor Jefferson. Six British warships had sailed into the Chesapeake with more than 2,000 troops aboard commanded by General Alexander Leslie. He had landed detachments of cavalry and infantry at Portsmouth and Newport News and was marching inland, committing, according to Jefferson, "horrid depredations."

The governor was summoning every force available to oppose the enemy incursion. Carleton immediately sent dispatches to the local militia commanders to rendezvous at Big Lick, and he and Andrews rode out at the head of their troops, leaving Isaiah's two light infantry companies behind to secure Thornlea.

It turned out to be a futile mission. They had gone only a day's ride when another express reached them, countermanding their summons. On receiving news of Ferguson's defeat and Cornwallis's withdrawal into South Carolina, Leslie had turned back to Portsmouth. Carleton and Andrews retraced their route, feeling somewhat deflated now that the prospect for action had evaporated.

They arrived home in time to confront another crisis. Just before dawn the next morning Marah shepherded another small flock of escaped slaves into the secluded valley behind the falls. As usual Carleton circumspectly absented himself while Elizabeth managed the transfer of supplies to the fugitives' hiding place. Jemma had no sooner than helped Elizabeth into a morning gown and done up her hair when a carriage drove up the valley road carrying a couple of local militia officers and their wives. They had just been passing on their way to Salem, the women declared cheerily, and thought to stop by to see their "dear friends".

It was not the first time that one or more local militia officers and their wives had appeared not long after slaves had escaped from one of the plantations in the region. By now it was becoming obvious that such visits were no coincidence.

A number of the officers had been Carleton's childhood friends. Like him, lean, tanned, and sharp-eyed, they demonstrated a similar keenness and charm. They had all grown up together, socializing with one another's families, wandering the forests while hunting, engaging in daring youthful escapades, and wooing the area's young ladies.

The majority of the men had inherited sprawling plantations or were in line to do so, and a couple had built prosperous businesses. All kept large establishments of slaves. Most had participated at one time or another in the fierce frontier wars against the Cherokee, Shawnee, and other native tribes.

On the surface the men's interactions with Carleton during the formal dinners and balls he and Elizabeth from time to time hosted or attended appeared easy and good natured. As did their banter about Carleton's having so spectacularly thrown over the British to take up their cause and laughing references to his being a pirate.

But underneath, in a subtle stiffness and occasional veiled, coldly assessing glances, Elizabeth sensed something darker. Seemingly casual remarks about the trials of managing slaves and dangers of uprisings, bloody Indian raids and the men's experiences in the equally bloody reprisals made it clear to her that these former childhood friends viewed Carleton with suspicion tinged with hostility.

She was sure that his former friends' sidelong looks and snide remarks made with feigned innocence had to cut. He gave no outward evidence of it, however, instead responding to them as she imagined he had always done.

When Elizabeth questioned him privately, he had shrugged the matter off. "I've a job to do," he told her. "My Rangers are assigned to Virginia's defense. I can't afford to be distracted by petty jealousies and ill will. I just want them to do their jobs."

With this in mind, she welcomed the latest batch of impromptu guests into the manor with outward delight. Inwardly she suppressed her annoyance with the reflection that they would find no more evidence of runaways in the valley than all those who had unexpectedly dropped by before them.

And so it had turned out. When the men mentioned that they had not yet viewed the encampment, Carleton obligingly took them on a tour of the entire estate. Meanwhile Elizabeth brightly suggested a tour of the manor, which the officers' wives happily accepted.

Elizabeth's mother joined them as they pried into every nook and cranny from the attics to the cellars, one of the women citing renovations to her plantation house as a pretext for her interest. When they returned to the drawing room, however, their conversation turned to intrusive personal questions and innuendoes about Elizabeth's medical work, activities as a spy, and sojourn aboard a British prison ship, subjects both she and her mother were hard pressed to respond to with civility

Carleton finally ushered the men back into the manor just as Elizabeth's father came in from the hospital. When Carleton invited the couples to stay for dinner, to everyone's relief they made excuses and took their leave, their frustration thinly concealed.

"Perhaps now our neighbors will finally be satisfied that escaped slaves are not harbored at Thornlea!" Elizabeth exclaimed as the carriage disappeared around the bend in the road.

Carleton responded with a rueful laugh. "We'll always be under suspicion, dear heart. There'll never be a time when we can let down our guard."

Chapter Twenty-nine

CARLETON REGARDED TEISSÈDRE suspiciously, eyes narrowed. "You've been gone so long I was beginning to think you'd sailed off the edge of the ocean, Louis. Where've you been?"

The Frenchman warmed himself at the fireplace in Thornlea's formal parlor, his brow knotting in an expression of wounded virtue. He had arrived unexpectedly half an hour earlier in the late afternoon of Saturday, 11 November. Carleton's attention had been happily focused on arrangements for the twins' first birthday celebration the next day, being expounded in detail by Elizabeth, Anne, Sarah, and Salome, and he wasn't entirely pleased at the interruption.

"Six months is hardly a long time considering all the business I had to conduct after sailing across a vast ocean to France amid a war with an implacable enemy," Teissèdre returned loftily.

"And I'm sure there were a great many critical affairs to keep you occupied while there."

Taking no note of Carleton's acid tone, Teissèdre inclined his head graciously in acknowledgement. He described the deadly hurricane that had wreaked havoc on the squadron he'd sailed with on his return, delaying their landing at York by more than a week. On arrival reports had reached them that the storm had ripped through the Caribbean on the tenth of October, passing along Martinique and Barbados and causing great loss of life. Both French and British fleets prowling the seas among the islands and along the American coast had lost ships and crews to the raging tempest.

"That must be what caused the storms that passed through here the middle of last month," Elizabeth said, frowning. "I wonder how the naval losses will affect the war."

Carleton shrugged and turned back to Teissèdre. "After all that I'm amazed you actually bothered to favor us with your presence in this insignificant backwater."

The Frenchman allowed a smug smile. He surveyed Elizabeth and her parents before fixing his gaze on Carleton, one eyebrow cocked ironically.

"As to that, your uncle wished me to report to you without delay the latest developments regarding your privateers."

He went on to remind them that after Carleton and Elizabeth had left for America, Caledonne had set himself to gather Carleton's scattered ships. He had managed to recover the merchantmen *Faire Winds* and *Horn of Africa,* which the British had sold off to a Portuguese shipping company, leaving only *Mandarin* lost. He had then brought the rest of Carleton's ships safely to L'Orient, where he had the merchantmen refitted as privateers, thus assembling his own formidable little fleet.

"I take it you mean *my* fleet since the ships belong to me and I'm paying for all of this," Carleton broke in, his voice steely.

Teissèdre bowed. "Of course, *mon général.* I misspoke." Ignoring Carleton's glower, he added dismissively, "Ah, by the by, *Destiny* is now also in his hands."

Carleton sat frozen for a moment, then shot out of his seat. *"What?"*

Elizabeth's mouth fell open, as did her parents'. "How did he manage that?" she demanded, echoed by Dr. Howard's and Anne's professions of amazement and delight. "You made a great deal of Portsmouth's strict security."

Teissèdre's smile broadened. "Indeed it was exceptionally strict. Which makes le comte's triumph all the more spectacular, simple though it was."

Carleton sank back onto the sofa, for the moment too astonished to speak.

"I confess I didn't think it possible for even Alexandre to accomplish such a feat," Dr. Howard exclaimed, laughing. "I'm relieved to hear that my doubts were entirely misplaced!"

"Oh, the English and their foolish attitude of superiority!" Teissèdre crowed in supreme disdain. "Their confidence in their invincibility is inevitably their undoing."

"Whereas, the French do not consider themselves at all superior," Carleton observed with asperity.

"In fact, our downfall is that we French are far too humble," Teissèdre countered, theatrically tipping up his nose.

Elizabeth met Carleton's gaze. His mouth quirked, his eyes alive with merriment. She couldn't help herself. She dissolved into hysterical laughter, while her parents stifled their own as best they could. Detecting a glimmer of humor in Teissèdre gaze, she laughed all the harder.

"Where's *Destiny* now?" Dr. Howard demanded when everyone finally subsided.

"Snugly secured in the harbor at L'Orient. Along with the rest of the general's ships."

At their urging, he recounted the 100-gun privateer's recapture. Sartine, France's naval minister and head of a vast spy network, had long had agents embedded throughout England, including in all of her ports and naval dockyards. Those holding trusted positions had followed every detail of *Destiny*'s repair and refitting by the British with great interest, soon acquiring exact details of the plan to move the ship once she was fully restored. She was to sail with a heavily armed squadron, under cover of night, to Land's End, where she would join a British fleet bound for the Mediterranean.

Caledonne's plan had been deceptively simple. Immediately after sunset the very night *Destiny*, now renamed *Prevail*, was to sail, and exactly two hours before the squadron assigned to escort her to the fleet was due to arrive, new orders came to the harbormaster's hand that she was instead to join up with her escorts off the Isle of Wight.

Meanwhile a large party of Caledonne's men, clothing and faces blackened, stealthily boarded her and with silent efficiency captured or eliminated all her officers and most of her crew. Happily, aboard had been a small but seething cohort of American, French, Irish, and Scottish sailors who had been pressed into service by the British and lusted to impose justice. Thus *Destiny* and her newly liberated and reinforced crew sailed out of the harbor with the blessing of the harbormaster, who had the added incentive of a French pistol pressed to his temple.

With an airy wave of his hand Teissedre concluded complacently, "By the time the genuine escorts arrived, your ship had long since vanished into the mists of the sea and was soon snugly berthed at L'Orient. Most accommodatingly, our old enemy did a magnificent job of restoring and then arming her with their finest, heaviest long-range guns and a full complement of every other instrument of destruction one could wish for.

"The only unhappy detail was that she'd been repainted in that disastrous British yellow and black scheme. I ask you, who'd choose such a combination? It puts one in mind of a giant bumblebee! But I digress. When I sailed, your uncle was already having her repainted to her original glorious navy blue, ivory, and crimson."

Eyes closed, Carleton rested his head against the sofa's back as he fought the swell of emotion that choked his throat. Evidently he failed as far as Elizabeth was concerned, for she gently laid her hand on his arm. He gathered her against his breast, his cheek pressed to hers.

"He's not forgotten us, you know," she murmured. "Our Lord still has all things covered—defeats, betrayals . . . and Uncle Alexandre too."

He cleared his throat and answered hoarsely, "I am learning, dear heart. Day by day."

Smiling, she turned his face to hers, tears glimmering in her eyes. "As am I." He brushed a kiss across her lips, which she returned sweetly before straightening and drawing out of his arms.

"This is heartening news indeed, Louis—and much needed. Should you see my uncle before I do, please tell him that I thank him with all my heart. I'm greatly in his debt."

Teissèdre had turned discreetly to the fire blazing on the hearth but now looked around with a smile. "Surely after all these years you can't have doubted le comte's determination and abilities."

Carleton went suddenly cold, a long-repressed memory emerging dimly at the edge of consciousness, too blurred for the moment to retrieve. Suppressing a shudder, he forced it back into the depths.

He felt Elizabeth's hand slip into his and gripped it tightly, steadying his breathing. He became aware that the others fixed him in a questioning look.

With a slight shrug, the Frenchman said, "I'm bound south for the winter so it's possible you may see him before I do. Your uncle mentioned that he plans to go to work at once to wreak vengeance on the British, but he hopes to come for a visit in the spring bearing some fruits of his endeavors for you and your lady." He gave Elizabeth a graceful half bow.

"If it's safe enough, I hope he'll bring my sister with him," Dr. Howard broke in. "I know it's unaccountable, but I do miss her," he added with a chuckle.

Both Elizabeth and her mother laughed, and Anne clasped her hands together. "Oh, I do hope he will! And perhaps Abby too—" She stopped abruptly, her face falling, and shook her head. "No, it's far too dangerous with this war still on. If something were to happen to my girl—"

"Now, my dear, perhaps the situation will have changed enough by then to allow it," Dr. Howard interjected hopefully.

Carleton ignored their byplay, keeping his expression guarded. "Caledonne means to come here? To Thornlea?"

"I took that for his meaning. I don't believe he's ever visited before."

"No. He hasn't."

"Then I imagine he's eager to finally see how the descriptions he's heard compare to the reality."

Carleton held the Frenchman in a steady gaze. An uncertain tension thickened the air in the room, the only sound the snap and crackle of the blazing logs on the hearth.

"I'll give it some thought," he said evenly.

For the first time in their entire acquaintance, he noted that Teissèdre's seemingly unshakable confidence slipped, though he quickly recovered it and made an elaborate bow. *"Certainement, général."* After a barely perceptible hesitation, he continued, "Le Marquis de Martieu-Broussard has sent you a supply of specie as an advance on the profits to come. Once your loans are paid back, *naturellement.*"

"*Naturellement.* I'll write to thank him." Carleton kept his tone cool.

Teissèdre dismissed the subject, with forced heartiness countering, "I hear you finally have a new commander for your Southern Department —and one of whom we can expect much."

Elizabeth and her parents quickly joined in praising General Greene and speculating on what changes in strategy he was likely to make in the Southern theater. Clearly bemused by the tension between Carleton and his agent, they seemed relieved that the matter was dropped.

Carleton stared into the air, their voices muting into the background. The too familiar black void yawned before him again. He had spent years refusing to gaze into its depths, denying that it existed at all. Telling himself it had merely been a dream.

Once he and Elizabeth had wed, he thought their shared confidences had exorcized the last of his demons. To a great extent they had. Yet at random times and places that despised, treacherous bog rematerialized to hover just out of his field of vision.

Haunting him in the nights. Keeping him from sleep. Filling him with a sickening dread.

He would not give in to it. Not ever. For he feared the consequences if he did.

Not for others. For himself.

Chapter Thirty

THE CELEBRATION OF the twins' first birthday the next day was a joyous affair, with gifts for the babies and a lavish dinner to which Carleton's officers were invited. Abundant food and merriment overflowed to the servants and throughout the camp as well.

Despite Carleton's outward good humor, Elizabeth could tell that whatever had caused the sudden clash between him and Teissèdre still rankled. The constant sparring between the two, whether thinly veiled or sharply open, had troubled her for some time, but whenever she broached the subject he shrugged off her concern. This time, however, she determined that for his own sake she must persuade him to confide in her what she suspected he had long concealed, perhaps even from himself.

He slept little that night, rising not long after midnight with the whispered excuse that he had reports to write. At breakfast the next morning he appeared bleary-eyed and preoccupied, his patience short. Although his interactions with Teissèdre were cordial enough on the surface, underneath she could feel the same taut wariness on both their parts, like boxers circling each other, looking for an opening to strike.

It was a fine November day, the wind cool, but with a warm sun shining out of a clear azure sky. When Teissèdre made his departure shortly after dinner, she persuaded Carleton to walk with her in the leaf-drifted gardens.

They spoke little, and then only of commonplaces. She had the unsettling impression that he had wrapped an impenetrable cloak around him even against her.

At last she slipped her hand into the crook of his arm and drew him around to face her. "Mama and Papa are delighted at the prospect of Uncle Alexandre bringing Aunt Tess here for a visit next spring. But you seemed far less so when Louis mentioned it."

"You know that Tess is always very welcome to visit," he answered gruffly.

"But not Uncle Alexandre."

He opened his mouth to speak, then stopped and looked quickly away, his face clouding.

"Dearest, please don't shut me out," she pleaded. "I've sensed almost from the beginning that something stands between you and Uncle Alexandre. And Louis, perhaps by extension. Some time ago you mentioned that Uncle Alexandre used you for his intelligence purposes when you were only a youth and the danger that put you in. I'm wondering . . . " She let the words trail off.

"That's long past," he growled. "There's no good in dredging it up."

She drew him down to sit beside her on a nearby bench. Taking his hand, she turned it over and placed hers palm to palm over his, then looked up and regarded him earnestly.

"But that's what's caused this rift between you, isn't it? Based on my own experience in France, I have a sense that it explains much about why you always keep your uncle at arm's length."

When he didn't meet her gaze or respond, she persisted, "Unless you confront what happened, you'll never come to terms with it. Don't you want to repair your relationship?"

Flinching, he muttered, "I'm not sure I do."

"Now that he's married to my aunt, it'll be difficult for you to avoid him." She studied him silently for a moment. "Did you ever confide in Sir Harry?"

His mouth tightened. Straightening, he pulled his hand away and sat back, arms folded as though barricading himself against emotions he refused to concede.

She waited patiently. But for a long interval he remained unbendingly silent.

HE HAD FOUGHT TO DENY the memory for so long. But now, without warning, out of the past the darkness enveloped him, tearing away all his defenses and casting him back into that moment of horror, smoking pistol in hand, when the shattering realization of what he had done crashed over him.

And broke him, forcing a groan from his throat.

"It happened the summer I turned seventeen," he blurted out, voice hitching. "The summer following the Battle of Quiberon Bay."

"In which Frédéric died," she murmured, referring to Caledonne's elder son. A lieutenant in the French Navy, he had been killed in France's decisive defeat by the British in November 1759 during the Seven Years' War.

He stared blankly into the distance, across the brown, frost-withered gardens to the river and forest beyond. "Frédéric had become like an elder brother to me, much more than merely a cousin even though the time we had together was always limited. I looked up to him, wanted to be like him. The news of his death reached me late the following spring, while I was in my last term at Harvard. I was . . . distressed, found it impossible to grasp that he was really gone.

"Sir Harry had never allowed such a long visit with the Bettárs before. But he arranged for me to take my final exams early, and then to spend the entire summer with them while he traveled between his European offices— a dangerous business with the war on and the British blockading French ports."

He looked up to meet Elizabeth's sorrowful gaze, took a shaky breath. "The family was shattered, as you can imagine. But they seemed to take as much comfort in having me with them as I did in being there. Aunt Luciana and Uncle Alexandre treated me as a son, you see. They never made any distinction between me and their own children."

Tears filled her eyes, and she laid her head on his shoulder.

Slowly he went on, reciting what had happened as though it involved someone else. Not himself.

"I'd always stayed with them at the Marseilles estate. But Uncle Alexandre kept an apartment at Versailles since he had to be there so often when not at sea. After losing Frédéric, he'd moved the family there so they'd be together as much as possible.

"It was my first experience of the palace and Paris. I found it overwhelming, just as you told me you felt when you were there. Daily mingling with people of the highest ranks of French society and government quite went to my head in spite of my grief. Or perhaps that made me more vulnerable to their influence."

During those last years of the war, he continued, voice empty of emotion, the British had been intercepting French ships with unnerving regularity despite efforts to maintain the utmost secrecy. Caledonne had concluded that one or more British agents had to be operating at the highest levels of France's naval establishment—operatives yet unknown to Sartine, who had not then developed his spy networks as fully as he did later. The Navy was bleeding men and money, and Caledonne wanted to make those responsible pay for it.

"Most of all he wanted vengeance for Frédéric's death. As did I."

Elizabeth sat up, thinking of the great whorls and ribbons of weapons, the Scottish Saltire, and the three portraits that adorned the Great Hall. "Sir Harry was certainly no lover of Britain. I can't imagine he taught you to be."

Carleton returned a short laugh and shook his head, his expression hardening.

It was common in France for youths to enter society at sixteen or seventeen years of age, he went on. At a ball he attended with his aunt and uncle soon after his arrival, Caledonne had introduced him to a Monsieur Penet, an acquaintance who had moved to Paris from the south two years earlier. By all appearances very well-connected in society and exceedingly wealthy, and more than willing to spread the largess around, the man had quickly become a confidante of many of the prominent naval personnel who were also in attendance that evening.

A widower, Penet had brought his lovely daughter, Madeline, with him. She was a year older than Carleton, small and slender, accomplished in music and the arts yet appealingly innocent, having been sheltered from the worst influences of French society. From their first meeting she aroused all of Carleton's protective instincts. It hadn't taken long for the two of them to become considerably more than friends, a relationship Penet happily encouraged.

And then one day Caledonne had confided alarming suspicions that Penet was a British agent and that he was using Carleton's relationship with his daughter to gain further entrée to Caledonne himself. Carleton's uncle was then quickly rising in King Louis V's favor and was in line for an appointment to admiral. And he was an intimate of Sartine. Such a relationship would be extremely useful to someone who was spying for the British.

Carleton had been immediately concerned for Madeline's safety, which his uncle claimed to share. Unfortunately Caledonne had no proof directly linking the man to any activity beyond simply knowing certain unsavory persons—hardly unusual in French high society. And Penet was frustratingly close-mouthed about his dealings and resistant to hiring any new household 'servants'.

After some discussion Caledonne had suggested that Carleton might have some luck finding out more about Penet's connections without arousing suspicion. It would involve no more than taking careful note of Penet's visitors, appointments, and discussions when Carleton called on the young woman. Possibly getting a look at her father's correspondence if the opportunity arose. Madeline might also have knowledge of her father's affairs that could be elicited through casual conversation.

Carleton's jaw hardened. "I readily agreed, thinking a bit of sleuthing a grand lark, especially if it led to vengeance for Frédéric's death. At the same time it provided more access to the lovely Madeline, an appealing prospect."

"But it turned out to be something other than a lark," Elizabeth guessed, her stomach in a knot.

He leaned forward, forearms braced across his thighs, head lowered. "Afterward I began to wonder whether it hadn't been Caledonne's plan all along and he'd subtly shaped me for his purposes. Of course, Sir Harry made sure I was skilled with firearms and tutored in the use of sword and rapier. Caledonne taught me to stay constantly alert, take careful note of small details others might miss, listen closely to what others said without appearing to, and forget nothing. And always to keep a weapon concealed on my person. By that summer I'd become very good at all of it."

Sitting up, he gave a caustic laugh. "For a seventeen-year-old, the feeling of newfound power was as heady as a drug."

She stared down at her clasped hands. "I'm too well acquainted with that same drug."

When she looked up, he met her gaze with an ironic smile. "You miss it, don't you? As much as I do even now in spite of my loathing for it."

She nodded, feeling the heat rise to her cheeks with the vivid memory of the masked ball she had attended in Paris with Caledonne's younger son, Lucien, the coldness with which he shot the man who threatened her, and then made the incident vanish as though it had never happened. It had all been so deftly done. So . . . planned.

She had wondered at the time whether Lucien had learned his skills from his father. She no longer had any doubt.

"Alas, pride goeth before a fall, as they say," Carleton muttered. "I grew too confident."

"What . . . what happened?" she faltered, dreading the answer.

He shrugged. "It wasn't long before I fully shared Caledonne's suspicions that Penet was somehow passing intelligence to the British. But I never could get my hands on decisive proof. I finally determined to get a look at his private correspondence if I had to create the opportunity myself. Which, as it turned out, I didn't need to."

He had arranged to take Madeline on a picnic in the Bois de la Boulogne one late September afternoon a month after his seventeenth birthday, with Sir Harry due to return from his travels in a little over a week. None of the servants was around, and Penet was absent from the house. So while waiting for Madeline to come downstairs, he slipped into her father's study.

Casting caution aside, he hastily rifled through the drawers of Penet's desk, then the cabinets in the room, but found nothing. He was on the verge of giving up when a hidden panel at the back of the last cabinet he tried yielded to his touch, revealing more than he could have hoped for: a thick packet of papers containing lists of French ship and troop movements, the names of contacts, drop points and times, even code keys.

As he scanned the evidence, stunned and exultant, the slight creak of the door opening and a light step behind him brought him sharply around. It was Penet's majordomo. Carleton had harbored a vague, uneasy feeling about the man from his first visit, but in his preoccupation with Madeline and efforts to uncover her father's clandestine activities, he had paid no attention to it.

Now the man stopped at sight of him, looked down at the opened packet he held, then back up to meet Carleton's alarmed gaze. But instead of appearing surprised or angry, a smug, calculating smile spread across the man's face.

"Did you really think you'd escape detection, little boy?" he drawled insolently. "Well, now we'll see what intelligence Caledonne will give up to get his precious nephew back unharmed."

Triumph and threat hanging heavy in his tone, the man slipped his hand inside his coat as he spoke. Raw instinct brought Carleton's loaded pistol to his hand from his pocket at the same instant the man withdrew his.

"I believed he intended to take me hostage. But when he saw the weapon in my hand, his eyes hardened. And he leveled his pistol.

"I knew both of us had only one shot, that if either of us fired, the report would draw everyone in the house. And I stared into his eyes, wondering whether he meant to kill me or merely wound me."

Elizabeth had listened to the grim recital, hardly breathing. Carleton stopped now and remained silent, face turned partially away, until her fingers ached under the pressure of her clenched hands. At last he spoke as though watching the scene play out in front of him.

"I saw his finger tighten on the trigger. I pulled mine by reflex, hardly aware of what I did. We fired at the same instant."

She pressed her hand over her mouth, strangling a cry.

"He was the first man I ever killed," he went on dispassionately. "I never told Sir Harry what happened, though a number of times he tried, kindly, to draw it out of me. But I couldn't speak of it. To this day I've not forgotten the man's face or how his eyes widened as he stared at me in shock . . . the crimson stain blooming across his white shirt . . . and how he fell."

With a shudder, he let the words trail off. Glancing around, he looked blankly through her as though he again stood in Penet's study, a youth barely seventeen, with smoking pistol in hand.

She ached to draw him into her arms, but intuition warned that he could not bear any touch in that moment. Not until he came to himself again.

"I'm glad you fired," she said fiercely, tears trickling down her cheeks. "He'd have killed you if you hadn't."

"His bullet passed so close to my head that if I hadn't flinched at his pistol's report, he'd have succeeded. Perhaps it would have been better if he had."

He uttered the last in a whisper, and the bleakness she read in the depths of his eyes shook her. "No, dearest of my heart! You were only defending yourself."

His gaze focused as though he only now saw her. "I was in another man's house. In his private study, going through his personal papers—"

"A man who was betraying your uncle's country, and who might well have been responsible for your cousin's death!" When he opened his mouth to protest, she rushed on, "Are not all the sins we've repented of covered by our dear Lord's blood? It isn't his desire for you to continue grieving what he's already forgiven and cast away."

The tightness of his features eased then, and a degree of peace returned to them. Tentatively she drew him into her embrace, felt him gradually relax, then his arms came around her, and she nestled against him.

"I needed to hear that," he said gruffly, then with a rueful laugh, added, "How did you become so wise so young?"

Sobering, he drew a breath and let it out. "I'm sorry I've put this burden on you, Beth. I never conceived of doing so. Never thought to confide this to anyone. I'd persuaded myself it was long dead and buried."

She bit her lip, afraid of his answer yet needing to know. "What happened afterward?"

A spasm of pain crossed his features. "The servant who always attended me burst into the room and dragged me outside to the carriage. I was too shaken to resist, unable to think clearly. After he shoved me inside, I looked down and saw I still held the packet of papers clenched in my left hand. I dropped them immediately, sickened. As the carriage drew away I caught a glimpse of Madeline through the window, running out of the house, looking after me with the same horror on her face that I felt. It was the last time I ever saw her . . . "

She pressed her brow to his chest, eyes closed, fighting back a sickening roil of nausea at the vivid memory of Lucien's hurrying her away from Veillars' body. "You gave Uncle Alexandre the papers, of course?" she managed to say.

He nodded absently. "I never learned what happened to Penet and his contacts . . . or Madeline. Caledonne told me only that she was well taken care of, that I was not to concern myself for her. In fact, all of them simply vanished. A couple of days later I got away and rode past the house. It was empty and shuttered as though no one had ever lived there.

"Sir Harry arrived the following week, as we'd arranged. And a week after that we were in Texel embarking on a ship bound for Virginia."

During that voyage it had become very clear to Sir Harry that something had gone very wrong. Carleton had insisted that he only grieved Frédéric's death. The events of that shattering summer, however, had deepened what had started as grief for his cousin's loss into an indefinable blackness that began to engulf him suddenly in the nights during their voyage home like the fierce assault of an implacable foe.

Unable to bear more, the night of their return to Thornlea with the household fast asleep, he had risen stealthily and, driven by something deeper than desperation, had saddled his horse and fled north as though hell-bound to the Shawnee, to Black Hawk. The sachem's wife, Owl Mother, had still been alive then, and as always she had had taken him to her bosom even as she did her own children. Carleton had sat at her fire with Pathfinder as a son, even as he had at the table of his Aunt Luciana.

"And you needed that more than anything else," Elizabeth ventured, straightening to look into his eyes. "Sir Harry seems to have been a kind, wise, and loving father, but he could never fill the office of the mother you'd lost."

Carleton jerked a nod as though her words pierced him to the core. "From the beginning I envied you your family. They're not perfect—no family is—but you've had them with you all your life. They love you unconditionally, and they've always been there when you needed them. Thank God, Beth, you've no idea what a void it leaves in your heart when that's taken away."

Remembering how he had left her after the angry confrontation with her parents the night they discovered that he was the Shawnee war chief, White Eagle, she bit her lip hard, blinking back tears. She understood even more painfully now how impossible it had been for him to even conceive of being the cause of a rift between her and her parents.

He went on to explain that through that long winter he had turned back each of the increasingly importunate messengers Sir Harry sent. He and Pathfinder had become blood brothers, strengthening Carleton's ties to Black Hawk's family. And he had found comfort in the games and story-telling in wigewa and council house and sweat lodge and on long hunting and fishing trips with Pathfinder; his cousins, Red Fox and Spotted Pony; and others, the peaceful ebb and flow of the life of the clan that was now his own. By this he had gained a measure of strength to hold at bay the oppressive, dark cloud that hovered over his mind.

"Did you ever confide what happened to Black Hawk or any of the others?"

"They wouldn't have understood. In fact, they'd have admired me for it. I couldn't have borne that. At any rate, early that spring when I returned to the town with a hunting party, I found Sir Harry there."

It had been a shock, he admitted, especially as it quickly became clear that there had been a confrontation between Sir Harry and Black Hawk, though neither man ever revealed what passed between them. It had been Owl Mother who had taken him aside and sorrowfully told him he must return home with his white father, that they could not allow him to come again. But as Carleton silently gathered his possessions for the journey back, Black Hawk had clasped him to his breast in a hard embrace, eyes burning. He pleaded for him to return whenever it became possible, secretly if he must, that he wished some day to make Carleton his own son.

It was the last time he had seen Black Hawk and his family until Pathfinder rescued him from the Seneca years later, and by then both Sir Harry and Owl Mother were in the grave. Sir Harry had forbidden Carleton to return to the Shawnee and to have any contact with his aunt and uncle—an indication of his suspicions, although he allowed Carleton to correspond with Cécile from time to time.

Carleton had obeyed. It had caused him much anguish, but he had disciplined himself to be obedient to the man who had adopted him and whom he dearly loved. That summer Sir Harry had sent him back to Boston to manage the import office there. The responsibilities had steadied him in the ensuing years, until Lord Carleton summoned him back to England from his deathbed.

"There's no more to tell," Carleton concluded, his voice catching. "Now you know my darkest secret, along with all that followed. The truth is that I fled to the Shawnee, then to Boston, to England, back home to Thornlea. And finally full circle to Boston again in the blind hope I'd find absolution or redemption. In the end I no more found either than I had before. Had God not brought you to me when he did, I don't know whether I could ever have found my way back to him. My life was in ruins."

"To all outward appearances you were entirely in control of your life," she ventured softly.

He let out a bitter laugh. "I'm quite skilled at dissembling. It's an old habit, one that's stood me in good stead on occasion."

"I can claim that talent too," she said, the words muffled. "Oh, Jonathan, how I wish you'd told me all this before. When you show me your heart, as now, far from thinking less of you, I love you all the more."

He turned his face quickly away, but not before she glimpsed the moisture in his eyes.

Again she took his hand. When she pressed it to her cheek, his fingers tightened over hers.

"You and Uncle Alexandre have never spoken of what happened that day?"

He shook his head, for a long moment remained silent. Then he said softly, "He's my mother's brother, my only connection to her. I trusted him! I did what he asked—what he'd trained me to do."

She released his hand and slipped her arm around his hunched shoulders. "Of course you trusted him! You were so young and had no reason not to. But, dearest, I've seen how he loves you. It wasn't unusual for him to have hopes for you or to teach you his own skills as you were growing into a man —ill conceived though it might have been in this case."

Carleton heaved a sigh. "I can understand that he wanted personal revenge for Frédéric's death and that of so many others. I shared it in every degree and he knew it. But what I find hard to forgive is that his deeper purpose was to wean me away from Sir Harry so he could make of me an officer in the French Navy and an agent in that country's service. Like him. To replace Frédéric."

"Surely not! I can't believe he'd—"

"*Sartine* was behind all of it, Beth!" he cut her off angrily, springing to his feet. He strode off several paces and back.

He reminded her that Antoine de Sartine, who had been Paris's Lieutenant General of Police at that time, was already developing the extensive network of intelligence services that soon became the best in Europe, with agents and spies ranging as far as America and India. Those skills and connections he later brought with him when he took control of France's Royal Navy.

"So don't tell me that my uncle didn't recruit me for Sartine's purposes or was ignorant of exactly what he was doing. Caledonne introduced us within days of when I arrived that summer, and Sartine showed flattering interest in me from then on despite my youth. He seemed a kind, fatherly figure, and because he was my uncle's friend, I asked no questions.

"No, they used me—*groomed* me—to serve their own ends without bothering to tell me the truth and ask whether I wanted to act as an agent for France! That summer I simply thought I was helping to protect a young woman I cared deeply for, while gaining some measure of the vengeance my uncle and I both wanted for Frédéric's death.

"Now, looking back, I see that Uncle Alexandre poured into me all his hopes for the son he'd lost, the one I most resembled in appearance and nature. And with Sir Harry restricting his access to me, when I was with him he tried all the harder to bind me to him and mold me into what Frédéric now could never be."

"What Lucien said was true," she whispered, stricken. "This is the root of his animosity toward you."

Carleton folded his arms. "It was clear even then that Lucien could never step into Frédéric's shoes, though he tried. That's not a criticism of Lucien. He must be his own person as all of us must be. I only wish I'd been wise enough to understand that back then."

"There are things I also wish I'd been wise enough to understand when I was that age," she murmured, looking away. Before he could respond, she stood and reached up to touch his cheek, deeply troubled.

"In spite of it all, will you not speak to Uncle Alexandre about this matter? As close as you've been, as much as you love each other, will you allow your relationship to remain effectively crippled."

His expression hardened. "I'll not demand an apology from him. If he chooses to give it, that's his affair. If not, we'll simply go on as we have these past—" he stopped, calculating, then shrugged, "—twenty years."

THAT NIGHT CARLETON lay drowsily in bed twined together with Elizabeth after their lovemaking, the chamber lit only by the fire's embers. She had been right in persisting until he confided to her the events of that long-ago summer in Paris, he reflected. Though as deeply wrenching as he had feared, it had also been a great relief. What he had most dreaded to confront had turned out to finally free him from the last of the painful shadows that had chained him to the past. His entire being felt lighter as a result.

She had also been right that his refusal to confront his uncle about the matter left a festering sore in their relationship, he conceded reluctantly, even as he thrust the thought away. Pondering their conversation, he realized that he had missed something else she had said. It gnawed at him now.

He released her and pushed up to sit with his back against the bed's headboard. Rousing, she gave him a questioning look before doing the same. He gathered her into his arms, tenderly smoothed back the tumbled curls from her face, and kissed her brow.

"This afternoon while we were talking you said there are things you wished you'd been wise enough to understand when you were seventeen," he prompted. "What did you mean?"

Her eyes darkened, and she looked away. Cupping her chin in his hand, he gently turned her head until she had to meet his gaze.

"Turnabout's fair play," he teased, smiling down at her. "I confided my most dreaded secret, dear heart, and you didn't throw me out. What's yours? I can't imagine it's all that bad."

She hesitated, finally said, "Just that I did some things I since have dearly wished I hadn't."

He regarded her earnestly for some moments before venturing softly, "With Hutchins?"

ELIZABETH FLINCHED at mention of the man to whom she'd become engaged at the age of seventeen—ironic, now she thought of it—the man ultimately responsible for Carleton's exposure and capture as a spy while serving as an aide to British General Thomas Gage in Boston. And for her own near capture as well, had Carleton not sent her to safety from the jaws of the trap.

Sighing, she nodded. "David's family moved to Roxbury near Aunt Tess not long before I turned sixteen. Our families became very close and spent much time together. David seemed so kind and good, and from the first he was exceptionally attentive to me. Before I knew it, I'd fallen entirely in love with him—or so I conceived. But who can know one's heart at such a young age?

"Afterward I came to understand Papa's opposition to our marrying, but at the time Mama felt it an excellent match. His family was wealthy and highly regarded in the community, and she was ecstatic when he pressed his suit for my hand. Over Papa's objections she insisted he approve it, as I did as well. Finally Papa gave in with great reluctance and the stipulation that we not wed until I turned twenty. Thank God that he did so, for I soon learned that he was right in his estimation of David's character."

When she fell silent, face downcast, he ventured gently, "I've wondered whether you told me everything that happened between the two of you. Things even your parents don't know."

She raised her face to his, blinking back tears. "I . . . I'm ashamed. If you know, you might . . . look at me differently. Think less of me. Stop loving me." She whispered the last.

His arms tightened around her. "Then we've harbored the same doubts of each other. Light of my life, there's nothing that could ever make me stop loving you. Especially since I too well remember how little I knew of the world and how foolishly I acted at that age. Isn't what you told me true for you as well?" he concluded, gazing into her eyes with such tender love that her heart melted.

A war waged inside her. He had opened his heart to her with the same unsparing honesty as he had at the beginning of their relationship, when he had confided what she now realized had been the cause of the even worse wreckage of his life that had followed: his sordid relationship with Lady Caroline Randolph and the resulting years of debauchery. She wanted to trust him equally. She had confessed all to the Lord and received forgiveness long ago. Yet still in unearthing what she had so long hidden, renewed fear and shame flooded over her, staining her cheeks with a scalding scarlet tide.

He slipped his arm around her and held her securely. By degrees the safety of his arms and the steady beat of his heart beneath her cheek eased her turmoil enough for her to find her voice.

"When we were first betrothed, I trusted him completely. So when he began . . . pressing me to allow him liberties, assuring me that since we were to be wed it was only natural . . . I finally agreed to clandestine meetings in which I let him kiss me. It seemed entirely innocent at first and sweet, but it lured me . . . and when his caresses began to go farther . . . I allowed him liberties I ought not to have." She finished in a rush, her face buried against his chest.

"How far—" He broke off and amended hastily, "Forgive me, Beth. Don't answer that. It happened before we met and is none of my concern." Bending his head until his cheek rested against the crown of her head, he added firmly, "Nor does it make a difference to me or change my opinion of you or my love in any way."

She looked up to meet his tender gaze. "He . . . we didn't . . . but he . . . " Her voice choked, and she chewed her lip.

"Touched you in places he oughtn't have," he finished for her.

She nodded, mute, dropped her gaze and drew in a shaky breath. "It aroused feelings in me that I wasn't prepared for, that shame me even now to think I allowed it. The verbal abuse started after I came to my senses and refused to let him go farther or repeat what he'd already done. First he apologized and promised he'd respect my wishes, and I thought all would be well. But then he began to bully me and criticize everything I did no matter how hard I tried to please him.

"He never struck me, but he might as well have. I felt dirty—used—believed I'd been so compromised that I was unworthy of another's love, that I now had no choice but to marry him. And I blamed myself, thinking I was at fault for tempting him and leading him on. Thankfully Papa learned he'd joined the Sons of Liberty, and shortly thereafter overheard him berating me. I've never seen him so violently angry. He immediately broke our engagement, threw David out of our house, and forbade him to ever come near me again and me to allow him to."

"I love him for that!" Carleton exclaimed. "I suspect I'll be equally harsh with any man who dares to mistreat our Julianne—if not more so."

"You'd better!" she returned with a muffled laugh.

Chuckling, he bent to kiss her with a tenderness and passion that drove away every other thought and the shame that had lingered so long in the guarded depths of her heart.

Chapter Thirty-One

"**M**ORGAN! You're a welcome sight!"

It was early afternoon, Sunday, 3 December, when Carleton and Andrews entered the ramshackle log cabin Greene had appropriated for his headquarters in the Southern Army's encampment at Charlotte, North Carolina. The giant bear of a man Carleton addressed swung from the crackling blaze in the stone fireplace to face him.

Beaming, he immediately crossed the room to grasp first Carleton's hand, then Andrews', in a bone-crushing shake. "I can say the same for both o' ye! It's been too long since we fought together."

"I couldn't agree more." Andrews winced as he gingerly pulled his glove off his aching hand and doffed his helmet. He regarded forty-four-year-old Brigadier General Daniel Morgan warily as though he feared the man might take hold of him again. Indicating Morgan's worn, rumpled Continental uniform, he added, "We were delighted by the news that you'd decided to come out of retirement."

Carleton divested himself of helmet and cloak. "And even more so to hear that not only did Gates put you in command of a light infantry corps, but also that you've finally gotten that promotion you've been wanting. Well deserved and long past due."

Morgan rubbed the back of his thick neck, his rugged face coloring at the praise as he met Carleton's smile with a rueful one. "Well, followin' on the debacle at Camden, I couldn't justify sittin' the war out any longer jist 'cause o' my pride. And Gates welcomed me with open arms."

Andrews gave a short laugh. "No surprise there considering his dire need of officers who know how to fight and aren't afraid to do so."

Carleton noted that Morgan had aged considerably since their last encounter at Monmouth. Welsh by descent, the man was as broad and muscular as the oxen he had driven as a youth that gained him the nickname the Old Wagoneer. He had also earned a well-deserved reputation for drinking, gambling, brawling, womanizing, and generally riotous living until marriage steadied him.

Morgan's weathered features were more deeply creased now, and his greying hair had thinned. He had long suffered from crippling back and joint pain that stiffened his movements, but his shoulders hunched more now than before.

Carleton eyed him with concern. "It appears you've been giving the British and their Tory minions the devil since your return. But how are you getting along, Dan? Truly."

Morgan grimaced. "Ridin's a trial, I won't lie. So is standin', sittin', and walkin' to be truthful. But it ain't yet gotten as bad as the four-hun-dred-ninety-nine lashes the British gave me back in the previous war. I sure ain't goin' to let a few aches and pains keep me from offerin' 'em my respects long as I can."

As always, Morgan made a point of noting the British error in count-ing out what should have been 500 lashes. His long military career had begun in the French and Indian War, during which he had earned the punishment for disobeying orders.

A livid scar disfigured his upper lip on the left side, along with another on the back of his neck giving testimony to a subsequent encounter with Indians. A musket ball had ripped through his neck and mouth, tearing away several teeth as it exited. That he had lived through injuries that would have killed most men and gone on to earn a reputation as the best backwoods fighter in the country despite poor health and continual pain testified to an indomitable will.

All three looked around as a brown-haired, keen-eyed officer in his early thirties stepped into the room. "Williams!" Andrews exclaimed. "I'm relieved to see you survived Camden."

Colonel Otho Williams' face eased into a wry smile as he glanced from Andrews to Carleton. Like Morgan of Welsh ancestry, the colonel had enlisted at the beginning of the war and been captured by the British early on at the Battle of Fort Washington on Manhattan Island. Imprisoned and finally exchanged after Saratoga, he had been awarded command of the 6th Maryland Regiment, a notably hapless unit incapable of standing firm against the enemy. Williams had transformed it into one of the army's most heralded regiments.

He had served most recently as adjutant general under De Kalb before the general's death at Camden. The Marylanders had constituted a sizeable portion of Gates's army and been one of the few units to hold their line during the battle until forced to withdraw in the general retreat.

Williams returned felicities, then said, "I apprised General Greene of your arrival, Morgan. Now that you're here, I know he'll be pleased to have you join us," he added, nodding to Carleton and Andrews.

As he was speaking, Farris pushed through the door and banged it shut behind him against the stiff wind. He pulled off his helmet, looking from one to the other and saluting before he returned Williams' broad smile.

"Glad to add you to the party, Farris," Williams said.

Charlotte lay on the border between the Carolinas and a two days' ride from the scene of the debacle at Camden, where Cornwallis's subordinate, Lord Francis Rawdon, currently commanded the occupying British garrison. Gates had established temporary headquarters there while waiting for his replacement to arrive.

Williams told them that Gates had issued his final orders earlier in the day, turning command over to Greene. "It was as elegant a lesson in propriety on the part of both men as I've ever seen," he concluded softly.

A welter of emotions beset Carleton, to his surprise including a pang of sympathy for the disgraced general.

He had ridden through the midst of the sprawling camp with his detachment on their arrival a short time earlier and had found what remained of the Southern Army a dismal sight. Officers occupied the village's sagging, weathered log cabins. But the ragged, gaunt, and dirty rank and file had few tents to shelter them against the chilly early December wind. Although rude huts were being thrown up to house them, the majority still huddled around meager, smoky campfires in the open air or under trees.

It reminded Carleton of his first discouraging sight of Washington's army four years earlier on his return from the Shawnee shortly before the Battle of Trenton. All that was missing was the raging nor'easter. At least in these climes temperatures rarely dropped below freezing at this time of year, but even so it was cold enough for misery.

Williams ushered them into one of the building's two back rooms, where General Nathanael Greene sat behind a rudely built table with South Carolina Governor John Rutledge seated in front of it. Greene sprang from his chair, his face brightening with surprise and pleasure as he took in Carleton and his companions and returned their salutes.

Greene, the son of a Quaker merchant, was Washington's most trusted subordinate. A year older than Carleton, he was equally tall and walked with a slight limp, the result of a childhood injury. He had served highly effectively for almost three years as Washington's quartermaster general, though very much against his will. Now that he had finally been granted the battlefield command for which he had passionately petitioned, he made no attempt to disguise his eagerness for action.

"I hoped you'd arrive while Morgan was here." Greene nodded at Rutledge, who had risen with him. "I believe you know Governor Rutledge."

"We had the pleasure at Hillsborough," Carleton said after they bowed to each other.

A man of distinguished appearance and manner, forty-one-year-old John Rutledge had been educated in the law in England. He had risen to prominence as a lawyer in Charlestown and had served as one of South Carolina's delegates to the Continental Congress before being elected as the state's governor.

For several moments they exchanged pleasantries and briefly touched on the events of the last few months. Rutledge finally excused himself and took his leave, while Williams and Farris pulled more chairs into the cramped space.

When everyone was seated, Greene launched into a detailed review of the situation they faced. He had been greatly enheartened on receiving news of the victory at King's Mountain, but the state of the Southern Army was pitiful, he told them bluntly. On paper he currently had under his command roughly 2,400 soldiers. The Maryland and Delaware lines, the army's finest, comprised the majority of the Continentals. The Virginia Line, reduced to the remnants of Buford's battered corps along with one other decimated unit and a few raw recruits, came to around 350 men.

Only about half of the army's supposed total was actually present at the camp and fit for duty. Of those, roughly 800 boasted proper clothing and equipment. Greene had gone so far as to forbid Major General Baron Frederick von Steuben, now stationed in Virginia gathering supplies and recruits, from sending down any more men who did not bring along full equipment.

With this bedraggled corps and nowhere near enough equipment they faced Cornwallis, camped for the winter with his 6,000 men at the village of Winnsborough across the South Carolina border barely seventy miles away. Add to that the various Tory militias roaming the area. And the fact that with the British controlling much of South Carolina and Georgia and poor harvests that year throughout the South, their state legislatures couldn't spare much in the way of men and provisions.

On the bright side, Greene continued, Gates had begun a much needed reorganization of the Southern Army's shattered remnants while waiting to be replaced. Morgan's brigade of handpicked light infantry included a corps of cavalry under General Washington's second cousin, Lieutenant Colonel William Washington. He and Davie continued to range into South Carolina, pressing raids against Cornwallis and the Tory militias, commandeering provisions, and encouraging patriots.

"The victory at King's Mountain and Sumter's defeating Tarleton at Blackstock's Farm are welcome rays of light against a sea of woes. I'll grant you the militias have been keeping this contest alive here in the backcountry. But the British will never relinquish South Carolina and Georgia until there's a formidable, unified force to oppose them on the field instead of these roving bands who emerge from the swamps when they please, only to run off when they face a real challenge."

Clearly frustrated, Greene fumed, "They seem more bent on pillage and plunder and their own private gain or personal glory than our cause! Most of the time they're of no more use than if they were on the moon. Like the locusts of Egypt they eat up every green thing the British haven't captured and leave our army to starve."

"Don't hold back, sir," Andrews urged, his expression droll. "Please do favor us with your frank opinion."

Carleton joined the others' laughter, while Greene regarded them with a rueful grin.

When everyone sobered, Williams pointed out that Sumter had been effective enough that Cornwallis had pulled Tarleton off his futile pursuit of Marion, who'd been wreaking havoc along the Pee Dee River, to hunt down the old Gamecock, as he was being called, in the hopes of reasserting control over the region and encouraging backcountry Tories. "He had over a thousand men at Blackstock's and actually placed them in a strong defensive position to take Tarleton on," he concluded.

"I'm bettin' he listened to the advice o' his colonels for a change," Morgan put in to the others' snickers.

"If so, it's a good thing he did," Williams returned. "He may have outnumbered Tarleton two to one, but Tarleton had more than five hundred men under his command, most of them Regulars. And up to that point he hadn't been defeated."

"Well, caution has never been one of Tarleton's virtues either," Carleton said dryly. "He's developed a habit of driving his men unmercifully over long distances. And then he presses a frontal attack without waiting for his infantry and artillery to catch up or bothering to properly scout the ground and determine the size and disposition of the opposing force. He depends on overwhelming the enemy by surprise and fury. But ordering an uphill cavalry charge against riflemen firing from cover isn't good policy under any circumstances."

Morgan shook his head dolefully. " 'Tis a shame Sumter took such a severe wound late in the battle with the British withdrawin'. Looks like he'll be out of action for several months."

"If you ask me, Tarleton suffered the greater loss though he escaped unscathed," Williams said. "Almost a hundred killed and a hundred more wounded, while Sumter's brigade only took three killed, four wounded, and fifty captured. That tells you something about what our militias can do when they're ably led. Absent an effective army, they've been our most valuable asset in the Carolinas."

Carleton shrugged. "Sumter may lack strategic sense and have a penchant for bloody and unnecessarily costly frontal assaults—just like Tarleton, I might add—but he does have the ability to recruit large numbers of men quickly even after suffering a defeat."

"It doesn't hurt that he allows his men to plunder freely," Farris said, his tone acid.

Greene shifted in his seat, considering. "Maybe I ought to pay a visit to Sumter as Rutledge is pressing me to do. I certainly can't count on His Excellency to send reinforcements since he's facing the same difficulties we are." He sighed. "Much as I hate to admit it, we'll have to rely on the militias' help if we're to retake South Carolina. Sumter's brigade will at least be of some use for scouting and harassing the enemy once he recovers."

He frowned, eyes narrowing. "As for Marion, Gates formed a low opinion of him. But he was formerly a Continental officer and has proven to be of some help in our cause." He picked up a letter from his desk and leaned back in his chair. "He wrote to Gates a number of times requesting guidance as to how he could be of the greatest use, and apparently Gates only answered once. Marion sent this last letter a couple of weeks ago from a place called Britton's Ferry on the Pee Dee."

The letter's tone reflected Marion's discouragement at Gates's lack of response. He was in dire need of clothing for his men and a surgeon to care for them. And now the British were making serious attempts to wrest back the area Marion controlled and to hunt him and his men down. Lacking sufficient men and supplies he could do nothing to stop them, and worst of all he had no idea when, or even if, the Southern Army would return to South Carolina.

"Many of my people have left me and gone over to the enemy, for they think that we have no army coming on, and have been deceived," Greene read soberly. "As we hear nothing from you in a great while, I hope to have a line from you in what manner to act, and some assurance to the people of support."

"It's unconscionable to ignore such a man!" Carleton burst out. "He clearly has no idea of how his successes are affecting the British."

Williams nodded. "I've heard Marion constantly sends out patrols to roam the countryside gathering intelligence, so it appears that he's here, then there, then someplace else in a matter of days or even hours. Makes the British think he has more men than he does, and they tie up substantial forces trying to run him to ground. All to our advantage."

Greene drummed his fingers on the table. He had studied maps, consulted with knowledgeable officers, and pondered the situation all during his journey south, he told them. Salisbury, forty-two miles north of Charlotte, was developing into a major collection point for supplies sent from states farther north. The town also had a jail large enough to house more prisoners in addition to those from Kings Mountain already held there. Local craftsmen manufactured a variety of needed items as well.

Greene planned to increase the production of clothing for the army by using the easily available and valuable commodity of salt as payment. He had also reluctantly concluded that the best strategy was to divide the army.

He would lead his main division southeast across the border into South Carolina. Meanwhile Morgan would head southwest into the back-country along the Catawba River where his light infantry would find ample forage. From there Morgan could strike the enemy's supply lines and hamper their movements while avoiding a confrontation that might destroy his brigade.

After some discussion the officers agreed that, although this strategy carried substantial risks, it would encourage the patriot militias and allow Greene time to build up his army.

He was already working on supplying the boats necessary for navigating South Carolina's rivers and swamps. More horsemen would also be essential to support Washington's and Carleton's cavalry.

"I'll call on Sumter," Greene allowed glumly. "But first I'm going to respond to Marion's concerns."

He skewered Carleton in a narrowed gaze. "Having a Continental officer personally deliver a letter should impress our regard on the old Swamp Fox, as Tarleton's taken to calling him. And since you have the most experience in irregular warfare, Carleton, I'd like you to hand carry it to him. Build him up. Let him know what's going on here and what's planned. Assure him that we value his efforts."

Carleton sat eagerly forward. "I'd be delighted, sir. I've been wanting to meet him."

Greene deliberated for several moments before sharing the latest intelligence report that a British fleet was being prepared to sail from New York to Virginia, where it would land a force under the command of Benedict Arnold, now a British general. Although Washington had sent agents to infiltrate the city in the attempt to capture the traitor, their success was far from certain. It was therefore vital that Carleton find Marion as quickly as possible, deliver his response back to Greene, then hurry north to meet any threat that might arise in Virginia.

After the meeting broke up, Carleton ordered Andrews to leave for Thornlea with the detachment early the following morning. Andrews' jaw dropped.

"I can't believe you'd be so foolhardy as to travel into enemy territory alone!" he protested.

"I'm taking Hutchinson and Stowe with me."

"That's not enough protection. If we all go, we'll easily return long before a fleet can reach Virginia."

"There's no way of knowing how long it'll take to track Marion down or what we'll encounter wandering through unfamiliar terrain. I need you and Farris back at Thornlea to alert the local militias and prepare for a possible invasion."

Andrews stared at him as though he had gone daft. "How long do you think it'll take Tarleton's scouts to discover your movements? Cornwallis will be salivating at the chance to capture you, and—"

"A large detachment will attract considerably more notice than a few backcountry-travelers," Carleton countered. "Besides, Cornwallis has more important concerns than me—"

"He certainly won't be loath to pounce if you blunder across his path!"

Carleton rolled his eyes. "I don't plan to go anywhere until I find a reliable, trustworthy guide to help us track Marion down without our mucking about the swamps interminably. We'll take every precaution to conceal our trail. There's nothing to worry about."

Andrews glowered at him for a moment. Then, shaking his head in frustration, he stalked away.

EARLY MONDAY MORNING Carleton saw a surly Andrews off with the Rangers on the road back to Virginia. While waiting impatiently for Greene to filter through his vast pile of correspondence and get to the letter to Marion, Carleton rode out to find Morgan, who, he calculated, must have a reliable guide familiar with South Carolina's Pee Dee River region. Bored to distraction and eager to get on the road, Hutchinson and Stowe accompanied him to the light infantry's camp several miles from Charlotte.

They found Morgan seated on a log at a campfire with several of his subordinates, polishing off with gusto the remains of a breakfast that appeared as appetizing as Carleton's had earlier. Brightening at sight of them, Morgan swallowed the dregs of the vicious-looking mixture that served as the army's coffee, when it could be found at all. After taking a cautious sip earlier, Carleton had spewed the bitter brew onto a patch of weeds, certain the liquid would rot the vegetation away in short order, and had followed with the entire cupful.

Morgan set his battered pewter plate and cup on the ground and pushed stiffly to his feet. "Well, here ye are! I intended to look ye up afore ye took off to hunt Marion down."

"That's why we're here," Carleton returned. "If we are going to find this so-called Swamp Fox, I'm going to need a trustworthy guide with intimate knowledge of his haunts. I figured if anyone knew of such a man, it would be you."

Morgan allowed a sly smile. "Then ye'd be right." Eying Stowe and Hutchinson, he added, "Nothin' 'gaist these boys, but ye'll need a bigger escort in case ye run into a British patrol. I know they'd be more'n happy to get their hands on ye. I can supply both."

Drawing Carleton aside before he could protest, he said, "There's another matter I want to broach with ye." At Carleton's questioning look, he continued, "I respect Greene's order to avoid a direct confrontation with the British. But after talkin' with a number o' the militiamen who've fought 'gainst Tarleton, I spent some time thinkin' on the matter. He ain't invulnerable. Given the right conditions and the right opponent, he can be whipped."

Carleton stifled a smile. "I can't say I'm opposed to taking him on. Considering our situation, Greene's policy is generally a wise one. But not necessarily in every case."

Morgan cast a cautious look around to make sure no one was close enough to hear. "I got only 'round six hundred effectives in my little flyin' army right now. We need to resupply and bring in a substantial number of militia afore we engage in any serious action. But if things develop the way I hope they do over the next few weeks, I figger I might be able to draw Tarleton after me till he's frustrated enough to cast caution to the wind. He's been known to do such on occasion."

Carleton gave a short laugh. "You might say that."

Morgan's eyes narrowed. "Should I happen on the proper ground, we just might have us a fight we can win. If ye're with me—"

Carleton didn't try to suppress his grin. "I am, but you heard Greene. I'll have to hurry back north in case the British do land an army on the Virginia coast. I'd love to get my hands on Arnold."

Morgan nodded. "I wish ye the best o' luck. What I'm thinkin' of is goin' to take some time. Month at least, I reckon."

"A great deal can happen in a month. You'll send a message to Thornlea the instant things start to shape up?"

Morgan's smile broadened. "Ye can count on it. Then if ye're free . . . "

Carleton took Morgan's hand in a hard grip. "I'll make every effort to put myself at your disposal."

Chapter Thirty-two

CARLETON THOUGHTFULLY assessed the man seated across the crackling fire from him, his features cast in sharp relief by the flickering light.

There was nothing about the ill-favored, short, slight, forty-eight-year-old descendant of French Huguenots that would have given anyone cause to recognize him as the most wily partisan leader in South Carolina.

Colonel Francis Marion could not be considered handsome by any measure of the word. A swarthy countenance; beaked nose; jutting chin; and high, broad brow distinguished a narrow face framed by lank black hair. Yet keen intelligence flashed in dark eyes that gave away nothing of what lay behind them. And a lean, wiry frame testified to a constitution that could endure considerable hardship with indifference.

Moments earlier, at the head of a small detachment, he had ridden into the camp where Carleton and his companions waited. Carleton noted that Marion sat his horse as though they were one creature, like the mythical centaur. When he dismounted, however, he moved clumsily on knock-knees and thickened, deformed ankles.

Carleton lifted the battered cup of vinegar water—his favorite drink for its healthful properties, Marion had mentioned laconically—and tipped it in his host's direction. "To your health then, sir," he said before swallowing the contents, suppressing a grimace.

In his usual position, squatting close behind Carleton's shoulder, Stowe kept his eyes on their surroundings and his hand on his pistol, his expression unreadable. But Hutchinson also lifted his cup and gulped his drink, though he squinted, mouth puckering.

A faint smile lighted Marion's face as he returned their gesture. "And to yours."

Marion's officers, lean, flint-eyed men mostly in their twenties and thirties who crouched in the circle with them, shared amused glances. On the fires' outer fringes lingered a motley assortment of others, some of whom appeared to be no more than youths, among them several Blacks and a couple of Catawba Indians.

Marion set down his empty cup and doffed his fitted leather helmet, handing it to his body servant, a black man of about his age called Buddy. Its front was ornamented with a silver crescent and inscribed with the word *Liberty*, Carleton noted with interest. From what he could see it was Marion's only remaining possession from the 2nd South Carolina Continental Regiment he had once commanded.

Marion and his men were garbed in rough, threadbare clothing, their coarse jackets crimson—the only cloth obtainable in the Carolinas since Charlestown's fall, Carleton's guide had explained with chagrin. Boots and other leathers were scuffed and worn.

Apparently only a small contingent of the partisan band was present, which, Carleton had gathered from the men's conversation, must number at least a couple of hundred. Judging from the present company, they were certainly well mounted despite their ragged, weather-beaten appearance. They would have to be, considering how much hard riding they were obliged to do.

Thomas Sumter and his partisans ranged through the forested uplands of the backcountry to the west. South Carolina militia Colonel Andrew Pickens covered the northwest third of the state bordering on Cherokee lands.

Marion's band patrolled the rivers and swamps of the state's eastern third, ranging from the low country up into portions of the backcountry. South Carolina's low country stretched roughly fifty miles inland from Charlestown and Georgetown on the coast. In this region the state's largest river, the Santee, held the greatest strategic importance to the war, flowing southeast to empty into the Atlantic below Georgetown. To the north the Black and Great Pee Dee rivers were also vital to Marion's theater of operation.

Nelson's Ferry on the Santee was the principal crossing between Charlestown and Cornwallis's winter headquarters at Winnsborough. Marion and his highly mobile band often camped nearby or at Witherspoon's, Britton's, or Port's Ferries where easy river crossings facilitated sudden raids and swift escape from pursuit.

After more than a week of frustration spent wandering through dismal swamps and seeking out fords and ferries, Carleton's small company including his aide and servant, their guide, and four of Morgan's soldiers, had finally run athwart of one of Marion's patrols on Thursday, 14 December, with dusk gathering. It had taken some effort to persuade the patrol's leader that they were friends carrying a letter for Marion from the Southern Army's new commander. But finally the detachment had led Carleton and his party to a well-concealed camp south of Witherspoon's Ferry near the tiny hamlet of Indiantown.

"We would have been here sooner, but Tarleton has the right of it," Carleton said dryly. "Finding you is harder than tracking a fox through these swamps."

Marion's mouth twitched. "If I'd known you were coming, I'd have arranged a better reception, general," he replied equably, his voice low and soft.

"We were off west on the Santee at Halfway Swamp pesterin' the latest regiment Cornwallis sent after us," volunteered Major John James, a burly Irishman about Marion's age, with a laugh. "Persuaded 'em to hightail it out'a our territory. We're not keen on sharin'."

"We're might' encouraged to finally see a couple o' Continental officers out here," drawled Peter Horry, who had intercepted their party.

With him had been his brother Hugh and militia Colonel Hugh Giles, who introduced himself as a surveyor, and whom, according to Horry, held intimate knowledge of the expansive area Marion and his men patrol-led. By appearance the Horry brothers were also of Huguenot descent, prosperous low country rice and indigo planters like Marion, and the patriot leader's close associates.

While waiting for Marion's return to camp, Carleton had been intro-duced to Major James, his son John, and cousin Captain John James. And to Captain Henry Mouzon, Marion's cousin, for whom the fight was personal as Tarleton had burned his home to the ground.

Other members of the band had slowly trickled in, followed finally by Marion, who had revealed no surprise at finding strangers among them. He calmly welcomed them and bade them to share in the meager supper steaming in a kettle over the fire.

Carleton first apologized for the lack of communication from Gates. He then went on to detail General Greene's appointment to the Southern Army's command, the meeting at Charlotte, Morgan's assignment, and everything that was being done and planned. At last he pulled Greene's letter out of his pouch and handed it to Marion.

"I assure you that Greene's a much different commander from Gates. He greatly appreciates your having kept Cornwallis and his minions so well occupied. Having served as Washington's quartermaster general for so long, you understand, he's not only very eager for action, but also . . . ah . . . extremely attentive to details. And very precise in what he expects. I believe he laid that out at length as far as gathering intelligence is concerned."

His expression inscrutable, Marion broke the letter's seal and scanned the contents of the closely written pages. Folding them again, he tucked them into his coat pocket.

"His instructions appear to be along the lines of what we've been doing. But I'll review them more closely as I have time. We'll pass on our intelligence as quickly as possible."

"You'll find Greene to be a good man and gratifying to work with in spite of his tendency to overmanage. He values the kind of address and effectiveness you and your men have shown."

Marion inclined his head, shrewdness and good humor flashing in his dark eyes. Carleton noted that his men listened to him attentively and with every sign of respect tinged with almost . . . veneration. Even though Marion's manner reflected nothing of inherent charisma, Carleton reckoned that every one of them served under him from a deep personal allegiance and would follow wherever he led.

"We were especially pleased to hear that you don't allow your men to plunder," Carleton continued. "I'm sure I needn't tell you that the same can't be said of all our militia leaders—and certainly not of the Tories—which appears to be the attraction for many of their followers."

Marion regarded him gravely. "The line between plunderin' and foragin' is a slim one, but I do my utmost to prevent the former. There's nothin' more guaranteed to lose the people's allegiance." He indicated the men clustered in the circle of firelight. "As to attractin' followers, I prefer the loyalty of a few good men to the fickleness of many uncommitted ones."

"We've had a goodly number of volunteers come in though, now the harvest is done," Hugh Horry, broke in, his eyes narrowed. "And we'll need 'em. Our intelligence indicates Cornwallis intends to send a larger force into this area to hunt us down. More Tory militias are risin' 'gainst us too."

Measuring his words, Marion said, "I can't disagree with Greene's assessment of the militias. When I held a Continental command, I too often found 'em to be not of the least service. And now that I've direct experience of commandin' 'em, their diffidence is even more frustratin'. They do come and go at will. But when their own homes, families, and crops are threatened, they rise, stand, and fight."

"Ferguson found that out at King's Mountain," Hutchinson said with a smile.

Marion nodded, his expression hardening. "Tarleton and others have torn through the area burnin' and plunderin' plantations and leavin' women, children, and the elderly with only the clothes on their backs. They've spared neither Whig nor Tory. That's the reason so many of 'em are joinin' us."

"Greene's anxious to support you in this fight, but I'm afraid as to your request for ammunition and clothing for your men, he hasn't enough to provision the army," Carleton said apologetically. "He outlined everything in his letter. Regrettably he also has no surgeon to spare but will see if he can find one to send you."

Marion's mouth tightened, but he said with weary resignation, "We'll continue to make do as best we can."

"I also talked to Governor Rutledge before I left Charlotte, and he means to commission you brigadier general of state troops. You should receive notice by the end of the month."

Whoops and murmurs of glee rose from the men around them. Several patted Marion on the back, but his face registered no emotion.

After a moment he said, "I'll organize a brigade then. We'll do everythin' we're able to hold this ground till Greene can get down here and finish the job."

Chapter Thirty-three

CARLETON SCRAPED the last spoonful of cold beans and salt pork off his battered tin plate and devoured it, stomach growling. After washing the unappetizing mouthful down with a swallow of brackish water, he set canteen, plate, and spoon aside and flexed his cold-stiffened fingers while dubiously assessing the smoky fire.

The feeble flames did nothing to ward off the damp, frigid wind, though thankfully the rain had abated for the moment. It was a miracle the wet wood burned at all, even sheltered as much as possible under the trees' dripping, low-hanging branches. Many other faint campfires glimmered beneath the dense pines and firs that cloaked the area, with the shadowy forms of soldiers moving wearily among them.

When he tipped his head up to look past his hat's sagging brim, a freezing stream of water poured down his back. Splendid. The only thing needed to increase the joy, he reflected, was for a nor'easter to blow in. It wouldn't have surprised him if one did.

It was Monday, 15 January 1781, and for a good deal of the past week he and his troops had ridden through repeated bands of rainstorms on their way south through Virginia and North Carolina. Instead of the new uniforms provided with coin Teissèdre supplied, they had donned frontier dress of buckskin breeches and hunting shirts, adding heavy woolen cloaks and slouch hats to better shed the rain. Even so, by the time they had passed into South Carolina with the deluge continuing undiminished, they were sodden and cold to the bone.

Morgan sat at the fire circle with him, Andrews, Isaiah, and Farris. His infantry commander, Lieutenant Colonel John Eager Howard, a handsome officer about Carleton's age who commanded the Continental Regulars; and Morgan's cavalry commander Lieutenant Colonel William Washington made up the rest of their company. The latter was immediately identifiable in the 3rd Light Dragoons' white jacket faced in dark blue and blue leather helmet with a white crest. Tall and corpulent but strong, Washington was deceptively amiable in nature. From his experience at the Battle of Trenton four years earlier, Carleton knew him to be a fierce and unyielding foe in battle.

Morgan's brigade had just settled into bivouac along Thicketty Creek near Burr's Mill when Carleton's detachment rode in. Red Fox, Spotted Pony, and their warriors had quickly joined a cluster of Catawba men on the far side of the mill while McLeod, Hutchinson, and Spencer commandeered the last stretch of dry ground above the flooded creek. They were currently overseeing distribution of food to the troops.

"I'm thankful our scouts ran across ye so ye didn't blunder into Tarleton," Morgan rumbled. "We was still camped at Grindal's Shoals this mornin' when they come in carryin' the news that ol' Benny was closin' in on the Pacelot River headin' our way. So we pushed on up here. Cornwallis is east of the Broad and word is he plans to head north toward Greene once Gen'l Leslie's reinforcements catch up with him. Last thing I'm goin' to allow is for him and Tarleton to squeeze me 'tween 'em."

Carleton exchanged an amused glance with Andrews at Morgan's habit of mockingly calling Banastre Tarleton 'Benny.' "You remember those rumors that Arnold might sail south with his new command?" he said. "Well, at the beginning of the month we got word that he'd landed troops at Portsmouth and was marching on Richmond."

Howard cocked an eyebrow at Carleton and his officers. "I don't suppose you managed to capture that . . . traitor."

"We received notice of his movements too late," Carleton growled.

"Failing that, we indulged in a deal of cussing, as I'm sure you can imagine," Farris said, grinning.

Andrews explained that since there hadn't been enough militia to oppose Arnold, he had destroyed a foundry, mills, warehouses, and stores of supplies outside Richmond with impunity. The governor, legislature, and most residents had fled by the time Arnold entered the town, leaving him to plunder and burn Richmond's public and private property unhindered.

"When we got there—through a downpour—he was already heading back east," he concluded with disgust.

"I brought out my entire division, but we had no cannon and were too heavily outnumbered to risk a general action even had the militia that showed up been fully equipped—which they weren't. We rendezvoused with General Nelson's men the first night intending to attack Arnold's rear. But then the gates of heaven opened and poured forth a deluge that all but drowned us and rendered our arms and ammunition unserviceable."

"We're intimately familiar with biblical floods down here, Carleton," Washington said dryly.

Andrews grimaced. "We noticed. What is it with this infernal rain?"

"At any rate, since we weren't in a position to stop Arnold, and General von Steuben's command lay in his path back to Portsmouth," Carleton said to Morgan, "I thought it wise to return to Thornlea and wait for word from you or Greene. As it happened, your courier arrived the day after we returned, and then Greene's not an hour later ordering us to link up with you. We left that same evening. The only time we stopped was to water and rest the horses, swallow a mouthful of food, and catch a few hours of sleep. If these storms hadn't washed out the fords and turned what passes for roads here in your backcountry into quagmires, we'd have arrived a couple of days sooner."

Morgan pulled off his battered hat, shook off the rain, then clamped it back on his head. "What with Tarleton on our heels, I was beginnin' to think we was goin' to have to hustle back and join up with Greene agin whether he likes it or no. Sumter wouldn't lend us men or supplies if Cornwallis hisself was bangin' at the door."

"You're better off with him out of the picture. In my humble opinion," Andrews amended wryly.

"You'll get no argument about that here," Howard returned with a smirk.

Morgan scowled. "Davidson didn't bring in near the number o' North Carolina militia he promised, but he's gone to beat the bushes for more. Thankfully, ever since we set up camp at Grindal's Shoals three weeks ago, Pickens has been rangin' 'tween us and Tarleton and alertin' us to his movements. He keeps directin' volunteers our way, too, with promise o' more. We couldn't do without him."

"Any idea of how many men Tarleton has?" Carleton asked.

"Accordin' to our scouts, 'tween eleven and twelve hundred. That don't count Tory militia that may yet join up. I got maybe six hundred foot and horse countin' my Regulars, Washington's eighty-two dragoons, and some Virginia state troops. Plus a fluctuatin' number o' militia. Trouble is, it's nigh on impossible to keep 'em collected at any one place! I don't 'spect even two-thirds of 'em to show up if Tarleton catches up with us."

"Your Maryland and Delaware regiments are the army's top Regulars," Washington reminded him, nodding to Howard.

"And the Virginians are all discharged Continental veterans," Howard pointed out as he propped a damp, rotted branch across the smoldering fire and stirred the coals back to a semblance of life.

"We can depend on them, Washington's cavalry, and Pickens' men," Morgan allowed, easing his position cautiously. Jutting his chin toward Carleton, he added, "And now your Rangers."

It was clear Morgan was suffering again, Carleton thought with concern. And the cold, rainy weather had to make things worse. He couldn't help wondering how much longer the older man would be able to endure, regardless of his legendary strength.

Morgan went on to explain that he had personally pleaded with the troops whose enlistments had expired to stay until the arrival of fresh state troops and militia from Virginia and North Carolina. So far his efforts to keep his small corps together had met with more success than not. But he was concerned that if he had to cross into North Carolina to stay ahead of Tarleton, he would lose the South Carolina militia units that made up half his brigade.

"How many men have ye brought? Couple hundred, I'm guessin'," he said hopefully to Carleton.

Carleton glanced at Isaiah, seated on his left staring into the fire's dying embers, his expression carefully blank. Carleton's insistence that he join them at the fire with Morgan's officers had not sat well with him. Nor did the occasional wary sidelong glance from the others, which Farris, who had made a point of sitting on his oppoiste side, countered with a level stare. Although far from ecstatic to have his black troops dragged into the Carolinas, Isaiah had made no objection to the order since all of them were as eager for battle as the rest of the Rangers following the vain chase after Arnold.

"Just in case Arnold decides to go on another raiding spree," Carleton answered, "I left my light infantry companies to guard Thornlea. They'd have slowed us down anyway. But I've over three hundred mounted troops and warriors, and we packed all the supplies and ammunition we could carry on horses so we could move fast."

Morgan brightened. "Well, that brings us nearer to squarin' the odds."

Washington slapped his hand on his knee. "With any luck, maybe this time we'll jerk a knot in Bloody Ban's tail that he won't soon undo."

"We jist need to see how many more reinforcements come in afore we can think about standin' and fightin'," Morgan cautioned. "Hard to say what might happen with this blasted rain! Makes movin' troops, scoutin', and keepin' up communications a right challenge."

He stared into the fire for some moments. "Both sides o' this contest have picked this area clean o' provisions. Fast as Tarleton moves, his men have no time to forage farther afield, and he wears 'em out on the march. We're pullin' him farther from Cornwallis, too, while we're movin' closer to reinforcements and supplies."

He nodded then, smiling, and murmured as though to himself, "If enough reinforcements come in, mebbe we ought to let Tarleton back us into a corner. Long as we can pick the corner."

RAIN AND FOG THICKENED as the long column wound northwest along the rutted track up hills, down ravines, and across swollen creeks and swamps through a dismal, densely forested landscape. Rattling wagons and tramping men churned up the boggy ground, making passage even more trying for those at the back and leaving a broad trail for pursuers. Progress had slowed to an exhausting slog, the ragged soldiers soaked to the skin and shivering, chilled by the cold, moisture-laden wind.

An hour before dawn, still full dark with a misty rain shrouding the surrounding forest, Morgan's stentorian voice had echoed through the camp. "Tarleton's 'crost the Pacelot not six miles off! Ain't no time for breakfast. Pack up! We're movin' out right now."

Contrary to Morgan's expectations, the arrival of additional militia companies overnight had swelled their numbers. The entire body had immediately launched into frantic motion. They had marched out in little more than a quarter hour, guttering fires and meager breakfast abandoned, leaving McDowell's North Carolina militia to cover their withdrawal while Pickens' men roamed between them and Tarleton's rapidly advancing troops.

"We're headin' for Island Ford higher up on the Broad, 'bout twenty miles above last night's camp," Morgan had told his officers. "On the other side o' the river 'round Thicketty Mountain lies rough hill country that might jist offer good terrain where we can stand and fight."

As the hours passed, the fog blew away on the wind, and the rain that had portended helpfully neglected to materialize. Flanked by his Life Guard, Morgan rode at the head of the main column in the company of his local guide and a couple of his officers, while Carleton's Rangers' roved ahead in the van and Washington held the column's rear.

Militia units were joining them now from all directions, small groups, entire companies, even battalions, all clearly scenting battle. Every man in the steadily growing column was spoiling to test his mettle against "Bloody Ban". Carleton heard many grumbling and cursing among themselves, believing that Morgan was retreating from a confrontation, but in his bones he could feel the battle brewing.

A couple of hours after midday he made his way to the column's rear to check with Washington. Tarleton's scouts were hanging on the column's tail like fleas on a dog, the colonel related cheerfully. Although they retreated at the approach of the details he sent to take their measure, as soon as they withdrew the enemy scouts filtered back.

"McDowell rejoined us a little while ago," he told Carleton. "He said they pulled out of Burr's Mill around noon just ahead of a party of Tarleton's dragoons probin' the area. Several parties of volunteers comin' up from the south brought in prisoners they captured in skirmishes with Tarleton's van."

Carleton rode back to the head of the column, reported to Morgan, then rejoined his Rangers. Another hour had passed when Morgan's guide directed the column onto a barely discernable byway even narrower and more arduous than the first. Companies and whole regiments lagged behind, forced to wade through flooded, densely grown thickets, undergrowth, and swamps.

With daylight fading, the advance scouts rode back in bringing the discouraging report that Island Ford still lay six miles ahead, and the river was running high and fast. Crossing the army would be not only time-consuming, but also dangerous, especially in the dark.

Morgan rubbed his hand across his mouth, considering his options. "If we should try it, and Tarleton were to come upon us—" He didn't bother to review the disheartening possibilities. "How far back is he?"

"Some of Pickens' men came in just before I rode up here," Washington answered. "They say Tarleton's bivouacked at Burr's Mill and his men are makin' free with our breakfast."

Morgan relaxed, a grin spreading over his face. "With all that marchin' double time the past four days tryin' to catch us, Tarleton's men done probly run out o' food. I imagine they're mighty hungry by now."

"He won't let them sleep the night away, but at least it buys us time," Andrews said.

Carleton looked back down the rutted track ankle-deep in mud, strewn with broken vegetation the army had left in its wake. "I'm sure he'll thank us heartily for the food—if not for the road we're so obligingly plowing up for him."

Morgan gave a bark of mirth, then, sobering, expelled a breath. "My first responsibility is to get this flyin' army back to Greene and the main army in one piece. Question is the best way to do that. Risk crossin' the Broad with ol' Ben closin' in—or find favorable ground, rest and feed our men, and figger out how we're goin' to fight him once he catches up with us?"

Washington exchanged glances with Carleton and Andrews. "I think we all prefer the latter, sir. Any favorable ground hereabouts?"

"The Old Fields lie not far away," the guide volunteered. "It's where the Over Mountain Men rendezvoused afore headin' on to King's Mountain. Captain Tramell of the Spartanburg Regiment makes his home nearby and is well acquainted with how the fields are situated."

"Let's go," Morgan responded.

THE OLD FIELDS, called by some the Cowpens, acquired its name from the broad meadowland where local cattle were penned to fatten on the lush grass before being driven to the Atlantic coast and sold for slaughter. It was near sunset when the advance party arrived. The hoarse bawling of cows being driven in echoed across the fields.

As the officers dismounted, Morgan's quartermaster and his assistants hurried past to intercept the drovers, intent on commandeering the entire herd. Carleton glanced toward the lagging column and saw that a number of officers strode purposefully back down it—likely rounding up volunteer butchers, he guessed, mouth already watering in anticipation of dining on steak.

They had taken the Green River Road, a dirt track that followed the high ground through heavy stands of pine, fir, and spruce interspersed with the denuded limbs of hardwoods before bisecting the Old Fields on its way to Island Ford. As Carleton and his officers trailed after Captain Dennis Tramell, who escorted Morgan, his aide, and Life Guard around the site, Carleton estimated that the open area bordered on all sides by woods was roughly five hundred yards long and wide.

He had thought the land level when their party emerged from the surrounding forest, but on foot it quickly became apparent that the impression was mistaken. In fact, the entire area sloped almost imperceptibly uphill, undulating in gentle folds that formed shallow depressions and slight rises indistinguishable unless one walked the ground.

Widely spaced trees dotted the landscape, with some of the low ridges more heavily wooded, but overall free of underbrush. A number of springs, rivulets, and creeks flowed through the area, concealed by stands of cane. Days of rain had turned low ground into bogs.

Gazing across the fields to the road that had led them there, Carleton mused that Tarleton would also have to follow it. And it would funnel his troops into an unfamiliar and deceptive landscape.

For a commander who disposed his army to the greatest tactical advantage, the site could become a deadly killing field. And there was no one more talented at placing his troops than Morgan.

One serious flaw nagged at Carleton, however. According to their guide, the Broad River lay five miles to the north, with the Pacolet an equal distance west. Hemmed in by flooded rivers difficult to cross, with the enemy at their backs, they would have no route of escape. In a hushed discussion with Andrews, the two colonels, Red Fox, and Spotted Pony, they all agreed that whatever the morrow might bring, retreat would not be an option.

Evidently Morgan had come to the same conclusion. When Carleton led his companions forward to join him and Tramell at the fields' upper end, they heard Morgan say grimly, "If Tarleton overtakes us while my men are fatigued and retreating, we'll have much less chance of success than if we choose to stand and fight. Captain, here is Morgan's grave or victory. On this ground I'll defeat the British or lay my bones."

Chapter Thirty-four

CARLETON SQUINTED, adjusting his spyglass's focus on where the Green River Road emerged from the woods. The sporadic crackle of rifle fire and answering musket fire echoed through the forest, gradually increasing in volume. Pickens' skirmishers were harassing Tarleton's advance troops, slowing them down, giving Morgan more time to dress his lines.

But that wasn't necessary at halfway past seven o'clock on this tentative, moisture-veiled dawn, Wednesday, 17 January 1781.

Two hours earlier, with darkness still at the full and thick frost blanketing the meadow, the pounding hoofbeats of Morgan's scouts galloping into camp had roused Carleton from what little sleep he'd gotten. He and Andrews had rolled out of their blankets and scrambled to their feet as one. With Isaiah and Farris on their heels and other officers scurrying in from all directions, they rushed to Morgan, who was conferring with Pickens and the scouts.

Tarleton had advanced within five miles of the Old Fields and was coming on fast, Morgan told them tersely as he levered himself painfully into the saddle. After ordering the baggage wagons away up Island Ford Road, he rode off with Pickens through the camp, bellowing to the sleeping, blanket-wrapped men, "Boys, get up! Benny's comin'!"

To a man they had obeyed eagerly. Morgan had ordered his officers to have their commands under arms and formed up before daybreak, and the various units had camped on the field in the order in which they would fight. Despite the bitter cold the men had been in their places well before first light.

They slapped their reddened, chapped hands together and stamped their feet to restore feeling while bantering quietly with each other and with Morgan, their breaths pluming in the frigid air. The general walked up and down the lines, joking and laughing with them as he had the previous night, when he had stopped by every campfire to explain to the militiamen exactly what he expected of them once the battle began.

With a hard glint in his eyes he had then shown his back scarred by 499 lashes and told them that the British owed him one more. But it was a debt they'd never collect, he'd assured them, for in the morning they were going to give ol' Ben a good whipping.

At the officers' meeting earlier that evening, while the rapidly growing army feasted on fresh roast beef, Morgan related what he had learned from men who had personally observed Tarleton's tactics: He never took the lead in launching an attack, instead sending two or three troops of dragoons to strike the unsuspecting foe. Then, with chaos at its height, he led his reserve in a furious sabre attack into the enemy's midst.

Morgan had gone on to detail what he intended for the morrow. Carleton judged his battle plan brilliant as it would use both militia and Regulars to the greatest effect, taking advantage of their abilities and weapons and the terrain. It would force Tarleton to attack across unfamiliar ground over which Morgan had personally walked, chosen for this confrontation, and judiciously distributed his army.

For the rest of the evening and all that night, increasing numbers of armed men had swarmed into the camp like hornets whose nest is threatened: Continental units, Virginia state troops and militia, North and South Carolina state dragoons, and additional volunteers from Georgia. Finally lean, dour-faced Colonel Andrew Pickens, the South Carolina militia leader renowned for action, not words, had ridden in at the head of close to 300 more men. By dawn's approach, Morgan's force had swelled to rival Tarleton's.

Carleton sat astride Devil with Andrews, Washington, and their aides on the crest of a low hill at the northern end of the Cowpens, well to the rear of the deployed American lines. They were screened from the road by a cluster of trees through which they had a clear view of the developing action while remaining unseen. On the other side of the shallow swale in front of them, the army's main line occupied a lightly wooded rise to their left.

Morgan had designated the cavalry to serve as his reserve, acting as opportunity arose, and they had formed their troops in long lines behind them facing south to allow rapid deployment to the army's right, left, or center as needed. Earlier, while waiting for the enemy to appear on the field, Carleton, Washington, and Andrews had consulted on tactics. Although mounted state troops and militia volunteers bolstered their force, Tarleton's cavalry still held a substantial advantage.

Carleton and Andrews had agreed with Washington that charging en masse in all actions and fighting at close quarters using only sabres would even the odds. Carleton privately cherished the hope that Tarleton would divide his cavalry, which would enable them to dissect his troops in detail.

Hutchinson blew on his hands to warm them. "Just once, couldn't we have a hot, sunny day for a fight?" he grumbled, eliciting a bark of laughter from Washington's aide.

"I seem to remember you complaining about the heat at Monmouth, Josiah," Spencer said with amusement, drawing Hutchinson's grimace.

"You'll be warm soon enough, boys," Washington reproved absently, his intent gaze fixed on the south end of the field.

The reverberation of gunfire was noticeably increasing in frequency and volume as Tarleton closed in. Isaiah and Farris rode along the Rangers' orderly lines, quietly reassuring men anxious for action that they didn't have much longer to wait.

Carleton flexed his hands to restore the bloodflow to his fingers and scanned the units arrayed down the slope ahead of them. Morgan was riding along their lines, encouraging and admonishing the men. Those who could be depended on to hold against the Legion's assault anchored the center under Howard's command: the corps of light infantry, 550 seasoned Continental Regulars of the Maryland and Delaware brigades augmented by battle-hardened militia from Georgia and Virginia, arranged in three battalions for firing in succession. A small detachment of North Carolina State Regulars guarded their right flank, where swampy lowlands, swales, and creeks would also impede a flanking movement by cavalry.

Roughly 150 yards ahead of the center, the main body of Pickens' militia stretched well across the meadow, a detachment of riflemen guarding their left flank. An equal distance in front of them stood a long, snaking line of clustered companies composed of lean, flint-eyed riflemen from Georgia and the Carolinas, the army's finest marksmen. These would greet Tarleton's advance parties, initiating the battle.

When Tarleton's men came onto the fields, they would naturally focus on the riflemen directly in front of them, Carleton reckoned. The shadows cast by the dim early morning light and the land's subtle folds and gentle upward slope would render Pickens' militia, stationed within a line of trees, almost invisible. The thicker woods on the rise behind them completely hid the main American line from Tarleton's view, nor would he have any warning that cavalry waited behind them.

Overall, the army made a motley appearance, the Continentals' blue-faced red uniform coats and those of the state troops virtually threadbare, as were the militias' and volunteers' fraying hunting shirts, breeches or overalls, and drooping hats. In most cases shoes and other leathers were worn almost to pieces.

Carleton's troopers in their frontier dress blended right in. His warriors, however, also including the Catawba men now, were arrayed in spectacularly impressive full war regalia that ought to intimidate any enemy, he reflected with satisfaction.

"What's taking them so blasted long?" Andrews rasped, staring through his spyglass.

"They can't show up soon enough for me," Washington responded, flashing a grin, which Carleton returned with a smirk.

Everyone was in high spirits, well rested and fed, sated on red meat. There had been much joking speculation on how much rest Tarleton's troops had gotten and whether they'd enjoyed as good a meal the previous night as Morgan's army had. Many had shared tales of cruelty and losses suffered at the hands of Tarleton's Legion that they meant to redress.

Morgan captured Carleton's attention as he reached his main line of Continentals. Drawing up to face them, his voice echoing across the field in the crystal air, he cried out, "My friends in arms, my dear boys, I request you to remember Saratoga, Monmouth, Paoli, and Brandywine, and this day play well your parts for your honor and liberty!"

A great roar went up from every man on the field as Morgan rejoined Howard behind the main line to keep an eye on the unfolding action. There was no fear in these gaunt, ragged men. Only the steely determination to settle bitter scores too long tallied.

The image of Elizabeth and their children formed fleetingly in Carleton's mind, but he dismissed it with hard determination, knowing that any distraction could cost not only his life but also that of others. As always with action imminent, the familiar battle fever seared through his veins, heightening every sense. His consciousness narrowed to the space of this field, these men, and the oncoming enemy.

He read the same emotions in the narrowed eyes of Andrews, Washington, and their aides, in the taut bodies of Red Fox and Spotted Pony and their warriors, in the officers and troopers behind them and the skittish movements of the horses.

On that clouded dawn at the Cowpens, Morgan's army was a powder keg with a lit fuse.

BY BARELY PERCEPTIBLE degrees the early morning gloom brightened, subtly defining the stark landscape and deepening the long shadows the hoarfrost-bearded trees laid across the icy grass.

Carleton adjusted his spyglass until the red- and green-jacketed soldiers came into focus as they hacked through the tangled underbrush bordering Thicketty Creek and filtered cautiously from between the trees. A few at a time they moved up Green River Road, fanning out onto the fields to make room for those on their heels, while confidently scanning the advance line of riflemen partially visible in the misty light on the rise directly in their front.

The horse and foot of Tarleton's provincial Legion were easily identifiable by their short green uniform jackets and close-fitting black leather helmets with bearskin crests. Whitened buckskin breeches and black boots and leathers complimented their distinctive look. The red-coated Seventh Regiment of Foot, the Royal Fusiliers, their tall bearskin caps replaced by regulation cocked hats sometime earlier during the American campaign, appeared equally formidable. As did the 17th Light Dragoons with their leather helmets sporting skull and crossbones on the front and a scarlet horsehair crest—his and Andrews' regiment in a long-ago lifetime.

Magnified in Carleton's spyglass, the enemy's uniforms appeared as tattered and dirty as those of Morgan's men. The Southern campaign had been punishing for both sides, though he couldn't summon any sympathy for the British.

He caught a glimpse of the Legion's infamous commander in the first rank of the woods behind them and to one side, partially camouflaged by the trees. Tarleton appeared to be conferring with several other mounted officers while they assessed the American lines. He was perhaps in his mid twenties, Carleton estimated.

Young, smart, arrogant, he thought. *By the end of the day he might not be quite so cocksure.*

He focused his spyglass on a large body of Legion cavalry behind the enemy van who were still fighting their way out of the underbrush along with companies of Fraser's Highlanders in their distinctive bonnets, red jackets, and plaid trews. Tarleton's reserves, most likely, which he'd unleash for the killing stroke when the Americans broke and ran, as he undoubtedly expected.

The sudden crackle of rifle fire drew his gaze back to the American front. Several of the sharpshooters had moved forward of the skirmish line and were picking off targets among the forming light infantry, still more than two hundred yards away. Here and there red and green coats dropped to the ground, with ensuing confusion in their ranks.

"Tarleton must be positively ecstatic that Morgan put militia out front," he observed dryly.

"As Gates did at Camden." Andrews snickered. "Everyone knows that our militias can't stand against a British bayonet charge."

"Thankfully Morgan's no Gates," Washington observed, his spyglass also fixed on the developing skirmish.

They watched a detachment of green-coated Legion dragoons trot forward. As the sharpshooters began slowly to pull back, Carleton made out a distant, hoarse shout he thought must be Tarleton's.

"Charge!"

Brandishing sabres, the dragoons charged. The rumble of hoofbeats resounded on the spongy turf as the detachment galloped along the high ground toward the American right. Still keeping up a sporadic fire as they reloaded their rifles, the sharpshooters gave way and rapidly melted back into the waiting skirmish line.

Morgan had ridden down moments before, and now, voice ringing like a trumpet, he shouted, "Hold yer fire till they're within fifty yards, boys!"

The militia officers echoed his order along the line. For a tense moment that seemed to stretch into eternity, the riflemen stood unmoving, squinting down the barrels of their leveled weapons at the oncoming cavalry. Thundering forward, the riders crossed the invisible line Carleton had mentally drawn.

"Fire!"

A massed volley engulfed the dragoons in a hailstorm of lead, the blast reverberating across the fields and briefly obscuring the skirmish line behind a cloud of smoke before the wind whipped it away.

The horsemen shuddered to an abrupt halt, more than a dozen troopers swept violently from their saddles. A shocked pause ensued, then the dragoons reined their mounts around and hastily vacated the field in the wake of the panicked riderless horses, leaving their fallen comrades sprawled motionless across the frosty grass. A deafening roar laced with taunts rose from the American lines.

British officers bawled commands. The rhythmic rattle of drums and shrill pipe of fifes filled the crisp air.

Without apparent regard for the Highlanders and main body of cavalry behind them still fighting clear of the underbrush along Thicketty Creek, the light infantry dropped their knapsacks and canteens where they stood. As one, with their customary measured precision, the oncoming force shook out into a loose two-row formation, the Fusiliers on the British left west of the road facing the American right and the Legion infantry and light infantry on the east side opposite the American left.

The 17th Light Dragoons rode forward to cover the light infantry's flank. The Legion dragoons veered to their left to flank the Fusiliers.

Carleton couldn't hold back a satisfied smile as Tarleton divided his cavalry, exactly as he had hoped the Legion commander would. Watching the scene unfold, he admired the enemy's orderly rows, their discipline, their efficiency. It was all he could do to wrestle down the raging impulse to order his Rangers to an immediate attack.

As the dragoons trotted forward, horses dragged two small cannon commonly called grasshoppers onto the road between the Fusiliers and the infantry. Their crews began to fire as soon as they came into position, the guns characteristically springing up almost four feet on the recoil as they sent solid shot arcing up the slope. Overshooting the American lines, the three-pound balls furrowed through the ground uncomfortably close to the troops in Washington's van, causing their horses to shy.

"If this keeps up, we might have to move," Washington drawled as another round of balls followed the first.

"I vote that we move to attack," Carleton muttered.

Long yards away at the base of the fields, three loud huzzahs rose from the British battle line. Again Morgan's voice rang out. "They give us the British halloo, boys! Let's give 'em the Indian halloo!"

The Americans instantly returned a wild, extended war whoop. Red Fox's warriors added their eerie, ululating cry.

Behind the light cloud cover the sun lifted above the eastern horizon, bringing the fields into clear focus and burnishing the enemy's ranks of keenly honed bayonets. They began to advance at quick step, Tarleton riding alongside.

"Remember, boys, don't fire till ye see the whites o' their eyes, then shoot for the epaulets!" Morgan called, the militia officers again repeating the command to their companies.

With the dragoons keeping pace on their flanks, the battle line scrambled up the long, treeless slope, heading for the American skirmishers while the crackle of rifle and musket fire and the cannons' simultaneous blasts reverberated from the surrounding hills. The riflemen began to back up the slope, pausing to fire from the cover of trees. When they reached Pickens' long militia line, they scurried into position on its flanks.

The artillery crews chambered grapeshot now. After each volley the horses dragged the small cannon up even with the moving battle line before their crews reloaded. A hail of lead balls pelted through the trees over-hanging Carleton and his companions, knocking twigs and bits of bark onto their helmets and shoulders. The next volley scattered grapeshot across the ground in front of the leading troop of Rangers, causing the horses to dance back.

"The British never get the elevation right," Carleton complained. "They always fire high."

Washington gave him a slit-eyed glance before ordering a shift to the west. Within minutes he and Andrews had reformed the cavalry behind the hill and now entirely out of the enemy's sight. Focused on the developing confrontation on the far end of the fields, Carleton hung back until another round of grapeshot ricocheted between the trees, barely missing him and causing Devil to snort and half rear, eyes rolling.

Andrews rode toward him, yelling, "Are you trying to get killed?"

Grinning, Carleton pocketed his spyglass and brought the stallion under control. He urged Devil toward the cavalry's new position but detoured to the crest of the rise, seeking a vantage behind a line of scrub trees. Washington and Andrews drew their mounts up on either side.

Fraser's Highlanders, finally clear of the woods, were gathering on the road well behind and to the Fusiliers' left with Tarleton's cavalry reserve close by, Carleton noted. Focusing his spyglass higher on the ridge in front of them, he watched the enemy's battle line close to within two hundred yards of Pickens' militia.

There they suddenly halted. The full extent of the militia line, stretching from one side of the field to the other, had come into sight, Carleton reckoned with amusement.

Some confusion ensued, the Legion infantry appearing to tangle with the Fusiliers. Tarleton galloped up, and the line quickly sorted out, again advancing at a quick step that rapidly ate up the ground.

As they closed, several small parties of riflemen stepped a few paces forward of Pickens' line, while Morgan ranged back and forth, calling out orders and urging them to stand firm. Carleton could clearly hear him and his subordinates' shouts borne on the steady south wind: *"Hold your fire!"*

Fewer than three minutes elapsed from the beginning of the enemy advance until the attackers entered musket range—now well within point-blank shot for a rifle, Carleton calculated, gut knotted as he timed their approach with his pocket watch. Abruptly a blast of rifle fire rent the air. Across the British line officers and soldiers stumbled and fell, while their comrades continued their inexorable advance.

The forward riflemen quickly stepped back into the militia line. *"Fire!"* bellowed Pickens, bringing his sword down in a sweeping arc.

A sheet of flame and boiling smoke instantly enveloped Pickens' men. This time the enemy soldiers visibly staggered backward, great gaps opening between them. The disoriented survivors' attempts to advance were immediately halted by a second devastating volley that ripped through their ranks doing even worse destruction.

Before the echoes of the second volley's discharge died away, Pickens's command began to fire by regiments, vivid points of flame rippling from one end of the line to the other. Grimly Carleton watched enemy dead and wounded fall like drifts of autumn leaves.

Yet in spite of the carnage Tarleton's battle line stubbornly righted itself. Those still on their feet clawed forward in a fierce rush, bayonets glittering, giving the militia no time to reload. Pickens' command broke in full-fledged retreat and raced toward the main American line at the hill's crest, the enemy's triumphant shouts following them.

At the militia's approach, Howard called out an order Carleton couldn't make out amid the battle din. He watched, breath held, as the Continentals' center immediately made a brisk right face. Then, moving like a well-oiled hinge, the men wheeled back, opening a gap for the militia to race through and down into the swale behind them and in the cavalry's front.

The instant the last man passed, the Continentals stepped back into position and faced the oncoming enemy, their line of fire down the slope now unobstructed and the full extent of the American center spread out in the enemy's view. Carleton shared his companions' exultant laughter as Tarleton's advance ground to a halt, his officers hastening to straighten and consolidate their shrunken battle line.

"The Seventeeth is moving to flank us!"

Carleton and Washington jerked around at Andrews' shout, and Carleton sucked in a sharp breath. The 17th Light Dragoons were charging toward the mixed battalions of South Carolina militia and Georgia volunteers anchoring the American left at a tree line along a shallow ravine fewer than 150 yards below Howard's Continentals.

The militia managed to get off a scattered fire. But the dragoons advanced so precipitously that before Carleton and his companions could react, they were riding through the American flankers, cutting down men left and right. Unable to reload, the flankers staggered back and ran, boiling into the swale crowded with Pickens' retreating militia, the dragoons hot on their heels.

Washington signaled his bugler, who immediately blew a ringing blast on his horn. The answering shouts of every trooper in the combined force echoed in the frosty air.

"Charge!" Washington shouted.

As one, he, Carleton, and Andrews tore their sabres from their sheaths. The turf shook under the thunder of hundreds of hoofs as they burst from concealment around the hill's eastern end. Washington's dragoons held the van with Carleton and Andrews storming after them at the head of the Rangers, warriors and troopers spreading out to each side, militia volunteers pressing hard on their heels at the rear of the mad stampede.

With cataclysmic force, screaming like banshees, they burst into the roiling mass in the swale, sabres slashing. The warriors wielded war clubs and tomahawks, their war cries chilling in the frosty early morning light as they struck red-coated dragoons from their panicked horses.

The flankers were scrambling to get out of the way, dragging their wounded with them, when Morgan rode up. Immediately taking charge of the disordered militia, he directed the men to turn on their attackers and fire a volley. They obeyed with alacrity.

In the melee several familiar faces impressed themselves fleetingly on Carleton's consciousness—acquaintances from his and Andrews' years in the regiment. It was obvious they recognized them as well by the impotent rage flooding their faces scarlet. But at his and Andrews' ferocious charge, they fled. The wholly unexpected onslaught, the militia's volley, and the sight of their comrades' bodies littering the ground shattered the heavily outnumbered 17th in moments. They made a desperate dash for their own lines, a small clutch of Washington's white-coated dragoons briefly pursuing. Together Washington and Carleton circled their troops around to their original position to reform.

"Well, that was extraordinarily satisfying!" Andrews shouted gleefully over the clamor when they drew up.

"It was that, but it'll be even more so if we can corner Tarleton and take him down!" Carleton answered.

His face stony, Washington swiped the sweat from his brow with the back of his gloved hand. "I want a shot at that devil so dearly I can taste it," he hissed through gritted teeth.

Carleton fully shared the sentiment. And he could tell by Andrews' grim expression that he was of the same temper.

THEIR CHARGE HAD TAKEN scant minutes. During that time Morgan and Pickens had formed the disorganized mass of militia back into a disciplined force. As Carleton watched from the crest of the cavalry's hill, more volunteers flooded in, every man eagerly loading his weapon.

Through his spyglass he scanned the Continentals' position at the top of the hill in front of him. A constant, jagged sheet of flame rippled from right to left, the gunsmoke quickly torn away on the wind. Fully engaged, the Virginians and the Delaware and Maryland Regulars fired by battalions and companies, pouring deadly buck and ball charges from rifles and muskets directly into Tarleton's battle line, now barely a hundred yards distant.

They received as hot a fire as they gave. On both sides men collapsed to the trampled grass in waves.

The strange, awful grandeur of the scene struck Carleton forcefully. If only one could ignore the hideousness of men marching to their deaths at the orders of strangers far away who enjoyed the manifold comforts of their tidy lives. Untainted by the blood shed at their command, they cared nothing for the individual agonies of those lost in a struggle they themselves took no part in.

McLeod's shout broke through his bitter reflections: "The Scots and Legion dragoons are turnin' our right!"

A louder wail of bagpipes punctuated the major's warning, the eerie, haunting drone unexpectedly rousing long-forgotten memories from his youth that sent a chill up Carleton's spine. With a shock of alarm he watched the Virginians suddenly give way. They began to pour into the right end of the swale, pursued by the advancing Highlanders. At the same instant the first ranks of green-clad dragoons came into view behind them as they stampeded around the far end of the American position.

Hearing Washington's bugler sound the charge, Carleton pocketed his spyglass and sent Devil down the slope and into the cavalry line, already in violent motion. They bolted at an angle through the swale to the west and burst across the slope on the American right flank.

Carleton kept his attention fixed on the advancing Legion dragoons, at the same time sharply aware that fewer than 200 yards beyond them Tarleton's reserve cavalry watched from the crest of the rise Pickens' militia had abandoned. All else fell away in the fierce resolve to serve Tarleton as he had served Buford's regiment at the Waxhaws.

They raged into Tarleton's dragoons in moments, heedless of the sting of wounds as they carved their way through the chaotic mass of green-coated troopers, leaving carnage in their wake. Wheeling around, they charged savagely back through the broken unit's rear, the scattering enemy dragoons leaving a large number of their fellows on the ground behind them.

Breathless, Carleton momentarily curbed his stallion and glanced warily around. Tarleton's reserve cavalry remained where they were, making no move to come to their comrades' aid. Even more reassuring, at the army's center Howard's Continentals now faced the enemy from a new position. Standing in a solid, unwavering wall, they jolted Tarleton's battle line to a halt at point blank range.

Howard rode imperturbably back and forth behind his men, his rasped commands and those of his own officers and the enemy's reaching Carleton over the paroxysm of gunfire, rattle of drums, pipe of fifes, skirl of bagpipes, and groans and screams of the wounded that engulfed the Old Fields. Their hoarse, rhythmic chants mingled on the acrid, gunpowder-tinged wind: "Prime and load! Shoulder! Make ready! Take aim! *Fire!*"

Carleton's chest clenched as the Highlanders suddenly made an impossible charge, screaming as they clawed toward the crest, where the Fusiliers and light infantry had stalled. He urged his mount to a gallop, quickly intercepted Washington and Andrews, who had passed the end of the battle line and were beginning to turn.

"The Scots are charging!"

Washington wheeled his mount all the way around, the rest of the cavalry following in one tight mass. Drawing up, he cast a swift glance toward the Highlanders, then beckoned his aide to his side.

"Tell Howard that if he'll give the Scots one fire, we'll charge them!" he shouted over the crash of musketry.

Grinning broadly, the aide touched his fingers to his helmet. As he galloped up the slope behind the Continentals, Washington and Carleton hurried to bring their troops back into line.

Just then Pickens' reformed brigade marched out of the swale at quick step and around the army's right flank. At his order they fired a resounding volley that reverberated through the fields and woods and dropped a swath of the attacking Highlanders in their tracks.

With his cavalry still in some disarray, Washington jerked his head in a nod. Immediately his bugler sounded the charge. By a miracle the disordered troops coalesced and raced after their commanders into the fray at full speed, screaming as they charged like madmen.

Above the pounding of hoofs and the Continentals' blazing volleys, Carleton caught Howard's ringing command: *"Charge bayonets!"*

Unleashing a mighty roar, the American center sprang forward, their deadly seventeen-inch bayonets leveled as they plunged into the oncoming Highlanders. At the same instant the cavalry collided with the Highlanders' left flank in a tremendous shock and hacked their way through to the Legion infantry.

Assaulted from both flanks in an astounding double envelopment, with nowhere to flee and a hot fire pouring in on them from all sides, resistance collapsed. All along Tarleton's wrecked battle line, the enemy soldiers began to drop their weapons in surrender, many falling to the ground as they pled for quarter.

AT CARLETON'S CALL, Andrews hastily drew his mount around.

"Tarleton's trying to get away! Washington's going after him and so am I!"

Andrews glanced past Carleton to where the troops of the 3rd Dragoons galloped south down the Green River Road. "I'll collect our troops and be on your heels," he shouted back.

They exchanged brisk salutes. As Carleton tore off down the road after Washington, Andrews ordered the bugler to signal their troops to form up.

The last moments of the battle had been a blur of fierce action as Tarleton's desperate efforts to rally his command had proven futile. Washington and Carleton had turned their sights on the reserve cavalry, only to run into the artillery on the way. As they were taking the crews prisoner, the horses' drivers attempted to flee, and after refusing repeated commands to surrender had been cut down.

Leaving the cannon for Howard to secure, Washington and Carleton had renewed their attack on the Legion's reserve cavalry, their men screaming, "Buford's play!" so loudly that their voices echoed across the fields.

Ignoring Tarleton's orders to form and oppose the American charge, the Legion dragoons abandoned their commander and fled into the woods.

Tarleton then retreated to the south end of the field and managed to persuade a small troop of dragoons to advance. These briefly checked the American cavalry's pursuit, inflicting their greatest number of casualties during the contest. Failing to drive the Americans off, they attacked Howard's infantry now swarming the guns. But by then Tarleton had given in to the inevitable and commanded a retreat.

While Farris and Isaiah brought their jubilant troopers into formation, Andrews consulted his pocket watch. The battle had joined at roughly seven o'clock that morning. It was now just past eight—little more than an hour later. He reined his mount around in a circle, scanning the trampled grass across which sprawled swaths of bloodied bodies, most closely piled where Pickens' militia had stood firm.

For a moment the bleakness that always followed battle's hot fever threatened to overwhelm him. He was staggered by an aching need to gather Blue Sky and their sons safely into his arms and the deep longing for home. For family. For love to blot out the cruel realities of war.

But time was fleeing too rapidly, and pursuit beckoned. His troops waited at the ready, Isaiah and Farris at their head.

He shook off the welling emotions, turned to lead them on. And halted at the sight of Morgan riding down to the men who surrounded the captured cannon.

Morgan's soldiers looked like demons, grins splitting faces that, like their clothing and cold-reddened, chapped hands, were fouled with the oily black residue of gunpowder mingled with mud and sweat. With their last shred of energy those not guarding prisoners gathered around their commander in high glee.

Beaming around at them, Morgan called out, "We sure done give 'em a devil of a whippin', didn't we, boys?"

In answer the men exuberantly brandished their weapons and let out a full-throated, jubilant roar.

Chapter Thirty-five

"I'M WOEFULLY out of practice!"

Elizabeth lowered her pistol and stared at the target with disgust. The bullet hole was an inch to the right of center, and none of the rest scattered across the target's surface were any closer.

"You're doing better than I am, and you haven't practiced since the twins were born," her father replied over the din of gunfire that filled the long, low stone barn adapted for the Rangers' use as a firing range. He reloaded his carbine, squinted down the length of the weapon's barrel and pulled off the shot.

Straightening, he groaned. "I was certain I had it this time. I keep overshooting on this blasted slope!"

Despite the frigid, blustery wind that made the late January day even bleaker, inside the stone walls it was warm enough that their breaths didn't cloud when they spoke. Elizabeth's muffatees kept her hands warm, while loading and firing prevented her bare fingers from freezing.

A line of Isaiah's light infantry soldiers stretched down the barn's length on Elizabeth's opposite side. Squinting down pistol or musket barrel, they blazed away at the targets anchored to the wall in front of them. A couple of the targets at the end where she and her father stood were set against the stone foundation below floor level, the ground dug away at a slant to simulate the downward slope of a hill. Which accounted for his overshooting.

Elizabeth set her pistol on the rude table between them and stepped to his side as he sighted his weapon. "I think you need to lower it a bit more."

Before he could fire Lieutenant Rob Atkin sauntered over and corrected his aim slightly lower. When Dr. Howard pulled the trigger the ball struck the center's edge.

He stared happily at the bullet hole. "Thank you, Rob. I'll try to keep that angle."

Returning a grin, Atkin sauntered back down the line.

Dr. Howard's gaze followed him and settled on Jemma, several yards away. Elizabeth saw his smile fade, a frown creasing his brow. The willowy young woman faced her target with her cloak thrown back, arms outstretched, the pistol she held cocked. Major Matheson stood behind her, his arms enclosing her shoulders, hands cupping hers as he steadied her aim.

While they watched, she looked up to meet the tall officer's sober gaze with one that glowed. She said something to him, and his face relaxed into a warm smile.

"So that's why she decided to learn how to shoot a pistol!" Elizabeth exclaimed.

"It appears so," Dr. Howard said, his tone dry. "Good thing Isaiah's not here. He's not happy about it. He thinks Apollos is too forward."

She turned back to him, eyebrows raised. "Isaiah talked to you about this?"

He nodded. "Evidently he allowed that it's her choice if she wants to walk out with him, but he admonished her to go slowly. He thinks she's too young and impressionable."

"Typical father," Elizabeth scoffed. "Jemma's almost twenty-one, well able to make her own decisions."

"Well, Apollos is about ten years older," he pointed out.

"And Isaiah was—what?—at least twenty-six and Sarah barely seventeen when they married?"

"It's always different when it's your own daughter," he conceded with a chuckle.

"There are eleven years between me and Jonathan," she returned smugly. "And I haven't suffered overmuch."

"I might disagree with your assessment," he objected, drawing Elizabeth's glare, at which he snickered.

"I shouldn't think Isaiah would distrust the man he chose as his second in command. What does Sarah have to say?" When he shrugged, she said firmly, "I'll have a talk with her."

She fixed Jemma in an assessing look. There was an unmistakable tenderness in the interactions between her and Matheson. Elizabeth was surprised she hadn't noticed it before.

They made a handsome couple, she thought, Jemma with her mother's graceful, fine-boned form and lovely coffee-colored complexion that enhanced her delicate features, and lean, muscular Matheson, with his cinnamon-tinged brown skin and handsome, hawk-like visage.

The realization pierced Elizabeth that the day was not far off when she was going to lose her—this girl, now a woman, whose childhood she had shared and who had been as much a younger sister to her as Abby. Just as her own children would one day grow up to leave her, she reflected, the thought bittersweet.

LATER THAT DAY, comfortably ensconced before the drawing room fire, Elizabeth gave Harry an affectionate glance. He was seated on the rug happily playing with—or mostly chewing on—his and Julianne's array of carved wooden toys.

Teething again, she thought. Thankfully he wasn't prone to the feverishness and ill humor that afflicted his sister when new teeth were coming in.

"Who is this Henri-François de Bonvouloir that Abby refers to all the time?" her father demanded, looking up from the letter he was writing at the escritoire across the room. "They seem to be quite often in each other's company. Do you know him? Has she developed a tendre? Surely she's too young to think of such things yet."

"Papa, she'll be seventeen in less than a month, and it's only natural that she's beginning to feel the stirrings of romance. Henri is only a year older than she and a very nice young man. He's Eugène's nephew by his youngest sister—her eldest son. Aunt Tess and I were both very taken with him."

"Well, Abby's obviously smitten." He blotted his pen and tossed it down.

"They've spent a good deal of time together since he's family. He's also very musical and an excellent tenor, not to mention quite handsome. Don't you remember? You and Mama met him and his parents while you were in France. They're wonderful people and devoted believers."

Dr. Howard considered for a moment before exclaiming, "He's the young man who sang at that dinner party not long before we came home!"

When she nodded, he conceded grudgingly, "I was rather impressed with his voice. And his address, for that matter." He nodded a reluctant approval. "Very courteous and well spoken."

"He and Abby are well suited, in my estimation, and Aunt Tess wholeheartedy agrees."

He lifted Abby's letter and scrutinized it. "To think that my little girl . . . " He broke off with a sigh, then directed a fierce glance at Elizabeth. "I suppose you, your mother, and Tess have already arranged the wedding!"

"We've not gone that far," she scoffed, laughing. "Papa, you know how responsible Eugène and Cécile are. They're keeping a close eye on the two, as are his parents. Naturally, as young as they are, there's no question of an offer being made, much less a betrothal, for some time to come."

Harry looked up, then pushed to his feet and toddled over, clutching a small horse and reaching for her as he demanded insistently, "Ma-ma, Ma-ma!"

She lifted him to stand on her lap and wiped the drool from his chin. "How big you've gotten, sweeting! You'll be full grown before I know it." A wave of sadness tempered her pride.

She held his fists while he bounced, crowing as though proud of himself and displaying two perfect white teeth. His eyes had changed to a striking hazel, but his hair, now curling thickly from beneath his lace-trimmed cap, remained as pale as tow—the same as Carleton's in his childhood, he had told her.

At fourteen and a half months old, both he and his sister had worn short clothes since learning to crawl, the bodice buttoning in the back and ankle-length skirts allowing greater freedom of movement. Today a wide blue sash adorned Harry's white gown of finely woven wool, with a matching blue woolen slip beneath. Thick, knitted, knee-length stockings and tiny shoes added warmth.

"Cécile and Aunt Tess have both mentioned more than once in their letters that they're becoming quite impatient to see the twins," Elizabeth said. "Since it's unlikely we'll be able to travel to France anytime soon, I'm going to send copies of the miniatures I'm having painted as soon as they're finished."

"Excellent," he returned absently without glancing up from the letter he had resumed writing.

Her gaze drifted to the gaily painted rocking horse standing in one corner that had been one of the twins' Christmas gifts. "Papa, how soon do you suppose the children will be able to safely ride their new rocking horse?"

Frowning, he looked up. "I'd wait until they're walking steadily, another couple of months to be safe, though Harry will likely be ready before Julianne."

Harry's brow creased and he reached his free hand toward the parlor door. "Ju-wee?"

"Your sister is with Grandmama," she told him, taking care as always to enunciate clearly when talking to the twins. "They'll come soon."

He tipped his head. "Ga-Ma-Ma? See-see?"

Smiling, she kissed his rosy cheek before settling him on her lap. He happily pounced his horse up and down her arm while she returned her attention to her father.

"Do you really think that separating them regularly like this is best as they get older? They've been together from the womb, after all, and both are distressed when the other is taken away."

Looking up, he considered the matter for a moment. "I must agree with your mother. It's good to wean them from each other a bit so they can develop their own individual personalities, interests, and friends, especially since they're not the same sex. A boy will be interested in different things than a girl."

"A girl may be interested in some of the same things as boy," she protested as Harry cast his horse onto the floor in an excess of exuberance. "If you'll remember, I was always much more interested in activities such as training, caring for, and riding horses and helping you in the surgery than I was in womanly domestic pursuits." She bent to pick up the toy Harry was straining to reach and returned it to his grasp.

Her father grimaced. "You don't need to remind me—not to say that was bad," he amended hastily. "You've been a tremendous help in my practice all these years, after all, and are quite capable of maintaining your own, were that possible. And some day it may be. But I can't visualize Julianne growing up to be as rough and tumble as Harry or as adventurous as you."

"I do have to agree with you," she admitted. "She's much more like Mama and Abby. But that's a good thing."

"Well, as much as I am proud of your . . . um . . . accomplishments, your mother and I both find it quite gratifying to see you settled down now with babes of your own and a great manor to manage."

She pursed her mouth but held her tongue.

Harry pulled himself up on her lap and directed a longing look toward the door. "Ba-ba?" he murmured sadly.

Elizabeth cuddled him against her shoulder. "I miss your Papa too. But he will come home soon, dearest. I promise."

"We've had no word from him, daughter," Dr. Howard pointed out gently. "It's all but certain he'll not arrive in time for your anniversary Monday. Two years in a row now. I know it can't be helped, but it must be trying."

She had been thinking the same thing, and her spirits sank. Quickly she said, "He feels it too, you know."

Her father nodded. "And he did make it back on Christmas Eve."

When he turned partially away to stare out the window at the bleak winter landscape, she wondered what he was thinking. She knew that in a private conversation before he left to join Morgan, Carleton had refused to allow her father to accompany the Rangers. Instead he would take Captain Lawton, his chief of surgery, along with a couple of the surgeon's assistants. If anything should happen to him in battle, Carleton had said, he wanted Elizabeth to have father with her and the twins.

The following day, moments before he rode off at the head of his troops, Carleton had told her that he could not promise when he would return. It would likely be several weeks if not months.

She had smiled and assured him that she and the children would be fine. Then she had watched him ride away yet again, vision blurred and throat choked. Emotions she knew he shared but held under stern control. Regardless of their own pain, however, she was very conscious that these separations were harder yet for Harry and Julianne, who could not understand their papa's reasons for leaving them so often for so long.

"It seems like this war will last forever," she sighed.

Her father turned back to her. "As a practical matter, it can't. And I'm fully confident that the British will give up before we do. All that's needed is for us to score one crucial victory, and if the French will finally do as they've promised, that's within sight."

Harry pressed his head into the crook of her neck, and she cuddled him more tightly against her breast. Half turning, he reached one hand out to his grandfather and called sadly, "Gam-ba-ba."

Dr. Howard immediately rose and came to gather the little boy into his arms. Harry popped his thumb into his mouth and laid his head on his grandfather's shoulder.

Elizabeth watched, fighting back tears. "He needs a man to love and guide him. I know it was difficult for you, but I'm glad Jonathan insisted that you stay behind to hold that office when he has to be absent for so long."

"I am glad too, though I admit it stung to be denied fulfilling my duties with the Rangers, especially if Jon should—" he cleared his throat "—should suffer harm, and I wouldn't be there to treat him. But he was right. You and the twins need both your mother and me here more than with him."

They both turned as Julianne appeared in the doorway. She toddled eagerly toward them, with Anne hovering over her, holding the leading strings attached to her gown, identical to her brother's. Her eyes had darkened to a warm brown, and her abundant red-gold curls now tumbled from beneath her cap.

"Ha-wee!" she squealed, reaching out for him.

"Ju-wee—See-see!"

Harry squirmed to get down from Dr. Howard's arms. As soon as he was on his feet, the two babies hurried unsteadily to hug each other. Julianne planted a slobbery kiss on Harry's cheek, which he happily returned. Both then came to receive Elizabeth's hugs and kisses before finally settling on the rug to play with their toys.

Shortly thereafter Mary entered carrying pretty, eleven-month-old Aileana, the sweetest natured, happiest babe one could wish for, Elizabeth thought with a smile. After greeting everyone Mary set her daughter on the rug. Aileana immediately crawled over to Harry, who met her half-way to hug and kiss her with enthusiasm, while Julianne watched indifferently, chewing on her toy. All the adults beamed.

Blue Sky soon followed with Leads the Way. Little Elk and Jimmy ran ahead of her. After them came Rain Woman, leading quiet, demure two-year-old Snow Flower, then Laughing Otter with her daughters and son. Jemma and Sarah drifted in on their heels.

Elizabeth's heart swelled as she observed the happy tumult that filled the room, gratitude welling up to overflowing for the blessings the Lord poured upon them without measure. Still, a deep pang of sorrow intruded that Carleton, who dearly loved these gatherings, had to be absent. And Andrews and McLeod, Red Fox and Spotted Pony, and all the other men who had become such an inextricable part of their company.

Ah, dearest Father, she prayed silently, *may it be your good pleasure that each one come home to us, to their wives and children again, well and whole!*

Her thoughts strayed back to the times that seemed now so long ago, when she'd played with the children of her cousin Will Stern and his wife Rebekah. How she had longed then for babes of her own, never guessing all that would lie between those innocent days and the present.

How precious the time. How quickly fled! And Will, torn so suddenly from their arms and borne home to heaven during the retreat from the battle on Breed's Hill. Almost six years ago—how distant that day seemed! Yet how near when, as so often, his beloved face filled her memory. And Sammy's too—Isaiah and Sarah's elder son, lost during the Battle of Brooklyn. Then there was dear Pieter Vander Groot, wrenched away in that terrible, haunting moment in New York Harbor when he had traded his life for hers.

Through tear-blurred eyes, she watched the children playing together in front of the fire as twilight gathered outside the windows. Oh, the hopes and dreams that filled her head and heart for her own wee ones—that they should never suffer such perils and griefs, but only goodness! Surely her parents had also dreamed this for hers and Abby's lives when they were small. And did still, for she felt the blessed results every day.

What lay ahead for her own babes? She watched them growing day by day, learning, wondering, developing into their own precious individual selves.

Doubtless there would be bumps, bruises, and detours along her children's road as there had been on hers. But she constantly prayed that through their own wanderings they would come to know the Lord and his perfect plan for their lives and in the Father's mercy choose to follow him.

Concerns for her children inevitably drew her thoughts back to their father. And again she fought the tide of fear that threatened to overtop her every time Carleton rode away on another mission, even more so now that a confrontation with Tarleton's Legion was all but certain.

WITH DUSK GATHERING, the babies and younger children were carried off to the nursery for their tea, while the older children joined the adults by the fire in the Great Hall for their own. Elizabeth was concentrating on crumbling her small slice of cake with her fork, thoughts wandering, when Burns ushered a courier inside.

He brought the slender young soldier directly to her, the man obviously half frozen and dead on his feet, wet and mud-spattered from what must have been a long, unsparing ride. "Sergeant Skain brings a letter for your hand only, Mistress."

Elizabeth pushed aside her cup and plate and sprang to her feet, her heart contracting sharply.

The courier pulled a sealed letter from his pouch and extended it to her. She snatched it with trembling fingers and drank in the sight of her name gracefully scrawled on its front, almost staggering with relief.

It was his own hand.

Her father drew the courier to the chair at the table nearest the fire. He sank into it as though he had no strength left. Everyone gathered around, faces reflecting the same mingled relief and fear that clenched Elizabeth's breast.

"We took on Tarleton," he croaked. "Gen'l Carleton sent me out soon's he could afterward."

Elizabeth pressed her free hand to her mouth to hold back a cry. Sarah immediately poured a cup of tea and offered it to the courier. He took it with hands that shook and downed the hot liquid gratefully.

A hubbub of exclamations and questions filled the Hall, but he could only shake his head, a weary grin splitting his face. When more tea was poured and a plate piled with an array of food from the table set before him, he fell upon it as though ravenous.

Elizabeth broke the letter's seal with shaking fingers and fearfully scanned its contents.

Friday, 19 January, 1781
Gilbert Town, North Carolina

Dearest one,

Don't fear—I am well. I've but a few moments before we must march, time enough only to share the barest details of the past days. We met Tarleton at a place called Cowpens and broke him. Our casualties were few, while his were great.

Surely our Lord covered us with his wings! I, my officers, and all but five troopers suffered only minor injuries despite being in the thick of the battle. Tell your father that those seriously wounded were quickly cared for and none lost, and assure the wives and children that their men are safe and well. Casualties in Morgan's brigade were similarly light.

I cannot praise Morgan and every man serving with us highly enough. They showed no fear or hesitancy in action, and even the militia held firm. The result is that Tarleton's Legion is destroyed. We took many prisoners, two cannon, and a large part of Tarleton's baggage train, with an abundance of supplies greatly needed for the army. Although Tarleton escaped to Cornwallis despite Lt. Col. Washington's and my best efforts to capture him, it will be long before he'll become the threat he was before, if ever.

How I've missed you and our babes! How I long to return to your arms! But I cannot tell whether it shall be weeks or months before I may do so. We just learned that Cornwallis pursues us, reinforced by General Leslie's brigade. Our greatest concern now is to avoid interception and link up with Greene and the main army. What follows will depend on Cornwallis.

I'll write when I can. Pray for us!

Light of my life, you are ever in my heart.
Jonathan

By the time she reached the letter's end, her throat ached and tears trickled down her cheeks. Looking up, she found her parents and the others regarding her with anxious expressions, faces drained of color. She forced a tremulous smile and quickly read the letter aloud, except for the endearments meant for her alone. Her audience reacted with exclamations of relief and delight, laughter and exuberant embraces.

She turned, then, with words of gratitude and anxious questions for the courier. But he was sound asleep, empty plate pushed aside, head buried in his arms, crossed on the table.

Chapter Thirty-six

"I'M SO GLAD YOU invited us to come for a visit, Dolly," Elizabeth said, dandling her giggling daughter on her knee as she took in the cozy scene in the Henry's parlor. "We've been hoping to meet you ever since Patrick visited Thornlea."

"I can't say how delighted we are that you were brave enough to come so far despite this deplorable weather," Patrick Henry's beautiful young wife, Dolly, returned in her sweet, soft drawl.

She was seated at one side of the blazing hearth with her husband's oldest child, Martha Fontaine. Called Patsey by everyone and just beginning to show her pregnancy, the latter was the same age as Elizabeth and two years older than her stepmother. Elizabeth's parents were seated opposite them while Elizabeth occupied the sofa with Julianne.

Harry played on the rug in front of the hissing fire alongside the Henrys' youngest daughters, two-and-a-half-year-old Dolly and thirteen-month-old Sallie; and Charlie, at not quite two the youngest of Patsey's three sons. Seated cross-legged on the floor near their mother, his brothers Pat and Neddy, six and five, were each occupied perusing a small book.

"It's only a couple of day's easy ride by carriage from Thornlea," Dr. Howard said dismissively, "and we were blessed to have a break in the weather just long enough for us to make it through."

Anne gave him a meaningful look. "We won't mention the state of the roads after all this rain and sleet. But at least it finally left off."

Outside the heavily curtained windows the wind picked up, moaning restlessly around the brick manor's eaves as though to dispute her remark.

"Well, this mornin' it's lookin' like that might not last, which means y'all may just have to stay till spring!" Dolly returned with a mischievous smile.

"Our spirits were gettin' right low, bein' stuck here in the house in this weather without any company to keep us lively," Patsey said, beaming at Elizabeth and her parents. "Why, we're so isolated way out here that we often don't have any company for days on end. As you can imagine, any-time we're so fortunate as to receive visitors, we're loath to give them up. You may find you've a hard time escapin' us."

"As comfortable as you've made us," Elizabeth protested as a young black maid brought in a steaming pot of tea, "I won't promise you'll see the back of us anytime soon."

They all shared a merry laugh. "Thank you, Deborah," Dolly said as the maid set the teapot on the tea table next to her. "That'll be all now."

Deborah curtsied. As she turned to withdraw, she gave Elizabeth a quick glance that brimmed with curiosity and another emotion Elizabeth could only guess at.

An older woman had brought hot water to Elizabeth's chamber early that morning. After exchanging pleasantries, she had gulped and mur-mured breathlessly, "We heard tell that your husban' . . . that the gen'l—" Clearly anxious, she had concluded in a rush, "—that he freed all his slaves."

Elizabeth had acknowledged it and assured the woman that she could speak to her in confidence. Dipping a curtsy, she had hurried from the room—and shared their encounter with others, Elizabeth guessed now, returning a faint smile to Deborah's surreptitious look before she slipped away.

Julianne fussed and reached out to Harry, who had picked up a carv-ed wooden soldier, its uniform painted in Continental blue. Elizabeth set her down, and she toddled over to her brother, plopped onto the rug beside him, and grabbed his toy out of his hand. Instead of reacting with outrage, he put his arms around her and kissed her cheek.

When Dolly's and Patsey's eyes widened, Anne said with amusement, "That's just Harry being Harry."

"Might I have one of those?" Patsey enquired drolly, drawing everyone's laugh as she went to separate Charlie and Sallie, who had begun to squabble over another toy.

Elizabeth's father rose and went to pry the toy out of Julianne's hand. When she began to screech, he wagged his finger, giving her a stern look that caused her to immediately subside, her lower lip protruding in a pout. He handed the toy soldier back to Harry, who took it with a happy grin and offered it to his sister. She looked beseechingly up at her grandfather, who threw up his hands and retreated to his seat, to the amusement of all the adults.

It was late morning on Thursday, 15 February. Elizabeth and her parents had arrived at Leatherwood the previous evening to a gracious welcome and had quickly been made at home.

The Henrys' extensive plantation in the foothills of the Blue Ridge in southern Virginia was named for the crystal-clear creek that crossed it on its way to Smith's River. The latter was a tributary of the wide Dan, a major waterway that flowed from the Blue Ridge foothills into North Carolina, then wound back over the Virginia border to form an informal boundary between the two states. The river stretched for more than two hundred miles before finally emptying into the ocean.

"I'm beginnin' to wonder what's become of those men of ours," Dolly said, frowning at Patsey. "They've been out in that cold wind for a sight of time since leavin' at daybreak."

"Knowin' John and Papa, they might have ridden all the way down to the Dan after all to see whether the army got across safely," Patsey replied. "That message from Gen'l Greene late last night said they planned to cross at the lower ferries while Gen'l Williams and his detachment tried to pull Cornwallis off toward the upper ones. What with Gen'l

Cornwallis not a day's ride behind them, Papa was worried we might end up in danger here."

Elizabeth exchanged a hopeful glance with her mother. "Then surely the army's across by now."

Patsey chewed her lip. "Unless the river was runnin' too high for a crossin' to be safe."

Dr. Howard gave Elizabeth a worried glance. "The cavalry will be holding the rear to delay Cornwallis, which means they'd cross last."

They were interrupted by the sound of the outer door in the foyer opening and quickly banging shut again. A cold draft wafted into the parlor, and footfalls echoed down the passage. Martha's husband, John Fontaine, strode into the room with Patrick Henry following him inside, both men bundled to the eyes.

Elizabeth's breath caught when Henry paused to usher Carleton out of the shadows behind him. He carried his helmet in the crook of his arm, and his hair was windblown, his ice-crusted uniform and cloak badly wrinkled and stained as though they had freeze-dried on his body.

His face was gaunt, and he appeared about to drop in his tracks. But when Dolly and Patsey rose and hurried over to the men, he forced a smile and returned a stiff bow to their curtsies while Henry introduced them.

"I apologize for my appearance and for tracking dirt across your clean floors, ladies, but Pat insisted I come in at once," Carleton said wearily as he peeled off his cold-stiffened gloves.

As always when he returned from an absence, a thrill went through Elizabeth at the sound of his voice, rough and hoarse though it was. Dolly graciously dismissed his apology and bade him welcome.

Harry had turned as the men entered. Catching a glimpse of his father, he pushed to his feet and ran to him, squealing, "Papa! Papa!"

Carleton was forced to stoop, astonishment erasing the strain from his face as he dropped helmet and gloves onto the floor and scooped his son up in his arms to keep the boy from colliding with his muddy boots.

His gaze immediately flew to Elizabeth, beaming now, and then to her smiling parents, while Harry clutched his neck as though he would never let go of his father again.

Julianne had also turned at the commotion and now, looking up at Carleton, she burst into a storm of tears. "Pa-pa!" she wailed repeatedly in desolate, hiccupping sobs.

Elizabeth hurried to snatch her up and carry her to Carleton, who took her in his free arm and kissed both their little heads as they clung to him. "Papa come!" Harry announced triumphantly, if unnecessarily, to his sister.

"Didn't I say I had a surprise for you?" Henry said as he retrieved Carleton's helmet and gloves from the floor and handed them to the black butler who had stepped quietly into the parlor behind them.

Holding Elizabeth in a tender gaze, Carleton answered, "The very best one I could ever hope for."

Dolly and Patsey retreated to their seats. Grinning, Fontaine managed to divest Carleton of his cloak and the thick woolen scarf wound around his neck without disturbing the twins, who were enthusiastically pressing moist kisses to their father's face.

The butler shook his head disapprovingly as he gathered the articles, looking askance at Carleton's mud-encrusted boots. Stowe had delivered Carleton's pack to the kitchens, he informed Carleton with wounded dignity, and insisted that he would personally clean and dry everything and deliver a change of clothing to Carleton before dinner.

Carleton's mouth twitched, but his grave assurance that those were Stowe's orders mollified the butler somewhat.

Elizabeth hardly noticed Henry and Fontaine stripping off their wet wrappings and adding them to the butler's burden before he disappeared down the passage. She only vaguely registered that the two men withdrew to the fire. As the twins contentedly laid their heads on Carleton's shoulders, she leaned in to receive his kiss.

"I've missed you abominably," he murmured, smiling deeply into her eyes. "I love you so."

She returned his smile. "I love you. Always." She reached up to cup his cheek in her hand. "Dearest, you look so tired."

He let his head droop against her hand. "All of us passed beyond tired weeks ago."

From across the room Dolly urged, "Please do sit down before you drop, general." To his protestation that he would sully the upholstery, she countered cheerfully, "Everything can be cleaned. I'm much more concerned with your comfort, sir."

With a relief he was hard pressed to conceal, Carleton followed Elizabeth to the sofa and sank onto it next to her. He settled the twins on his lap and, too spent to hold himself erect any longer, rested his head against the sofa's back. Elizabeth leaned into his shoulder, and a merciful warmth and peace enveloped him. It was all he could do to keep his eyes open.

It was nothing less than God's grace that had brought her and their babies so far to meet him, he reflected, overwhelmed with gratitude. Despite the turmoil of battle and pursuit, despite his present exhaustion and the uncertainties the army still faced, their presence deepened the settled confidence and contentment that filled him since they had wed.

His reverie was interrupted by the other children who, seeing their new playfellows cuddled on their father's lap, began to demand the attention of their own. Henry was soon sprawled on the rug in front of the fire wrestling with the squealing boys, while Fontaine bounced laughing Sallie and little Dolly on his knees.

"General Andrews will come up to join us for dinner?" Dolly asked.

Forcing his limbs to move, Carleton levered himself erect, carefully shifting the twins, who remained attached to him like limpets to rock. "He promised he would as soon as the camp is organized and pickets and scouts sent out."

"How did Lawton manage?" Dr. Howard asked anxiously.

He was interrupted by a maid, who entered carrying a tray of glasses and bottles of Scotch and sherry. Fontaine poured whisky for the men, while Dolly passed sherry to the women. As the maid went out, Carleton registered absently that she paused in the doorway to look back and meet his gaze with a veiled look before hurrying off.

Gratefully he accepted the glass Fontaine offered. "Lawton did all that could be wanted at Cowpens and in the actions we were involved in coming up through North Carolina, Samuel. You made a good choice in enlisting him as your chief of surgery and obviously trained him well."

Dr. Howard sighed in relief, his expression reflecting gratification.

Taking a sip of the amber fluid, Carleton deftly fended off Harry's grasping fingers. "When you're older, my lad," he murmured. "Much older." He made a face at his son that caused the little boy to giggle.

The whisky's warmth spread through his veins, dispelling the strains of the past month, and Carleton finally allowed himself to relax. "We were involved in a number of skirmishes on our way north. The day before we passed into Virginia, Ensign O'Neil in Farris's regiment took a deep cut on the thigh. Lawton told me this morning that the wound has begun to fester, and he wondered whether it would be wise to send for you—"

Before he could finish, Dr. Howard set aside his drink and sprang to his feet. "I'll go down at once. Where's the camp setting up?"

Henry sat up, holding Neddy imprisoned, laughing and squirming, in his arms. "Down in the meadow along the creek where it'll be most convenient for your patrols to come and go. I'll have my man take you down."

Anne immediately hurried upstairs to fetch her husband's cloak, gloves, and helmet, and Dolly dispatched one of the servants to carry down his medical case.

While they were gone, Henry told Carleton that there were two empty tobacco barns on the meadow and another large barn nearby that between them should accommodate all of Carleton's troops. The hay stored in the larger barn would provide forage for the horses as well as bedding for the men. Earlier in the week he'd had enough wood chopped to last several days in case the army came through the area, and he had also managed to commandeer a supply of wool blankets for the militia.

All of it was available to Carleton's troops. In addition, on their arrival Henry had ordered all the foodstuffs and other necessary supplies that could be spared to be sent down to the camp. The news cheered Carleton immensely.

Anne and the servant soon returned, and bundled heavily against the cold, Dr. Howard followed Henry's body servant outside.

IT HAD TAKEN considerable wheedling, comforting, and promises that he would see them in a little while to pry the twins away from Carleton. But at length the black nurse and a maid had borne them off to the nursery with the other children. Already his arms felt empty, and he longed to feel their tiny, solid bodies cuddled against him again.

Andrews had come up to join them for dinner, bringing along Dr. Howard, who gave a reassuring report on the ensign's wound, which he had cleansed and redressed. After everyone had gathered around the large dining room table and grace had been offered, the servants brought in bowls and platters of food whose aromas made Carleton's mouth water.

He swallowed a long draught of wine and set the glass aside, only marginally registering the conversation flowing around him. Having watched a maid help Elizabeth into a claret-colored gown for dinner upstairs half an hour earlier, he was more than conscious of her seated beside him. He reached under the table to capture her hand, exchanging a smile tinged with heady promise that dispelled the dregs of his exhaustion.

"You look much refreshed, General Carleton. I trust you received everything you needed from the servants and your man."

He wrenched his thoughts back to the present and returned a grin to Dolly's knowing smile from the end of the table opposite her husband.

"I did. I haven't words to thank you for your kind hospitality. I feel like a new man."

Indeed he did after washing off the long journey's filth in gloriously hot water. Stowe had arrayed him in his spare uniform, clean linens, and polished boots. Despite the wear and tear the past weeks had caused to his effects, he was confident he looked the proper officer again.

So did Andrews, seated across the table from him and Elizabeth. Before coming up to the house he had washed in creekwater heated over a campfire, he had assured Carleton, and changed into a dry uniform. Their men were comfortably accommodated in the barns with blazing fires outside and food and drink and warm blankets for the night. The horses had been cared for, pickets posted, and patrols sent out to keep watch along the rivers. The report eased Carleton's mind.

As their gaze met, he read the emotion in Andrews' eyes and returned it with understanding and sympathy. He at least had his family with him, while his friend did not. Nor ever could at a gathering such as this one.

The private discussion he'd had with Elizabeth before they rejoined the rest of the company nagged at him. He had noticed the servants' masked glances and asked her about it.

After relating her brief conversation with the maid early that morning, she had concluded with considerable distress, "The Henrys are truly dear persons. They couldn't be kinder or more thoughtful. I respect them and thoroughly enjoy their company. Perhaps that's why this bothers me so. Even though it appears they treat their slaves reasonably well, I simply can't dismiss this evil as inconsequential. I don't want to be discourteous, but I marvel that they remain blind to the inconsistency of their beliefs."

"I meet it at every turn, dear heart," he had responded. "Seeing slavery so openly defended is well nigh intolerable. And believe me, once our country's independence is secured and I'm no longer dependent on slaveholders' goodwill, I'll not hold my tongue or stay my hand no matter how much I might esteem some of them personally. I couldn't be happier that we're able to assist Marah's endeavors in the meantime."

Now he forced a smile and responded to the lighthearted conversations around the Henrys' dinner table as though no dark thoughts clouded his mind.

Seated across the table from Carleton and Elizabeth, Andrews resolutely banished his envy. He was delighted that they were together. Truly. But that did not lessen the longing that wrenched his heart.

How he ached to hold Blue Sky and their sons. With every separation he missed them more painfully. In Blue Sky's tender, passionate love, he grew stronger, felt that he could do anything, bear any trial as long as she was by his side. And their boys—how much they were changed whenever he returned from an absence! The loss of so many precious moments of their lives as they grew lodged in his chest like a heavy rock.

"Your wife and children are well?" Patsey's polite question drew him back to the present.

"So I've been told." He directed a grateful look at Elizabeth.

"You have two sons, I believe." Although Dolly spoke kindly, he sensed wariness in her manner.

"I do."

"Joshua is three and a half, and Daniel turned two in December," Anne broke in. "They're quite handsome boys and quick to learn."

Andrews noted that as usual she used their Christian names—appropriate here, of course. Considering her reservations about the Shawnee, it touched him that despite of it she was always quick to take the children's part.

"I met their mother at Thornlea," Henry said. Turning to Andrews, he added, "You're most fortunate to have such a lovely wife, one from a powerful and distinguished native nation."

"I am indeed blessed."

He meant it, even knowing that his wife and children would be no more comfortable at such a table as this than their hosts would be to have them, no matter their outward courtesy. Nor would Red Fox, Spotted Pony, or any of his and Carleton's clan and nation ever really be welcome in white society.

Glancing across the table, he met Carleton's meaningful gaze; clearly his thoughts matched Andrews' own. Nor was Henry—alone of the others except for Elizabeth—insensible to them. It was telling that no one brought up what surely all of them must be thinking: that he and Carleton took their kinship with the Shawnee seriously and would never put it off for any other.

A deep divide stood between their people and the white world, even as it stood between the white world and the slaves. It was one that pretense could not conceal any more than it could the unsettling apprehension that those divides would only widen in the years to come.

WHEN THEY WERE FORTIFIED by warmth, food, and drink, at the others' prodding Carleton and Andrews described the battle at Cowpens, then their twenty-eight-day forced march back to Virginia.

Cornwallis had begun his pursuit of Morgan immediately on learning of Tarleton's debacle. Determined to take back Morgan's prisoners and prevent his linking up with Greene, he had burned his excess baggage and wagons in order to move all the faster.

Morgan, in turn, did the same. With Carleton's and Washington's cavalry screening his rear, Morgan had eluded Cornwallis and delivered his brigade and the prisoners taken at Cowpens to Greene at a nondescript village called Guilford Court House.

That Greene's army had reunited only served to fuel Cornwallis's fury. Having already crossed into North Carolina, he had evidently thrown every restraint to the wind and determined to follow Greene to the end of the world. His army ruthlessly plundered private homes all along their route, and civilians soon clogged the roads ahead of him, carrying with them whatever possessions they could on their panicked flight. Greene sent orders to Lieutenant Colonel Henry Lee, whose Legion was off raiding with Marion, to join the army on the double. On the way Lee met up with General Huger and his command, and they arrived at Guilford Court House together. By then Morgan was in such pain that he couldn't sit a horse and was forced to return home by carriage, leaving Colonel Williams to take over his command.

The same day Morgan departed, Greene learned that Cornwallis had crossed the Yadkin River. Intelligence indicated that he believed Greene would head for the rain-swollen Dan's shallower upper fords since the lower fords were running too high to cross and no boats were available there to ferry his army.

Thankfully the British commander's intelligence was badly flawed. Greene had already sent orders for boats to be collected at the Dan's lower fords. After dispatching Williams' brigade, Lee's Legion, and Carleton's Rangers straight north to draw Cornwallis off toward the upper fords, Greene had marched the rest of the army at all possible speed northeast toward the lower ones.

The deception's success had depended on Williams and his cavalry keeping to their course until the last possible instant before making a break to rejoin Greene. Maintaining speed, communication, and fierce resistance to the pursuing enemy across miles of rugged terrain became their sole focus.

Their audience listened spellbound while Carleton and Andrews described that perilous journey marked by desperate clashes with the British van as they and Lee constantly harassed their pursuers in the effort to delay Cornwallis's unrelenting progress and prevent him from learning that he was being led farther and farther astray. They had taken time only to rest their horses, devour whatever food was at hand when there was any, and catch an hour of sleep as they dared.

Guarding Williams' brigade as his exhausted men pressed forward with all the speed they could muster, they had repeatedly clashed with Tarleton and what remained of his still lethal Legion, while ranging through rain and ice, forests, hills, and meadows over rutted, miry roads, tracks, no path at all, and uncountable crossings of flooded rivers, creeks, and swamps. The brigade had never been more than a couple of days ahead of their pursuers. Often only a few miles separated them.

Cornwallis's scouts had come into view more than once, with only Lee's Legion and Carleton's Rangers standing between them. But every man had faced the trial with cheerful fortitude, and all the while Greene continued to withdraw steadily toward safety.

Carleton noted that Elizabeth listened with rapt attention, her face pale. But far from appearing distressed as did the other women, she did not flinch at any detail, instead regarding him with a fierce pride and admiration flashing in her eyes—and something akin to envy. His heart swelled with renewed delight that this passionate woman belonged to him, and he to her.

They had won a victory just by crossing the Dan with the army intact, the Rangers the last detachment to cross late the previous night. Cornwallis's van had pressed through to the Dan at daybreak that morning. When Greene learned that the main British force had halted a few miles below the border, he had headed for Halifax Court House to rest and reprovision his army and wait to see what Cornwallis intended to do.

"He posted us here temporarily to protect Leatherwood and keep watch along the river in this area while Williams and Lee patrol the Dan east of here," Carleton explained.

Apologetically Henry related that Greene had asked him to send fourteen or fifteen hundred volunteers to the Virginia border to meet the army when they crossed into Virginia. Although he had immediately called out all the militias in the surrounding counties, they hadn't yet come in for lack of supplies.

"We can't oppose Cornwallis without reinforcements!" Andrews burst out. "Not with the casualties we've taken and the majority of the North

Carolina militia deserting us to go home. The men we have left are worn to the bone."

"Greene met us at the crossing last night, and I felt something implacable in him," Carleton broke in. "He was as spent as we were and disappointed that no reinforcements were waiting for us. But when I asked what he means to do now, he told me without hesitation that he won't leave Cornwallis to operate unmolested in North Carolina."

Henry fixed him in a keen look. "I thought Cornwallis's orders from Clinton were to remain in South Carolina and protect Charlestown and his outposts this winter."

"That didn't keep him from pursuing us all the way through North Carolina," Andrews pointed out.

Henry sat back in his chair, arms folded, expression thoughtful. "That Greene managed a retreat across such difficult terrain in the dead of winter with the speed and efficiency he did is an astounding display of military skill and exertion. You drew Cornwallis well over two hundred miles from his supply base in Camden. He'll find no provisions for his army in North Carolina, and I think it unlikely he'll cross into Virginia."

A shrewd glint in his eyes, he continued, "It'll be interesting to see what he does. With the Dutch and Spanish joining our fight against Britain, I've a feeling that the next few months are going to be crucial to this war—either for our victory or defeat."

THREE DAYS LATER Carleton received Greene's orders to move back across the Dan into North Carolina with Lee and two companies of the Maryland line. Their assignment was to assist Pickens and his now 700-man militia corps in gathering intelligence and harassing Cornwallis.

If Carleton had ever harbored doubts about how deeply his leaving affected Elizabeth and the twins, he could have none now. For the first time it was Harry who caused the greatest commotion, repeatedly imploring, "Papa, stay!" as he clung to him, while Julianne sobbed uncontrollably in Elizabeth's arms. She, in turn, leaned into her own mother's arms, tears trickling down her cheeks.

When Dr. Howard finally succeeded in prying Harry out of Carleton's arms, he would not be comforted. Carleton kissed his screaming son, feeling as though his heart was being torn out of his chest, went to kiss Julianne, and then Elizabeth. They exchanged choked pledges of love before he turned on his heel and blindly followed Andrews outside into the clouded afternoon, the children's anguished cries torn away by the blustery wind.

"What do you think, Charles? Is it better to spend time with them whenever you can or to stay away until this blasted war is over instead of leaving them thus?" he asked in desolation as they strode to where their servants held their mounts' reins.

Andrews directed an unreadable glance at him before saying, voice breaking, "I can't say. I suppose it's entirely selfish of me, but there's nothing on earth I'd not give to hold Blue Sky and my sons in my arms for just one hour."

They came to a halt beside the horses. Looking earnestly from one to the other, Stowe said in a gruff voice, "It'll all come right in the end, sirs. Be sure o' it."

Carleton stared bleakly off toward the distant river. "That's what you always say, Stowe," he growled.

"And ain't it always been so, sir?" Stowe responded.

Carleton turned back to study the older man for a long moment. Then blowing out a breath, he conceded, "So it has."

The four of them mounted their horses. With their servants trailing and Andrews silent at his side, Carleton turned his face resolutely to the east where their troops waited to ride out again into the shadowed, uncertain future.

Chapter Thirty-seven

THE WEEKS THAT FOLLOWED their return to Thornlea impressed Elizabeth anew with the vital importance of a father's presence in his children's lives. Carleton's leaving this time had been the most traumatic for them, especially for Harry. The more the twins comprehension of their world and those around them expanded, the more painfully the repeated separations from their father affected them.

The two-day journey back to Thornlea had been a trial, and not only because of the cold, unsettled weather. Julianne had dissolved into tears with every slightest provocation, while for the first time ever Harry's sunny nature had been replaced by a sulky refusal to cooperate punctuated by screaming temper tantrums. Only his grandfather had been able to placate him, and that with difficulty.

Once settled again into their familiar environment and routines at home, the twins had for the most part resumed their normal behavior, though both clung to their grandfather more than usual. Julianne showed less outward distress, and then she was more easily comforted by her mother and grandmother. Elizabeth unhappily noted a subtle, pervading sadness in Harry, however, that had not been there before.

Anxiety for the twins added yet another burden to her loneliness in Carleton's absence and nagging fears for his safety, along with her responsibilities in hospital and estate and the worrisome news of the war that regularly trickled in to Thornlea. She often felt desperately overwhelmed

and more deeply than before comprehended the concerns of her own parents for her and Abby from their childhood that remained yet today, with their elder daughter as a new wife and mother and their younger one far away across a wide ocean in France. Elizabeth found herself increasingly leaning on them, grateful beyond measure for their steadying love and support.

At the same time, through their shared concerns for their men and children, she, the Shawnee women, and Mary, Sarah, and Jemma, formed ever tighter bonds. Together they prayed passionately for their loved ones' safe return and clung with all their hearts to each other and to the promises gleaned from God's word.

As FEBRUARY WORE into March, a letter finally reached Elizabeth from Carleton, written from the vicinity of Hillsborough, where Cornwallis had retreated. After leading his army back over the Dan into North Carolina, Greene had dispatched him along with Lee, Williams, and Pickens to bait Cornwallis into coming out against them.

Greene's corps had been received by the inhabitants of the wealthy county of Halifax, Virginia, with all the affection of brothers, and for the time they wanted for nothing in the way of food, materiel, and other supplies, Carleton wrote. But Cornwallis's army, which had previously plundered Hillsborough, was now reduced to robbing local farmers of what little sustenance they had left. They had even begun butchering their own draft horses to stave off starvation.

He included little detail of skirmishes and maneuvers with Cornwallis's forces. Instead he poured out his abiding love for her and their children, his gratitude that they had come to meet him at Leatherwood, his concerns for their welfare, and how very dearly he missed them.

Later, seated on the chair nearest Carleton's portrait in the Great Hall, Elizabeth took Julianne and Harry on her lap, forcing a smile even as she choked back tears. She read their father's loving words to them in a steady voice while they listened, wide-eyed.

Then she helped them to trace his signature with their tiny fingers. Both listened attentively and seemed to understand when she explained that this was their papa's name which he had written with his own hand.

When she set them on their feet, led them to his portrait, and lifted each in turn, Julianne leaned eagerly forward to kiss her father's cheek on the painted canvas. Harry, however, laid his head on Elizabeth's shoulder, his face turned away.

The memory of Carleton's confession that he always averted his face from his own father's portrait, believing Lord Carleton did not love him, haunted her. How confusing a father's extended absences must seem to children so small.

She responded to Carleton's letter with tender assurances of her and the twins' love and that they were well and as happy as possible for missing him. She made no reference to Julianne's and Harry's distress nor how painfully she ached to be at his side through every adventure and danger he faced. For the knowledge would weigh on him too heavily when he needed all the strength and resolve he could muster to make it through each day.

MARCH BROUGHT WITH IT alternating rain and snow that kept the manor's residents inside a good deal of the time. Of necessity, however, the routines of the hospital and the estate's employees continued as normal, as did the drills, exercises, and patrols of the troops guarding Thornlea.

News of the wider world continued to filter into the valley. At Philadelphia early that month, the United States Congress adopted Articles of Confederation, forming a new, and hopefully, in Dr. Howard's estimation, a more financially stable government for the fledgling nation.

Closer at hand, Arnold continued his destructive raids north along the Chesapeake shore, burning stores that could benefit the American militias and army. In response, the local militias were also becoming more aggressive, probing Arnold's lines around Portsmouth and skirmishing with his pickets, although the lack of sufficient weapons and ammunition ruled out any major engagement. Elizabeth took comfort in the assurance that Thornlea's distance from the conflict and the area's mountainous terrain made a strike against the Rangers' encampment unlikely.

Reinforcements were finally beginning to pour into Virginia, and she had the sense that the state was destined to become a crucial battleground. Early in March, 1,200 of Washington's most seasoned light infantry from New England and New York reached Annapolis, Maryland, under the command of young Major General le Marquis de Lafayette. Equally encouraging, a powerful French fleet was on its way south to wrest control of the Hampton Roads from the British, then send a squadron to transport Lafayette's troops south to the Virginia peninsula.

On 20 March a report from General von Steuben reached Thornlea that a few days earlier French and British fleets had clashed off Cape Henry. Both had suffered extensive damage and casualties in a fierce, but ultimately indecisive battle. The British had finally broken off the engagement and sailed into Chesapeake Bay, thereby blocking the French from entering. The latter had consequently departed for the fleet's base at Newport, Rhode Island, to make repairs, leaving Lafayette's force stranded on the bay's northern end.

It seemed to Elizabeth that every time events began to turn in the patriots' favor, they inevitably stalled. But when a courier arrived the next evening bearing a packet from Carleton, her hopes bubbled up again. Sarah, Jemma, Mary, and the Shawnee women had joined her and her parents for a late supper as they often did, and Elizabeth eagerly read the enclosed pages aloud.

Their efforts had at last succeeded in drawing Cornwallis out of his lair, Carleton related in the letter, dated Saturday morning, 17 March, and the British commander had pursued his tormentors with a vengeance. Three weeks of constant maneuvering and increasingly violent skirmishes between the two armies had followed as Cornwallis vainly tried to corner Greene. From Carleton's terse descriptions Elizabeth gained the impression that the two armies had circled each other like enraged pugilists in a ring, each inflicting sharp jabs, but unable to take down his opponent with a decisive blow.

Cornwallis had marched hundreds of miles in his pursuit of Greene, driving his army to rags and exhaustion, Carleton wrote. But finally on 14 March, with reinforcements from Virginia and North Carolina doubling his army to over 4,000 men, Greene had lured Cornwallis to the small town of Guilford Court House.

On Thursday, 15 March, drawn into a number of increasingly fierce skirmishes on the town's fringes, Cornwallis had finally launched a full-scale assault while still uncertain of the terrain, how many men Greene had, and their dispositions. It had been a fateful decision.

Basing his strategy on Morgan's at Cowpens, Greene had arranged his militia, Continentals, and cavalry in similar order. The fight had been brutal and unrelenting, the battle lines of the two armies so close at times that the flashes of fire from the musket's muzzles seemed to meld into one rippling extended blaze. Lee's Legion had been pulled away into vicious battles with enemy units scattered through the dense woods bordering the town, while, as at Cowpens, Washington's and Carleton's cavalry had repeatedly driven through the charging British, sabres swinging.

Elizabeth's heart clenched as she read how achingly close Greene's force had come to holding the ground. With victory all but within their grasp, Cornwallis in desperation had ordered his artillery to fire grapeshot into the battle line, indiscriminately cutting down his own troops as well as Greene's. In the resulting carnage Greene's left flank had begun to collapse, and, left no choice, he had withdrawn from the battlefield. Carleton assured her that his Rangers had suffered few casualties, news that she and her audience rejoiced to hear.

In the end none of it would matter, he concluded grimly. Cornwallis had won at best a Pyrrhic victory, for he left behind on the battlefield at

Guilford Court House many more men than did Greene. A quarter of his effective force and a large number of his best officers, men he could ill afford to lose as they could not be replaced, lay dead or wounded. Indeed, by inflicting additional devastating losses in addition to those the British had already suffered at King's Mountain and Cowpens, Greene had ruined Cornwallis's army, while preserving his own to fight another day.

Carleton concluded by noting that Cornwallis's army was withdrawing from the town as he wrote. Where the British commander meant to go next was as yet uncertain, but Carleton suspected he would move southeast toward Wilmington on the North Carolina coast hoping to resupply his army by sea. All he could relate with any certainty was that Greene was intent on blocking Cornwallis from moving north, and he promised to write again as soon as he learned more.

More reports followed at the beginning of April, causing the spirits of the valley's inhabitants to sink once more. A tough, experienced British officer, Major General William Phillips, had arrived at Portsmouth with more than 30 ships carrying 2,300 troops. Intelligence indicated that his orders were to take command from Arnold, who had requested a new assignment, and then to increase raids against American military stores along the Chesapeake. Concluding that his corps was too far outnumbered for any effective action, Lafayette was returning north to rejoin Washington.

Then, to everyone's surprise and jubilation, on Tuesday afternoon, 10 April, Carleton and Andrews rode into the valley at the Rangers' head, everyone weary and travel stained, but greatly relieved to be home. A multitude of joyful gatherings ensued for all those with families in camp, even though the realization that the men's stay could not be long hovered in the back of everyone's mind.

Elizabeth and Carleton's reunion was especially wrenching for its effect on the twins. Although Julianne clung to her father as before, Harry pulled back and turned his face away until Carleton swept the squirming boy up into his arms and kissed him, murmuring tender endearments in a voice that shook. At last Harry turned to clutch him and buried his face against Carleton's neck, tears pouring down his rosy cheeks and tiny shoulders heaving.

"I—wuv—you, Papa!" he sobbed.

"I love you too, my own dear wee lad, more than I can say," Carleton replied gruffly and repeated the same to his little lass.

HE WAS ENTIRELY undone, couldn't banish the memory of the Anglican priest who had married him and Elizabeth describing his own father's grief on sending him away for his protection at such a tender age. And now he himself was forced by duty to leave his little daughter and son too often, for reasons they could not understand. If there ever came a time when he did not return, they would carry that sorrow throughout their lives as he did for the loss of his mother when he'd been only a little older than they were now, and his father when he'd been hardly more than a youth.

The thought stung bitterly. Already he dreaded the day, coming all too soon, when duty would again call him away from the ones dearer to him than any others, those who were his whole world.

AT SUPPER THAT EVENING, he and Andrews related that Cornwallis had, in fact, marched his corps to Wilmington, with Greene's army shadowing him every step of the way. The report of General Phillips' arrival in Virginia had reached them there.

Concerned that Thornlea might eventually become a target of Phillips's raids despite its distance from the coast, Carleton had pressed Greene to release him to return home. Greene had been loath to do so, but within hours new orders had come from Washington.

Their commander had ordered Lafayette back to Virginia. He directed Carleton to rendezvous with the marquis and coordinate his future actions with him. Greene was to retain Washington's and Lee's legions to pursue the war in the Carolinas.

Carleton and Andrews had immediately ridden out with their detachment toward the place that appeared to them now most likely to become the war's final stand: Virginia.

Chapter Thirty-eight

CARLETON PACED UP and down along the Appomattox River's bank, his boots scuffing through the dry grass and dirt that coated the polished black leather with a film of dust. From time to time he directed an anxious glance across Goode's Bridge to the south; northwest toward Manchester, thirty miles away, from where his detachment had come; or at his troops. Many of the men lounged in the shade of the nearby trees in damp uniforms. Others still soaked in the shallows or were watering their horses at the river's edge.

"Where the deuce is Wayne?" he growled, swiping the sweat from his face with his handkerchief. "He had only a little farther to come than we did."

"It takes longer for infantry to march this far in the heat, Jon," Andrews reminded him, adding wryly, "In case you hadn't noticed, it is July, and this is Virginia."

Farris exchanged amused glances with Isaiah, McLeod, and the aides gathered around them. "I hate to point this out, sir, but the pace you set slightly fatigued our men and horses."

Studying the river's sluggish flow, Isaiah muttered, "Had a hard time draggin' my ol' self out o' the water, truth be told."

"Just be grateful we were ordered to rendezvous at a river," Carleton snapped.

He had resisted the urge to dive into the water with his troops but had to admit that he was glad it was nearing sundown. The sun's orb hovered close to the horizon, its glow an intense red behind the early evening haze.

He indicated the broad track of hoofprints that trampled the road, continuing over the weathered timber bridge and out of sight beyond. Through gritted teeth, he added, "After Cowpens I thought—hoped—that butcher's effectiveness would be much reduced, if not altogether destroyed."

"It would have been if Tarleton had died in the battle or we'd captured him afterward," Andrews noted glumly. "Somehow the slippery devil always manages to escape."

"We did put a crimp in his tail."

"Apparently only the tail, James," Carleton returned with a rueful glance at McLeod. "The head of the snake still strikes."

"It would've helped if we'd learned sooner that Cornwallis sent him out," Farris grumbled. "He's at least two days ahead of us."

Grim-faced and silent, all of them stared across the river to the west, where a small detail trailing dust was just coming into view from behind a low, tree-covered rise, still a mile off. Carleton pulled out his spyglass and assured himself that it was only his warriors heading back.

Several minutes later they thundered over the bridge and drew to a halt. Red Fox and Spotted Pony slid from their mounts, while their warriors headed for the river.

None of them were happy. In deference to local sensibilities and to avoid attracting undue attention, Carleton insisted that while on campaign they wear hunting shirts over their leggings and refrain from painting their faces or shaving their hair to a war lock. Avoiding his gaze, they stripped to the skin and splashed into the river. The lounging troopers watched with envy, knowing that their colonels would have their hides if they followed the warriors' example.

"Tarleton's track continues on the road west," Red Fox reported. "It gives no sign he means to turn south."

"Then I'd say Lafayette's wrong in thinking he's leading Cornwallis's vanguard on a move back to the Carolinas."

McLeod's expression reflected Carleton's concern. "Lynchburg's a hundred miles west, but what else lies out in that direction?"

"Prince Edward Court House is maybe thirty miles away. Some military stores are held there. New London is seventy miles farther on near the juncture of the Great Wagon Road and the Wilderness Road."

"There's an arsenal there," Farris contributed.

Carleton nodded, his breath strangely constricted. "The materiel they manufacture and store supplies Greene. And General Clark, too, for his campaign in the Ohio Valley."

"How much farther be Thornlea from there?" Isaiah demanded before the others could speak.

Carleton swallowed with an effort, after a long pause managed to say hoarsely, "Forty miles."

He watched the color drain from his companions' faces, read in their eyes the same sickening comprehension that clenched his chest. Even Red Fox and Spotted Pony, normally stoic, tensed and exchanged alarmed glances.

"That's where he's headed then," Andrews finally said, voice choked.

Farris pulled out a damp, wrinkled handkerchief and mopped the sweat from his face, flushed scarlet by sun and searing wind. "How fast can he travel in this heat?"

"The real question, Matt," Carleton countered, "is how fast can we?"

Carleton was at the end of his patience and on the point of heading after Tarleton, the devil be hanged, when Wayne finally rode up. His brigade of 500 Pennsylvania Continentals, almost doubled by the 400 New England Continentals Lafayette had assigned to him, trailed in his wake, spreading a billowing cloud of dust through the fields and trees to each side.

Every man appeared as overheated and weary as Carleton's troops, with the exception of Wayne himself. He dismounted with aplomb and joined them, moving with an energy that forced his subordinates to scurry in his wake.

Of middling height and handsome despite a long, sharp nose, Brigadier General Anthony Wayne exuded an attractive, good-humored self-confidence. Although he harbored a hot temper and tendency to impulsiveness that had led to a couple of notable defeats during the war, he was a highly effective officer with a solid reputation for battlefield prowess. Just a week earlier at Green Spring near Jamestown, when trapped by a British force greatly outnumbering his own, he had led a fierce charge that broke through the enemy lines and checked their advance.

After everyone exchanged salutes and greetings, Wayne turned to survey his sweat-drenched men with exasperation. "It isn't just the heat. This blasted humidity is about to kill us."

Carleton gestured expansively toward the river. "Feel free to refresh yourselves—that is, if my troops have left you anything except mud."

Wayne grimaced and issued orders to his subordinates. In moments the new arrivals crowded the stream and its banks for some distance to either side.

Glancing from Carleton to his officers and back, Wayne frowned. "I apologize if I've kept you waiting, but—.

"No matter," Carleton cut him off. "You're here now." Tersely he related what they had learned of Tarleton's movements and what they surmised to be his mission.

Wayne digested the unwelcome news and finally allowed reluctantly, "Well, there's nothing we can do to stop him. He's too far ahead. And you heard Lafayette. He doesn't want us taking off after him. We've no idea what Cornwallis is likely to do, and Lafayette wants us within reach in case we're needed."

Carleton gritted his teeth, fighting to keep his temper in check. And his fear.

"Besides, I doubt Cornwallis would send Tarleton that far out," Wayne went on, shrugging. "To get all the way to your camp and back to Portsmouth would take him more than a fortnight."

"Even though we keep the militias in our area supplied, Thornlea still holds more ammunition, weapons, and other provisions than von Steuben lost to that British raiding party at Point of Fork last month," Andrews broke in stiffly. "*I* doubt Cornwallis would pass up such a chance."

THANKFULLY WAYNE did not outrank him, Carleton ruminated near midnight while his troops prepared to mount up, restored by a meal and several hours' sleep. And he hadn't protested Carleton's decision though, to be honest, it would have made no difference in either case.

After a frustrating three months, on that Thursday night, 12 July, American forces appeared little closer to driving the British from the country's shores than they had been when he and Elizabeth returned from France two years prior. His most immediate and pressing concern on reassignment to Lafayette's division had been to strengthen and expand his camp's defenses from the valley's entrance back to the manor. Happily his efforts had received substantial assistance with the delivery of a generous supply of materiel, plunder from British ships and privateers Caledonne had taken prize and shipped from Philadelphia down the Great Wagon Road to the estate.

Carleton had not had long to dread the summons to leave his family again. Barely had the new fortifications been completed when an express arrived from Jefferson with the news that Phillips and Arnold were leading a force of over 2,000 up the James River toward Richmond. The governor called for all militia units to muster and for Carleton, von Steuben, and Brigadier General Peter Muhlenberg to march to Richmond at all speed.

Carleton had immediately sent orders accompanied by additional arms and other supplies to the area's militias before riding out. He and Andrews had taken along a force of more than 400 men, Farris's and Isaiah's cavalry troops, Farris's mounted light infantry, and Red Fox's warriors. Isaiah's two light infantry companies under Matheson's command remained behind to defend Thornlea in case of an attack Carleton prayed fervently would never come.

Reaching the city's outskirts on 26 April, they had linked up with Muhlenberg to wait for Lafayette's arrival. By then Jefferson and the majority of the House delegates had fled to Charlotte, while most of the city's inhabitants scattered.

From Muhlenberg Carleton and Andrews had learned that a British detachment had routed the artillery garrison at York on the Virginia Peninsula and occupied the town. Closer at hand another detachment sent out by Phillips had destroyed the Virginia State Naval Shipyard on the Chickahominy River before rejoining their commander at Petersburg, south of Richmond, thereby forcing von Steuben and his small force to hastily retreat. As if that were not disaster enough, Phillips had then put Petersburg's supply depot to the torch.

The most disheartening news had been von Steuben's withdrawal a good distance northeast of Richmond while Lafayette was still a hundred miles distant at Alexandria with his 900 Continentals, and Wayne and his reinforcements were nowhere to be seen. Even with Carleton's Rangers added to Muhlenberg's command, they did not have enough troops and equipment to have a realistic hope of stopping the British from taking Richmond. The next day they had stood helplessly by while Arnold captured a couple of the last few ships remaining to the Virginia navy and destroyed the rest.

The outlook had become more promising when Lafayette finally marched his Continental light infantry corps into Richmond at the end of April, regardless that his baggage and artillery lagged a couple of days behind. From previous encounters Carleton knew the first impression

tall, slender twenty-three-year-old Gilbert du Motier, le Marquis de Lafayette, projected was deceptive.

Although the young Frenchman could not be described as handsome
with his fair complexion marked by ruddiness and his red-tinged hair, an
amiable nature, lively intelligence, an attractive energy radiated from him
that made him welcome everywhere he went. But beneath that layer of
Gallic sophistication lay the qualities of a decisive battle commander.

Lafayette had quickly taken the place of a son to Washington, who
made no secret of his deep affection for him. Carleton also enjoyed his
company immensely. Although the young marquis' command of English
was excellent, each time they met Lafayette greeted him with an exuberant kiss on each cheek followed by a flurry of greetings, exclamations, and
questions in his native tongue.

There had been little time to celebrate his timely arrival, however.
After marching into Manchester on the opposite bank of the James the
following day, Phillips promptly set more military stores ablaze. In coun-
terpoint, the portly von Steuben had arrived with his troops in a flurry
the next morning, flamboyantly garbed, as usual, in an ornate Continental dress uniform, with his young aide-de-camp, military secretary, and
Italian greyhound at his heels.

Lafayette had seized the opportunity to post every available soldier on
the heights above Richmond in the hope that the British would remain
ignorant of his small force and temporary lack of artillery. It was a cha-
rade that proved effective. The British commander re-embarked his army
aboard his transports and sailed back down the river.

Blessedly, Lafayette's artillery and baggage arrived soon thereafter,
for the news that Phillips had suddenly reversed course and was on his
way back to Petersburg set them on alert again. And when intelligence
arrived warning that Cornwallis had left his subordinate, Lord Rawdon, in
command in South Carolina and was on his way north with what remained
of his army to take command in Virginia, tensions heightened even more.

Lafayette had immediately sent Carleton south with several additional units of light infantry and cavalry. Their mission was to harass Cornwallis's rear guard in small parties, slow his progress, and give the impression that Lafayette commanded a larger force than he did. A week of frenzied skirmishing ensued as they harried Cornwallis all the way to Petersburg.

The British commander entered the town on 20 May only to discover that Phillips had died of a fever a week earlier. He had left Arnold in temporary command, of which Cornwallis speedily relieved him. The only tears shed in the American camp at Arnold's departure soon thereafter for Portsmouth—and, it was rumored, New York—were out of frustration at not managing to capture and hang the man despite Jefferson's tempting promised reward.

One evening, while supping with his officers in his marquee, Lafayette had confided that Washington had authorized him to summarily hang Arnold should he capture him. In fact, he added, to everyone's surprise, he had received several letters from Arnold before he left for Portsmouth, which Lafayette had returned unopened.

Noting the astonished expressions all around the table, le marquis had downed a draught of wine and leaned back in his camp chair, an amused gleam in his eyes. "I sent one of my officers to meet with Arnold about exchanging prisoners. He actually asked what you Americans would do to him if you captured him."

"And what was the reply?" Carleton had drawled.

"I understand he responded without hesitation: 'We should cut off the leg which was wounded when you fought so gloriously for the cause of liberty and bury it with the honors of war, then hang the rest of you on a gibbet.'"

In answer to the approving nods and laughter of those around the table, Lafayette had lifted his glass in salute. "I'm keeping that in mind should I ever be so fortunate as to have the opportunity."

It appeared that was not to be the case. The following day Cornwallis had circled them, crossing the James and marching north. With little over

2,000 men to oppose an army of more than 7,000, the only possibility was to take a course parallel to the enemy's, hoping to rendezvous with Wayne's approaching Continentals.

All they could make of Cornwallis's movements thereafter was that he intended to draw Lafayette away from his real objective. Two weeks later on 2 June he had suddenly turned toward Charlottesville, where the Virginia legislature was in session. Two detachments raced ahead of the main column, Tarleton leading one on the road to Charlotte, the other detouring toward the nearby Point of Fork Arsenal.

Before Lafayette could learn of the enemy's change in direction and hurry to catch up, Tarleton had reached Charlottesville and captured several of the delegates while the rest fled. Alerted to the enemy's approach, Jefferson had sent his family to safety and escaped from his home at Monticello bare minutes before a small enemy party burst in.

At Point of Fork the second detachment drove off von Steuben's militia and captured a vast hoard of arms and munitions. Cornwallis had soon reunited the two detachments and moved downriver to camp at a small plantation owned by Jefferson, which the British thoroughly plundered and laid waste to, going so far as to slit all the horses' throats.

Wayne's arrival had been one of few bright notes that dismal June. Lafayette had succeeded in again interposing himself between Cornwallis and the rest of the Americans' military stores. Almost 2,000 Virginia militia commanded by their new governor, Thomas Nelson, and several hundred riflemen under Colonel Campbell swelled Lafayette's army, with von Steuben on the way back with his 500-man militia brigade.

At the end of the month Cornwallis had unexpectedly withdrawn all the way to Williamsburg—on Clinton's orders from New York, according to intelligence received a few days later. Several short but fierce battles ended the month, and although the Americans had held their own against the British, in the end they were forced to retreat once again.

Shortly after Cornwallis had crossed his army back over the James on his way to Portsmouth, one of Carleton's patrols galloped into camp.

Tarleton had abruptly separated from Cornwallis's column leading a detachment estimated to include at least 350 cavalry and mounted infantry and was riding west at all speed.

Which had brought Carleton and his Rangers to this bridge at Lafayette's command. Orders he was about to cast to the wind, giving no heed to the fact that Lafayette did, technically, outrank him in seniority.

❋ ❋ ❋

THE NEXT DAY, stopping briefly at Prince Edward Court House after a hard, swift ride, they learned from the town's residents that Tarleton had swatted off the local militia as if they were gnats buzzing about his head. After destroying the militia's small store of materiel, he had ridden off down the road to New London, seventy miles west. The heat and rigors of the journey appeared to be wearing on Tarleton's men and their mounts, however, the angry locals informed Carleton and Andrews. When his regiment rode out, many straggled well behind.

The heat was oppressive, but Carleton allowed only a brief rest to water the horses and for the men to devour their rations. There were no complaints for everyone was anxious to press ahead, especially those with families at Thornlea. Dusty, weary, and about to faint from the heat, they nevertheless all eagerly resumed the pursuit when Andrews shouted the command to move out.

Two and a half days later they rode up the main street of the normally bustling town of New London. Its location at the intersection of the Great Wagon Road and the Wilderness Road made it the center of the area's trade and an important stop for settlers moving west or south. The county militia also mustered at the town for drills and stockpiled their military stores there.

The small community appeared almost deserted, and the few residents they saw scrutinized them warily from windows and behind partially closed doors. The column passed a number of substantial houses and finally drew to a halt across from the courthouse and jail, entirely blocking the street for some distance. Every man was sunburned and drooping, the lathered horses' heads down as they steamed under the hot sun.

All cast longing but resigned looks toward Mead's Tavern on their near side. There was no doubt that serving so large a force was beyond the expansive establishment's capacity even if they wanted to waste the time.

It didn't take long to learn that Tarleton had torn through the town late the previous day. As at Prince Edward Court House he had driven off the outnumbered militia and destroyed the arsenal's military stores, another great loss. No sooner had his stragglers caught up with him than Tarleton had abandoned the town in a furious race west toward Salem, thirty-five miles off, a weathered old militia captain told Carleton and Andrews.

Staring west down the road to where the sun hovered above the distant mountain ranges, hands clenched, Carleton said in a tight voice, "If he so much as touches even one of our women or children, I'll have his heart out."

"You'll have to fight me for the privilege," Andrews rasped, his whole body shaking.

Chapter Thirty-nine

T HE SHARP, ROLLING reverberation of musket and rifle fire to the north had grown distinctly closer.

Mouth dry, Elizabeth carefully plucked the lead ball from the wound in the corporal's side and dropped it into the basin on the table beside her. Laying the bloodied extractor next to it, she looked up, swiping the stinging sweat from her eyes with the back of her blood-smeared hand.

"They must be closing in on the dairy."

Her father finished bandaging the sutured bayonet gash in Atkin's scalp. He returned a nod to Elizabeth's worried glance as a surgeon's mate helped the lieutenant down from the surgery table.

"I'm afraid they won't be able to hold Tarleton below the manor much longer."

"We fight to the last drop o' blood," Atkin said grimly, grabbing his musket propped against the surgery table.

Only twenty, the slight, short black officer appeared hardly old enough to qualify as a soldier. But the hardness in Atkin's gaze testified to harsh experience gained on the streets of New York City well before Isaiah drafted him into his regiment four years earlier on the night Carleton stormed the prison ship *Erebus* to rescue Elizabeth. He had more than proven his worth since then.

Elizabeth watched him weave through the wounded men crowding the hospital and disappear out the door before again bending over her patient. She focused on cleansing the wound with spirits as the corporal stirred sluggishly, wincing, the hefty dose of whisky he'd swallowed to numb the pain beginning to wear off.

"Even with all Rufus's workers and the Indian youths pressed to service, Tarleton's force still outnumbers us at least two to one. And obviously we're taking quite a few casualties."

"So're they," the corporal mumbled, speech slurred. "We takin' out plenty of 'em, and we gonna stand!"

She pressed him back onto the table as he struggled to sit up. "I'm sorry, but you're not going anywhere."

After placing a thick gauze pad over his wound, winding a bandage snugly around his abdomen, and tying it off, she motioned to Blue Sky, who hurried over, followed by two of the estate's workers bringing a stretcher. They carried the weakly protesting corporal outside into the shade of the trees where a number of the Shawnee women were assessing wounds, treating the less serious injuries, and caring for those recovering from surgery.

Elizabeth hastily washed her hands in the basin of clear water Mary McLeod delivered. The loud hubbub of voices and rush of movement to and fro echoed inside the hospital's stone walls, but their patients gave only an occasional low groan or stifled gasp. The realization that they were too proud to cry out brought tears to Elizabeth's eyes.

She dabbed the trickling moisture from her flushed face with her stained apron. The air felt hot as a bake oven in the overcrowded building with the July sun beaming serenely from a cloudless sky over the fierce battle that raged between the manor and the valley's northern end.

The alarm had been raised at midmorning that Tuesday, 17 July, that a large, mounted British force of cavalry and infantry was headed their way from the direction of Salem, moving fast. The cavalry wore the green jackets of Tarleton's Legion, Matheson's aide noted tersely.

Elizabeth had immediately donned the breeches she wore for riding and hiking, thinking they'd free her movements if it became necessary to flee into the uplands. Over them she'd tied on her thinnest petticoat to avoid scandalizing the men, not to mention her parents, and strapped on her holstered pistol. Now, in the wilting heat, she ruefully contemplated casting the petticoat aside regardless of decency.

Adding to the chaos, Rufus and his men were bringing in a steady stream of casualties loaded on ox-drawn wagons returning from delivering more powder, shot, and weapons to the valley's defenders. By now all the hospital's beds were filled. A growing number of wounded took up the floor, leaving only a narrow walkway through the building's center.

It didn't help that Lawton and more than half of the surgeon's mates had ridden off with the Rangers. They were desperately needed now. In their absence, a large number of the woman in camp had been pressed to service. Depending on their skills, they attended the wounded; fetched needed equipment, bandages, and medicines from the dispensary at the building's back; carried away what was discarded; or emptied basins of bloody water and refilled them.

Brief reports of the Rangers' movements and battles had regularly reached Thornlea over the past weeks. The most recent, sent by Andrews, had arrived several days earlier with the news that they were traveling southeast down the James ahead of Lafayette's army, shadowing Cornwallis as he moved back toward Portsmouth.

She hastily calculated the miles between them and Thornlea. Her anxious thoughts were interrupted when a sergeant burst in through the door, his face, arms, and torn uniform liberally streaked with sweat, dirt, and blood. He hastily saluted Dr. Howard.

"Major says to tell you we're makin' a stand at the dairy. Rufus's men are settin' fire to the lower grain barns."

"Which means the battle line is only two miles down the road now," Elizabeth said breathlessly.

"We'll hold 'em back long as we can," the sergeant rasped, "but we haven't the men to extend our lines far enough to keep 'em from flankin' us. The major advises movin' the hospital farther up the valley."

Dr. Howard beckoned to the surgeon's mates to gather around him. To the sergeant he said, "Inform the major that we'll move all the wounded back to the barn on the riverbank just beyond the sawmill as quickly as possible."

"Assure him also that the children and all the women except those helping us here or packing up goods in the manor have been taken into the uplands, along with provisions enough for several days as well as ammunition and weapons," Elizabeth put in. "Everyone who can fire a gun is armed."

The sergeant gave them both a grateful look, saluted Dr. Howard, and pushed his way out the door just as Rufus stepped inside. The older man was equally sweat-stained and dirty. Breathing hard, he wiped his brow with a handkerchief.

The cattle had been driven from the northern pastures to the horses' pastures south of the manor, he reported. His drovers were waiting for the shepherds to finish moving their flocks into the uplands before driving the horses and cattle after them. All the poultry that could be caught had been caged and transported there by wagon as well. And Durie had sent more wagons loaded with ammunition and barrels of water and rum up to the battle line.

While Dr. Howard explained to Rufus all that needed to be done to move the hospital and the wounded, Elizabeth began working her way through the melee to the door. "I'm going inside to speak with Alistair," she called to him over her shoulder.

LEAVING THE HOSPITAL, Elizabeth stopped and looked down the road toward the battle line. A long, dark smudge of smoke rose above the trees, blown toward the northeast by the wind. The small grains and hay harvested several weeks earlier and stored in the lower barns, now being torched, she reckoned. Most likely Rufus would burn the hayfields too.

She glanced toward the near gardens as she detoured around the ox teams and their wagons lined up in front of the courtyard gate, thankful that the ripe produce had been picked that morning, leaving little for the invaders to forage. The green corn in the valley's upper fields well south of the manor would only be destroyed if Tarleton's troops came that far.

When she entered the Great Hall she found her mother, Sarah, Jemma, and Durie still there overseeing a handful of workers hastily securing the last boxes and packs. Her mother ran to her.

"You've removed all of Jonathan's family portraits and coat of arms, the Saltire, and the trunk containing his plaids"

Anne brushed loose strands of hair out of her face. "Of course, dear. We've only to load the last boxes into the wagons. Oh, and Alistair brought Jonathan's lockbox full of coin from the safe in his study too."

Elizabeth gave a sigh of relief as her mother hurried back to her work. Durie strode across the Hall to her, appearing, as usual, entirely composed in spite of all he had accomplished that day and still had to do.

"We took down as many o' the weapons as we could reach without bringin' up the ladders," he told her, indicating the almost completely denuded walls. "And we loaded up all o' the ammunition we'll have time to move."

"I want to make sure enough is left."

He gave a slight bow and motioned her to precede him. She led the way to the fireplace set into the massive wall between the Great Hall and the dining room and stepped inside its broad, neatly swept hearth.

When she pushed against a brick on the near end wall, it shifted. A hidden door beside it swung inward, revealing the shadowed top of a spiral stairway within the dark opening.

She descended quickly ahead of him, holding up her petticoat with one hand while gripping the cool iron handrail with the other. At the stairs' end they stepped into the wide, bricked magazine that normally held a great store of munitions.

Large quantities of lead, bullets, and boxes of cartridges had been removed, along with about half the gunpowder. A great many casks of the latter still remained, however, stacked neatly against the sixteen-foot-thick central foundation wall.

For a long moment Elizabeth studied her surroundings. At length she crossed to a stout oaken door with iron hinges set in the manor's rear outer wall. Cool, dank air smelling of damp earth wafted inside when she pulled it open.

In front of her a bricked tunnel stretched out of sight underneath the terrace into the darkness. Brackets for torches were set at regular intervals along its walls. Carleton had led her the length of it once to its secret exit amid a stand of trees behind the renovated former slave cabins that now housed the manor's married employees and the Rangers' officers.

She closed and latched the door and turned to face Durie. "I don't want one single thing left that Tarleton's men can wield against us or plunder for their own use," she said fiercely. "Whatever it takes, I want it all gone."

Durie studied her intently before saying with a faint smile, " 'Tis what Sir Harry planned should Thornlea ever be attacked, mistress, as yer husband knows. I'll make verra sure it's done if 'tis what *ye* want."

She blinked back stinging tears and forced a tremulous smile. "It is, Alistair. We'll not be able to stop Tarleton, and Jonathan's too far away to reach us even if he knew."

"Then ye'd best be off. Get the wounded as far from here as ye can. I'll have all the others away afore Major Matheson's pushed back here."

She jerked a nod, then turned and fled back up the stairs.

THE SUN HAD DIPPED below the western ridgetop when Rufus's men retreated to take up posts among the trees bordering the hospital's new location. A short distance beyond, at the verge of the upland forest, the Indian youths spread out to hold a third line of defense.

Heavy gunfire sounded from the direction of the manor. From where she stood with Durie on the high clifftop above the falls, she could see through her spyglass a portion of the building's steep slate roof with its tall chimneys pointing toward the sky above the surrounding trees. On the ground below she caught brief glimpses of tiny, indistinct forms moving rapidly between the trees, the pinpoints of gunfire puncturing the shadows.

For what seemed an eternity she waited, breath choked, while the attackers swarmed into the building, driving back the stubborn defense. Desecrating Carleton's home. Hers and their children's. The place grown dear that she had believed to be their inviolable sanctuary.

By slow degrees the reverberating crackle of gunfire dwindled away. An uneasy silence wrapped the valley, unsettling after the long day's ceaseless clamor.

With shocking suddenness an incandescent flash of flaming light erupted upward on a billowing black cloud toward the clear, dusky heavens that spanned the wooded ridgetops. For one brief, tenuous moment the chimneys stood out in high relief. Then, as she watched with mingled horror and triumph, they began to crumble, sliding downward out of her sight, the rooftop disappearing as abruptly.

She stood transfixed, vaguely aware that at her side Durie seemed equally held in thrall. A long, thundering blast of deafening sound, rolled over them then in a monstrous wave, followed in seconds by a tremor that shook the rock beneath their feet.

The trees all around them shivered. Small avalanches of stones and dirt dislodged from the cliff's face on either side of where they stood and cascaded into the pool's dark waters far below, stirring them to a froth.

She gulped in a breath that seared and turned abruptly away. When Durie pulled her into his arms, she pressed her face against his shoulder, her body shaking with silent sobs.

❋ ❋ ❋

Hearing the distant, muffled echo of an explosion, Carleton drew up so sharply that the lathered, long-legged roan gelding he rode half reared. He brought the animal back under control and reined him around, exchanging an anxious look with Andrews, who immediately came up beside him. Their aides and servants urged their mounts forward as well, Farris, Isaiah, and McLeod close behind. The long column trailing back down the road slowed to a halt, the dust cloud they had raised settling over them.

The sun hovered just above the western ridges by the time they had ridden out of Salem with six miles yet to travel. Carleton had fought a despair more wrenching than he had ever known, pleading ceaselessly with the Almighty to keep Elizabeth and the twins and all the rest at Thornlea under the shelter of his wings.

Now, breath seizing, he reined his mount back around and waved the weary column forward, resolved to press an attack regardless that he, his troops, and their horses were on the point of collapse. As one they urged their drooping mounts forward.

They were within sight of the valley's entrance a mile down the road when a body of green- and red-jacketed horsemen suddenly flooded out between the broken barricades. Their leader—Tarleton no doubt—first turned in their direction as though to head back to Salem, only to pull up at sight of the rapidly closing Rangers.

Bending over the gelding's neck, Carleton fiercely urged him to a run. For the briefest of instants Tarleton appeared to assess the advancing force. Then he signaled to his troops and led them in a stampede away down the river road in the direction of Big Lick.

Carleton cursed profoundly as the enemy's fresher horses outpaced the Rangers' laboring mounts. But gradually the realization sank in that their numbers were noticeably short of what Tarleton had been reported to have.

"Shall we pursue?" Andrews shouted.

"Our horses are on their last legs and so are we," Carleton shouted back. "Tarleton can go to the devil for all I care—he's the least of my concerns right now!"

HE VAULTED FROM the saddle before the roan fully halted and raced toward the shadowy figures clustered by the pond's edge. *"Beth! Beth!"* he shouted, heart pounding so hard he felt lightheaded.

A slight figure detached from the indistinct cluster and ran to him. The shock of their collision drove the breath from his lungs in a rush. Staggering and stepping back to regain his balance, he snatched her into his arms.

Relief was so intense that his knees went weak. He cupped her up-turned face in one hand, with the other arm clenched her against him. She pressed into him as though seeking to meld their bodies into one, and their lips met in hard, desperate kisses that left them both breathless and shaken.

At last he pulled back, hastily ran his hands over her shoulders and back. "You're not hurt?" When she shook her head wordlessly, he said, "Thank God! Harry and Julianne—"

"Back at the old barn with the others—"

Pounding hoofbeats cut her off. As their horses slid to a stop, both riders slid from their saddles, crying out at the same time.

"Blue Sky—'

"Mary—"

"All the women and children are safe in the back valley," Elizabeth called to them.

Before she finished speaking, the two women came running toward them together, crying out their husbands' names and assuring them that they and their children were well.

"Alistair and I were watching from the clifftop when the magazine exploded," Elizabeth told Carleton, voice trembling, while Andrews and

McLeod anxiously questioned their wives. "We saw Tarleton form up the survivors of the blast and lead them back down the valley at a run. At that point we came back down to determine whether they'd all gone."

He briefly explained how the past days had unfolded.

When he finished, she said woefully, "We didn't believe it possible for you to come so far in time even if you'd learned of the attack. If only we'd known you'd arrive before—"

He gently pressed his fingers to her lips to stop her. "But you didn't."

"And now your home is gone," she murmured, face downcast, tears gathering.

He drew her back into his arms and bent over her, cheek resting on the crown of her head. "My home is where you and our children are, dearest of my heart. All that matters is that you're all safe. You did everything needed to ensure that—and very well, too, from the look of it."

When she returned a tearful look to his smile, he added, "The moment I heard the blast, I was so proud of you, my fierce little Oriole, that I thought I'd burst!"

Chapter Forty

THE FIRST FAINT GREY light of dawn had just begun to lighten the barn's interior through its high windows and half-open doors. Elizabeth awakened from an exhausted sleep to find Carleton already sitting up and reaching groggily for his carbine.

Red Fox, Spotted Pony, the other Indian men, and Andrews had escorted their families back to their untouched camp late in the night. Carleton had come in even later after everyone else gathered in the barn had fallen asleep, his uniform rumpled, sweat-stained, and dirty. With the events of the long day continuing to revolve in her mind, Elizabeth had not given in to slumber until he kissed her and laid down with her and the children.

He leaned over to kiss her again now, taking care not to jostle Harry and Julianne, cuddled deep in slumber between them on the blanket-covered hay, before pushing to his feet. The air had cooled enough to be comfortable overnight, and in the crowded barn it was preternaturally still, as though the world still reeled from the previous day's clamor and destruction.

She watched him ease soundlessly between the estate's slumbering workers, moving with the catlike grace she always marked in him, until he disappeared from her view outside. By the time she had shaken out her clothing, done her best to pin up her hair in some semblance of order, and covered the unruly mass with her cap, her mother had done the same, and the rest of the barn's occupants were also stirring.

The twins roused, their anxious questions subsiding when Elizabeth assured them that their father remained nearby. Harry's lower lip quivered for a moment, but he quickly calmed. Elizabeth was proud of him, relieved that he was beginning understand that his father's absences were only temporary and that he would return.

Her mother took charge of the children, and Mary soon joined them, bringing along Jimmy and Aileana, who engaged the twins in happy play. Elizabeth went outside, where Salome and the kitchen maids had built up the fire and begun to prepare breakfast with Sarah's and Jemma's help. The savory fragrance filling the still, early morning air caused Elizabeth's stomach to cramp, reminding her that she had not eaten since breakfast the previous day.

Carleton returned while everyone was gathering for the meal. As soon as he sat cross-legged on the ground, the twins tumbled gleefully onto his lap. Between trying to eat and feeding them bites from his plate, he soberly recounted what had happened during night and what he had learned that morning.

Isaiah's and Farris's troops had swept the entire lower valley from its entrance to the uplands. A large number of enemy dead had been found at the manor's site. Among them had been several enemy wounded and a few of Matheson's troops who had fallen during the final battle. Still more casualties from both sides lay along the battle's route from the fortifications at the valley's mouth to the manor.

All those requiring surgery, friend and foe alike, had been transported to the hospital's temporary location. Dr. Howard, Captain Lawton, and the surgeon's mates had tended to the most urgent injuries into the wee hours of the morning before making impromptu beds wherever they found space to snatch a few hours' sleep. With a strong guard posted at the valley's entrance, the troopers and Rufus's men had collapsed beneath trees or out in the open in the warm air.

All told, their own casualties were relatively light: several Indian youths with serious injuries and one dead; a number of Rufus's men wounded and a handful dead. Of Matheson's 140 troopers, thirty-nine had suffered wounds, ten severe, while an additional seven had died in the ferocious running battle during their withdrawal toward the manor. The rest had escaped unharmed through the tunnel while Matheson lit the fuse to the magazine.

Not all of Tarleton's dead had yet been counted, but there were many. They were to be buried behind Thornlea's burial ground, while Matheson's slain troopers would be interred within its boundaries.

Her voice quavering, Anne asked the question Elizabeth could not. "The manor . . . how . . . how bad is it?"

He regarded her for a long moment, his expression unreadable. At last he said gruffly, "I'm going to take Beth down first. It's best if you stay here with the children for now, Anne. There'll be a considerable amount to sort out later, and we'll need you and Samuel to help us."

THE FIRST THING SHE noted was an unsettling void where the steep slate roofs, massive chimneys, and crow-stepped gables of the great, castle-like manor had brooded over the landscape from atop a low rise. She had been so used to seeing it there. It did not seem right that it had simply . . . vanished.

Wafted by a light breeze, a shifting mist wrapped the valley laden with the acrid stench of gunpowder, wood smoke, and earth when she and Carleton rode down from the upland. As they drew nearer, between the fringe of trees and dark billows of smoke that still rose from the fire's dying embers, she caught brief glimpses of jagged, blackened fragments of walls.

She kept her gaze averted as though not looking at the manor's ruins would hold at bay the reality of the destruction. Instead she focused on what remained intact: the barns, cornfields and hayfields, orchard and vineyard, gardens, camps and barracks, workrooms, and cabins they passed.

That was a very great deal, she determinedly assured herself. It could have been so much worse.

From the manor north to the valley's entrance was another matter, Carleton had warned her. The valley's defensive outer perimeter would require a great deal of repair. But the dairy barns, poultry yard, and hay and grain barns had been reduced to charred, smoking rubble. All of that year's grain, the hay already stored in the barns and still standing in the lower fields had been lost.

He said nothing of the manor. But as they rode up the slope on its south side, to her left Elizabeth saw that the laundry house, summer kitchen, and, a short distance away, the springhouse had been destroyed. She kept her attention on those minor details and on the trampled gardens to keep from looking ahead of her.

She drew to halt when he did, allowed him to help her dismount. All around them troopers and crews of Rufus's men were busy clearing away rubble and assessing needed repairs. Andrews and Durie came by and after greeting Elizabeth with sympathetic looks conferred briefly with Carleton before hurrying off again.

She staggered as they approached the hospital, overcome by the sensation that they stepped into an utterly alien world. The force of the blast had brought down the building's roof and its rear and side walls. Only a shattered façade remained.

Nausea swelled as Carleton lead her by the hand around the ruin to the road outside the broken courtyard walls. She kept her gaze fixed on the path in front of her, afraid to raise her head, breath choking in her throat.

He stopped, took her in his arms, and held her tightly. At last he gently turned her to face what she most dreaded to see and waited patiently for her to gather her courage.

When she finally did, she immediately swung back, pressed her face against his chest, and wept, hard sobs shaking her shoulders. She was grateful beyond measure that he held her like an unmoveable rock, for surely she would have fallen had he not.

"Shhh," he murmured when the worst of her grief had begun to ease. He bent to look into her down-turned face, his own eyes glimmering with moisture. "Please don't cry, Beth. Please don't be sad. A house is easy enough to come by. The lives of those you love, once lost, can never be replaced."

Crying all the harder, she sobbed, "I—I was able—to save your plaids—all the portraits, the Saltire—and your—your family's coat of arms."

"All of it?" he exclaimed, astounded.

She nodded, gulping back a sob. "Everything that I—I was afraid you'd grieve losing. All the specie from your safe, too, of course. We've enough to tide us over until Louis returns with another supply," she concluded tearfully.

He gave a soft laugh and kissed her, then pulled out his handkerchief and tenderly blotted away her tears and his own. "I should have known. You always do exactly what's best."

"And I should have known you'd come," she whispered, pressing into his arms. "You always have."

His arms tightened around her. "You couldn't be sure of it, dear heart. Both of us know a time may come when . . . when I'm not able to."

Together they turned back to take in sorrowfully the ruin in front of them. It was all she could do not to break down again.

All that was left of the manor's central core, from the magazine, storerooms, cellars, and kitchens on the ground floor to the attics at its top and the broad terrace at its back, was a vast, blackened chasm lying open to the sky. Where the Great Hall had been was empty space. Thick spirals of smoke rose from a bed of seething embers at the crater's bottom.

To their left the south wing had been reduced to a jagged, roofless section at its former end. There a truncated length of the first floor hung

at a slant into space, empty window frames blindly overlooking the ravaged scene of devastation, glass panes blown out. On their right the
lower portion of the short north wing's outer wall farthest from the
explosion's center canted unsteadily backward. On all sides blasted, broken trees framed the spectral, charred remains.

Hand in hand they picked their way around the outer edge of the destruction, stepping carefully through the debris that remained of roofs
and chimneys, chamber walls and floors and broken bits of furnishings
flung far and wide across the marred expanse of lawns.

"Oh, Jonathan, this was your home—the home Sir Harry built," she
mourned when they stopped amid the smashed kitchen garden. "It would
cost a fortune to rebuild, even if that were possible. But it would never
be the same."

He remained silent for some time, looking around them. Her heart
contracted painfully to see the grief he struggled to contain.

At length he said resolutely, "Thornlea was Sir Harry's vision, not
mine. I've always loved this place. The happiest memories of my youth
are here. But perhaps it's as well that the physical substance of it is gone.
I'll always cherish the memory of it as it was when Sir Harry was alive.
That can never be taken from me."

When he looked down to meet her sorrowful gaze, she said sadly,
"It was our first home. Julianne and Harry were born here."

"I regret that the most." Forcing a teasing tone, he added, "However, I'd feel a great deal better if we'd at least managed to eliminate Tarleton."

She let out a rueful chuckle. "You were right. All that really matters is
that we're all here and safe. We do still have much more to be grateful
for than we've lost."

Smiling, he cupped her face in his hands and kissed her. "As long as
I have you and our children, beloved, I've more wealth than there is in
all the world."

✳ ✳ ✳

OVER THEIR PROTESTS, Durie insisted that Carleton, Elizabeth, and the twins, and the Howards take over the second floor of his small stone house nestled in a glen west of the river. He set up a bed in his first-floor study, while Salome and her kitchen maids commandeered the cottage's smaller kitchens, where they were soon turning out plentiful feasts for every meal.

The most immediate concern was housing for Rufus's dairy workers, drovers and the other employees whose homes had suffered the same fate as the dairy barns. The camps with their barracks and officers' cabins had survived the attack with minimal damage, and as the late July days remained hot, the troopers happily shifted into tents. This opened space in the barracks for the displaced workers and their families to settle temporarily. Life resumed some semblance of normality, while efforts at cleanup, repair, and rebuilding continued.

That Friday Carleton sent Hutchinson to Lafayette at his camp at Malvern Hill north of Williamsburg to deliver a report on the attack and apologies for Carleton's delaying his return. A courier rode off with copies for Governor Nelson and Washington. After them went Durie and Stowe to seek a suitable location for the Rangers' camp in Williamsburg's vicinity.

In the evening, with dusk coming on, Carleton walked with Elizabeth along the riverbank. "Have you thought about what we should do about Thornlea?" he asked tentatively.

She tipped her head to study him, frowning, questions in her eyes. "If we were to stay, we'd have to build a house, whatever it might be."

He hesitated, then said slowly, "It troubles me that it's too far for my clan to come here easily and safely. Even after the war with Britain is over, the war between the United States and the Shawnee—all the native peoples—will continue. As I told you back in France, someday I want to build you a home in Ohio Territory nearer our clan."

She considered for several moments before looking up with a warm smile. "Whither thou goest, I will go, my love. Your people are mine as well, and our children's. And, I confess, moving to Ohio Territory is an adventure I find quite enticing."

He returned her smile, his heart lifting. "I hoped you might. Then as soon as possible I'll buy a tract of land from the Shawnee where they can come to us and always be welcome and safe. But Thornlea is yours, and you must decide what to do with it."

Thoughtfully she said, "It's in my mind to bequeath it to Harry. When he's grown and ready to establish his own family, he can decide whether he wants to make it his home or sell it. In the meantime, if he's agreeable, Alistair can oversee building the house and continue managing the estate for us so it remains a source of income and a place for us to stay when needed."

"Yes, I'd like that very much," he agreed, greatly pleased. "It occurs to me, too, that we might be able to arrange things so Marah can continue using the valley as a safe haven for her fugitives. Only Isaiah's troops know about her endeavors. All anyone else ever needs to know is that the valley's our secret refuge in case of attack or any other need."

She clasped her hands, beaming. "Oh, yes! Surely after all that's happened everyone will be eager to keep the valley's existence secret."

They spent some time discussing the construction of a modest manor house that Harry could expand after taking possession when he came of age. Finally, indicating the ruins across the river, he said, "I have a sense that all this had to be taken away for us to move forward into the life God has for us. This belongs to the old world. We are of the new—the one that's to come."

She slipped her hand into his, linking their fingers. " 'Forgetting those things which are behind, and reaching forth unto those things which are before, we press toward the mark,' " she quoted.

He smiled down at her. "We'll throw ourselves on His mercy and trust in his sustaining grace."

"What is this?" she teased. "Can this be General Jonathan Carleton actually choosing to trust?"

He drew a wry face. "Even so, at the ancient age of thirty-seven, though doubtless I'll still fail on occasion."

He sobered and took her hands. Raising them to his lips, he turned them to kiss her palms, then pressed them to his breast and regarded her earnestly, deep emotions overwelling. Each time he thought he could not love her more, she proved him wrong.

"One thing I've learned through all of this is that our lives are not tied to earthly things, not even to each other," he said huskily. "Our true home is where our Lord dwells forever among us. Not here. And on the day we're welcomed there, nothing will be able to separate you and me ever again."

"No turning back," she said, nodding firmly as she smiled up at him.

Chapter Forty-one

THE FOLLOWING AFTERNOON, standing at the head of the *msikahmiqui*, Andrews led the gathered men and women in the death chant. Every face was painted, clothing and hair hanging loose in mourning, as together they sang the mournful, drawn out notes, tears falling. Gradually their voices dwindled away, and for some time the assembly sat in silence, smoke twining upward from their pipes.

At midmorning White Horse, a runner for Black Hawk's clan, had arrived from Grey Cloud's Town bearing news of the sudden, untimely death of Andrews' adoptive father. Carleton and Elizabeth had immediately set aside all other concerns to join him, the warriors, and their wives in grieving the dead sachem.

At length each warrior stood in turn to recount Grey Cloud's notable deeds in war and peace. When all those who wished to speak had done so, Andrews stood up, shoulders bowed.

In a ragged voice he spoke of all that Grey Cloud had been to him as a father. His natural father had not been one, he told them. In fact the man had abused him and been responsible for his birth mother's death. It was Grey Cloud and Autumn Wind who had taken him to their hearts, made him a member of their clan and nation, and done for him all that parents should do. It had been Grey Cloud who had taught him the legends, traditions, and rituals of their people and provided for him the wife and children he cherished. For this he would never forget the man who had taken him as a son.

When he sat, tears streaming, Blue Sky gathered him into her arms, their sons pressing into them both. Seated beside them, Elizabeth squeezed Andrews' hand while Carleton briefly grasped his shoulder in a tight grip.

Finally Red Fox rose and opened his Bible, his face set in sorrowful lines. Surveying those assembled, he said sadly, "White Horse has told us that our brother Grey Cloud never returned to the faith in Jesus that he once professed. There are also those among us who do not share this faith. But as his wife, Autumn Wind, is a true disciple of our Great Father in Heaven, even as many of us here are, I will read the words of comfort that Jesus spoke before his own death on a cross.

" 'Let not your heart be troubled; ye believe in God, believe also in me. In my Father's house are many mansions: If it were not so, I would have told you. I go to prepare a place for you. And if I go and prepare a place for you, I will come again, and receive you unto Myself; that where I am, there ye may be also.' "

He raised his head, again looking earnestly from face to face. "These words are the promise of the one who died to save us and rose again from the dead to those who place their trust and faith in him and follow as a disciple in his footsteps. We mourn Grey Cloud more deeply as it appears to our eyes that he put away this promise. But in truth only the Great Father can judge what is in one's heart when breath leaves him. We pray our brother may have turned back.

"It is for us who live, then, to grasp onto these words, to cling to them, and to never let them go. For at the end of days Jesus will come to catch up to the heavens with him all those who call on his name."

AFTER THE SERVICE ended those gathered filed outside where a fire had been lit and a meal prepared. Andrews stared at his dish of food, unable to eat, aggrieved yet hopeful that, as Red Fox had said, Grey Cloud might yet have had a change of heart before his spirit left his body.

That Autumn Wind was said to be in deep mourning also weighed heavily on his heart, its burden eased only partially by White Horse's assurance that Walk on Water, the leader of their Christian fellowship and all of its members, along with the rest of their clan, cared lovingly for all her needs. He ached to return home that he might comfort her himself.

While they ate, they discussed the implications for the clan of their sachem's loss. Blue Crane, the clan women's peace chief asked to know their thoughts before the women brought forward their recommendation for Grey Cloud's successor. When White Horse described General Clark's renewed campaign on the western frontier, the reason for Blue Crane's hesitation became apparent: Many of the young men were agitating for the clan to join the majority of the Shawnee in allying with Britain in the war against the Long Knives. A few even threatened to join in the fight whether the clan agreed or not.

Carleton and Andrews detailed the most recent developments in the war between the Americans and Britain, the indications that a major confrontation with Cornwallis was brewing, and what that might mean for the Americans and for the native nations. Neither of them offered a hopeful assessment on the latter.

Both pressed a strong case that Red Fox would wield the most power within the clan as sachem, that he really was the only viable candidate if the clan's young men were to be reined in and the clan's peace stance maintained. White Horse told them that the women had brought up Red Fox's name the most favorably. Their feeling was that until White Eagle and Golden Elk could return, Red Fox, with Spotted Pony as his right hand, were urgently needed back with the clan.

Although Red Fox expressed concerns and doubts about his possible role in the matter, he could not dispute the need for a strong leader to ensure the clan's welfare. In the end Spotted Pony prevailed on him, and the two men determined to leave with White Horse as quickly as they could gather provisions for the journey.

After further discussion everyone reluctantly agreed that the best course was for all the warriors of Black Hawk's clan to return home with their families. Blue Sky and her children and Sweetgrass would stay behind with their husbands, and for the time being Yellow Feather and Morning Dew would continue as the twins' nursemaids. Carleton also released the men from other tribes who had fought with them.

Several days later the warriors and their families gathered on the road in front of the ruined manor with several packhorses loaded with provisions for the long journey and whatever could be spared from Thornlea's diminished stores as gifts for Black Hawk's clan and the clans of the other departing warriors. Both sadness and eager anticipation filled them as they took leave of those staying behind, receiving and giving blessings with tears and promising to convey their love to those at home.

THAT NIGHT WHILE the others slept, Carleton lingered late in the cottage's parlor feeling lost. Cast out. Parting with his cousins and their families and the rest of the warriors had been especially painful. In spite of promises that they would soon see one another again, the bleak fear that they never would unexpectedly assailed him.

His spirit felt parched and empty, and the piercing longing to return to his clan and nation overwhelmed him. Since his first youthful wanderings the great wilderness of the Ohio Territory had called to his soul. Its verdant hills and densely forested ridges, rushing streams and crystal air bearing the rich, earthy scent of the land powerfully drew his spirit ever farther westward to new lands yet unseen.

There lay the home of his heart. As long as Elizabeth and their children were a part of it, for he could not live if they were not within reach of his arms.

Yet what of his people? What was to be their future? Questions that seemed to have no answers haunted him.

Blindly he stared through the window into the night's blackness, beyond which lay the unknown. He had spoken bravely to Elizabeth of trust. Yet despite the times he had given himself into the Father's hand before, it remained a great rending each time to surrender to the One who alone knew the future.

He became aware that the candles guttered even though the curtains at the windows did not stir and the air in the room hung motionless. Then abruptly the flames extinguished. Instead of darkness shrouding his surroundings, however, a strange light filled the vast empty space that seemed to stretch out into limitless distance on every side. The sensation of an unseeable Presence raised the hairs on the back of his neck and arms.

He could hear no voice, yet words formed quite distinctly in his mind.

"Go and tell this People, 'Hear ye indeed, but understand not; and see ye indeed, but perceive not.' Make the heart of this People fat, and make their ears heavy, and shut their eyes; lest they see with their eyes, and hear with their ears, and understand with their heart, and convert, and be healed.' Then said I, 'Lord, how long?' And He answered, 'Until the cities be wast-ed without inhabitant, and the houses without man, and the land be utter-ly desolate, and the Lord have removed men far away, and there be a great forsaking in the midst of the land.' "

As suddenly the room's walls hemmed him in again. Everything was as it had been before, with the candles' flames shivering though no breeze wafted in through the open windows. Yet he could hear a distant roaring as of wind rushing through the surrounding forest.

He sprang to his feet, a deep sense of dread shortening his breath and causing his heart to pound. The prophet Isaiah's unyielding words reverberated in his mind, and questions immediately arose:

For which people was the warning meant? The Shawnee alone? The native nations as a whole? The Americans?

All?

"Lord God, no!" he whispered hoarsely. "Let it not be so!" But he knew certainly that his plea was futile.

Without warning the rushing wind engulfed him, and the heavily charged air sent a sharp prickling sensation like lightning through his body. Then, as abruptly as it had begun, it ceased.

He stood motionless for some moments, stunned. Finally he sank back into his chair, numbly struggling to make sense of what had just occurred.

By degrees a murmur filtered into his consciousness, a familiar voice that had often assured him of what it whispered now: *It'll all come right, sir. In the end.*

Shuddering, he let out his breath and unclenched his fists. Gratitude flooded over him for his servant and all the others the Lord had sent to him over the years who so often bore him up and reminded him of God's faithfulness. For Elizabeth most of all and the steady love she brought into his life.

In a choked voice he whispered, "*Seela.* All will come right in the end. In your time, Father, and according to your perfect will."

His heart did not cease to ache even though he knew the truth of that assurance. It had taken many years and much heartbreak to learn that he could safely rest in it, even when he could not discern how it could come about.

And again, humbly, he made the choice to do so.

Chapter Forty-two

CARLETON SLOUCHED BACK in his chair, watching with amusement as his uncle and Elizabeth's aunt conversed animatedly with Elizabeth's parents.

"I know you're concerned, but they're very much in love and have settled on marrying once Abby reaches twenty," Tess was saying while cuddling her squirming grandniece. "That's almost four years from now," she continued, gently deflecting Julianne's tiny fingers from the jeweled brooch pinned to the bodice of her flatteringly fitted blue-green silk gown and substituting a trinket from her reticule. "His parents as well as Eugène and Cécile are quite determined to hold them to that. And both Abby and Henri are in full agreement."

"But why conclude an engagement so soon?" Dr. Howard demanded, drumming his fingers on the arm of his chair. "It's very likely they'll change their minds in the interim."

Tess exchanged a meaningful glance with Caledonne, who countered, "Everyone close to them is persuaded they will not. They are extraordinarily mature for their ages and show every evidence of a settled affection."

Returning his attention to Harry, ensconced on his lap, he smiled down at the little boy, who reached up to touch his face, studying him with an expression akin to wonder. *"Quel beau garçon tu es, Harry! Je suis tres heureux de faire enfin votre connaissance et celle de votre soeur."* What a fine lad you are, Harry! I'm very pleased to finally make your acquaintance and that of your sister.

Harry looked anxiously from his great-uncle to his father and back again, a faint line creasing his brow.

"He looks a bit dubious about making *your* acquaintance, Uncle Alexandre," Carleton said with a chuckle.

"The two of you look too much alike," Elizabeth pointed out. "He doesn't know what to make of it."

Carleton had to concede that there could be no question of their relationship. Indeed Alexandre Bettár, le comte de Caledonne, currently commanding Carleton's privateer fleet, was an older image of himself.

Deeply tanned from years of service at sea, the sixty-three-year-old retired French admiral was slightly shorter than Carleton, but equally lean and muscular, with the same deep blue-grey eyes though his once-blond hair had gone entirely white. In spite of the fine lines that etched his forehead and the corners of his eyes, he appeared to Carleton to have shed some years since his marriage to Elizabeth's aunt.

So had Tess, for that matter. She looked uncommonly fine and not just because she had spent the past two years availing herself of Parisian styles at her doting husband's insistence.

Ah, the power of an affaire de coeur, Carleton reflected smugly. Elizabeth's amused smile told him she was thinking the same thing. He returned his attention to Tess, who continued the conversation undeterred.

"Alexandre and I have the highest regard for both Abby and Henri," she said firmly to Elizabeth's hearty agreement. "They insist they'll not marry until the two of you meet Henri and give your blessing to their union."

"Then the instant this war is over and the seas are safe again, Samuel and I are going to Paris," Anne stated decidedly, to which Dr. Howard gave grudging assent.

"Hopefully that's in the offing at last," Carleton put in, exchanging a significant look with Caledonne.

It was shortly past noon on Thursday, 13 September, another oppressively hot, humid day in a summer characterized by them. Early that morning Carleton, Andrews, and their aides and servants had ridden down to the American front lines outside the small river town of York just off Chesapeake Bay, where Cornwallis had barricaded his army. Lafayette's entrenchments now ringed the town and ran all the way across the Virginia Peninsula between the York and James rivers.

British cavalry had ravaged the once serene, fertile area between Williamsburg and York, leaving pastures strewn with the rotting carcasses of horses and cattle. The land lay stripped and deserted, houses empty, fields and roads trampled and overgrown with weeds. In the worst of the depredations a pregnant woman had been found on a bed in her plantation home brutally bayoneted to death, with the inscription "Thou shalt never give birth to a rebel" above the canopy.

By sheer good fortune, they had detoured to Jamestown on their return to Williamsburg, hoping for news of the French navy. There they had run into Tess, Caledonne, and a small cluster of their servants just debarked from *Destiny,* which rode at anchor off the docks in her original splendor, surrounded by five of Carleton's other heavily armed privateers. Learning that they had planned to travel overland to Thornlea, Carleton gave a brief account of the attack and the manor's destruction, thus sparing them an exhausting and ultimately futile journey.

Their unexpected appearance at the Rangers' encampment a short distance outside Williamsburg had occasioned joyful exclamations, embraces, kisses, and laughter from Elizabeth and her parents. A flood of questions from both sides had followed, which everyone was doing their best to answer amid the excitement of introducing the twins to their grand-aunt and uncle.

Wide-eyed, Julianne and Harry hung on every word spoken, and their enchantment with their new relatives was fully mutual. Just turned twenty-two months old, the twins could not have looked more like cherubs in matching white gauze gowns with pink slips and sashes. Harry continued to outpace his more delicate sister in stature, but both children were now able to run freely and chattered away using a daily expanding vocabulary of English intermixed with the Shawnee words Yellow Feather and Morning Dew assiduously taught them.

Converstion paused when Tess offered the gifts she and Caledonne had brought for them. They tore the toys from their wrappings with excited squeals and were quickly occupied at play on the rug.

With the issue of Abby and Henri's betrothal temporarily laid to rest, Carleton asked Caledonne whether he had any news of French Admiral François Joseph Paul, le comte de Grasse.

"He brought twenty-nine ships of the line up from the Caribbean at the end of last month and landed munitions and over three thousand troops. He also posted several frigates at the mouths of the York and the James, which happily blocked in Cornwallis's ships. The rest of his fleet was anchored off Cape Henry, but last week every single one suddenly vanished out to sea. We heard gunfire echoing from that direction sometime later, but nothing since. Needless to say, there's a considerable level of anxiety in Lafayette's camp."

"It so happened that we arrived at the Chesapeake yesterday the same time as Admiral de Barras," Caledonne answered, referring to Jacques-Melchior Saint-Laurent, le comte de Barras. "In fact, we entered in his fleet's wake, and I went aboard his flagship. He's brought heavy siege equipment and other supplies for Lafayette, by the way, but he also shared his latest communication from de Grasse.

"It seems he detected a fleet under Admiral Thomas Graves attempting to enter Chesapeake Bay and drove them off. The British took such heavy casualties and damage during the battle that Graves was forced to limp back to New York for repairs," Caledonne concluded with relish.

A burst of gleeful exclamations met the news. His smile wide, Caledonne added, "Even better, de Grasse himself sailed up to join us, his fleet augmented by two captured British frigates. At this moment he's again anchored off Cape Henry and has sent transports up the bay to bring Washington's troops down to Williamsburg."

Carleton shared the others' exultant laughter. "Excellent! Our first inkling that something was afoot was when de Grasse appeared unexpectedly last month. That same day Lafayette received notice from General Washington that the combined American and French Army was already well on its way south. They maintained such tight security that not only did they keep General Clinton in the dark, but Lafayette as well."

"We're expecting Washington and General Rochambeau to show up at any time," Dr. Howard put in. "With all of our forces converging here now and Graves out of action, I'd say Cornwallis has lost any hope of salvation."

Elizabeth shook her head. "What I'd like to know is why in the world he chose to move his entire army to the end of a peninsula where he could so easily be penned in. The merest lieutenant should know better."

"The British believe that their navy will always save them," Caledonne replied with a shrug. "Cornwallis obviously didn't take into account that Clinton might drag his feet in sending a fleet to his rescue. Or the proximity of one the size of de Grasse's in the Caribbean."

As he was speaking the two Shawnee maidens slipped in and led the twins off to the nursery. A short time later Andrews and Blue Sky joined them for dinner.

When the first course had been served, Caledonne turned to Carleton. "I cannot imagine the grief you must feel at Thornlea's loss, Jonathan, and I'm sorry for it. But at least you're able to have your family close during this campaign. That must be a comfort. "

"This is a little too close if you ask me," Tess said sharply. "You're almost within sight of the enemy, Jon! Doesn't that put Beth and the children at too great a risk?"

"This was the only place we could find in the area large enough to quarter my troops and officers and house my family," Carleton explained. "My troops are on constant alert, and should Cornwallis show any sign of trying to break through our lines—which so far he hasn't—I'm prepared to remove Beth, Anne, and the children from here on the instant."

"Well, I'm sure you know what you're doing," Tess conceded, frowning. "This certainly is an impressive establishment."

"Not nearly as much as Thornlea was." Anne sighed. "The manor was incomparable, Tess. Oh, we're comfortable enough here, but the house is smaller, and we've had to make shifts to accommodate everyone."

Caledonne gave Carleton an assessing look. "Do you not desire retribution for the destruction of your home? I know I would in the case of such a personal attack."

Pulling a wry face, Carleton downed a swallow of wine. "There's immense satisfaction in being just close enough to Cornwallis's lines that he knows we're here, but secure enough that he can't get at us. I hope Tarleton's gnashing his teeth at Beth's outwitting him so spectacularly when he was certain he was finally going to put an end to my operations."

Dr. Howard raised his glass. "To Tarleton's . . . health."

"Hear, hear," Tess responded dryly, raising her own along with the others.

Meeting Elizabeth's affectionate gaze, Carleton noted that she appeared unusually pale and somewhat drawn. Moving their household so far had put too great a strain on her, coming on the heels of the attack as it had, he reflected, a shadow of anxiety settling at the back of his mind.

It hadn't helped that the journey had been slowed by Rufus and his drovers bringing down extra horses for his Rangers and a large herd of cattle to feed them. To which had been added constant concern for Marah and her latest band of fugitives, who had melted in among the black drovers and servants until they could safely break off toward City Point.

Thankfully the twins had been fully weaned by early that summer. And Elizabeth had her mother, Laughing Otter's daughters, and the other women to help in managing daily routines. Still, he decided to speak with her father about curtailing her medical duties for a time.

A discussion of the latest developments in the war drew his attention back to present concerns. Andrews related a report that early in the month Arnold had led a raid against New London, Connecticut, just a few miles downriver from where he had grown up. After setting the town to the torch, he had captured the fort across the river and slaughtered its garrison regardless of their surrender.

"Nearly a quarter of his force was either killed or wounded in the action, however," Andrews concluded with grim satisfaction. "Greene's had his defeats down in South Carolina, too, but in the process he's taking a heavy toll as well. As he says, 'We fight, get beat, rise, and fight again.' If he can keep that up, the British will eventually be finished."

Dr. Howard rubbed his chin ruefully. "But it's costing us a great deal as well, Charles. Maintaining an army is only going to get harder since our currency is essentially worthless."

"Personally, I'm just hoping Congress can hold on," Carleton interjected ruefully. "It isn't unusual if there isn't a single representative present from several of our states. Those who do show up spend their time scrambling to find enough militia and supplies to keep the army in the field. And trying to hold off creditors and patch up holes in our Articles of Confederation, among other puzzles like figuring out what territory Vermont actually comprises! Our legislators are going to have to come up with a better system or this nation won't survive even if we do hold out long enough that Britain gives up."

"The Virginia General Assembly isn't doing any better!" Andrews exclaimed. "This ongoing inquiry into Jefferson's actions during the British incursion while he was governor only hinders efforts to win the war. Jefferson used to be good friends with Patrick Henry but has turned on him now because he's participating in the investigation. We can't afford political rows at this precise moment!"

He subsided as Sarah ushered Hutchinson into the room. The major saluted Carleton, Andrews, and Dr. Howard, bowed to Caledonne and the ladies, and apologized for intruding.

"I just got this from one of our advanced sentries who received it from one of his counterparts across the lines," he explained, withdrawing a sealed letter from his pocket. "It's from Colonel Tarleton to—"

Astonished outcries around the table cut him off. Both Andrews and Carleton were on their feet, their faces drained of color. When Carleton reached to take the letter, Hutchinson hesitated and gulped.

"Sir, it's addressed to . . . Mrs. Carleton."

A collective intake of breath met this announcement. Everyone exchanged astonished looks and a deathly silence settled over the room. Stunned, Carleton turned to Elizabeth.

"I've no interest whatever in anything that person has to say," she said stonily.

Swinging around to face his aide, eyes narrowed, Carleton held out his hand. Hutchinson turned the letter over, and Andrews sat abruptly down.

"Burn it, Jonathan," Caledonne rasped. "Better yet, send it back unopened."

Carleton hesitated, staring hard at Elizabeth, then cracked the letter's seal with suppressed violence, wishing intensely that it was Tarleton's neck. He tore open the page and scanned the lines therein. By the time he reached the end he was livid and shaking with rage.

"Would you care to read it to us, Jon?" Dr. Howard prompted cautiously.

For a moment Carleton pressed his eyes shut, fighting to wrestle his fury under sufficient control that he could speak without cursing. Finally he did so, his voice low but every word spoken savagely.

13 Instant
Gloucester Point, Virginia

My dear Mrs. Carleton,
Please allow me to offer my sincerest apologies for any inconvenience my Legion's

incursion onto your estate may have caused. It was a great disappointment to me that I was unable to convey my respects to you and your young son and daughter in person. I'm confident, however, that you understand the unfortunate necessities of war, especially considering your own involvement as a combatant in these colonies' unwarranted rebellion against their lawful sovereign. Certainly an arsenal such as your husband amassed in your home could not be allowed to continue supplying Britain's enemies.

I hope that you and your children remain in good health. Please relate my greetings to your parents and to le Comte de Caledonne and his bride, who, I understand, is your aunt. I eagerly anticipate meeting all of you one day soon so that I may personally tender my kindest regards. Until then, I remain

Your most humble servant,
Lt. Col. Banastre Tarleton

Anne gasped. "The nerve of the man!"

"How insufferably insolent!" Tess fumed.

Carleton stared at the name inscribed with a flourish at the letter's end through a blood-red haze. He looked up when Andrews rose so abruptly that had Blue Sky not hastily caught his chair it would have crashed to the floor. Coming to Carleton's side, he plucked the letter out of his hand, carried it to the table, and held one corner to a candle in the branch at its center. When the page began to yellow and char, blue flames licking upward along its edge, he strode to the fireplace and flung it onto the cold hearthstone, where it reduced to ash in seconds.

"It's nothing but bluff, Jon," Dr. Howard growled. "He wants you to believe that his spies are better than yours, and that he knows everything about you and your family."

"We all know Cornwallis sends small boats past our ships under cover of night and up along the coast to spy on us," Andrews observed, tight-lipped. "And Tarleton stays in close contact with loyalist spies all over this peninsula. Why, the man took a small detail out one night, drove off a picket *west* of Williamsburg, rode right into the town to probe Lafayette's lines, then returned to his own without encountering the slightest opposition."

"Cornwallis knows our every move within hours, if not minutes," Carleton conceded. "But he isn't the only one who has spies. One of ours is making himself useful as the general's personal servant at his headquarters. I have mine as well, along with strong detachments patrolling far out from this camp, keeping watch and gathering intelligence. The night of Tarleton's little jaunt a small body of horsemen got close to us—undoubtedly him and his detail riding between us and Williamsburg —but they took off in a great hurry when my men fired on them. No one's tried since."

He dismissed the issue with an airy wave of his hand. "So if it amuses Tarleton to think he can threaten me through my family, let him enjoy his little delusion until we finish pounding Cornwallis's camp into oblivion and the colonel and his cohorts march out to surrender—if they survive."

"I'll be first in line to cut—" Breaking off as Carleton swung around to fix him in a narrowed look, Hutchinson cleared his throat, then finished in a mutter, "—punch the blackguard in the nose."

Carleton strode around the table to stand behind Elizabeth. Placing his hands on her shoulders, he bent to kiss her neck and murmur tenderly into her ear, "You've nothing to fear, dear heart. He'll never get near you and our family while I draw breath."

She laid her hand over one of his and turned to press her lips to his. "I know," she whispered, giving him an affectionate smile. "And as you know, I'm very capable of defending myself. And them. And you, for that matter."

Snickering, he straightened and grinned down at her. "Which you've demonstrated quite effectively, my love. Tarleton better pray he never faces *you* at the end of a gun barrel."

Chapter Forty-three

ANDREWS AND BLUE SKY withdrew after dinner, and Tess suggested that Elizabeth and her parents accompany her on a tour of the estate's gardens. "I suspect Jonathan and Alexandre have matters to discuss that would bore the rest of us," she added.

She spoke lightly, but Carleton noted that she directed a significant glance at Caledonne. A pang went though him at the vulnerability in his uncle's expression as he watched her leave with the others. It was quickly erased when he turned back to Carleton, however.

"You mentioned a spy at Cornwallis's headquarters," he said gruffly. "You know his identity?"

Carleton cast a wary glance toward the doorway before saying softly, "He's a slave named James Armistead. He volunteered to spy on Arnold, and when that traitor returned to New York, Armistead was assigned to Cornwallis's personal staff. His intelligence enabled us to prevent Cornwallis from escaping York, among other things."

Caledonne fixed him in a keen look. *"Mais, bien sûr:"* But of course. "It is essential to know the mind of your enemy. And regardless of what Tarleton may have learned, he doesn't know yours."

Carleton inclined his head. "Not yet. But if Providence smiles on us, he soon will."

The earl seemed suddenly unable to meet Carleton's gaze. The suspicion of what was coming aroused a welter of deeply conflicted emotions.

After the painful conversation with Elizabeth about the subject, he had no desire whatever to discuss it with his uncle. Their relationship had been characterized by a wary distrust on his part and a determined avoidance of the issue on his uncle's for so long, he realized, that he was loath to let go of it.

After all, he had forgiven Caledonne. Why dredge up all the pain again? Would it be possible for them to rebuild their relationship on a new foundation?

Yet as they moved into the drawing room and found seats, the realization sank in that Caledonne needed to confess, needed to receive Carleton's spoken forgiveness. Without it he could never fully release the past and move on any more than Carleton could even after confiding everything to Elizabeth.

"You've had stunning success commanding my privateers," he said, knowing full well that he was stalling. "I hope it's made giving up your rank in France's navy worth it."

Caledonne shrugged. "For the first time since Frédéric died, I'm truly enjoying the freedom to face the enemy head-on to win at all odds. Since marrying Thérèsa, I've taken a cold, hard look at the reality that all these years I've turned a blind eye to the corruption of my country's society and government. I've been seriously reconsidering my allegiances, and it may surprise you to know that I'm no longer a staunch supporter of France's monarchy."

Carleton regarded him with raised eyebrows. "You're serious?"

"In that and much more, my bride has influenced me for good. The best thing I ever did was to marry that magnificent woman."

"But—what will you do after this war is over?" Carleton spluttered.

"Move here, to America, of course. Your republican ideals have infected me." Caledonne gave a rueful laugh. Sobering, he continued, "This United States of yours is the future. There's nothing more exciting happening in the world, and in these waning years of my life I want to be a part of it."

Carleton could only stare at him, speechless. After a long moment, Caledonne cleared his throat and regarded him cautiously.

"Thérèsa and I will share more of our plans later. First there's another matter I wish to address—one that has stood between you and me far too long. *Le bon Dieu* has used my good wife to convict me of my faults most gently and lovingly. Some years ago I caused you grave offense—"

When Carleton began to speak, Caledonne raised his hand to forestall him. "You were not ready for the entanglements in which I involved you that summer after Frédéric's death. Nor should I have done so in any case. It's pained me greatly ever since, but all these years I've endeavored to silence my conscience. I feared that to address the matter would give you excuse to finally turn your back on me forever. I could not bear to lose you when on her deathbed I promised my dear Julianne to always watch over you. So to face the truth that I willfully exposed you to such danger in the incident with Penet—"

"Incident?" Carleton snapped. "I killed the man."

"You acted in self defense!"

Through gritted teeth, Carleton returned, "Which wouldn't have been necessary had you not recruited me to unwittingly spy for France, thus placing me in a situation no seventeen-year-old should ever be in. You knew what you were doing and the dangers involved. I—did—not."

The earl slumped forward in his chair, arms braced across his thighs, hands gripped tightly between his knees. "I was wrong in all of it. My actions were inexcusable. It's my pride that's kept me from confessing my fault to you and to God, but with Thérèsa's encouragement I've brought it before our Lord and received his forgiveness. I don't deserve yours, but ask it of you nevertheless. I understand if you cannot . . . " He broke off, his gaze fixed on the floor.

Silence stretched out for what seemed to Carleton an eternity while the two of them remained frozen in place. The raw tightness of his throat and pain in his chest made speech impossible. Sight blurred with tears, he dragged air into his lungs and let out a shaky breath.

"Then I ask one thing of you as well." When Caledonne looked up hopefully, Carleton continued, "That you also forgive me for allowing my pride to keep me from speaking of the matter and for holding a grudge against you ever since. I too am responsible for the choices I made—"

Caledonne shoved to his feet. "You weren't mature enough to freely make the choices I asked you to, Jonathan!" he cried. "If I could make any defense, which I will not, it's that you were extraordinarily mature for your age, for which I give what is due to Sir Harry. That made it all too easy for me to forget how young you really were. And that streak of the daredevil in you added to the talents that persuaded me you'd develop into a highly effective agent for our cause—"

"You never asked whether that was what *I* wanted!"

Caledonne bent his head. "I did not, to my shame. When I confided this to Thérèsa, she brought me to see the great wrong I did you, and that it was past time for me to confess my sin and ask forgiveness of you and of God."

Pain and hope in his gaze, he faltered, "I pray that you are able to forgive such . . . such grievous offense from one who ought to have cared for your welfare much better than I did."

Carleton got to his feet and strode over to him. "You have my forgiveness freely, uncle," he said in a choked voice. "Let there finally be peace between you and me."

They drew each other into a fierce embrace. After some moments they pulled back to regard each other earnestly.

"You know you hold the place in my heart that Frédéric did while he lived. Have I such a place in your heart, Jonathan?"

Hearing the longing in his uncle's voice, Carleton said, "You know you do. We've the precious bonds of family between us, and those will always endure. I never really knew my mother, and you're the only one I have left who loved her. You've said that I'm very like her, but so are you. It's through you that I can know a little of her, and that means more to me than I can say."

Caledonne took him by the shoulders. "And in you I have my Juli-anne back too."

Troubled, Carleton asked hesitantly, "But where does that leave Lucien?"

Letting out his breath, Caledonne released him and turned away.

"I always thought you cared more for me than for him," Carleton ventured, measuring his words. "Right or wrong, he clearly feels the same way."

Caledonne raked his fingers through his hair. "When I lost Frédéric I came to believe that all my hopes lay in you." He paced across the room, then turned abruptly to face Carleton. "It's unfair to Lucien, I know, but from the beginning he was different from my other children. One could not have asked for a more contrary child!"

"Do you think he's not felt your disappointment from the very first? He's your son, Uncle Alexandre! He needs to know that he has your love regardless of anything he might do. If my father had been able to give me that, the path I followed might have been a different one."

"And perhaps you'd not be the man you are today. In spite of our failings, in his mercy our Sovereign Lord always works out his perfect plan in our lives."

"It doesn't always seem so perfect," Carleton returned soberly. "But, yes, though it isn't clear to me yet, I do feel there's a greater purpose in all I've endured, even in suffering."

"You see, this is why I love you, Jonathan! You embrace the lessons suffering teaches. Even as a child Lucien pushed away every effort I made to teach him these things, to take him under my wing and be a father to him. And he blames me for it!"

"Like the prodigal son, who in effect wished his father dead by demanding his inheritance? Yet his story wasn't finished. *He returned.* Perhaps when Lucien gets to the end of his pride, he'll also return. But he'll only do so if he has reason to hope that his father might welcome him home."

For a tense moment Caledonne regarded Carleton, stricken. Then, shoulders bowed, he covered his face with his hands, tears trickling down his cheeks.

"I've not done that, have I? I've not welcomed my son just as he is. Always I've demanded that he be what I want him to be."

"Tout comprendre c'est tout pardoner." To understand all is to forgive all. Striding over to Caledonne, Carleton pulled him into his arms again. "Make every effort to find him, Uncle Alexandre. Let him know that he's the son of your heart no matter what he does or what he is, and that you love him for himself alone. And if he still turns away, tell him that the door will always remain open for his return. It may be that will be the saving of him."

HE HELD ELIZABETH against the curve of his body as they lay together in bed, skin to skin. He had thrown the windows wide to admit the desultory breeze, but the night remained too sultry for any covering.

He and Andrews had taken Caledonne down to the Rangers' camp to review the troops late that afternoon. They had returned in time for a simple supper, and after the twins had been carried off to the nursery lingered to visit with Dr. Howard and the women until well after dark. It had been almost midnight before everyone had finally drifted off to bed.

When he slowly slipped his hand along her side to her thigh, she shifted drowsily to snuggle closer. "I love you," he murmured, his lips brushing her shoulder.

She half turned to seek his mouth. "I love you."

"This move has been hard on you, I think. Are you getting enough rest?"

"I'm fine. Truly. Don't worry so over me, dearest."

"I can't help it," he returned on a sigh. Sliding his hand around, he splayed his fingers across her abdomen, testing the firm, silky flatness— which didn't allay his fears.

"How far along are you?"

She hesitated before answering, "Two months."

"Just after the attack on Thornlea then."

Meeting his anxious gaze she teased, "Well, we did rather—"

"I know," he cut her off with a rueful grin. "Your fault."

She giggled. "You're totally innocent, of course." Turning fully around, she said, "Has Charles told you that Blue Sky is with child again too?"

"He did, this evening while we were down at the camp. That's what started me thinking."

"Blue Sky says we're going to have our babies together—in April, *Pooshkwiitha,* the Half Moon." After a moment she murmured, "You are happy?"

"Yes, of course. You know I'll always welcome additions to our brood as long as you and the child are well. Have you told anyone—except Blue Sky, of course?"

"I wasn't going to before I told you. But you know Mama. And Blue Sky, who told me she knew," she added with a soft laugh. "But I swore them to secrecy. Even Papa doesn't suspect."

He chuckled, then sobered. "I'm going to have a talk with him. I don't want you working in the hospital during the siege." When she began to object, he said firmly, "You know what battle is like, Beth. I absolutely forbid you to be anywhere near the lines while you're pregnant. It's bad enough when you're not."

She sat up abruptly. "I'm perfectly capable of—"

"Beth!" he exclaimed reproachfully, drawing her back down to the pillow. "Please heed me for once."

Frowning, she subsided, muttering, "I'll talk to Papa tomorrow."

"Don't think you can win him over. You know he's as intractable on this subject as I am."

She fixed him in an assessing gaze. "We'll see."

Chapter Forty-four

T HE NEXT AFTERNOON Carleton and Andrews escorted Caledonne to Williamsburg, trailed by their aides and servants. Lafayette was still sick with the miseries of the intermittent fever that had kept him abed for weeks, but they hoped he was well enough for an introduction to Carleton's uncle. And they were eager to learn whether the young marquis had received any further communications from Washington and Rochambeau.

Carleton was in a disgruntled mood and Andrews no happier. Despite fighting a bout of nausea; her mother's, aunt's, and Carleton's vehement objections; and the silent disapproval of Andrews who had learned the futility of opposing anything his own wife determined to do, Elizabeth had managed to negotiate a reluctant compromise with her father.

Carleton allowed that his father-in-law could ill afford to spare his most skilled surgeon and her best assistant. Thankfully the agreement was one he and Andrews could live with, though grudgingly.

Neither woman would be allowed to set foot in the field hospital in the Rangers' camp at York, but Elizabeth would manage a reserve hospital a couple of miles from the siege line where the most severely wounded would be brought for surgery. Blue Sky would assist, as would Sweetgrass and Mary McLeod, whose training was proceeding nicely in Laughing Otter's and Rain Woman's absence. Dr. Howard and Captain Lawton would divide their time between the two hospitals as needed.

Carleton glanced at Andrews, who rolled his eyes, evidently mulling over the same subject and equally out of humor. "Women," he growled.

"Just remember, Charles, if they're not happy, neither will we be."

Andrews returned an ill-tempered grunt, while Caledonne observed the passing landscape, maintaining an expression of bland innocence.

It was shortly after four o'clock when they rode into the once bustling town that had served as Virginia's capital until the previous year. The College of William and Mary bracketed the town on its west side, with the imposing Governor's Palace nearby at the far end of the Palace Green. A mile opposite on the east side, the old Capitol building, currently surrounded by Lafayette's camp, stood shuttered at the terminus of the wide Duke of Gloucester Street.

Williamsburg had once been a charming place, Carleton reflected morosely. Cornwallis's brief encampment there before moving a dozen miles southeast and digging in at York, had changed that. Piles of debris littered its broad streets and pleasant greens, nor did the detritus contributed by the American and French camps improve the situation. Its 300 or so buildings, varying from the impressive brick college and state buildings to graceful mansions and mean huts, had formerly been devoid of flies. It was now so plagued by them that one could hardly eat, drink, sleep, or indulge in any activity at all in peace. They consequently avoided the town whenever possible.

Since Caledonne was eager to confer with the French West India division's commander, Claude-Anne de Rouvroy, le marquis de Saint-Simon-Montbléru, they first headed to his camp. It sprawled across open ground west of the college, with the Virginia militia's camp beyond it.

They rode straight into a melee of jubilant, shouting men surrounding a cluster of familiar, travel-worn figures who stood in front of the marquis' tent. Carleton immediately took note of the horsehair-crested leather helmets of Washington's Life Guard, who waited, dismounted and formed up, along one side of the marquee.

Reining his mount to a halt, he directed Stowe and Briggs to ride back to camp at all speed and alert the women that they likely would not return until late that night, if at all. He added instructions for the two colonels to ready their troops to parade the following day.

After sending them off, he hastily dismounted, his companions doing likewise, and strode into the melee. Caledonne, Andrews, and the aides crowded on his heels in a phalanx, forcing their way toward the two commanding figures at the crowd's center.

Forty-nine years old, with auburn hair and keen blue-grey eyes, General George Washington was a born horseman, powerful in build despite narrow, sloping shoulders. A natural charm that drew men and women to him equally balanced the immense, and intimidating, physical energy he radiated. Despite the dust and wrinkles of travel, his dark blue uniform coat faced in buff, each shoulder crowned with a gold epaulette; buff waistcoat and breeches; and black knee-length boots added to his imposing appearance.

Carleton turned his attention to the graceful, dignified, fifty-six-year-old French commander. Jean-Baptiste Donatien de Vimeur, le comte de Rochambeau was an equally arresting figure in his ornate dark blue uniform coat and red waistcoat and breeches, all liberally adorned with gold braid. He was well known for his exceptional capability as an officer and skill at diplomacy. And as Carleton observed the interaction between the two generals, he was heartened by the evidence that they had developed a warm friendship—an encouraging omen for the coming siege.

Shouting over the tumult to Washington's nearest aide, Carleton learned that the General's party had spent two and a half days on the road from Mount Vernon, riding at a pace that left a number of officers miles behind in the dust. Only Will Lee, Washington's mulatto body servant who as usual clung to his side like a burr; Rochambeau; Adjutant General Edward Hand; and several aides had been able to maintain the unsparing pace the American commander set.

It was clear that the news of their arrival had spread through the town like wildfire. Even as Carleton was speaking with the aide, Lafayette, trailed by stout, energetic Governor Nelson and burly General Saint-Simon, galloped up Duke of Gloucester Street toward them.

Still flushed with fever, Lafayette drew up so abruptly that his mount reared. Springing heedlessly from the saddle, he threw the reins across his horse's neck and with wide-spread arms ran to Washington, flung his arms around his commander, and proceeded to kiss him from ear to ear—as ardently as a lover would his mistress, Carleton thought with amusement. He laughed heartily with his companions and everyone present, certain it was a sight none of them would ever forget.

Motioning his companions to follow, he pushed his way into the circle around the generals. Washington and Lafayette turned as they approached, and noting it, Rochambeau did so as well.

On catching sight of Caledonne, the latter's face brightened, and he strode to meet him, exclaiming volubly in French, "Caledonne! I should have known you'd find your way to the center of the action!"

"It's been far too long since last we met!" Caledonne returned heartily as the two men embraced and exchanged kisses on the cheek.

When they stepped apart Rochambeau turned his attention to Carleton. "And this is, *sans doute,* your nephew, the celebrated General Carleton. The resemblance between you is remarkable, to say nothing of the spirit you both so admirably demonstrate in battle."

Carleton began to bow, but finding himself in Rochambeau's enthusiastic embrace and receiving the earl's kiss on his cheek, returned it in high good humor before introducing Andrews and their aides.

Washington and Lafayette came over to them, with Saint-Simon and as many officers and aides who could find standing room clustering around to exchange bows, greetings, and introductions.

The two commanding generals were the center of focus, as Carleton expected. To his surprise, however, he received a share of attention along with Caledonne, especially from the French officers, who made it clear they claimed both of them as their own.

When the initial clamor died down, Washington exchanged bows with Caledonne, then glanced from him to Carleton and back, smiling broadly. "I have heard a great deal about you from General Carleton, Admiral. I am delighted to finally have the opportunity to thank you in person for your efforts on our country's behalf."

"It is I who am most honored to meet you, Your Excellency," Caledonne responded. "Everything my nephew has told me is surpassed by the real man."

Washington inclined his head with a smile, faint color tingeing cheeks. Turning to Carleton, he sobered and said, "I cannot express my gratitude for all you have done, sir. I was very sorry to hear of Thornlea's destruction. It is an incalculable loss, I know. If I can assist you in any way, you have only to ask."

"We're quite comfortably situated for now, but I thank you," Carleton said. "My wife sends her greetings and good wishes."

"Please tell her that I am grateful as well for her sacrifice and courage in service of our great cause and return my kindest regards to her."

At Carleton's bow, Washington turned back to Lafayette, worry creasing his brow. "Have you any news of de Grasse?"

Lafayette shook his head, his face falling. "No, Your Excellency. I'm sorry to say we've received no communications since his fleet disappeared out to sea."

Carleton directed a meaningful glance at Caledonne, who stepped hastily forward to relate all that he had learned from de Barras and de Grasse himself. The report caused an outburst of celebration that resounded across the camp.

"We have finally cooped Cornwallis up like a fox in his lair!" Washington shouted above the clamor. "And this time we are going to have his hide for a trophy!"

Saint-Simon's regiments had been forming up on both sides of the road ever since Washington and Rochambeau's arrival. The exceptionally tall, muscular men, striking in their white uniforms faced in pale blue, stood rigidly at attention while straining to get a glimpse of the American commander out of the corners of their eyes without turning their heads.

Carleton and his party accompanied the officers as Saint-Simon escorted Washington and Rochambeau in an informal review. A mounted procession east down Duke of Gloucester Street followed. The cavalcade passed Bruton Parish Church and the Palace Green, the town's market square, and the inns, shops, and other businesses and residences lining the street. Finally they detoured around the Capitol to Lafayette's camp, where the ragged, fever-plagued American regiments were drawn up for inspection.

Carleton nodded to Wayne, who stood among the officers leaning heavily on a cane. The general had taken a musket ball in the leg the previous week on failing to heed a sentry's challenge. Carleton sympathized but had to suppress a smirk, knowing the high-spirited general's penchant for riding roughshod through any obstacle.

Tamping down his uncharitable mirth, he focused on the line of field pieces ahead of them, which thundered a twenty-one gun salute. At the procession's head Washington and Rochambeau acknowledged the honor with bows while the troops cheered.

It was, as Carleton had anticipated, a long, exhausting day, and Washington weathered it better than anyone. Escorted back into town, he established his headquarters at the home of his friend George Wythe north of the church, while Rochambeau settled a short distance away in the home of Mrs. Peyton Randolph, the widow of Congress's first president.

Afterward Saint-Simon held a reception at his quarters where the two commanders personally greeted every officer, Hand and Wayne introducing those unfamiliar to them while the entire corps marched by. This was succeeded late in the evening by a lavish repast for the senior officers, at which a French band played popular tunes to everyone's pleasure.

It was nearing eleven o'clock before the assembly finally broke up in a happy flurry of congratulations and well-wishes. Carleton, Andrews, and their aides rode back to camp, weary but in an exuberant mood enhanced by the wine that had flowed freely at dinner.

✹ ✹ ✹

ADDITIONAL UNITS OF the combined army continued to trickle in over the next days. Some had marched overland along rough roads in the hot, dry weather, raising choking clouds of dust. Others, sailing down the Chesapeake aboard small boats, had been bedeviled by contrary winds and storms.

The majority of the American troops, including children as young as fourteen, were gaunt and barefoot, their motley clothing in tatters. The only units distinguished by uniforms were former Boston bookseller General Henry Knox's elite artillerymen and the splendidly turned-out Rhode Island Regiment, black soldiers renowned as among the Americans' best troops under arms.

On a cloudy, windy Friday morning, 21 September, a Massachusetts brigade marched into camp. At its head rode Elizabeth's uncle, Brigadier General Joshua Stern, with his son Levi and nephew Caleb, both majors now. Elizabeth and her parents immediately insisted on hosting them at dinner that evening, delighted at the prospect of a reunion after their long separation.

Barely an hour later Teissèdre showed up, unexpectedly as usual. In a private meeting, he reported to Carleton and Andrews that late the previous month Thayendanegea, the Iroquois' principal sachem also known as Joseph Brant, had ambushed a detachment of Pennsylvania militia sent to reinforce General Clark's latest expedition against the British at Detroit. He didn't volunteer where he had traveled and how he came by that information, and Carleton didn't press him.

He and Andrews received the news with mixed emotions. While they could take no joy in the militia's defeat, neither could they deny their relief that the debacle effectively ended Clark's western campaign for that year. Peace would reign on the western frontier through the winter for the Shawnee and the other tribes who had lost people, homes, and crops in Clark's attacks, though it would likely be only temporarily.

✴ ✴ ✴

THAT EVENING, WITH THEIR company gathered around the dining room table, Elizabeth watched her uncle and cousins, a pang of sadness mingling with pleasure. The years of war had taken a toll on them, she noted, as indeed it had on everyone.

Deeper grooves marked Stern's square, genial face, weathered by sun and wind. His unruly mop of curly grey hair had thinned, but she was pleased to see that his stance remained unbowed, charged with vitality, his gaze keen and direct.

His wife, Jane, was very well, he assured her parents. Rebekah, the widow of their elder son, Will, killed in action at Breed's Hill, had recently married a parson of simple means who was proving to be a loving father to her three children. The latter also continued to benefit greatly from the inheritance and education Carleton funded.

Smiling, Elizabeth turned her attention to Levi and Caleb, for the moment engaged in a lively conversation with Carleton, Andrews, Caledonne, and Teissèdre. It especially pleased her that tall, lanky, Levi, almost thirty now, displayed an ease and confidence he had lacked before. The welcome news that he and his long-time sweetheart planned to wed early in the new year had elicited a chorus of delighted cheers and heartfelt congratulations.

Of middling height, muscular, and dark-haired, Caleb had served as butler to her and Tess during their stay first at New York City, then at Philadelphia while they gathered intelligence on British General William Howe. Caleb appeared the least changed of their visitors, still reticent, but demonstrating the steady level-headedness she had depended heavily on in planning and carrying out her clandestine missions.

Behind their happy fellowship loomed the dark shadow of the coming siege, Elizabeth reflected uneasily as the evening progressed. Their conversation inevitably turned to it. Carleton related that Washington, Rochambeau, and Knox, currently conferring with de Grasse aboard his flagship, were expected back at camp by that weekend. The two commanders would then set the date for advancing their lines to York's perimeter.

Their allied army decisively outnumbered Cornwallis's force entrenched at York and in fortifications across the river at Gloucester Point. To be sure the British Army included seven regiments of Regulars, formidable enough under other circumstances. But not now.

With de Grasse blocking access to the bay, the British commander could not place any hope in reinforcement by either land or sea even if Clinton made a belated attempt. Once the allied Armies had dug their trenches, built their fortifications, and set up the heavy, long-range French cannon, the siege would open with a bombardment that would flatten everything standing within that town's environs.

Chapter Forty-five

THE WIDE, TWENTY-MILE long estuary called York River constricted to less than half a mile at the tip of the Virginia Peninsula, where Gloucester Point projected from the north bank into the surging tidal flow at the Narrows. Reaching ninety feet in depth, the river's channel provided sufficient anchorage for the largest ships, which at the moment included the French warships warily facing off with a twenty-gun British corsair, several transports, and a number of smaller vessels trapped by de Grasse's fleet.

One of Cornwallis's first acts on investing the small harbor town of York, just above the river's mouth on its south bank, had been to fortify the Point. A line of earthworks ran along the edge of its bluff, from which a battery of cannon overlooked the waterway. Behind it lay a log palisade, small triangular fort, and clustered tents that housed what currently remained of a detachment of Tarleton's dragoons.

Astride Devil, Carleton reflected with satisfaction that the infamous Legion commander had lost fifty men three days earlier. While out foraging, his dragoons had been shattered in a clash with a mixed force of Virginia militia and French troops, an action in which Carleton wished fervently he had participated.

Although Tarleton had beaten a hasty retreat into the fort, the arrival of French hussars the next day had deprived him not only of forage, but also of land communications. The only connection remaining between the Point and York was via the river under the protection of Cornwallis's ships—as long as they could hold their positions against the French.

Carleton surveyed the fortification through his spyglass, Andrews, Farris, Isaiah, and McLeod doing the same on either side, while their aides and servants loitered nearby. Carleton had grown so used to the incessant din of cannon fire from both sides that he no longer paid it much attention. He didn't flinch when a cannonball from the nearest British battery landed so close it threw grit into their faces and sand and small stones across the horses' hooves, causing them to toss their heads and dance backward. Realizing that they had drawn the attention of the enemy gunners, he impatiently beckoned his companions to pull back to a copse of trees a short distance behind them.

From its verge he transferred his attention to what was visible of the town behind the British lines. He remembered the small community well from numerous visits in his youth. Established almost a hundred years earlier and about the same size as Williamsburg, it boasted several churches and a courthouse. He could make out the row of houses, some built of fine brick, that ran along the crest of the cliff overlooking the river and the bay beyond it.

A lower street skirted the water's edge at its base, he knew. It was bordered by taverns, shops, wharves, and warehouses in addition to a collection of more modest houses. Far beyond, where the river passed through marshland and into the Chesapeake, he caught a hazy glimpse of the nearest of de Grasse's ships riding peacefully at anchor.

York had flourished for a number of years as the home of many of the area's leading families and the principal port on the Chesapeake for shipping tobacco to markets domestic and foreign. Over time much of the business had drifted away to more favored ports, and the town had fallen into a slow decline. It now displayed the ravages of the enemy's occupation, as did its environs.

Just before the allied army moved out of Williamsburg on a late September morning so hot the sandy road burned the soldiers' feet, a report had arrived from Greene detailing his engagement with a British force early in the month at a place called Eutaw Springs. Greene had been forced to withdraw, but not before inflicting crippling casualties on the enemy. According to the latest intelligence the British commander, Lord Rawdon, had abandoned Camden and withdrawn his army all the way to Charlestown, in effect ceding South Carolina's interior to patriot control. The Southern Army's defeats were costing the British more than they gained, Carleton reckoned, and did not bode well for the war now concentrating in Virginia.

After nightfall this Friday, 5 October, American sappers and miners were finally to lay out the allies' first parallel, laying out strips of pine to mark the path where the trench would be dug the following night. Carleton and Andrews had reconnoitered the enemy lines numerous times the past week with Washington and a coterie of his officers. But that day with the weather cooling, Caledonne and Teissèdre happily ensconced with Rochambeau, and nothing else to occupy them, they and their companions had spent the day tracing the parallel's proposed path while surveying the enemy's fortifications.

Starting at the town's far eastern end, they had curved around back toward the west, then followed the deep ravine carved by York Creek north all the way to Williamstown Road. The trees where they had taken shelter fringed a rise out of range of the British Fusiliers' Redoubt off to their left at the edge of the river's high bank, where a French sortie had received a bloody repulse a few days earlier.

In front of the British lines' center, the land rose in a barren, sandy plain, which fell away on the right to a sheer bluff forty feet above the river. Cornwallis's troops had spent the past two months digging trenches, leveling the ground, and tearing down houses to provide a clear field of fire for their artillery. All the trees fronting the trenches had been reduced to stumps, and barricades of sharpened logs blocked every road.

Cornwallis's inner ring of defenses was even more formidable, interspersed with seven redoubts and a number of gun batteries. British guns remained silent at night, however, allowing the allies' sappers and miners to work feverishly from sunset to sunrise expanding and strengthening what had been Cornwallis's outermost defenses, which he had inexplicably abandoned when the siege began. Meanwhile French and American engineers were industriously laying out positions for the heavy siege guns.

According to the allies' spies, an estimated 3,000 escaped slaves had sought shelter and freedom behind the British lines. A steadily growing stream flowed in the opposite direction as well: deserters from the British Army following the fleeing residents. A great deal of useful intelligence had been gleaned from captured enemy soldiers.

Cornwallis's headquarters had been identified, located in an elegant brick house at the town's southern end—no doubt destined to become a prime target of the allied batteries, Carleton reckoned. It had also been learned that many enemy troops were sick and supplies were growing dangerously low in the beleaguered town. With forage lacking, the British were being forced to slaughter hundreds of horses. Their carcasses lay rotting on the beach or bobbed in the river.

Cornwallis's puzzling withdrawal of his troops from his outer defensive works had also been explained: The British commander had consolidated his lines after receiving a message from Clinton promising to send a large relief force within a week—intelligence immediately conveyed to de Grasse and de Barras.

With the sun lowering in a sky beginning to cloud over, Carleton and his companions passed back inside the American lines. The sprawling allied encampment lay about a mile outside the town. The French camp occupied its left, the Americans holding the position of honor in a wooded area on the army's right, facing the British left.

Carleton glanced toward Washington's two weathered field tents, pitched well beyond cannon range near the camp's center. He slept in the smaller while the large one next to it served as his office and accommodated up to fifty officers for meetings and dinners. Members of his Life Guard surrounded both, but the detail was noticeably smaller at the moment. Washington's new mount, Nelson, a tall chestnut with a white face and stockings, was also absent. Their commander was out roaming around, Carleton surmised with a wry smile, no more able to sit idle than he was.

His Rangers were stationed on the camp's far right side with Lafayette's corps. He had appropriated a relatively level, dry area between the marquis's light infantry and Wayne's Pennsylvanians and in front of the Rhode Island and New Jersey regiments.

Happily there was no lack of food in the allies' camps. Packs of hogs ranged through the surrounding woods—fine provender for the troops —and Carleton caught the rich aroma of roasting pork on the cool, rising wind as they entered the camp's environs. Leaving their aides and servants to their supper, he and Andrews continued through the burgeoning area belonging to the camp followers that bordered the army's rear.

On every side roughly clad women, mostly the wives or sweethearts of soldiers, and their children raised a ruckus. The children raced around at play, shouting to one another. The women visited or argued vociferously while stirring steaming kettles of stew or laundry hanging over open fires, carrying armloads of provisions to and fro, or sitting in small clusters mending soldiers' clothing by the fire's light.

After passing through the picket line at the camp's rear, the two men proceeded alone down the shadowed road through the bleak, war-torn landscape in the gathering darkness toward the large tent a mile farther on that housed the Rangers' reserve hospital, where the two women they loved were busy at their healing work.

THE TORCHES LIGHTING the tent flared in a gust of the increasingly damp, chilly wind, causing Elizabeth to draw her shawl more snugly around her shoulders. When Carleton entered she looked up from the young woman who lay unconscious on the cot beside her. Andrews followed, turning aside to Blue Sky, who bent over a middle-aged soldier struck by a cannonball, his mangled leg amputated earlier that day.

Elizabeth gave Carleton a weary smile as he strode over to her. They had relatively few patients that night, and she motioned to him to sit on the cot next to her. He did so, glancing from the young woman, whose flushed face she was gently wiping with a damp cloth, to the bloodstained pinner apron covering her plain blue linen gown.

"The siege has hardly begun, and your duties are already wearing you out," he murmured reproachfully, regarding her with a frown. "I hate to see you so wan, with dark circles under your eyes." He looked around at the two surgeon's mates occupied with other patients, then at Blue Sky in Andrews' arms, leaning against his chest. "She looks as exhausted as you do."

"We're both fine, just a bit tired. It's been a long day, but we're almost finished for the night. Papa sent Captain Lawton to assist for a while, and the surgeon's mates, Mary, and Sweetgrass are a great help." She dropped the cloth into the basin of water by her feet and swiped back a wayward curl that had escaped from her chignon. Nodding at her patient, she said, "I just want to make sure her fever doesn't worsen."

Carleton studied the young woman who lay motionless on the cot, her tangled hair fever-damp on the pillow, her linen gown threadbare and dirt-streaked. She had clearly once been pretty, but her face was now gaunt, her form wasted.

"What happened to her?"

"A couple of the camp followers brought her in shortly after noon. They found her this morning curled up by one of the wagons, incoherent and bleeding. She was able to tell them that she'd slipped out of York last night. Evidently she'd been ill used by several British soldiers when Cornwallis first invested the town."

Elizabeth gently smoothed the tangled hair back from the girl's brow, feeling the familiar sense of healing flowing through her hand. Her patient let out a sigh, briefly opening her eyes before drifting back into insensibility.

"They'd gotten her with child, and she . . . tried to rid herself of it, then developed an infection. I've done all I can for her medically and have talked with her, encouraged her, prayed over her. The fever has moderated, and she seems a little better. I'm hopeful she'll recover."

Carleton clenched his jaw, face taut with anger. "She lost the child?" When Elizabeth nodded sorrowfully, he swore under his breath. "Men like that ought to be horsewhipped. Or worse. Of course, even if it were discovered, nothing would be done."

He cast a grim glance at the cot on his other side where a young black man lay moaning. More bone than flesh, he was covered with oozing sores.

"We see so many of these poor starving fellows lying in the woods outside the camp, many already dead. They're being driven out of York because there's hardly food enough to feed the troops. And they're spreading the pox. We've orders to avoid them, but I can't bear the thought of leaving them to such a miserable death. I hate to add to your work here—"

"Papa told me you talked to him, and I'm glad. Since we've all either had the pox or been inoculated, we can safely minister to as many as we can find place for. I only wish we could do more. But once the assault begins and we've larger numbers of casualties coming in—"

"This is the last thing you need right now, Beth," he growled. Taking her hand, he kissed it. "You take too much on yourself, and I'm only adding to your burdens. I wish I could spare you all this."

She smiled and cupped his cheek tenderly with her free hand. "It's what I'm called to do, dearest. Blue Sky reminded me that each day I must surrender you to the Lord's care. And you must do the same for me."

"Do you find that easy to do?"

"No," she admitted. "But I keep striving after it."

He made an impatient gesture. "As often as I've vowed to trust the Lord, I still find myself trying to wrest matters back into my own hands. I feel as though if I don't—or can't—protect the ones I love, something terrible will happen to them. But all I end up doing is mucking everything up."

She returned an amused look. "I often think that the Lord's hardest task is to save us from ourselves."

Grimacing, he muttered, "This thing about trust is a deuced nuisance."

"It all depends on whom you trust."

His nod was grudging, but his expression softened. When he drew her to him, she sighed and settled into his embrace, inexpressibly grateful for the haven of his arms. And even more for their Savior's.

SHORTLY AFTER NIGHTFALL the following day, with thunderstorms sweeping through the area and temperatures dropping, Washington inaugurated the first allied parallel by striking several ceremonial blows in the ground with a pickaxe. At this signal the details of sappers and miners dug their shovels into the sandy soil. None minded the drenching rain, for the heavy clouds obscured the full moon and concealed their work from the enemy.

When completed, the trench stretched 2,000 yards from the west side of Hampton Road all the way east to the river, lying just beyond musket range from the enemy with command divided equally between the allies. The French extended a supporting trench on its northernmost end to a new battery from which they could bombard the British ships in the river.

When the sun dawned on Sunday, 7 October, revealing the new line, the British artillery immediately set up a furious assault. Undeterred, the allies completed their batteries and dragged the heavy artillery into place in two days: Knox's three twenty-four pounders, three eighteen pounders, two eight-inch howitzers, and six mortars added to the eighty heavy siege cannon and mortars de Barras had delivered. As they continued bolstering their batteries, British fire gradually dwindled, the reality of their situation apparently sinking in.

At mid afternoon on 9 October the French opened the barrage. Driven across the river to the north shore, the frigate HMS *Guadeloupe* was scuttled to prevent her capture.

Two hours later the Stars and Stripes rose majestically over the American front, and Washington set a match to the first cannon. Standing in the trench nearest York with his own officers and several others, Carleton watched the blazing ball arc into the town. They could clearly hear the shot bouncing through the streets and crashing into walls.

A loud roar went up from everyone in the line, quickly drowned out by the deafening thunder of cannon and mortar fire as Knox's gunners joined the French in full force. With deadly efficiency they went to work dismantling the British defenses and maintained the barrage all night at Washington's command to make it impossible for the enemy to repair their ruined works.

The following day four more batteries joined the barrage. Every gun on the British left was soon silenced. American batteries obliterated the house rumored to be Cornwallis's headquarters. The British hastily sank more than a dozen small boats clustered along the shore to prevent their capture.

The French battery on the allies' far left now targeted the rest of the British ships trapped in the Narrows, lobbing red-hot shot that reached all the way across the river to the Point. A direct hit on forty-four-gun HMS *Charon* set it ablaze. The wind fanned the flames to the vessels around it, and in moments their riggings were all engulfed in a spectacular inferno, going up in smoke and flame like torches. Drifting helplessly to the Gloucester shore, the ships burned to the waterline.

Enemy soldiers began to pitch their tents in the trenches in a desperate bid to escape shot raining from the air. Increasing numbers slipped through the lines at night, either to attempt escape or to surrender. Most of the town's remaining residents fled down to the river on the town's east end, where they dug into the sand cliffs for shelter from cannonballs and the whirling fragments of exploding bombs.

At Washington's orders, during the night of 11 October, details dug a second parallel line 400 yards closer to the British entrenchments. The work proceeded unnoticed, the enemy's dwindling barrages continuing to send shot overhead to land behind them in the first parallel. All the while, undeterred by the cannonballs flinging through the air and furrowing the ground around them, the camp women continued to trudge tirelessly back and forth carrying bread and large pots of coffee and boiled beef to fortify their men on the siege line.

By sunrise Lafayette's division had pushed the trench within 250 yards of the enemy lines. It remained short of the river, however, the sappers and miners blocked by two formidable British redoubts, numbers 9 and 10, from extending it all the way.

Chapter Forty-six

"H IS EXCELLENCY APPOINTED me to the command," Alexander Hamilton said, his chin jutting truculently. He directed a suspicious glance from Carleton to Andrews, then to Isaiah and Farris, who hovered behind them in Hamilton's small marquee.

Carleton raised his hands, palms outward. "We're well aware of it. We're merely offering our services as volunteers."

"His Excellency doubts my abilities and sent you to prop me up, I suppose."

"Not a bit of it!" Andrews objected hotly. "We asked him if we might be of use, and he simply directed us to you."

"I've no need of cavalry," Hamilton snapped.

"Believe it or not," Carleton drawled, "both our cavalry and light infantry have considerable experience fighting on foot. It appears to me that if you're to take that redoubt, the more support you have, the more likely you are to succeed."

Hamilton hesitated, eyes narrowing. "I've never heard of generals placing themselves under the command of a mere *lieutenant* colonel."

Carleton understood the reasons for Hamilton's hostility, truly he did, and he determinedly reminded himself of them. Washington's young, ambitious former aide had gone toe to toe with the General to gain this long-denied field command, even going so far as to resign his commission to make his point. But Carleton was rapidly losing patience.

It was early afternoon on Sunday, 14 October. That morning Washington had ordered the American artillery to concentrate their fire on redoubts 9 and 10 in preparation for an assault that night. There would be no moonlight to expose the attackers, and they were to advance in complete silence using cold steel alone. Muskets were not even to be loaded until the men reached the fortifications' walls. Considering the din of the incessant bombardment on both sides, Carleton had to wonder how likely the British were to hear them even if they advanced on the redoubts screaming and banging drums.

Leaning in close over the short, slight officer, Carleton said through gritted teeth, "Tarleton laid my estate in ruins. As if that were not enough, he sent a personal letter to my wife threatening her and our children. I've a score to settle, and I'll not stand idly by when the opportunity is at hand to settle it!"

His vehemence drove Hamilton a step backward. "I understand," he said, wavering between conciliation and defiance. "As long as we're clear who's in command here, I've no objection to your assisting in the assault."

"We're clear," Andrews said, shifting a warning gaze from Hamilton to Carleton.

"Perfectly. What's your plan?"

Hamilton's mouth tightened. "Why, to take Redoubt Number 10 . . . sir."

Carleton let out an exasperated sigh, but returned a thin smile. "Just as I prefer—the direct, straightforward approach. Let's get at it then. Whenever you're ready . . . sir."

ALL DAY A DEAFENING, unrelenting barrage from the American and French batteries had filled the air over York and the outlying British entrenchments with concussions that shook the earth, flinging geysers of dirt and debris to all sides. Then moments earlier, with night coming on, the batteries in their quarter had suddenly fallen silent.

Carleton squinted to make out the dial of his pocket watch in the rapidly fading light. As the minute hand ticked over to 6:30, a crash of gunfire suddenly erupted along the riverbank beyond the French camp, well off to the town's west. It was answered immediately by renewed enemy barrages.

He returned Andrews' eager grin. The diversionary attack on the Fusiers' redoubt signaled similar feints to begin at other points along the parallel in the pretense that the allies meant to assault the town.

At Hamilton's hushed command the detachment rapidly formed up, bayonets fixed, and crawled stealthily over the entrenchment's top. As soon as they were in the clear, everyone fell prone on the ground to wait for three signal shells to be fired from one of the nearby batteries.

For long, suspended minutes the guns heralding the feints continued to blast away at the answering British batteries, their clamor intense, while those in their own line maintained silence. Carleton glanced anxiously toward the signal guns, then tensed, for a moment thinking that a shell had burst overhead though he heard no sound. Before he could command his detail to advance, he realized that what he saw was the planets Jupiter and Venus. They appeared unusually close to each other in the moonless night sky, their brilliant light steady against the star-spangled indigo heavens from which the last glow of sunset was fading.

He took a breath and forced the tension of his muscles to relax. As always when facing battle, he determinedly put from his mind all thoughts of Elizabeth and the twins, and this time of the babe to come. Committing himself to God, he returned his attention to his immediate vicinity.

Their goal, Redoubt Number 10, loomed straight ahead, its walls indistinct in the deepening gloom. According to intelligence the fortress held around seventy men. Along the wall on its right, a steep, almost perpendicular bank dropped off to the narrow beach edging the river. Carleton caught a glimpse of starlight sparkling across the dark waves visible below.

Four hundred Regulars of the French Deux-Ponts regiment would endeavor to take Redoubt Number 9, roughly 300 yards inland to their left and manned by well over a hundred Hessians. Rows of ditches and abatis surrounded both fortifications to complicate the two detachments' efforts.

Hamilton's command included the elite, smartly uniformed, all-black First Rhode Island Regiment that, among other impressive exploits, had driven back three fierce British assaults at Newport, Rhode Island, three years earlier. Carleton's volunteers added to the effort one light infantry company and one unmounted cavalry troop from each of Farris's and Isaiah's regiments, plus their aides, servants, and McLeod, who refused to be left behind. A couple of companies from Stern's Massachusetts brigade under Levi's command rounded out the detachment.

Hamilton's low voice was barely audible above the blast of cannon fire as he ordered Lieutenant Colonel John Laurens to circle around to the redoubt's rear with his detail and intercept any defenders attempting to escape. The men moved off at a crouch.

Their dim forms had hardly dissolved into the darkness when with startling suddenness the signal battery sprang to life. One after the other, three shells arced fiery trails across the sky.

"Up! Up!" The urgently hissed order snaked down the line.

On his feet in an instant with Andrews at his side, Carleton repeated the command. Waving their men to follow, the two of them charged, their men surging on their heels amid the moving shadows surrounding them who raced silently forward on every side, unloaded muskets in hand, the burnished steel of bayonets reflecting glimmers of starlight. Carleton was distantly conscious that well off to the left another great mass of men barreled toward the inner redoubt.

Ahead of them the sappers and miners were already furiously hacking with their axes at the abatis. The earlier barrage had done little damage to the dense tangles of downed trees fixed to the ground, sharpened limbs pointing outward. But Carleton and Andrews, with McLeod on their heels, crowded through side by side, following the lead of the soldiers ahead of them who forced their way through any break they could find, heedless of the sting of cuts and scratches. After making sure Isaiah and Farris followed with their companies, they scrambled across a ditch and closed cautiously on the redoubt amid the roiling sea of silent black figures.

In a moment of alarm Carleton noted that here and there men ahead of them were abruptly vanishing from sight. McLeod grabbed his arm, wrenching him to a halt just as he realized that the ground between them and the redoubt was heavily pocked with craters blasted by American shells. He could barely make out the one directly in front of his feet.

"Looks to be big enough to bury an ox," Andrews muttered at his other side before passing a low warning back down the detail to watch their steps.

At that moment a shouted challenge reached them from the redoubt's wall. Everyone kept silent, but the roar of a volley quickly followed.

"Rochambeau!" screamed Hamilton from the direction of the palisade ahead of them. Together Carleton and Andrews repeated the watchword for the night at the top of their lungs, echoed by every man in a shout that drowned the din of gunfire and the multiple explosions of hand grenades erupting from the fortress. Atop the parapets the flames of massed volleys set the defenders who bent over them in vivid relief, the flickering light and shadow giving them the appearance of veritable devils.

The watchword "Rochambeau" quickly mutated into a fierce cry of "Rush on boys!" along with screams of "The fort's ours!" that spurred the entire force pell-mell onward. Tasting victory, the attackers poured into the ditch at the palisade's base, many hastily loading their guns, while Carleton hoarsely ordered his men to charge with bayonets. Climbing onto the shoulders of comrades, the horde clambered over the parapet in an unstoppable tide despite blistering enemy fire, which those with loaded weapons returned to deadly effect.

Carleton vaulted over the wall, sabre in hand as he savagely warded off the defenders' attempts to pull him down. Unceremoniously he dragged Andrews and McLeod after him, then Farris and Isaiah jumped in and helped those coming behind, each man doing the same for those who followed.

In the high pitch of battle fever, Carleton and his detail waded into the boiling fray. Resistance began quickly to collapse. Before they could be stopped, a number of the redoubt's defenders escaped over the rear and side walls, but the rest, trapped, laid down their weapons in surrender.

With the clamor subsiding as prisoners were secured, Lafayette came up to join them. The French detachment had been slowed down by the abatis at the other fort but should be in possession of it shortly, the young marquis announced with undisguised glee.

He was still speaking when a shout of *"Vive le Roi"* reached them from the direction of Redoubt Number 9, quickly repeated in a triumphant cheer by the troops of the Deux-Ponts Regiment. Lafayette, Hamilton and all their men joined in exuberant huzzahs. At the same moment the British unleashed every gun along their main line in a violent, but impotent barrage.

EVEN BEFORE PRISONERS were led off, sappers and miners were at work digging new trenches to link the captured redoubts to the allies' second parallel. By morning the works extended to the river, and the heaviest guns were in the redoubts, trained to enfilade the entire enemy line. Deserters streamed from York in a flood.

In the days that followed, the British subjected the closest allied line to a desperate bombardment. A raiding party managed to infiltrate the second parallel, kill and wound several soldiers, and spike half a dozen cannon before being killed or captured. But within hours the guns were back in service and rejoined the allies' bombardment along with new batteries that were brought online.

The allied barrage intensified to the point that it seemed to Carleton even the heavens reeled. He could not imagine how anyone in York could survive the assault.

Most of the British cannonades passed over the American sector to fall on the French, and their hospitals overflowed with the injured. When

Carleton checked with Elizabeth and her father, he found them and their staffs busy with a tide of casualties, but not, to his relief, entirely overwhelmed.

On the night of Tuesday, 16 October, Cornwallis attempted to evacuate his remaining force in small boats across the river to Gloucester Point. The effort ended abruptly when a squall raged downriver, lashing the water into a froth and drenching the peninsula in a cold rain. The troops already evacuated were brought back the next day, no doubt to report the unhappy truth that even had the evacuation succeeded, an extensive cordon of trenches backed by French hussars hemmed in Tarleton's small garrison so tightly that there was no hope of escape in that direction.

By then the allies had extended their entrenchments far enough to capture Cornwallis's strongest remaining redoubt, which they furnished with yet another powerful battery of guns. And on the cold dawn of 17 October, a screaming barrage of shot and shells from at least a hundred guns crashed into York from deadly close range, the British capable of only sporadic mortar fire in response.

Carleton checked his pocket watch when a small red-coated drummer mounted a parapet at the British center and began to strike a steady roll. It was nine a.m.

For some moments the boy drummed unheard above the explosion of shells. But before Carleton could send Hutchinson to alert the nearest battery, it ceased firing. One by one every gun along the allies' lines did the same.

While the drummer continued his furious tattoo signaling for a parlay, a British officer emerged from beneath the parapet waving a white handkerchief over his head. Soon an American officer picked his way across the heavily furrowed no man's land to his side. Taking the man's handkerchief, he blindfolded him and as the drum fell silent led him back behind the allied lines.

Standing at Carleton's side, Andrews said softly, "Four years ago this day Burgoyne surrendered at Saratoga."

Carleton met his gaze with a sober one. "So he did, Charles. And today, perhaps, we'll finally see come to pass what we hoped for then."

NEGOTIATIONS TURNED contentious, the quick settlement Washington expected dragging out while the officers commissioned to work out an agreement haggled over every article. The greatest impediment centered on Washington's stipulation that Cornwallis's army march out with flags furled, their band playing one of their own marches. The article was too harsh, the British officers protested. According to tradition vanquished troops surrendered their arms with flying colors, playing an enemy tune in derision.

At this the American commissioner, John Laurens, whom Andrews remembered with great fondness, coldly reminded the British that he had been present when the same terms had been imposed on General Lincoln at Charlestown. "This remains an article," he seethed, "or I cease to be a commissioner."

The article remained.

Washington carefully weighed the proposed agreement and granted most of its provisions, while denying several. The British were to sign the final document at eleven that morning, October 19, he informed Cornwallis by messenger, the army then to surrender its arms at two o'clock. The garrison at Gloucester Point would surrender their post and arms at the same hour.

The signed agreement was duly submitted, and now with American regimental flags flying above the British earthworks, the two allied commanders led their armies onto the broad plain between their camp and York. Every face beamed with satisfaction and joy.

The troops formed into two long ranks, French and Americans standing several yards apart facing each other. While they waited for the British to appear, regimental bands on both sides played jubilant tunes, the French musicians employing timbrels to delightful effect.

This is going to be quite a spectacle, Carleton ruminated as he took in the scene.

News of the allies' victory had spread far and wide, and a huge, jubilant throng, vying in size with the army, had gathered behind it with the camp followers to witness their enemy's humiliation. On the sprawling camp's left the French troops stood at rigid attention, resplendent in spotless white uniforms faced in a variety of pastel hues according to regiment. On the right the American soldiers appeared even more gaunt, dirty, and ragged than they had on their arrival weeks earlier. Only the highest ranking Continental officers and a few others presented an impressive appearance. In spite of it, all of them had won the admiration of the French for their ability to fight.

The few units that were well turned-out included Light Horse Harry Lee's Legion, the First Rhode Island Regiment, and Carleton's impeccably uniformed Rangers, with their new dun-colored short jackets faced in forest green and striking dark-green leather helmets with gold chains and flowing, blond horsehair crests. He sat astride Devil at their head, Andrews on his right with Isaiah and Farris next to him. Caledonne, brilliantly clad in his French admiral's uniform, and Teissèdre in high French style held Carleton's left. Behind them ranged their aides, servants, subordinate officers, and neatly formed troops. Carleton wished intensely that Elizabeth could share the moment at his side, but she remained with Dr. Howard, Blue Sky, and the rest of the medical corps at the division's rear.

A sustained drumroll reached them from the direction of the town. Along with everyone on the plain, Carleton focused his gaze on the enemy vanguard emerging at a slow march from York's ruins. The remainder of Cornwallis's army trickled after them, the entire body in their finest uniforms and carrying their flags cased.

The advancing officers appeared to Carleton like whipped schoolboys, some biting their lips, some with sullen pouts, others with unrestrained tears. Resentment, grief, and anger contorted the soldiers' faces as well, and their tread and ranks were broken. In contrast the German troops maintained their order and dignity though like all the rest appearing much daunted by the vast army that stretched across the plain in front of them.

As they drew nearer their band struck up a slow tune more a dirge than a march, muffled by drums covered in black cloth and fifes wrapped in black ribbons. Indeed the ceremony must seem a funeral to their vanquished enemy, Carleton reflected.

He scanned the lines for Cornwallis, but could identify no officer who fit his memory of the man: short and thickset, blind in one eye from an injury as a youth. He recalled him vaguely from their brief acquaintance in England as an affable fellow in the main, though prone to fits of bad temper and sulking.

Instead a red-faced, black-haired officer rode stiffly erect in the British Army's van, garbed in an older style of uniform and jackbooted. Count Dumas, one of the French officers, rode out to meet him. After introducing himself as General Charles O'Hara, he asked where General Rochambeau was.

Dumas indicated the general at the head of the French Army, and O'Hara turned his mount in that direction. Apparently realizing O'Hara's intent too late, Dumas hastily circled around in an effort to block his path. O'Hara reached Rochambeau first and offered his sword.

The French commander shook his head with great dignity. Gracefully indicating Washington in the opposite line, he said firmly, "We are subordinate to the Americans. General Washington will give you orders."

Carleton exchanged an amused glance with Caledonne as O'Hara reined his mount around with obvious reluctance and crossed to Washington. Although he put on a bold front, he seemed more than a little chagrined as he held out his sword to the American commander.

Washington drew stiffly back. "Never from such a good hand."

His face flushing an even deeper red, O'Hara apologized for Cornwallis's absence, explaining that the British commander had fallen ill.

"Heartsick, no doubt," Andrews muttered, a shade of sympathy in his tone, as Washington passed O'Hara to General Lincoln with a nod.

Lincoln accepted the sword and held it for a moment before returning it to O'Hara. Then he motioned to a large circle of French hussars holding drawn sabres and lancers with raised spears a short distance away. Each regiment was to enter there in turn, lay down their arms, and march back between the allies' lines, Lincoln directed crisply.

As at Saratoga, Carleton could take no joy in a valiant enemy's defeat, no matter the cause of their dispute. Nor did anyone on the field, civilian or soldier, seem to take any pleasure in the sight of the British troops filing into the circle to cast down their weapons.

Many sobbed, even the German soldiers now. An officer called out commands with tears streaming down his cheeks: "Present arms! Lay down arms! Put off swords and cartridge boxes!"

As he scanned the long, somber lines filing in and out of the circle, their scorn for the tattered American soldiers all too obvious, Carleton thought grimly, *Fiat justitia ruat caelum.* Let justice be done though the heavens fall.

He glanced back at the neatly formed mounted ranks of his Rangers with their colorful regimental standards snapping in the cool breeze. Most were backcountry settlers, many ruffians of one sort or another, others free or fugitive blacks who, if not for his provision, would lack clothing, food, shelter, and weapons. And then there were his absent warriors.

And for them also, Lord God, the humble, the slave, the freeman, the fugitive, the native. For if justice is not done for them as well, how can you, the Great Judge of all, ever bless this land?

On his left, Caledonne murmured, *"Tout est perdu fors l'honneur."* All is lost save honor.

"The only honor worth having is that given from on high," Carleton returned quietly. "Today, I think, we've received a measure of it."

Caledonne gave him a searching look. "Indeed. In my old age, I'm learning to desire that honor above all others."

Chapter Forty-seven

S EATED WITH THE OTHERS around the fire circle between Carleton and her parents, who held the twins, Elizabeth watched, smiling, as Andrews proudly handed his swaddled daughter over to Red Fox on Saturday, 27 April 1782. At his side Blue Sky beamed at their baby, who squirmed, protesting, before stilling to look up into Red Fox's face.

They had every reason for joy, Elizabeth thought, hardly able to contain her own. Born ten days earlier, the little girl was perfect in every way, a tiny replica of her mother, blessed with a soft, dusky complexion and abundant silky black hair. Her English name had been given earlier in the week when McLeod baptized her: Dorothea, Gift of God. And so she was. Clearly about to burst with happiness, Andrews enfolded his two boys in his arms as they watched, eyes wide.

Red Fox considered the infant, his smile broad. Then, nodding to John Walk on Water, who stood at his left hand, and Spotted Pony on his right, he lifted her in his arms, presenting her to heaven and to those gathered with them at his delegations' temporary camp.

"Little sister, I name you Willow by Flowing Waters, for your life will bear much fruit for our Heavenly Father."

Both Blue Sky and Andrews blinked back tears. Leads the Way, now three-and-a half-years old, and Little Elk, two-and-a half, handsome boys tall for their ages, looked up at them questioningly.

Feeling her own new babe stir, Elizabeth gazed down at the bundle on her lap as Carleton's arm went around her. She met his warm gaze, the tide of emotion that washed over her all but impossible to contain.

Red Fox returned tiny Willow to her parents and now turned to them. Carleton took their new son from her and rose to hand him to his elder cousin. Named Jonathan Stuart Alexandre after his father, he had been born two days after Willow and baptized along with her. With Harry's hazel eyes and face that was increasingly taking on the contours of his paternal grandfather, Lord Oliver Carleton, the boy they had already taken to calling Jon-Stuart resembled Carleton the most closely now in his features and vivid blue-grey eyes in spite of having hair as dark as Elizabeth's father's.

When Red Fox took him, Julianne protested worriedly to her grandmother, "Why's he taking my brother? He belongs to us!"

A chorus of guffaws rippled along the circle of onlookers. Hastily Anne hushed the two-and-a-half-year-old, Dr. Howard leaning to whisper in her ear. Harry, his normal imperturbable self, reached from his grandfather's lap to encircle his sister's shoulders reassuringly with one arm.

Elizabeth could feel heat flaming in her cheeks. She determinedly averted her face from Red Fox and Carleton, who were grinning at each other.

Shifting sideways to bump her shoulder with his, Carleton murmured, "That's our girl."

It was too much. Elizabeth bent over, clutching her middle, but it was impossible to strangle her hysterical laughter. Julianne let out a wail.

When order was finally restored and Red Fox managed a sober mien, he lifted the boy before them. "Little brother, I name you Soaring Eagle. Like your father, White Eagle, you will grow to be a renowned warrior of Black Hawk's clan of the Shawnee nation."

A chill went through Elizabeth as Red Fox returned her son to her arms. And as Walk on Water blessed the two infants, she was pierced by

a foreboding that she and Carleton would ponder this prophecy often in the years to come.

✳ ✳ ✳

THE PREVIOUS DECEMBER, when reports reached Carleton that the British had evacuated Charlestown, South Carolina, he had released half his Rangers to return home and leased an estate a short distance west of Philadelphia for the greatly reduced division's winter quarters. The troops and their officers were comfortably accommodated in the barns and other outbuildings on the gently rolling, tree-dotted property, while Carleton's and Andrews' families occupied the graceful Palladian-style mansion.

Red Fox, Spotted Pony, their wives, and a number of others from the clan had arrived at the beginning of April, bringing with them the leader of the clan's Christian fellowship, the Oneida John Walk on Water. But the happy welcome they received quickly gave way to horror as they related shocking news of a massacre of peaceful Christian Lenape and Mahicans.

In early March a Pennsylvania militia detachment commanded by Lieutenant Colonel David Williamson had marched into the Moravian town of Gnadenhütten in Ohio Territory and accused the people they found there of having aided Indian parties raiding into Pennsylvania—a laughable charge considering the Moravians' firmly held nonresistant stance. The townspeople's denials of the false charges had been dismissed out of hand, and Williamson ordered their execution. Although more than a dozen soldiers protested and left the town rather than take part in such an atrocity, the majority agreed.

The following morning the remaining soldiers had bound and divided men, women, and children into separate groups. Then, while the Moravian Indians knelt before them praying and singing hymns, Williamson and his men scalped and beat to death ninety-six people with mallet blows to the head. Only two young boys, one scalped, survived.

Their bloody work finished, the militia then looted the village, piled the bodies in the mission buildings, and burned the village to the ground. They proceeded to loot and burn other abandoned Moravian villages in a trail of destruction, taking so much plunder that eighty horses were needed to carry it.

News of the massacre had not only outraged Black Hawk's clan, but also aroused fear that they were in danger as well. If the peaceful Moravian Indians were slaughtered, would it matter that their clan had supported the Americans in the war and even sent warriors to fight and die on their behalf?

Reports of reprisals being planned by large groups of Lenape and Shawnee warriors were spreading like wildfire throughout the tribes in Ohio Territory. And with many men of the clan speaking of joining their brothers in the raids, the women's peace sachem, Blue Crane, had formed the delegation to carry a protest to Pennsylvania's governor and legislature and warn of the coming vengeance.

The news struck everyone like a thunderbolt. Carleton, Andrews, and their aides along with Isaiah, Farris, and McLeod joined the delegation at once. Carleton succeeded in arranging a meeting with the state's leaders the week following the naming ceremony.

They were received politely enough by the state's leaders, though several pointed out that many of the militiamen had lost relatives and friends in Indians raids. They maintained that in their anger the soldiers likely did not distinguish between peaceful Indians and hostile ones.

Red Fox's cold response that the native peoples had suffered even more losses, in addition to the theft of their tribal lands, and felt the same anger made no apparent impression. Walk on Water's explanation that Indians allied with the British had forcibly removed the Moravians from their towns for refusing to fight with them and that they had only returned to collect crops and stored food because they were starving aroused some sympathy. But in the end Pennsylvania's leaders shrugged off the delegation's warning of a coming whirlwind as well as their demand that the men responsible be arrested, tried, and punished according to their crimes.

After they returned to the estate Red Fox characterized the meetings succinctly: "They make fine speeches, but they do not hear our words."

"They do not consider us to be human beings or to have any rights," Spotted Pony fumed. "But they will learn that we Indians do not give up our rights as men cheaply."

Without a word Carleton drew Hutchinson into his office. After writing reports describing the massacre and the meeting with Pennsylvania's governor and legislative representatives in detail, he sent the major off to Congress at the Pennsylvania State House and to Washington at the army's camp at Newburgh, New York.

Later that night in private, Carleton told Elizabeth bitterly, "I thought I was done with war, Beth. It's been my fondest hope all these years. But I'm seriously considering returning with Red Fox to wage such war upon those invading our lands and killing our people as they've never seen. Spotted Pony and Charles are for it. Even Red Fox—"

Gently she took his face between her hands, tears glistening in her eyes. "I can't blame you, dearest. I feel it equally. But you know as well as I that such a course will only lead to even greater tragedy. And it'll undo everything you've striven for thus far."

He bent his head, tears stinging his own eyes, his throat so tight he could hardly speak. "We can never win," he managed, his voice breaking. "There'll never be justice for my people or any of the others."

She slipped her arms around his neck and rested her head against his shoulder. "Though we may not see justice done for them on this earth, there's yet a righteous Judge in heaven who won't allow evil to prevail forever."

He could make no reply. Though he knew the truth of what she said, his entire being ached to impose his own justice now—in his own time, not God's.

It was a bitter surrender. Pressing his cheek against the crown of her head, he clung to her until, by degrees, the agonizing knot in his chest eased enough that he could breathe.

THE PROSPECT OF LEAVING Elizabeth and their children again, especially with the recent birth of Jon-Stuart, was wrenching. But when a runner from Red Fox's Town reported that a Wyandot raiding party had attacked a fort in Kentucky a fortnight after the massacre at Gnadenhütten, then routed a detachment pursuing them, Carleton felt he had no choice, a sentiment Andrews shared. Reluctantly they decided to accompany the delegation back to Ohio Territory at the end of the month to confer with clan and tribal leaders.

The day of their leaving was made more difficult as Yellow Feather and Morning Dew were going home with Laughing Otter and Red Fox, who had missed their daughters as much as the maidens had missed them. Thankfully Anne was able to engage a nursemaid for the children who came highly recommended and who proved her worth as she and the twins quickly bonded. Julianne and Harry bade farewell to the two Shawnee maidens with no more tears than anyone could expect.

Before Elizabeth's parents shepherded the children away, Dr. Howard paused to give Carleton a penetrating look. "Jon . . . you'll not involve yourself in these raids, I hope. Not that I could blame you after this, but you've a wife and children to consider, after all."

Carleton returned a hard look. "That's something I never forget, Samuel. I'm striving to stay my hand. But at this point I can guarantee nothing."

Turning abruptly away, he led Elizabeth outside onto the front stoop. It was the last day of April, sunny and unseasonably warm. Andrews and their servants were mounted, waiting on the carriageway below.

When he drew her into his arms she leaned into him, feeling anger in the tension of his body, but also beneath it the inexpressible longing that drew him always to the wilderness and to his clan and nation. It was a force as powerful as his love for her and for their children, she knew, ever tearing his soul between the two worlds.

"You'll return by fall?" she ventured.

"The beginning of September at the latest, I should think," he answered gruffly. He took her hands in his, head bent. "If I should find good land to build us a home along the Ohio, will you come and bring our children. I know everything is uncertain now, but—"

"Must you ask?!" She smiled up at him, eager anticipation suddenly welling up. "Of course I shall if that's God's will for us."

He met her gaze with a sober one. "I feel it is. And neither Charles nor I can bear being apart from our clan and nation much longer. Not now."

"Our Lord has always gone before us," she reminded him. "As long as we follow where he leads, nothing will come into our lives that he doesn't ordain.

"Besides, I've grown bored with this settled life," she continued mischievously. "I need a new adventure! I want to see with my own eyes the lands and people that constantly draw you. I want our children to see them, too, and to know their clan. Promise you'll take us to see the great Mississippi one day!"

His tension dissolved, and he threw back his head, laughing heartily. "My brave little Oriole! How God has blessed me in you!"

She tiptoed to kiss him. "And me in you. Always."

Chapter Forty-eight

CALEDONNE AND TESS had sailed for France aboard *Destiny* late the previous month, Teissèdre accompanying them to help facilitate their permanent move to Philadelphia. They hoped to bring Abby back with them and perhaps Henri, too, a possibility Carleton, Elizabeth, and her parents eagerly anticipated.

A large portion of Carleton's fortune had been expended in the war effort, and he was determined to rebuild it as quickly as possible. So while in France, Caledonne also intended to oversee the conversion of half of Carleton's privateers back into merchantmen, equipped with heavy armaments to repel attacks at sea.

The savage battles between Loyalist and patriot militias in the Carolinas were gradually dying away. In the north the Continental Army remained idle at Newburgh. The prisoners taken at York had been dispersed to various locations, while the rest of the British Army in America remained holed up in New York and Savannah waiting on the tentative peace negotiations underway in England and France.

With De Grasse's return to the West Indies to secure France's possessions there, Britain's navy had resumed its blockade of ports along the American coast, stifling trade and causing inflation to soar. No further loans were available from France as the war had bled her coffers dry, and Congress lacked funds to pay Washington's soldiers. Peace appeared the best option on all sides, but reconciling conflicting terms proposed by

British, French, Spanish, and Dutch negotiators remained a daunting task.

That spring the flames of war again exploded into an inferno all along the frontier. The Revolution's end unleashed a flood of westward migration that was met with savage resistance. By midsummer white settlers beyond the Appalachians were calling 1782 the Bloody Year.

The runners Carleton regularly sent from Red Fox's Town delivered news of the spreading conflict, and newspapers filled with details of the violence. But his report on Gnadenhütten along with those of others had outraged Congress, and hope rose that they might take some action even though they lacked jurisdiction over the militias.

Washington's response reflected that of Congress, and he took the precaution of ordering American soldiers to make every effort to avoid being captured by Indians. But in June, while leading an expedition against Shawnee and Lenape warriors in Ohio, one of the General's close friends, Colonel William Crawford, was captured along with a number of his men when their force was routed near Sandusky in Ohio Territory. Although Crawford had not been present at the massacre, the warriors exacted brutal revenge, torturing and burning him to death along with other prisoners they believed had participated.

The appalling accounts inflamed emotions even further, and more raids spread death and destruction. Elizabeth began to wonder how far the conflict would rage and whether Carleton and Andrews would be drawn into its conflagration. With the situation on the frontier changing day by day, the runners' assurances that Black Hawk's clan held firm against joining in the violence couldn't completely calm her fears and those of her parents, Blue Sky, and Sweetgrass.

Carleton, Andrews, and their servants returned early in August to the great relief of everyone in household and camp. The news they brought that the British had evacuated Savannah the previous month and that peace negotiations were underway in Paris was received with renewed hope for a speedy end to the war.

Carleton had found a suitable property for their new home, he told Elizabeth and her parents privately, a 30,000 acre tract along the Ohio River. He had brought up the matter with the Shawnee leaders, proposing that it would always be a haven for members of their nation and provide a base from which he could easily travel to and from their towns. The elders had responded favorably, and in his absence Red Fox would carry out negotiations to conclude the purchase.

Carleton's description of the building site he had chosen, a broad, wooded rise atop a bluff that offered a splendid view of the Ohio River, delighted Elizabeth. He proposed to begin clearing the land the following spring, with building beginning on the house and outbuildings by early summer.

Elizabeth had discussed the matter with her parents while he was gone. To his surprise, they accepted their decision to move into Ohio Territory without argument, though they remained hesitant to accompany them.

To allay their concerns Carleton told them that a small settlement lay across the river on the Virginia shore, and Red Fox planned to move his town onto the land as soon as the purchase was completed. Carleton intended to bring Durie up from Thornlea to supervise the project, along with Rufus and a number of his men, who would manage the livestock. In time Salome, the kitchen maids, and the majority of the household servants would be installed at the new estate as well, with only those necessary for Thornlea's operations and maintenance left behind.

He also intended to offer parcels of land for farms to any of his troops who wished to move west, for their free use as long as they wished to stay. The only requirement was that they live at peace with their neighbors, whether white, black, or native, and that they help to defend the estate should it ever come under attack.

McLeod and Mary had already expressed interest, with McLeod proposing to establish a church and school for the new community. Elizabeth and her father could provide medical care to their neighbors at the dispensary and surgery Carleton planned to build. He also reminded them that the great Ohio provided a convenient highway to speed the transport of needed goods as well as travel east to Pittsburgh and Philadelphia, whether for safety if war threatened, or for visits to Caledonne and Tess in Philadelphia. Abby and Henri might eventually settle there as well.

His arguments proved persuasive. There was Abby's homecoming and marriage to consider, but Elizabeth's parents admitted that they couldn't bear the thought of parting from their grandchildren. At least for now they would plan to move with Carleton and Elizabeth to Ohio Territory when building was completed.

JAW CLENCHED, CARLETON surveyed Lucien coldly as he made a deep bow to him and to Elizabeth. "Général Carleton, Madame Carleton," he said, his voice holding a tremor, eyes downcast as he straightened.

Carleton turned his attention to his cousin's companion, a slip of a woman with delicately modeled features, curly black hair, and lustrous dark eyes, who curtsied gracefully. Marie Glasière, risen, it seemed, from the dead.

She must be in her mid twenties now, Carleton estimated. Her beauty had not diminished since he'd last seen her aboard *Destiny* when he'd breached New York Harbor to rescue Elizabeth. Her expression remained as serene as it had been then.

Following dinner on that golden late September afternoon, Carleton, Elizabeth, and her parents had been relaxing in the drawing room with the twins and five-month-old Jon-Stuart when Sarah interrupted them with the announcement that they had guests newly arrived from France: Lucien Bettár and his wife. Elizabeth's parents had discreetly whisked the children outside for an airing, while Sarah ushered the couple in.

As soon as the housekeeper withdrew to bring tea, Elizabeth rushed to embrace Lucien's companion. "Marie! We could learn nothing of your fate after *Destiny*'s capture and feared you were dead. We never thought to see you again."

Marie returned her embrace, a warm smile lighting her face. "As you see, I am here. With my husband," she added, turning to indicate Lucien.

"Your husband."

"Please let me explain, *Gén*—"

"You know my name. Use it," Carleton cut Lucien off. He strode to a small table where a decanter half full of amber fluid sat on a tray with several glasses.

"Please sit down," Elizabeth broke in hastily, motioning their guests to seats.

Lucian perched on the sofa as though he might flee at any moment. Marie settled at his side and laid her hand reassuringly on his arm. While Carleton poured a generous portion from the decanter into one of the glasses, Sarah slipped unobtrusively into the room bringing the tea tray and again quietly withdrew.

"I assume you'd prefer armagnac, Lucien," Carleton rasped as Elizabeth began to pour the tea.

"Yes. Th-thank you, Jon—Jonathan." He could hardly get the words out.

Aware that Elizabeth watched him with unconcealed apprehension, Carleton brought Lucien's glass to him, then slouched into a chair opposite the sofa and tossed back his own drink in one swallow.

Lucien stared at his glass, finally took a sip, almost choking on it. "I won't blame you if you dismiss me. It's no more than I deserve, after all. But . . . I've come to seek your forgiveness."

Since his confrontation with Caledonne, Carleton had envisioned a more congenial scene if he and Lucien ever met again. But now that they actually faced each other, he found himself bristling.

He gave a short, harsh laugh. "It seems I've heard this before, cousin. Yet we always end up back in the same place, don't we?"

Lucien drew in a steadying breath, but before he could respond Marie pleaded, "Please hear him out, *mon général.* My husband is a changed man, as you will see."

"So he's pledged more times than I can count." Carleton fixed Lucien in a hard look. "I think, perhaps, you ought to seek your father's forgiveness first."

"I've done so, I assure you—not long after he and Thérèsa returned to Passy." Lucien leaned eagerly forward and with a warm glance at Marie, continued, "Had it not been for the grace shown me by our Savior through this dear woman I'd never have had the courage to confront him."

"Jonathan, ought we not to at least listen to what they have to say?"

Carleton met Elizabeth's pleading gaze. "Very well," he returned brusquely. "Let's hear it then."

A tense silence stretched out for several moments. Finally, gripping Marie's hand, Lucien admitted that he had been blinded by rage at Carleton's humiliating set down in refusing his challenge to a duel, and by what he conceived to be his father's preference for his nephew over his own son. He had determined to subject them both to the betrayal he felt, and on reaching England immediately contacted William Eden, the head of Britain's Secret Intelligence Service. Lucien's credentials had guaranteed an enthusiastic reception and a generous reward for the intelligence he provided.

"So we heard," Carleton drawled, his tone caustic.

Lucien ducked his head. "I was naïve enough to believe that if my intelligence led to a British triumph, I'd become the toast of London. But, *naturellement,* all was done in the greatest secrecy. I was charged to keep quiet and stay out of the public eye. Evidently my expectations made me a nuisance to the few who knew of my existence, however. I soon found myself persona non grata. They had what they wanted and didn't need me any longer."

When he learned the full consequences of his actions in the British attacks on Caledonne's fleet and the destruction of Carleton's privateer squadron, Lucien continued, he unexpectedly found himself shocked and appalled. The reality of what he had done had finally broken him. Unable to return home, incapable of facing the person he had become, he had descended to the point of taking his own life.

"But thankfully you did not do so," Elizabeth said softly. "And what of you in all that time, Marie? How did you and Lucien find each other?"

Marie looked down at her clasped hands. "You know that Jean did not survive the battle in which *Destiny* was taken," she said, referring to Jean Lemaire, the doctor whom she had assisted as a nurse. "It was a day I will never forget, though I have tried. Jean and I had fallen in love and pledged to marry, you see."

"I suspected as much."

Marie returned Elizabeth's sympathetic smile with a sad one. "To have him snatched from me so suddenly, all our hopes erased in an instant . . . " She stopped, for a moment unable to go on. Then drawing herself up, she continued steadily, "But the worst was yet to come. The other women were carried away to the fate that awaited them. And the captain in command of the squadron that attacked us took me to London as . . . his whore."

"Oh, Marie, I'm so sorry!"

Springing from her chair, Elizabeth went to kneel before the young woman and gathered her into her arms. Their tears mingled as Lucien pressed Marie's hand to his lips.

"I conceived but lost the babe, a little girl, at six months," Marie whispered, voice shaking.

Abruptly Carleton shoved to his feet and crossed to the window, where he stood staring through the panes. By degrees the scene before him took focus: Julianne and Harry running joyfully across the emerald leaf-strewn lawn, while Elizabeth's parents followed, Anne carrying Jon-Stuart.

How can anyone desecrate something so beautiful and innocent? he thought bleakly. *Yet they do, just as at Gnadenhütten. And all of us are guilty in some measure. It's a wonder the Almighty hasn't destroyed this world a long time since.*

"A few days later," Marie continued with an effort, "I was left alone. The captain was gone and the maid who attended me went out on an errand. I'd gained her trust, and she thought me too unwell to leave my bed. But I . . . I did and found my way to a small Catholic mission in the city. The priest and nuns took me in and kept me from discovery. I received healing, and some months later Lucien found his way there too."

"I was at my lowest ebb," Lucien admitted, his voice gruff. "She saved me as much as the priest's and nuns' ministry did. Together they introduced me to the Lord Jesus, who restored me to my right mind. And after we married, Marie persuaded me to go home to *mon père* and confess the great injury I'd done him."

Carleton turned back to regard Lucien intently, the realization coming forcibly to him that God's purpose had always been, not to destroy his corrupted creation, but to reverse the work of the Evil One. To make all things new. He'd had a dim grasp of this truth for a good part of his life, but now the reality of it struck deep into his heart.

"I knew Sartine's agents would quickly learn that I'd gone to England. Father confirmed it when I spoke to him. But his reaction on learning that—" clearing his throat, Lucien continued raggedly "—that I gave the British all the information they needed to intercept and attack his fleet and your privateers, Jonathan, was . . . was *mercy,* not condemnation!"

He bent his head, fighting to regain his composure. "He actually asked for my forgiveness for not loving me as he ought to have from the time I was a boy." Looking up with wonder, he added, "Can you believe that?"

Convicted, Carleton said, "You've always been seeking the father whose love you keenly felt the lack of, haven't you? Just as I also did."

"But you took the course of honor—"

"I can't make that claim. But all that matters in the end is that each of us has found our earthly father. And our heavenly one."

Lucien gulped in a breath and turned to Elizabeth. "I must ask your forgiveness as well for the great wrong I did to you."

She returned a tearful smile. "You have it freely."

Lucien's troubled expression eased. Pushing to his feet, he strode to Carleton, who came forward to meet him.

"If I could only undo all the wrong I did—but I cannot! Will you forgive me even so, Jonathan?"

A flood of emotions swept through Carleton, and he took his cousin by the hand. "The Lord has forgiven my sins, which are many and grievous. How could I withhold such grace from you?"

Chapter Forty-nine

H ENRI-FRANÇOIS DE BONVOULOIR was no longer the lanky youth Elizabeth remembered from four years earlier. He had grown into a darkly handsome man of twenty-three, fashionably, though conservatively dressed, who demonstrated an attractive grace and unpretentious charm. That he was besotted with Abby was obvious to everyone in the room.

And so he should be, Elizabeth thought admiration mingled with something akin to regret. And, to be honest, a tinge of envy. Her little sister was no longer little. Now nineteen, slender and matching Elizabeth in height, she was a young lady in the first glorious bloom of womanhood, her delicate features; blonde, loosely curling hair; and sky-blue eyes reflecting their mother.

Five years of schooling at Passy, France, in the household of Caledonne's son-in-law, Eugène Sevier, le marquis de Martieu-Broussard, and his wife, Cécile, had accomplished all their parents had hoped. It had been quickly evident that although, thankfully, her naturally sweet, loving nature had not changed, she had matured and developed all the graces one could hope for in a woman.

Elizabeth suppressed a sigh. She felt positively dowdy in comparison despite her moss-green India jaconet gown that set off her figure and coloring to perfection. Abby's rose and white satin jacquard cut in the latest French fashion was more stylish and perfectly enhanced her flawless complexion. As if that was not enough, just that morning Elizabeth had noted in the mirror that the fine lines at the corners of her eyes and the slight one between her eyes had deepened.

Feeling Carleton's gaze on her she glanced toward him and was rewarded with a smoldering look that brought heat to her cheeks. She returned one laden with promise, then, her spirits lifting, returned her attention to her sister.

Unaware of their byplay, Abby appeared as enchanted with her small niece and nephews as they were entranced by her. Sixteen-month-old Jon-Stuart, garbed in a short white gown with a blue underskirt and sash, sat happily enthroned on Abby's lap, fascinated with the lace that edged her sleeves, while the three-year-old twins stood, beaming, at her knees. Julianne looked particularly fetching in a floor-length gown that matched Jon-Stuart's. Harry appeared much more a boy now, having graduated on his last birthday to ankle-length trousers buttoned onto a short jacket with a ruffled, wide-collared white shirt beneath, while his light golden-brown hair fell loose around his shoulders.

Looking up, Abby exclaimed, "Are they not the dearest creatures one could imagine, Henri? Oh, I do hope we shall have such angelic children when we are married!"

Carleton leaned toward Elizabeth and muttered under his breath, "I might dispute the word *angelic*."

She rolled her eyes, stifling a laugh.

A blush tinted Henri's cheeks. "I cannot think it unlikely, my dear, as long as they take after their mother."

"A nicely diplomatic response," Dr. Howard approved with a chuckle.

"You might do well to remember it," Tess countered dryly while Caledonne, mouth twitching, pretended preoccupation with the twins.

It was nearing dinnertime, Tuesday, 19 August, 1783. Their company had only arrived an hour since, Elizabeth reflected, and already her father had shed the stiffness he had displayed on being introduced to his youngest daughter's fiancé. In fact, he now regarded Henri with tentative approval. Abby noticed it, too, for she sent her father a grateful look.

The children's nurse, a quiet, plain young woman in her early thirties, stepped unobtrusively into the parlor, and Anne rose. "Come, children. Thompson will take you to play outside until your dinner is ready."

"But Grandmama," Julianne began, only to be instantly squelched by her father's reprimanding look.

"Mr. Stowe promised to let us sit in the saddle today, Juli!"

She brightened at Harry's excited reminder. When Anne tipped her chin meaningfully, the twins made graceful courtesies, receiving Abby's and Henri's delighted smiles. Thompson came to take Jon-Stuart's hand, and beckoning the twins, ushered them from the room.

"You have them riding already?" Caledonne questioned, eyebrows raised.

"Their ponies are docile and well trained," Elizabeth explained. "Stowe is a hard taskmaster who brooks no nonsense—they adore him, of course —and they won't be allowed to do more than sit on the ponies until every-one concerned is satisfied with their steadiness."

Dr. Howard leaned back in his chair, fingers laced across his abdomen. "They have grandparents who are quite unbending about the matter."

"And a Papa who's determined that they learn to be excellent riders as quickly as possible so he can take them for a gallop," Carleton added wryly, both drawing the others' laughter.

Lucien and Marie received a warm welcome when they arrived shortly thereafter to join them at dinner. While temporarily living in the imposing mansion in town that Teissèdre had purchased on Caledonne's behalf, they had managed the renovations Tess wanted, then the distribution throughout of furnishings and supplies shipped from France over the past year. All that was left for Tess and Caledonne to do was to finish moving in. Abby and Henri were to stay with them until they married in the spring of 1785.

Lucien and Marie planned to settle in New York as soon as the British evacuated the city, plans that were approved by everyone as they would be close enough for frequent visits. By now the majority of Carleton's ships had been refitted as merchantmen, the remaining privateers to serve as escorts. Lucien had accepted Carleton's offer that he manage his import office in New York when it reopened, and Carleton was confident that he would do well. Caledonne would continue to command Carleton's fleet, and Teissèdre would assist in any way needed as Carleton's business offices were reestablished down the coast from Boston to Savannah.

That spring when Carleton had learned that his uncle had placed Pete Moghrab in command of the 50-gun privateer *Pursuit,* assigned to Boston, he had persuaded Isaiah to take over management of that office. In early summer he and Sarah had returned to the town along with Jemma and her new husband, Apollos Matheson, who had agreed to serve as Isaiah's assistant.

Elizabeth shared a wistful smile with her mother. Both of them greatly missed the family who had been their mainstay for so many years, but joined in the Moghrabs' joy in returning home, where they would have their son with them when he was not at sea.

The company's conversation inevitably turned to progress being made toward finalizing a peace treaty with Britain. Washington had ordered all hostilities to cease when Congress endorsed the preliminary peace accord in April. Canada's former governor, Sir Guy Carleton, who had replaced General Henry Clinton as the North American commander in New York City, Britain's last remaining stronghold in America, had done the same. By the beginning of June the army in the field had been disbanded, and Carleton had discharged the rest of his Rangers.

"Britain's not likely to allow American ships to ply the oceans unmolested even after the peace treaty is officially concluded," Caledonne warned when everyone was settled around the table. "They'll use any pretext to intercept vessels flying your Stars and Stripes and press your sailors into their navy."

"I've no doubt of it, which is why I wanted all my ships to remain heavily armed, even though they fly the fleur de lis," Carleton returned grimly. "I'm also certain the British will continue to supply and goad their Indian allies to continue the war on our northwestern frontier, regardless that they're turning over to us all lands between the Mississippi, Florida, and Canada."

He had just returned from Ohio Territory a fortnight earlier and went on to describe the new estate he and Elizabeth were calling Sycamore Spring for the towering sycamore trees abundant on the site and the spring that fed the river flowing through it. He added that Red Fox had moved his town there after the clan's harvest festival the previous fall, not long after General Clark led another expedition through the region, destroying Piqua and other Shawnee towns along the Great Miami River.

As a result, many members of Black Hawk's clan who had been living elsewhere had gravitated to Red Fox's Town along with families from other Shawnee divisions, the Lenape, and several other tribes looking for a safe haven from the fighting. By now the town had swelled to more than 300 residents.

"But what's to keep Clark or the militias from attacking them there?" Tess demanded.

"The property is registered in my name with the Commonwealth of Virginia," Carleton answered. "If anyone tries it, they'll be trespassing, and I'll be justified in taking any measures needed to drive them off."

Besides the men living at Red Fox's Town, which included Andrews, who had moved his family there permanently that summer, Carleton continued, the estate's workers and their families would make their homes on the land as well. Most of Carleton's troops had returned to their former lives since their discharge, but McLeod, whose wife Mary had recently given birth to a son, and several others were building homes for their families on acreage Carleton allotted to them.

"So you see, we'll have a fair number of men to guard the place."

"There's to be a building that will serve as both church and school," Elizabeth chimed in excitedly. "Sawmills and a gristmill are already in place. And according to Jonathan our trading post is almost completed at a landing on the rivershore just a short distance from the mansion."

"Jon promised that our dispensary and surgery will be ready by the time we move there next fall," Dr. Howard said with satisfaction.

Elizabeth returned his nod with a smile. "Sycamore Spring is well on the way to becoming a respectable community."

Henri and Abby had been intently following their conversation, and now Abby exclaimed, "Oh, I can't wait to see it, and the Ohio River!"

Henri agreed enthusiastically. "I'm quite intrigued by the descriptions I've heard of your frontier. In fact Abigail and I have discussed the possibility of settling in St. Louis or New Orleans in time, after we're wed."

"Oh, not so far, surely!" Anne protested, reaching for her youngest daughter's hand.

Watching them, Elizabeth mused, "All this talk of the future has me wondering whether our children and grandchildren and the generations that follow will carry on the work we started—building a strong nation that ensures freedom and justice for all its citizens. Our Articles of Confederation are so weak a foundation that I fear our government won't be able to meet the challenges sure to arise."

"We can only pray that they'll choose virtue and wisdom," Dr. Howard responded. "But I'm less than sanguine on that score. We humans are too prone to doing whatever is good in our own sight."

Tess shook her head sadly. "History offers more than enough examples of the consequences of that policy. You only have to read the Bible. When the ancient Israelites turned their backs on the one true God to worship idols of their own making, they were overtaken by their enemies and carried away into exile."

"I hold concerns for France on that score as well," Caledonne noted, his expression grave. "Though I have left the old for the new, I devoutly pray that *le bon Dieu* is merciful and spares both countries from such a fate."

✱ ✱ ✱

FOUR MONTHS LATER Carleton stood somberly at the rear of the Maryland State House's Old Senate Chamber with Hutchinson at his side. Even crowded among a large cluster of other finely uniformed Continental Army officers, local officials, and prominent Annapolis residents, he was uncomfortably aware that the two of them drew more attention in their striking uniforms than he wished. But he shrugged off the distraction and, vision blurred, focused his attention on Washington.

Flanked by two former aides, the General cleared his throat, fighting back his own tears. He took a deep breath and stared down at the paper he clutched in trembling hands before continuing in a resonant voice that steadied and grew stronger as he spoke.

"I consider it an indispensable duty to close this last solemn act of my official life, by commending the interests of our dearest country to the protection of Almighty God, and those who have the superintendence of them, to his holy keeping. Having now finished the work assigned me, I retire from the great theatre of action, and bidding an affectionate farewell to this august body, under whose orders I have so long acted, I here offer my commission, and take my leave of all the employments of public life."

Washington had entered the building promptly at noon, Tuesday, 23 December, 1783, attired in full uniform, and strode into the large chamber with its muted yellow walls and cream-colored moldings. Although the fire blazing on the hearth at one side did little to dispel the cold day's chill creeping inside on drafts from the blustery wind, none of those gathered seemed to notice.

With the overflowing Ladies' Balcony at the chamber's rear behind him, the General faced the president of the Congress, Thomas Mifflin, who sat at a table at the head of the chamber in front of an ornately framed alcove set between two windows. The assembled members of Congress seated in the rows of chairs facing him neither rose nor removed their hats.

Washington had begun his address in a low voice choked with emotion. Finished now, he withdrew his commission from inside his uniform coat and went forward to hand it to Mifflin, who received it and read a short note of thanks.

Turning, Washington bowed deeply to the Congress. When the representatives rose to their feet and removed their hats as one, he hurriedly withdrew from the room, visibly overcome, his two former aides following him out.

Carleton exchanged a sober glance with Hutchinson, who murmured, "I feel as though it's the end of an era."

"I think it is," Carleton agreed. "The question is what follows. I believe it's a good omen for our future as a nation that the General has subjected the nation's military power to its civil authority."

They were interrupted when Washington stepped back into the chamber, emotions again under tight control. As he made his way around the room, taking final leave of all those who thronged it, Carleton thought at first that the General avoided him. But after bidding the rest farewell one by one, he came over to greet the two of them.

After shaking Hutchinson's hand, he reached for Carleton's. "We've had our differences, Jon," he said earnestly. "But in spite of it, I'll always count you as a good friend. I hope you feel the same."

"I do, sir," Carleton said, his voice rough. "I'm more grateful than I can say for your leadership and your kindness to me and my wife. I wish you and Mrs. Washington every felicity."

Washington's hand tightened over his, then he released him, smiling faintly. "I know I can speak for her in wishing you the same. You will bring your family to visit us?"

"I will."

They exchanged an embrace and wishes for safe journeys home. Then, with his aides' assistance, Washington shrugged on his greatcoat and went outside into the cold, blustery day. Carleton and Hutchinson followed the crowd streaming outside to watch the now retired commander ride alone down the street toward the south.

The final peace treaty between Britain and the United States had been signed on September 2, 1783, in Paris. General Greene resigned his commission not long thereafter, the war in the South over except for lingering personal vendettas. The Revolution was officially ended.

Sir Guy Carleton evacuated the last British troops from New York in late November. Washington had entered the city the same day to ecstatic crowds, a welcome by New York Governor George Clinton, speeches, banquets, and other week-long fetes. After bidding an emotional farewell to those of his officers who were present, Washington had then taken the road to Philadelphia.

The city had given him another enthusiastic welcome, and he endured yet more speeches and celebrations. Carleton, Elizabeth, and their family had taken part in many of the events and hosted Washington at a private dinner at their home as well.

A week later Washington left for Annapolis, where Congress was then meeting. At Carleton's request Hutchinson traveled from his home in Connecticut and accompanied him to witness the General's last formal act as commander in chief of the Continental Army.

They had arrived in time to attend the public dinner given by Congress the previous day and the illuminated ball that followed, at which Washington danced with every lady present. Although both he and Hutchinson participated in the festivities, Carleton had found little enjoyment in them, his spirits dampened by Elizabeth's absence and the prospect of taking a final farewell from his former commander after the better part of a decade at war.

His and Hutchinson's own leave-taking was deeply emotional as well, both feeling that all they had endured together bound them inextricably as brothers. But separate futures beckoned. And after a swift, hard ride, they bade each other farewell with embraces and tears on the road south of Philadelphia late on the afternoon of Christmas Day.

Chapter Fifty

CARLETON PAUSED in the entryway of the graceful Georgian-style mansion and scanned the list he held. "You'll have the changes Mrs. Carleton wants completed by the time we arrive in October?"

Durie nodded. "I'll ha' the carpenters start on 'em at once. Everythin' else is to yer satisfaction?"

Carleton surveyed the spacious foyer, glancing through the doors on either hand that opened into the sunlit parlor and dining room, along the passage where doors opened to the rest of the rooms on the first floor, then up the broad stairway. Beautiful moldings had been installed and paneled doors of solid hickory hung. Smoothly honed wide-plank pine floors extended throughout the building, their fresh fragrance filling the air.

Walls throughout the building were finely plastered. Those in the entry and dining room boasted lovely hand-painted murals depicting picturesque vistas of the estate and riverside. The rest had been variously painted in a soft cream color, covered with lovely papers in fresh light hues, or finished with elegant paneling.

A swarm of workmen moved in and out of the building completing the last details. Others carried in furniture and goods delivered in the most recent shipment from Pittsburgh, where Elizabeth, the children, and her parents were living until the house was ready for occupancy. Below on the ground floor Salome and her assistants were busily stocking the kitchens with every needful thing.

He grinned, chest swelling. "It is. She'll be very pleased."

He and Durie went outside and descended the mansion's wide front steps to the circle carriageway, passing Stowe, who waited with his and Carleton's saddled horses. Crossing to the sun-dappled lawn, they strode the length of its broad sweep beneath the trees' overhanging branches, alive with the chime of birdsong.

That Monday, 23 August, 1784, in *Po'kamawi kiishthwa,* the Plum Moon, had dawned blazing hot, and Carleton was grateful for the shade cast by the stately sycamores, oaks, and hickories that dotted the lawn. Even though he had donned only breechcloth, leggings, and moccasins that morning and pulled up his hair into a roach ornamented with three white eagle feathers, sweat already trickled down his brow and beaded his bare chest and arms.

They stopped before reaching the bluff's edge and turned their backs to the stunning vista of the broad river below. Durie unrolled the building plans he carried. A pang of pleasure coursed through Carleton as he compared the drawings to the façade of the massive three-story manor house that crested the rise in front of them. He nodded his approval.

The building was perfectly symmetrical, the windows and doors of the main block and wings on either side exactly centered and matched top to bottom. The walls were faced all around with expertly dressed limestone blocks brought up from Virginia and topped with a deep grey-blue slate roof. Surrounded by planting beds and gardens that overflowed with flowers and ornamental shrubbery and with redbud and dogwood saplings transplanted among the trees, the house appeared to be as integral a part of its site as if it had thrust up from the native soil instead of being built there.

The dense woodlands belonging to the estate extended some distance to either side along the north bank of the *Spelewathiipi,* the Ohio River. On the manor's east side the main road ran north to south, a branch veering west to form the circle drive at its front. The single-story stone building that housed the dispensary and surgery stood where the second branch turned east and passed out of sight behind a stand of pines and hardwoods before descending to a sheltered cove below.

There the log trading post built on the riverbank the previous year carried on a burgeoning business with settlers on both sides of the river, native and white. A broad, level area in its front allowed for landing canoes and bateaux. A couple of docks extended into the deeper water to accommodate a ferry and the flatboats and other sturdy craft that plied the river in ever increasing numbers.

The weatherworn cabins of a settlement called Holderby's Landing clustered near the mouth of the Guyandotte River on the Virginia shore a short distance upriver, with the Kanawha forty miles beyond and Pittsburgh roughly 250 miles farther east. Less than a two-day ride north of the estate lay Chillicothe, the principal town of the Shawnee's Chillicothe division, which controlled all political matters that affected the tribe, including relationships between the Shawnee and other native nations. And west lay the wide Mississippi, giving access to St Louis and New Orleans.

Carving the community Carleton had envisioned out of virgin forest had been a daunting undertaking, but Durie had coordinated every detail. Crops now thrived in fields, gardens, and orchards, while heavily forested outlying areas offered abundant game for hunting. Substantial barns stored the first cuttings of hay and would soon overflow with the grain harvest. Flocks of chickens, geese, and ducks filled the poultry yards, while the dairy supplied milk, butter, and cheese. Herds of cattle, sheep, horses, and hogs grazed peacefully in pasture and woodland.

Spotted Pony and Golden Elk rode around the side of the manor, interrupting Carleton's reverie. He and Durie strode back across the lawn to meet them.

Grasping Durie's hand, Carleton said, "I can't thank you enough for all your hard work, Alistair. I don't know what I'd do without you."

Durie grinned. " 'Tis a pleasure workin' with ye, sir. I'll make sure 'tis all finished properly and see ye next when ye bring yer family home." Nodding respectfully to Spotted Pony and Golden Elk as they drew their mounts to a halt, he went back into the house.

Andrews was almost indistinguishable now from his adoptive kin with his deep tan and identical garb, Carleton noted with a pang of longing, except for his sun-bleached brown hair and blue eyes. Answering only to the name Golden Elk since moving with his family to Red Fox's Town, he appeared entirely content at having cast his lot among their clan and nation as he had intended ever since marrying Blue Sky.

If only he also— Quickly Carleton brushed the thought aside.

He had been called to a different path, he reminded himself resolutely. And it was the right one despite Black Hawk's prophecy that he was destined always to wander, never finding a true home either among the Shawnee or among the Whites.

For he knew that a greater home had been prepared for him, Elizabeth, and their children. And one day they would all meet there in unshadowed joy.

HE MOUNTED AND reined Devil around, Little Running Heron doing the same behind him.

Spotted Pony cocked one eye at the house and nodded his approval before saying in the Shawnee tongue, "The people are gathering at the *msikahmiqui,* White Eagle."

Assessing the angle of the sun's rays, White Eagle said, "I promised Healer Woman I'd return by my birthday. I can't delay longer if I'm to reach Pittsburgh in time. And the season grows late. I'd have my family settled in their new home before *Kini kiishthwa,* the Long Moon, if possible."

"But Healer Woman is to give birth in *Ha'shimini kiishthwa,* the Papaw

Moon," Golden Elk pointed out, frowning. "Surely that will delay your return."

"When White Horse came back to us last week he said she does well," White Eagle responded, mentally calculating. "The babe is not expected for three weeks, and hopefully the birth will be easy. But you are right. It may be toward the end of *Sha'teepakanootha,* the Wilted Moon, before they can travel so far."

Spotted Pony turned his mount onto the road, heading north as the others followed. "The winds will be cold by then and the river rough."

White Eagle exchanged a worried glance with his cousin, but made no answer.

At intervals other tracks intersected the one they followed. A short distance past a crossroads they came to the McLeods' tidy log cabin, with its barn and outbuildings. Across the road lay the new clapboard church building that before long would also serve as a school.

McLeod emerged from the stable leading his horse, with Jimmy, almost seven years-old now, skipping at his side. Mary stepped out of the cabin to wave a greeting, the latest addition to their brood, five-month-old Aaran, in her arms, while shy, four-year-old Aileana peered, wide-eyed, around her petticoat. Jimmy ran to them.

Mounting, McLeod waved to Mary and the children and urged his horse onto the road to Red Fox's Town with White Eagle and his companions. As they passed more farm tracts they called greetings to former Rangers at work in garden and field with their families.

While they rode White Eagle mulled over the disheartening situation his clan and nation faced. Even though Elizabeth had been pregnant again, due to give birth in September, he had reluctantly left for Sycamore Spring early in March. He had been needed to supervise the final stages of the manor's completion and more so to counsel with Shawnee, Lenape, and other tribal leaders. He, his two cousins, Blue Crane, and other leaders of Black Hawk's clan had returned from Chillicothe just the previous week from yet another contentious meeting, which had delayed his return to Pittsburgh longer than he had hoped.

Tensions were once more building toward war between the Shawnee and the American settlers, who since the end of the Revolution were flooding in a great tide ever farther west into Kentucky and tribal lands north of the Ohio River. At the same time the influence of the clan's peace faction was eroding, and many of the clan's men, young and old, were agitating to join their Kispokotha division in taking up the war tomahawk. White Eagle could not say that he blamed them, and Red Fox, Spotted Pony, and Golden Elk privately held the same opinion, though they all recognized the futility of such a course.

The Treaty of Paris remained an open sore. None of the tribes, whether allied with Britain or America, had been given any voice in the negotiations or a single mention in the final terms. The ultimate hypocrisy was that, as White Eagle had predicted, the British still held their forts on territory they had formally surrendered and were quietly goading their former allies into raids against the Americans, which they then provisioned. Anyone with eyes could see that events were rapidly spiraling toward another round of bloodshed that would affect the British not at all, but would have tragic consequences for the inhabitants of the Ohio Territory, most of all for the native peoples.

As they approached the woods' verge, without warning a flock of crows burst from the long grasses ahead of them in a raucous, sooty flurry of flapping wings and hoarse caws. Heart pounding and breath shortened, White Eagle brought his stallion under control, his companions doing the same with their mounts. They all drew to a halt.

The crows' flight drew his gaze to the highest branches of a towering tulip poplar that stood where the woods opened out onto a long, wide, wildflower-strewn meadow. He wiped trickling sweat from his eyes and squinted upward against the sun's glare.

The great white eagle appeared as a brighter glow against the soft blush of morning light behind it. Its flaming eyes pierced him through.

After a suspended moment it gracefully spread its wings and pushed off from its perch to soar upward, beckoning White Eagle's gaze to the high heavens, where it dissolved into the cloudless azure blue.

He became aware that his companions had followed his gaze. When he turned to them, they returned puzzled, questioning looks. Letting out his breath, he motioned them forward.

High, rocky bluffs guarded the meadow on three sides, much of the land divided between pasture for cattle and horses and fields densely planted in hills of corn, beans, and squash, their broad leaves shining in the bright sunlight. Directly ahead of them the log cabins of Red Fox's Town spread a long distance between the nearest bluff and the bank of the sparkling Sycamore River that snaked southward through the area.

As they drew closer they saw clusters of men, women, and children hurrying to join those already gathered on the grassy clearing in front of the long council house, at the town's center. The moment they drew up and dismounted, they were instantly enveloped by the cheerful throng.

Walks Far, Wolfslayer's widow, was the first to embrace White Eagle. Then Blue Sky came forward, her children following, with Autumn Wind leaning on her arm, her steps faltering. The old widow was growing ever more frail and bent, he noted with a pang, yet her devotion to the fellowship of believers did not waver in spite of Grey Cloud's turning back from the faith.

Red Fox, Laughing Otter, and Rain Woman with all their children crowded around as well. Sweetgrass greeted him as she came to meet Little Running Heron. Then Walk on Water stepped forward with his wife, their daughter, and her husband and children.

McLeod immediately gravitated to Walk on Water's side. The two men had become great friends and were often together discussing the Scriptures or the needs of the believers each of them shepherded.

The warriors of the clan who had fought faithfully with White Eagle despite deep misgivings, pressed in as well. And so many others who had long been dear to him, with many new faces who were also becoming good and trusted friends. They all made it clear how eagerly they looked forward to Healer Woman's coming with her children to live among them.

He stood before his gathered clan, heart aching for what lay ahead of them. By earthly standards the battle the Shawnee and the other tribes faced was a losing one, but it was yet a worthy one: to dwell with their families in peace and safety in their ancient lands, to prosper, to do no harm nor suffer it. If their quest was ever to come to pass, however, weapons of flesh and blood would do them no good. Only spiritual power could prevail.

Truly he longed to be done with war and never to leave family and home again. But he knew that war would never cease until the hearts of men were changed, for there was no other cure. And unless the Savior changed them, he would inevitably be drawn again into war's toils in some measure.

He could freely say now that he did not hate those he'd fought against—those who had harmed him, his family, and his people. He held no grudges, not even against Tarleton. Nor against any other.

He wanted only to defend the right of his people to live!

Looking around at all those who held his heart, he thought to plead with them again to hold to the path of peace. But it came to him then that this was not a day to air grievances or to counsel one way or another. All that could be said had been. Let those who had ears to hear, hear.

No, today was a day for blessing.

The sun neared its zenith, and he must be on the road that led to Elizabeth and their children—and her parents, too, as much his own now as hers. To bring them back to live among this fierce, unyielding people.

Let the future be what it would. The Almighty God held all things in his hands. Their part was to trust.

To his wonder, despite the clouds of war that threatened on the horizon, despite the north wind that carried the breath of coming winter, he felt beneath his feet new life pressing upward through fertile ground, seeking light. He also would follow the Great Spirit's light wherever it led, for its path was always life and health and blessing. And one day his eyes would see it.

Looking from one beloved face to another, he was overcome by the reality that all of them were indeed one people, not by blood, but by faith. And by the abiding love that knit hearts to one another and to their Creator.

Lifting his gaze to the heavens then, he raised open hands, vowing that in this truth he would live and die.

Chapter Fifty-one

ELIZABETH STOOD at the window, as she had too often the past days. She had meant only to direct one quick, hopeful glance down the dusty dirt road to where it emerged from the forest's shade a quarter of a mile to the west. But it remained stubbornly deserted no matter how long she peered at it.

She roused at the sound of children's laughter outside. Smiling, she turned her gaze to the scene below at the far end of the house where Harry and Julianne, almost five now, rode their ponies in a circle on the lawn under her father's supervision. Her mother stood close by, holding squealing two-year-old Jon-Stuart to keep him from running after them.

It was Monday, 30 August, Carleton's birthday. Noting that the sun hung not far above the western treetops now, subtly lengthening the shadows and casting the landscape in a melting, lambent light, she fought back disappointment. She had so hoped that he would come.

All Carleton had been able to find for their temporary accommodation had been this cramped two-story log cabin. It stood along the bank of the Allegheny near the juncture of a path north to French Creek and another west to Big Beaver Creek. At the Point across the river where its rushing waters crashed into those of the Monongahela in a great froth to form the Ohio, she could see the clustered buildings of the rapidly expanding frontier town of Pittsburgh.

Fort Pitt still loomed over the Point. For now. No longer of strategic importance with the frontier moving ever westward, its buildings were progressively being torn down for wood and other materials that could be used for new structures. The once renowned fortress was a great deal reduced from the one she and Andrews had passed through almost eight years earlier on their quest to find Carleton, rumored to be the Shawnee's implacable war chief White Eagle. And then again on their subsequent return, bringing him reluctantly back with them to rejoin Washington's army.

Now that war was done. But judging by what she had learned from the runners Carleton sent, she felt in her bones that yet another conflagration was sparking to flame along the western frontier.

Releasing a muffled sigh, she started to turn away. Sudden movement arrested her, however, and she leaned eagerly forward to peer west through the cloudy panes.

A rider emerged from beneath the branches overhanging the road where it curved between the trees bordering the Ohio. As he drew nearer she could make out the dark bay stallion with black mane and tail, black blaze, and four black stockings, and her heart leaped.

The rider's identity was soon also unmistakable though the dying sun's melting glow blurred his form. Tall, lean, and broad-shouldered, garbed in a blue linen shirt, buckskin leggings, and moccasins, with his long blond hair tied back, he rode with an easy grace as though he and his mount were one. Close behind came another rider, also familiar by his shorter, stocky frame and the way he kept his horse protectively near his master's.

She first thought they approached at a slow walk. But for an instant, whether by a trick of the light or by its refraction across the panes' wavy glass, she suddenly had the impression that they rode away from her, as they had that morning five months earlier. And so many times before.

She stood shrouded in darkness, buffeted by a cold wind amid a foreign, heavily wooded landscape far distant in time and miles. Her surroundings' wild beauty bore the shattering of battle. And she knew, without seeing the evidence of it, that there his body lay with many others beneath that unknown, unforgiving, blood-drenched sod.

She staggered, clutched the windowsill to keep her legs from giving way beneath her. But as quickly as it had come, the illusion dissipated, and below, through the window, she saw that the riders were dismounting inside the gate in the yard's fence.

I'll not grieve, she thought fiercely. *Not now.*

Sorrow would wait for that future, yet far off. Until then she refused to allow any shadow of worry or fear to darken the years that lay ahead. She would fill each day, each hour their Father gave them with joy and laughter and love.

Hearing a soft mewling in the cradle at her side, she hastily finished pinning her bodice closed over the top of her shift, then bent to lift the tiny form into her arms. She wrapped a shawl around her shoulders, enclosing the swaddled babe, and left the bedchamber to descend the narrow stairs with careful steps.

By the time she emerged through the front door onto the porch that spanned the cabin's width, the children were running to their father with joyful cries, her parents following more slowly. Carleton knelt, reaching for them, and in their eagerness they collided with him, almost knocking him over. Laughing, he managed to keep his balance and gathered them into his arms. Stowe stood with Elizabeth's parents, all of them laughing at the merry reunion and the children's excited chatter about their doings while their papa had been away.

When Carleton pushed to his feet, Jon-Stuart in his arms, the sun's slanting rays lit up the boy's curly hair with a fire that matched Elizabeth's own dark auburn locks. Carleton noted it, too, for he ran his fingers through the unruly mass and made a laughing comment that caused her father to beam. In spite of his darker hair, their youngest son resembled his father more every year in the contours of his face and the color of his eyes, Elizabeth thought, smiling.

She descended the steps, a great wave of joy overflowing. Her mother said something to Carleton that caused him to glance toward her, then set Jon-Stuart on his feet.

Turning, he strode toward her as Stowe led the horses off to the stable while her parents herded the children over to the ponies, Julianne protesting as she looked back. Seeing Carleton's rueful grin, Elizabeth couldn't help laughing.

He looked younger now than when he had gone, rested and carefree once more, almost as on that day nine years earlier when they had collided in the doorway of what was to be his bedchamber in her parents' Boston townhouse. The lines that fatigue and pain and worry had etched into his features during the war had smoothed with the wind and sun of the wilderness, as always. The indescribable grace and vitality that had captured her from their first meeting charged his body, and that same light shone in his eyes when his gaze captured hers.

Suddenly his steps faltered, his eyes widening as he caught sight of the shawl-wrapped bundle nodding against her shoulder. He glanced from the babe to her as he took the last few, quick steps to catch her in his arms.

She encircled his neck with her free arm, and his mouth found hers, his kisses holding a hunger she returned in equal measure. At length, hearing a muffled, protesting squeak, they disentangled, breathless, both looking at the swaddled bundle pressed to her shoulder.

"But White Horse said—"

"My pains started not long after he left us." She gazed doubtfully down at her daughter. "She was apparently determined to make her entrance three weeks early—or perhaps I conceived earlier than I thought."

When she looked up, she saw the worry in his eyes. "There were no complications, dearest. I'm fine, and she's quite vigorous and healthy, as you see," she said as she lifted the babe into his eager arms.

He cuddled the little bundle to his chest and nudged the wrappings away from her face with his free hand, brushed his cheek against her dark fluff of downy hair, and kissed the top of her head. Caressing the softly rounded, rose-tinted porcelain of his tiny girl's cheek with one finger, he drank in the sight of her, whispering unintelligible endearments, while she blinked sleepily up at him, a slight frown creasing her brow as she attempted to focus a wondering gaze on his face.

When he finally pulled his gaze back to Elizabeth, he said gruffly, "I always forget how tiny newborns are and how afraid I am that I might break them."

"She is a bit smaller even than the twins were when they were born. Jon-Stuart was huge in comparison."

"He was," he agreed with a chuckle before returning his attention to his newborn daughter, who had drifted back to sleep. "She's as beautiful as her mother. I couldn't ask for a dearer birthday present."

"Well, I'd almost given up hope you'd return in time to celebrate it," she teased. "If you hadn't appeared this evening, the consequences might not have been to your liking. But I suppose I shouldn't complain, considering that I blew up Thornlea just before you arrived to save us."

He threw back his head in a shout of laughter. It took some moments before he was able to contain his mirth, but at last he sobered, his expression contrite.

"My wife and children are far more precious to me than any house. Beth, I'm so sorry I wasn't with you when she was born. I was delayed by another infernal meeting at Chillicothe that I'd happily have foregone had I known she'd come so early. Alistair is more than capable of overseeing the final details on the house after all."

"It's finished?" she asked, beaming.

"It will be by the time we get there—and everything as you wished." Transferring his gaze back to their newborn, he said, "You named her Elizabeth Anne as we'd decided?"

"I wanted to wait until you returned." She hesitated before continuing, "It's in my mind to name her Mercy for God's great mercy to us. In French *merci* means thank you, and I do thank our Lord for her with all my heart."

"As do I." Bending to kiss the babe again, tears welling, he whispered, "Mercy Elizabeth Anne. Indeed you are our mercy."

As Elizabeth smiled up at him, he indicated her parents and the children, who accompanied Stowe as he led their ponies back to the stable while her parents trailed after, her father carrying Jon-Stuart in his arms with the little boy's head resting sleepily on his shoulder.

"This is the greatest blessing I could ever have hoped for. Our family. And you."

Unbidden, the memories of the years at war tumbled through her mind. How passionately the two of them had fought for a grand ideal of liberty even while hungering for the deep intimacy of their own earthly love! Yet deep inside, she reflected now, the cry of their hearts had really always been for the true peace and lasting freedom only God could provide.

Her musings were interrupted when her mother came over to them and reached for the baby. "Here, let me take her inside. She'll need to have her clout changed, and supper will be ready shortly." When Carleton hesitated, she said affectionately, "I promise you'll have her back directly after we eat. I assume you are hungry."

He conceded that he was but still surrendered his daughter reluctantly.

After she carried the baby off, he took Elizabeth's hand on his arm and led her to where they had an unobstructed view of the fort's bulk across the river. Its decaying battlements momentarily reflected the golden gleam of the sun's declining rays.

But his gaze was not drawn there. "How is it possible that you're more beautiful each time I see you," he murmured, looking down at her.

She laughed softly. "You always say that."

"Because it's always true. When I'm away I think I remember. And when I return, I see how wrong I was."

She bit her lip and looked down. "I'm older now, and worn, I fear."

He gently tipped up her chin until she met his steady gaze. "You're more beautiful to me now than that day back in Boston when I first laid eyes on you and thought I saw an angel. Do you remember?"

"How could I ever forget?" she asked, everything in her melting. "I told myself that I'd have to guard my heart with all my strength to prevent your breaking down my defenses. But I doubted heartily that I'd be able to. Or even wanted to."

Turning, he indicated the beaming faces of their children, now gleefully chasing fireflies across the lawn in the gathering dusk, Julianne calling for the two of them to join in. "I told myself the same thing, you know. And I'm glad that neither of us did."

"We'd have forfeited all this." With a wistful sigh she went on, "That morning we stood in Aunt Tess's garden after escaping from Boston, we heard the oriole's song and pledged our lives to each other. I never dreamed so many years would pass until the war was ended."

His fingers tightened over hers. "None of those years were wasted, Beth. God worked out his plan for us in every part of it."

Longing etched his face as he looked away to the west, across the rolling lawn to the willows that bordered the river, hazy shadows in the gathering twilight. She followed his gaze down the broad stream of the Ohio, its turbulent waters catching the declining sun's fiery red-gold rays on its way toward the twilight-shrouded line of the distant mountains. Her heart contracted sharply.

"What lies beyond?" she whispered, uncertain whether she meant the river or the looming war.

His keen gaze told her that he read her thoughts. But he only drew her closer and said, "Rich lands stretching out for unimaginable miles where we've never yet been. Our people—all of them. And adventures yet to be found."

He hesitated before adding, "The world's changing, and it'll only change more rapidly now with settlers moving west in greater numbers. Whether the Shawnee will find a home in it any more than I shall remains to be seen. Yet as long as we're together, I am content."

She responded with mischievous laughter. "Neither of us will ever be content, dearest. God has given us both a bent to wandering. Always we must see what lies beyond the next river and mountain."

"My little Oriole will never be caged, I see," he returned with a teasing smile. "She'll always soar and sing to delight my heart. Come away with me, my love."

She nestled against him, feeling that the Almighty had created her to lie there trustingly against his heart no matter what their future might hold. As indeed he had.

"Light of my life," he murmured, "you're all I've ever desired in this world or ever will. As you told me on our wedding night, let's not waste another moment of the rest of our lives."

It felt as though the fading amber glow of sunset warmed her through with the very incandescence of noontide, beckoning them on to the years that stretched before them. They would be blessed as long as they were together. And safe as long at the Lord held them in his hand.

They did not need to know what the coming days would bring, only to trust the One who guided them all and guarded their steps.

Her heart too full for speech, she turned her face up to his as she had on that day when, by God's grace, she had snatched him from a British noose. She had thought then that she glimpsed heaven in his eyes.

Now, as she searched their depths alight with love for her, she knew that she had.

The Shawnee's continued fight for independance...

WHAT IS TODAY CALLED the Northwest Indian War began in 1785 and involved a confederacy of Indian nations that included at various times the Shawnee, Miami, Lenape, Wyandot, Odowa, Mohawk, and a number of others. Prominent among its leaders were the Shawnee chief Blue Jacket and the Miami war chief Little Turtle. The war ended with the Treaty of Greenville in 1795.

Determined resistance to the influx of settlers into Ohio and Illinois territories and the seizure of Indian lands continued into the nineteenth century, however. The renowned Shawnee leader Tecumseh formed a new pan-Indian confederacy only to have it collapse when he was killed at the Battle of the Thames in Canada on October 5, 1813, while fighting against William Henry Harrison's pursuing army.

It is known that American soldiers scalped him on the battlefield and stripped his body. Some cut off pieces of his skin for souvenirs. But the location of Tecumseh's remains has never been identified with any certainty. Although various burial places have been claimed, most likely he was buried on the battlefield or in a concealed location elsewhere.

The Shawnee suffered great loss as a result of their determined, but ultimately futile battle to hold onto their ancestral lands. The last band forced to leave Ohio Territory relocated to Kansas in August 1831. In 1854 their land holdings were significantly reduced and in 1858 were broken up into individual allotments, removing Indian land from tribal management, diminishing tribal authority over its members, and facilitating sale of the allotted lands to outsiders.

If you enjoyed this story and series and would like to offer feedback, we invite you to email the editor, Joan Shoup, at jmshoup@gmail.com. We'd love to receive your comments.

You can find more information about The American Patriot Series at www.theamericanpatriotseries.com. To learn more about J. M. Hochstetler, please visit www.jmhochstetler.com.

We greatly appreciate thoughtful reviews posted on the book's detail page on Amazon, Christianbook.com, Barnes and Noble, Goodreads, and other online sites. Thank you for telling other readers about this series!

Historical Notes

WHAT DID JOHN PAUL JONES REALLY SAY?

Scholars have debated for years what, precisely, John Paul Jones replied when Captain Pearson asked whether he had called for quarter during the battle between *USS Bonhomme Richard* and *HMS Serapis*. The famous line, "I have not yet begun to fight!" is truly heroic. Would that it were so!

That line first appears in an 1825 biography of Jones by Henry Sherburne, quoting Richard Dale, Jones' First Lieutenant, at that time a sixty-five-year-old retired U.S. Navy officer. Not only was the event forty-six years past, but also while the battle was in full clamor, Dale was at his station on the gun deck, two levels below Jones on the quarterdeck.

The line is also suspect since Jones wrote a very different account of what he said in his official report within days of the battle. Others participants recorded versions of Jones' words, many of them longer and more pompous than the captain of a mortally wounded ship in the midst of a life-or-death brawl would be likely to say.

After considering the issue, no matter how much I wanted to use that famous line I simply couldn't justify perpetuating a myth when Jones himself didn't corroborate it. Instead I ended up using a quote that appeared in the *Edinburgh Advisor*'s report a few days afterward, varying it slightly to avoid the use of profanity, even though I'm sure there was plenty of it during the battle: "I may sink, but I'll be cursed if I strike!"

CHARLESTOWN, SOUTH CAROLINA

Charleston, SC, was named Charles Towne at its founding. Early in the eighteenth century, the name was commonly written Charlestown, and after the Revolution it was changed to Charleston, as it is today.

Fort Putnam

During the American Revolution Fort Putnam was the largest military garrison at West Point, New York. Built by Colonel Rufus Putnam's 5th Massachusetts Regiment and completed in 1778, it sits 500 feet above sea level and is currently preserved as a historical site.

York, Virginia

Originally named York, the town and the battle were renamed Yorktown after the war.

Virginia

At the time of the Revolution, Virginia claimed lands extending to the Mississippi River that were later divided into the states of Ohio, West Virginia, Tennessee, Kentucky, Indiana, and Illinois.

The tune the British played during the surrender at York

According to legend, British fifes and drums played "The World Turned Upside Down" as the British marched out to surrender to the combined American-French Army at York, Virginia. But the truth is that there are no details at all in official accounts about any songs played on either side during the surrender.

The sole record of this claim appears in a memoir written by Alexander Garden in 1828, in which he describes the surrender and mentions this tune. Garden admitted, however, that not only did he never hear the tune played, but also that he got the information at second and maybe even third hand. Since there's no way to validate that the tune was actually played at the surrender, I chose not to include it.

Glossary

ENGLISH

Ague or intermittent fever: malaria.

lawn: a fine linen cloth.

muffatees: fingerless gloves.

pilch: a knit wrapper worn over a baby's diaper to keep outer clothing dry.

FRENCH

affaire de coeur: affair of the heart.

bien: good.

certainement: certainly.

Dieu: God.

général: general.

lustrine: lustring, a silk fabric with a shiny finish

mais, bien sûr: but, of course.

Mère de Dieu: Mother of God

merci: thank you.

naturellement: naturally.

notre: our.

père: father.

sans doute: without doubt.

seize: sixteen.

serviteur: your servant.

tarte: pie.

tout est perdu fors l'honneur: all is lost save honor.

tout comprendre c'est tout pardoner: to understand all is to forgive all.

vive le Roi: long live the king.

Gaelic

arisaid: traditional Scottish Highland women's dress.

auld: old.

bairn: baby, child.

Bhiodh tu nas bòidhche às aonais, a ghràidh: You would be even more beautiful without it, my love.

braw: fine, splendid, brave.

Cho brèagha ris á bhan-dia Diana: As lovely as the goddess Diana.

Nollaig Chridhheil, mo chridhe: Merry Christmas, my heart.

sasannach: an English person; something considered typical of England.

trews: plaid trousers.

Shawnee

Ha'shimini kiishthwa: Papaw Moon, September.

Kini kiishthwa: Long Moon, November.

Long Knives: originally the Virginians and later all Americans, so called because their soldiers carried swords.

msikahmiqui: a long log structure with a gabled roof that served as council house and temple for religious rites.

Po'kamawi kiishthwa: Plum Moon, August.

Pooshkwiitha: the Half Moon, April.

seela: yes.

Sha'teepakanootha: Wilted Moon, October.

Spelewathiipi: Ohio River.

wigewa: a large rectangular or square dwelling for one family framed with poles and overlaid with bark, woven mats, or animal hides.

Military Terms

legion: a regiment-sized military unit that consisted of infantry, cavalry, and sometimes artillery, all under one command.

partisan or irregular warfare: today known as guerilla warfare.

rangers: a division composed of cavalry and dismounted troops or light infantry trained in partisan or irregular warfare.

regulars: well-disciplined, battle-hardened soldiers who were the backbone of the British and American armies in the eighteenth century.

NAVAL TERMS

courses: the lowest row of sails on a square-rigged ship.

ratline: a small rope that forms a rung of a rope ladder on a ship.

shrouds: ropes supporting a ship's mast.

taffrail: railing around the stern of a ship.

top: a platform at the top of a mast, designated as fore-, main-, and mizzen-top.

yard: a spar tapered on both ends and attached to a mast to spread the head of a square sail.

www.ingramcontent.com/pod-product-compliance
Lightning Source LLC
Chambersburg PA
CBHW051933020726
47501CB00001B/105